Spirit of the Stone

Also by Maggie Furey

The Artefacts of Power

AURIAN
HARP OF WINDS
THE SWORD OF FLAME
DHIAMMARA

The Shadowleague

THE HEART OF MYRIAL

Spirit of the Stone

Book Two of The Shadowleague

www.orbitbooks.co.uk

An *Orbit* Book

First published in Great Britain by Orbit 2001

All characters and events in this publication are fictitious and any resemblance to real persons, living or dead, is purely coincidental.

A CIP catalogue record for this book is available from the British Library.

ISBN 1 85723 952 0

Typeset by Palimpsest Book Production Limited,
Polmont, Stirlingshire
Printed and bound in Great Britain
by Clays Ltd, St Ives plc

Orbit
A Division of
Little, Brown and Company (UK)
Brettenham House
Lancaster Place
London WC2E 7EN

Sometimes, very special people come into our lives,
just when we need them most.
I would like to dedicate this book, with gratitude,
affection and respect, to
Professor John Deanfield and Mr Victor Tsang.

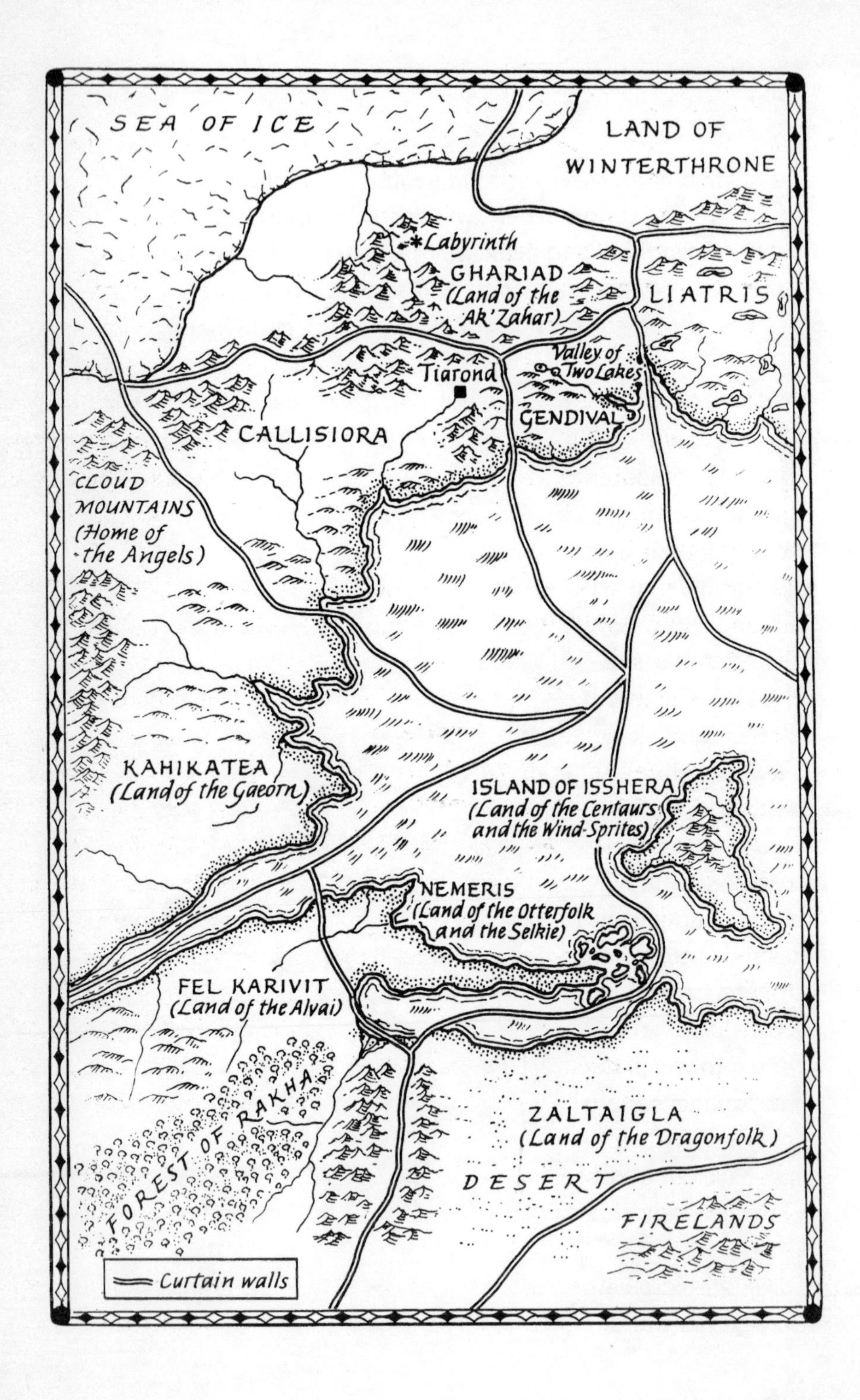
SEA OF ICE
LAND OF WINTERTHRONE
Labyrinth
GHARIAD
(Land of the Ak'Zahar)
LIATRIS
Valley of Two Lakes
Tiarond
GENDIVAL
CALLISIORA
CLOUD MOUNTAINS
(Home of the Angels)
KAHIKATEA
(Land of the Gaeorn)
ISLAND OF ISSHERA
(Land of the Centaurs and the Wind-Sprites)
NEMERIS
(Land of the Otterfolk and the Selkie)
FEL KARIVIT
(Land of the Alvai)
FOREST OF RAKHA
ZALTAIGLA
(Land of the Dragonfolk)
DESERT
FIRELANDS
Curtain walls

One

Nightfall

Dawn was still a long way off when Seriema and her companions escaped from Tiarond. The horses galloped through the waterlogged fields of the townlands, threading their way between the ghastly pyres, the biggest of which still smouldered with a dull red glow, the others extinguished by rain and snow. As she raced away from the beleaguered city, it took all Seriema's self-control to keep from looking back over her shoulder. She was certain that the horror she had left behind must be following.

It was raining: a cold, thin rain that chilled exposed flesh and penetrated clothing like steel needles, but being wet was the least of Seriema's problems. On this dreadful day, the bastions of power, wealth and privilege she had built around herself had come crashing down, and she had turned from the richest woman in Tiarond into a homeless vagabond, threatened by all manner of dangers, her future uncertain and her survival hanging by a thread.

Only pride sustained her. She was angry, hurting and afraid; she wanted to weep, to curse, to shriek like a harridan – but no matter what setbacks the world might hurl at her, she was determined to face them with courage and determination. Seriema would rather walk barefoot over broken glass than give way to weakness and fear before her new companions, but it was hard to keep up her mask of courage.

Disconnected images from the last few hours kept flashing through her mind. Pain and terror. The taste of blood and the stink of her own fear. The face of the man who had attacked her, contorted with rage and hatred. The hideous winged creature that had hurtled through the shattered window, moving preternaturally fast, its fanged maw agape and dripping gore. Marutha, the old housekeeper who had played such a significant – and vocal – part in her upbringing, lying dead on the kitchen floor, her skull bashed in, her grey hair clotted with blood, brain, and bits of bone. Seriema stifled a sob. She had sent the old woman away in the midst of a quarrel, and the last words Marutha had heard from her beloved mistress had been harsh, and spoken in anger.

'Don't think about it,' Seriema ordered herself. If she let herself fall apart now, she would be lost. 'Concentrate on practicalities – like where that trader is taking us, and what he plans to do when we get there.' That was better. She could do nothing to change the past, but her future, no matter how uncertain, was something she could influence. Urging her horse onward through the gathering gloom, she went to speak to Tormon.

My child. My child. My child. My child. The hooves of the racing horses pounded out the words. Tormon held tightly to the blanket-wrapped form in front of him: so small, so infinitely precious.

I have you back, my little Annas. I'll keep you safe. So long as we're together, nothing else matters. Who cares what happens to their accursed city?

Bold words – yet a shudder ran through the trader as he remembered the winged abomination in Lady Seriema's mansion, and the unclean swarm of its brethren thronging the sky. His mind replayed the screaming as the helpless Tiarondians, trapped in the enclosed confines of the Sacred Precincts like sheep in a pen, were slaughtered. Tormon clutched Annas even tighter, until the child whimpered, and wriggled in protest.

Why should I trouble myself about their fate? They killed Kanella, my lifemate. They deserved to die.

In his heart, however, he knew it wasn't true. Those Tiarondians were ordinary men, women and children, just like his own sundered family. They had not murdered Kanella. Zavahl had done that – at least, he had ordered her death. And now the Hierarch himself was surely dead. Elion, the mysterious young man Tormon had encountered on the trail last night, had planned a rescue for reasons known only to himself, but the trader was sure he had no chance of succeeding. No, Zavahl must either have been sacrificed on the pyre to appease an angry god, or killed by the monstrosities that even now assailed the city. Tormon hardly knew which he would prefer. Death by fire must be an agonising end – but in this climate, the smoke from damp fuel would suffocate Zavahl before his flesh could sear. Perhaps the skyborne invaders were the better option. He imagined the Hierarch writhing and screaming, his body ripped open, the feral creatures clawing out his eyeballs and quarrelling over the glistening lengths of his gut . . .

Once, the trader would have been shocked to the core by such bloodthirsty, vengeful thoughts. Not any more.

Night had fallen. The hooves of the labouring horses splashed through the thick mud that stretched beyond the city. Tormon tried to keep his eyes fixed directly in front of him, for on either side the great pyres loomed, their smouldering glow casting a dim, smoky light into the darkness. The charred remains of bodies were still hideously distinct, despite the gathering gloom. He tried to protect Annas from the dreadful sights, turning her face into his chest, and pulling up her blanket to form a shield.

A shadowy shape loomed up at his side, and resolved itself into Lady Seriema, astride the great black horse that was the twin of his own. In his preoccupation, the trader had almost forgotten the companions of his flight: Presvel, the Lady's assistant, shivering in stylish city clothes unfit, as was their wearer, for a journey such as this, riding double with a young lass, unknown to the trader, whose hair was a mass of silvery-blond curls; Scall, the long, skinny youth who had attached himself to Tormon for good or ill, and of course the Lady Seriema herself, until today the most powerful merchant in Tiarond.

The woman who approached the trader, her white face blotched with ugly bruises and spattered with mud and gore, and her coarse brown hair flying loose in a witch's tangle, was unrecognisable as the well-groomed, richly-clad head of the Mercantile Association and Miners' Consortium. Her dishevelment was scarcely surprising. Not an hour ago, she had been attacked in her own home by a madman. She had been beaten and almost raped. Her city had been conquered by ravening monstrosities from the skies. Seriema had lost everything: wealth, home, rank and empire. Everything but her life and her indomitable pride, Tormon realised, noting her sword-stiff spine, her steely gaze and the hard, grim set of her mouth. Though he respected such determination, he also feared for her. She had mastered her emotions as tightly as she held in the powerful horse she rode, and the trader shuddered at the effort it must be costing her.

Seriema's voice betrayed no sign of the strain she must be feeling. Pulling her horse abreast of his own, she leaned across so that she could be heard over the thin whine of the rising wind. The trader could almost see the question on her lips.

Oh, please don't ask me what we're going to do now, Seriema. Why should I be able to answer that any better than you can?

'Where are we going, Tormon?' The words came slurred from her bruised and swollen mouth. 'Do you have a plan in mind?'

Why in Myrial's name does it have to be me *who comes up with a plan?*

Up to this point, the trader had been concentrating on what he did *not* want. He never wished to see Tiarond again. He didn't want his child to be put at any further risk, and he had absolutely no desire whatever to lay eyes on any more of the fell creatures that had attacked the city. All reasonable goals, as far as they went – but it had taken Seriema to remind him that he needed something positive to put in their place.

Away. Go far away. The rest could wait. All Tormon wanted right now was to put as much distance as possible between himself and Callisiora's capital city, with its politics, its arcane ceremonies, its secrets and intrigues – and its Hierarch, who thought nothing of murdering a young wife and mother in cold blood. He hoped this rain was also falling higher up the mountain, for even now it would be sluicing away the snow that had choked the pass last night. Maybe, for once, the wet weather might actually work in his favour.

The trader called the others to him. 'I'm taking Annas over the Snaketail.' Even as he spoke, the plan took shape in his mind. 'We'll be safe among the Reivers of the eastern hills. You can . . .' He realised that Seriema was no longer listening. Instead, she was looking back over her shoulder, her expression a peculiar mixture of relief and dismay. Tormon, following the direction of her gaze, felt his heart contract with dread. Unbelievable as it might seem, given the utter chaos in the city, they were being pursued.

Seriema, glancing back, saw a cluster of bobbing lights as a knot of Godsword soldiers, each one bearing a smoking torch, burst out of the city gates. Even at this distance, it was clear that they were following the muddy track of the fleeing travellers, and moving at a tremendous pace. The reins of her horse began to slip through hands that had suddenly turned damp, and she clenched her fingers tighter round the slippery leather.

Surely that was Blade? She squinted, trying to peer through the murk of drizzle and smoke. A curse on this imperfect eyesight!

She was torn at the thought of encountering the Godsword Commander. *How can I face him, looking like this?* was the first thought that shot into her mind, followed by a blaze of anger at her own stupidity. *You fool! He doesn't care what you look like. Why should he? You've served your purpose now.*

Seriema writhed at the memory of such gullibility. Blade had used her as a cat's paw in his vendetta against the Hierarch and she, or rather the plain, lonely old maid concealed beneath her veneer of confidence and power, had let him. Flattered by the attentions of the powerful, charismatic Commander, she had walked into his trap with open eyes.

How can I face him after I let him make such a fool of me? Yet despite her dismay and mortification, there remained a part of her that observed the approach of the Godsword troops with joy and relief. *It's all right now. I'm safe. Lord Blade will deal with this crisis. He'll take care of me.*

Tormon's curse cut across her deliberations. It was the first time she had ever heard him swear. There was fear in his eyes when he glanced down at his daughter – but that oath had contained a good deal of anger, too. Seriema felt an unaccustomed stab of guilt. She had been so preoccupied with her own selfish concerns, she had forgotten that Blade represented great danger to the trader and his child. Though she had no idea what lay behind his actions, the Suffragan Gilarra had told her that the Godsword Commander, together with the Hierarch Zavahl, had been responsible for the murder of Tormon's wife.

Tormon glanced behind once more, and shook his head. 'It's no good. They'll catch us in no time. The Sefrians are built for sustained power, not bursts of speed.'

Seriema knew he was right. There could be no escape. The Godswords, on their lighter, faster mounts, were catching up already. She turned back to speak to the trader, but he had dropped behind to ride with Scall, who was still insisting on leading Tormon's ridiculous donkey. The two drew close together for a moment, then the boy fell back, seeming to melt into the dusk, and vanished into the shadowy, smoke-wreathed area between the pyres.

When the trader turned back to Seriema, his arms were empty. There was a bleak look on his face as he loosened his sword in its sheath. She realised that having done all he could to save his child, he was determined to take his revenge on as many of the Godswords as he could manage: perhaps, if he could reach him, upon Blade himself.

No! Don't hurt him.

Yes! Let me help you.

How she cursed her ambivalent heart.

Then there was no more time for thought. The Godswords were

upon them in a blaze of torchlight, the hooves of their racing horses throwing up gouts of mud to either side. Seriema gasped in utter disbelief as a voice cried, 'Clear the road, you rabble.' Then her horse was shouldered aside by the sheer press of riders, as the column of soldiers barged past the travellers without a second glance. Within moments the Godswords were gone, hurtling up the road towards the pass.

The little mud-spattered band were left by the roadside, staring at one another in bemusement. Presvel frowned. 'What was *that* about?' He was aware of the trader's plight, Seriema knew, due to his unfortunate habit of eavesdropping on her business. She suspected that his feelings were somewhat similar to her own in that moment: glad that Tormon and his daughter had escaped Blade's notice, but also partly dismayed at his departure. The Godswords represented authority, security and order, all of which had been the keystones of Presvel's existence and her own.

There was a stir of movement among the shadows, and as Seriema's eyes grew accustomed once more to the gloom, she saw Scall slip out from between the smoking pyres on his little chestnut mare, the tired donkey trailing after. He returned a scowling, rumpled child to her father with an air of relief. Annas, wriggling herself comfortable in Tormon's arms, appeared to share his sentiments. '*He* put his hand over my mouth,' she complained shrilly. 'And it was *all dirty*.'

'Well, you wouldn't keep quiet,' Scall defended himself. 'Anyway, a little bit of dirt never hurt no-one.'

'You taste *horrible*.' Annas was not to be quashed so easily.

'If you hadn't bit me, you wouldn't know that, would you?'

At first, Tormon scarcely heard them. As the soldiers had rushed by, he had glimpsed the rearmost rider, who rode a little more slowly than the others, apparently because he had difficulty managing his horse. Elion? Out here with Blade? What was going on? His thoughts followed the Godswords up the trail, until the squabble between Scall and his daughter jerked him back. 'Quiet,' he growled. 'This is no time for your nonsense. I'm trying to think.' He nudged his horse closer to Seriema's mount. 'You see a lot of Lord Blade. Have you any idea what he's up to, my Lady? I don't understand why he should go tearing off up the mountain like that when the city is in danger.'

Seriema drew herself up in the saddle. 'What makes you think that I have any connection whatsoever with Lord Blade?' Her voice was whetted steel. 'Whatever you may have heard, it's a pack of lies.'

The trader looked at her in surprise. What ailed the woman? Well, whatever it might be, he had no time for it now. He had a decision to make – but was there really anything to decide? Since Blade was at large in the vicinity of the Snaketail, Tormon and his party had just run out of alternatives. He turned to the others. 'This changes everything. It will be too dangerous to go over the mountain now. I'm taking the cliff road down from the plateau to the lowlands, but the rest of you may want to take your chances elsewhere. The way will probably be guarded, and it'll be a nightmare in the dark, but . . .'

'Tormon, what are you saying?' Seriema interrupted. 'You can't take the lowland route. Didn't you know? The floodwater draining down from the plateau has turned the trail into a torrent.'

The trader turned cold all over. 'Are you sure? Maybe it's not as bad as you think. It could be passable with care—'

'We don't know. The folk who tried it never came back to report. We presume they were swept away to their deaths,' Seriema told him flatly. With flashing eyes and lifted chin, suddenly she was the imperious great lady once more. 'To try that path would be suicide. You can drag the others to their deaths if they're mad enough to follow you, but Presvel and I are staying right here.'

'Damn and blast!' Tormon turned his gaze up to the mountain, where a string of tiny lights showed the Godswords beginning to ascend the winding road. He took a deep breath. 'I'm going to try it anyway. As the Lady Seriema has pointed out, you folk have another choice: you can follow the Godswords if you prefer, or wait here for their return. If you go back to the city with them, maybe they can protect you. It's up to you, but anyone who wants to join with me had better come now. I want to get to the edge tonight with some time left to rest ourselves and the horses. If the cliff road is as bad as you say, I want to wait until daylight before trying to go down.' Without waiting for objections, Tormon turned towards the south and urged his horse forward. Now that he had made his decision, he was anxious to press on quickly.

There was a stir of movement at his side, and Scall came up abreast of him, tugging the reluctant Esmeralda behind his horse. The boy was scowling. 'Were you planning just to leave this poor donkey?' he demanded.

Tormon shook his head. 'No, lad, and I'd no plans to leave *you* behind, either. It was important that you chose for yourself, but I was counting on you to join me, and I'm very glad to have you along.'

'And what about the other Sefrian? They're a pair. You can't break them up.'

The trader chuckled. 'Just wait for a moment.'

Even as he spoke, Seriema came galloping up, splashing mud in all directions in her haste. Behind her came Presvel and the girl, their horse working hard to keep up the pace with its double burden. Judging by the stormy expressions on the faces of the Lady and her assistant, a short, sharp quarrel had taken place – and evidently, Seriema had lost. 'Damn you,' she snarled at Tormon. 'You leave us no choice.'

'That's right, Lady. Just as Blade left me with none.'

Up on the mountain, the two women and the firedrake stood high on a slope above the trail to the Snaketail pass. Veldan and Toulac were stretching their legs, and giving Kaz's back a rest after their headlong race across the upper slopes. While they paused, the firedrake was using the time to scan the track below for any signs of pursuit. In his darksight, the route lay quiet and peaceful and, to human senses, seemingly unoccupied behind the drifting veils of rain. Nevertheless, Kaz was far from convinced. 'There are soldiers somewhere nearby,' he insisted. 'It's a wonder you can't smell them yourself – they stink of iron, unwashed sweat and old blood.'

This news came as no surprise to Toulac. It was exactly what she'd been expecting. 'Didn't I tell you, girlie?' she asked Veldan. 'That son of a bitch Blade would never sit tamely in Tiarond without at least trying to catch us. Though he sent some men after us through the tithe caves, I bet you he'll be racing up the mountain himself, to see if he can get ahead of us on the trail.'

'That's mucked it.' Veldan growled a lurid curse that could have come straight out of Toulac's own mouth. The veteran looked at her in approving surprise. Despite the instant friendship that had sprung up between the two women, they really knew very little about one another. In the three days of their acquaintance, Veldan had spent much of the time unconscious after her encounter with the landslide. She was still recovering from the battering she had taken, and until now had been fairly quiet and subdued. Toulac rejoiced at the signs of returning health and confidence in her younger friend, and looked forward to knowing her better. First, however, they must win their way through the next few hours. Sitting up here in the freezing rain wouldn't accomplish anything.

Nor would taking unnecessary risks, and forcing the others to take them too. Toulac the old campaigner was wise enough to know the difference between want and need. They had been on their way back to the sawmill, to rescue Mazal, her warhorse, who'd been left behind during the escape from Blade and his men. She had persuaded Veldan to return, but if Kaz could scent soldiers on the trail, it would be suicide to go back for an animal, no matter how precious, and nothing short of murder to ask Veldan and the firedrake to come with her.

When Veldan had agreed to go back for the horse, the veteran had blessed her good fortune in having such an understanding companion. Now, however, she saw a faint frown on the younger woman's face. Was she having doubts? Toulac could scarcely blame her. If they went back now, they would be running right into Blade's clutches.

It's no good. I'll have to give him up. It just can't be helped.

It was the right decision, but it went hard with her. Mazal was the last reminder of her glory days as a warrior. He had been a faithful friend, had saved her life in battle times without number – and he was the very last of her old companions-in-arms. Whatever happened, Toulac knew in her bones that she would never be coming back to this place. She must abandon Mazal, and leave him behind to face an unknown fate.

When she turned back to Veldan, the younger woman's eyes were on her face. 'Look, Toulac. If you still want to go back we will. We have Kaz to help us. We'll manage somehow.'

The veteran swallowed hard. 'Don't be daft, girlie. We can't go back now and you know it. Let's get ourselves away over the pass, before we lose what little lead we have.'

'Are you sure?'

'Certain.' She turned away from Veldan, so that the younger woman could not see her face. 'Come on, let's go.' Using a rock to boost herself, she scrambled clumsily onto the firedrake's back.

Veldan was relieved that Toulac had given up her plan to rescue the horse. She appreciated the extent of the sacrifice, and knew better than to diminish it by discussing the matter any further. It was time to get moving. Those men that Kaz had scented downtrail could not be too far behind. 'Got your breath back, Kaz? Are you ready?'

'Any time you like, Boss.' He held out a foreleg, and Veldan sprang to his shoulders. The graceful, fluid movement with which she usually mounted turned into a scramble as clumsy as Toulac's ascent, when her knee caught on the recumbent body of Zavahl, who was bound across the firedrake's back between the two women.

'Plague on it!' Veldan rubbed her knee where it had hit the side of the former Hierarch's head. He stirred and moaned, but she took no notice. Why should she be concerned about hurting him? At their first meeting he had flinched away from her scarred face as though she was too hideous to contemplate, and called her a *creature*, as though she wasn't even human. After that, she didn't feel she owed him any particular consideration. Had it not been for the fact that he shared his body, however unwillingly, with the consciousness of Aethon, Seer of the Dragonfolk, she would quite happily have let him burn on the sacrificial pyre from which she and her companions had saved him.

'Are you ready?' the firedrake's telepathic voice broke into her thoughts. 'Because I think I hear riders in the distance.'

'Damn. Let's go!'

'Hold tight, ladies.' Kaz was off with a rush and a slither, speeding down through the trees towards the trail. No-one had any doubts that the Commander of the Godswords could not be far behind them.

For a man whose plans had been smashed to splinters, Blade was surprisingly calm. He was amazed that he could contemplate this setback – no, catastrophe – with such composure, and he had a feeling it wouldn't last. But surely anger would be forgivable, appropriate even, under the circumstances. The Hierarch had escaped his clutches, and though Zavahl was no great loss in himself, Blade strongly suspected that the Hierarch carried within him the mind and essence of one of the Dragonfolk, who might recognise the renegade former Loremaster from the past, and betray him to the others. Worse still, there would be no chance now of using Callisiora as a base from which to conquer the Shadowleague and snatch the leadership from that hidebound fool Cergorn.

Before he'd realised what was happening, it had all slipped out of his grasp. Those endless years of self-sacrifice and single-minded determination; all the intrigue, the manoeuvring and manipulating: all wiped out in a single day by a skinny, scar-faced woman and a firedrake. Not to mention a couple of thousand deadly winged predators from the north, he reminded himself. What were the odds against *them* turning up today of all days, to snatch away the city which had figured so largely in his schemes? And worst of all was the bitter knowledge that they had only come at all because *he* had seen fit to tamper with the Curtain Walls.

It was almost enough to make one believe that Myrial was a god, after all.

Blade mastered his rising anger until he was calm once more. Rage would get him nowhere. Now he must think, must plan, must calculate how much could be salvaged from this disaster. The path he had been travelling was closed to him, but he could always trample out a new route. Experience – and expedience – had taught him that.

It was hard for his subordinates to see beyond the globe of amber light cast by the smoking torches, but Blade was Mageborn, with the acute night vision of his kind. He took the head of the column, and led them unerringly up the trail. Trustingly they followed him. Once, he had been proud of this efficient, disciplined body of fighters he had trained. Now, however, they had become nothing more than the means to an end. It was vital that he found the Loremaster and her firedrake partner, and stopped them returning to Gendival with the Hierarch. They would return to the trail, of that he was certain. The pass carved its way through a craggy wilderness of cliffs and broken pinnacles that would surely be too much even for a firedrake. First, however, they must make their way across from the far side of the mountain. If he hurried, there was still a chance to catch them at the Snaketail.

Kaz came out onto the track, and Veldan turned cold as she saw the glittering lights of torches, coming up fast from the direction of Tiarond. The approaching riders were still a few hundred yards away and, once again, Veldan blessed the firedrake's remarkable eyes as he changed focus to bridge the distance and bring the figures into clear view. Just as Toulac had said, the Godswords were led by their Commander himself. Digging his taloned toes into the ground for leverage, Kaz swerved to the right, his tail sending up a spray of soil and gravel. As he shot up the track, Veldan sent him an urgent thought, 'We've got to delay them somehow.'

'Why worry, Boss? I can outrun those slugs any time.'

'I know, but you'll be slowed right up in that narrow place on the trail, and last time I looked, you hadn't perfected the art of outrunning an arrow.'

'I'm working on it – but you're right. Maybe we should hold them up a little.' Kaz veered aside to where the tree-clad slopes came down to meet the track. Abruptly he lashed his tail back and forth, scattering earth, stones, broken underbrush and a couple of sapling trees across the only route the Godswords could take.

Veldan heard curses and shouts from the approaching soldiers. She glanced back over her shoulder to see them closing the distance between themselves and their prey. One or two of them were already lifting crossbows, and a few bolts embedded themselves in the muddy track, short of the Loremasters' position, but too close for her liking. 'Time to go,' she warned the firedrake.

Kaz ran on out of bowshot, speeding ahead of the Godswords until the trail narrowed, and the tree-covered slopes gave way to steep crags on the right. To the left, the distance between the track and the cliff edge had narrowed, until the route now skirted the very brink of the precipice. It had taken the soldiers a few minutes to get round the initial blockade, but still they were following. To Veldan's dismay, Blade was far out ahead of the others. Though he did not carry a crossbow, the look on his face boded ill for the women should he catch up to them.

'Oh, how I wish I hadn't lost my own bow in that landslide,' she muttered.

'Never mind that – I have a better idea. Hold tight, girls.' Kaz reared up on his haunches, with Veldan and Toulac clinging precariously to his neck spines. He leaned against a battered old fir tree at the side of the trail, pushing hard. The roots, loosened by months of rain and wind, held but lightly to the soil, and tore loose with a sound like the ripping of a gigantic bolt of canvas.

The firedrake sprang back hastily as the tree came crashing down across the trail. 'Not bad, eh?' he said smugly, and with a jerk that nearly unseated his riders, he dashed off again at top speed. Confident that their pursuers had been foiled for a time at least, and with their minds on the road ahead, neither the firedrake nor the two women he carried looked back to see the results of their efforts.

Consumed by the urge to reach his prey, Blade was running far out in front of his men, urging his horse on and on to greater efforts. Looking ahead, he saw the firedrake pause at the fir tree, and realised what was about to happen, but it was too late to stop. He tried to rein the beast in but it had caught his own wild mood, resisting his commands, fighting bit and rein, and running headlong towards disaster.

The tree came crashing down. The horse shied violently aside, almost from underneath the fallen giant. One leg found a pothole in the rutted track, and the beast floundered and lurched to one side with a scream of agony and the sickening snap of breaking bone. Blade, thrown over its shoulder, hit the ground hard and rolled to escape the crushing weight of his mount as it went down. Without warning, the ground dropped out from beneath him. Disorientated by the fall, he had rolled right to the edge of the track and over the precipice.

For a horrifying instant, Blade's body twisted in empty space, then he struck a stony projection, slowing his fall. Despite the jarring pain of the impact, the cold terror searing through him loaned him sufficient strength to jerk his body round and slam it into the cliff, where he clawed at the rock for a handhold. The escarpment became less steep as it dropped: he slithered down its rough, sloping face for a few more yards until his scrabbling fingers found a hold, bringing him up with a jolt that drove the breath from his lungs, wrenched every muscle in his hands and arms, and threatened to dislocate his bones from their sockets.

Fighting for breath, Blade braced his toes hard against the rock, trying to take some of the strain from fingers that were braced into a narrow niche where erosion had cracked the stone away. He was hanging on through sheer willpower, though soon his ebbing strength would fail him. He knew he had only a few minutes at most – but at long last his men had caught up with him and he could hear them at the top of the cliff. Looking up with difficulty, he saw sparks of torchlight clustering at the edge of the trail. Voices came from high above him:

'Did you see where he went over?'

'About here, I reckon.'

'Torchlight doesn't reach that far – it's all shadows down there.'

'Don't see no sign of him. Do you?'

'Nah. I reckon the bastard's still bouncing.'

There was a harsh guffaw of laughter, then another voice spoke, this time with more authority. 'Well, sod this for a lark. It was a stupid idea anyway, this wild goose chase up the mountain. Both Blade and the Hierarch are probably frying in perdition by now, and serve them right, I say. Come on lads, let's go back to the city and report to Lieutenant Galveron. We'll have problems enough when we get there, thanks to those flying sons of bitches, but I reckon we can do far more good in Tiarond than we can out here.'

They were actually leaving! Blade had always known he was hated; that his men obeyed him out of fear, not love. It had never mattered to him until now. But surely if they knew he was still alive . . . He opened his mouth to shout – but no sound would come. He had never asked anybody for help since he had ceased to be Amaurn; since his beloved Aveole had been torn from him forever. He couldn't do it now, not even to save his own life. Couldn't humble himself, let go of his pride, betray a weakness.

You fool. What good is your pride if it gets you killed? Across the void of years, Aveole's voice came back to him, and for a moment it seemed that his beloved was there beside him. His men were leaving. This was his only chance.

'Help. I'm down here. Help me!' It was as though the words ripped their way with bloody claws out of the depths of his being. Even as he shouted, he despised himself for the moment of weakness that had lured him into giving in.

For a moment there was nothing but silence from above, then the voices came again.

'Was that Blade? Did you hear him?'

'I didn't hear a thing, and nor did you.'

'Leave him be. Vicious bastard – we're better off without him.'

'You're right. It was probably only a bird or something.'

'Well if it wasn't, it had better learn to fly pretty bloody quick!'

The voices faded, and diminishing hoofbeats sounded on the trail. They had left him deliberately, knowing that he needed help, knowing he would soon die without it. Blade, consumed by anger at their treachery, suddenly felt his fingers slipping . . .

Terror speared again through him as he dropped, slithering down the cliff faster and faster, tearing his fingers on the unyielding rock as he scrabbled frantically for another hold. His headlong slide was brought to an abrupt halt as his feet hit a level surface. His knees buckled and gave way beneath him, and he found himself kneeling on a narrow shelf of rock, barely wide enough to accommodate his body. Reaction set in and he doubled over, gasping for breath, his body wracked by tremors as his muscles unlocked from their dreadful tension. He pulled himself up short when he realised that the harsh, quick rasp of his breathing stood in danger of turning into hysterical laughter or sobs. Since losing Aveole, he had never allowed free rein to his feelings. Emotions only led to confusion, mistakes and endless pain, and he had no intention of making himself so vulnerable. Not ever again.

At first Blade was incredulous, then euphoric at his own survival. He had done it! For the second time in his life, he had cheated imminent, almost certain death. But as the reality of his situation began to sink in, he sobered quickly. He was marooned halfway up a cliff face with no food or water, and a bruised, battered body that was already beginning to stiffen and ache from the punishment it had taken. Even if he managed to make it back up to the trail, he was miles from anywhere and he had no horse. Worse still, he had lost his grip on the city he had striven for so long to control, and all his plans were in ruins.

Well, he had pulled himself out of worse situations than this before, and had returned to fight another day. If he'd been the kind of man who was daunted by setbacks, he would have given up on life years ago. So what if his men had chosen to betray and abandon him? They would pay sooner or later. Blade had a long memory for grudges. In the meantime, he would damn well manage without them.

Shakily, he got to his feet, balancing precariously on his narrow perch. He had been a renegade Loremaster, then the Commander of Tiarond's Godsword troops – what would he become next? Only time would tell. Gritting his teeth, Blade hunted for his first hand- and footholds, and began to climb.

Two

Hard Lessons

As the Godsword troop departed, Elion doused his torch in the mud that covered the trail, and hung back, guiding his horse into the shadows beneath the fallen tree. He could make out the progress of the soldiers from the movement of their lights in the darkness, and it was clear that without Blade they had abandoned their orderly double file and had set off down the mountain in a shifting, loose-knit bunch. That suited the Loremaster just fine. With luck, everyone would think that the missing trooper was riding with someone else, and his absence would not be noticed. In their hurry to get back to the city, it was highly unlikely that anyone would think of stopping to count heads, so he should be safe enough.

While he waited for their lights to pass out of sight, Elion sought the mind of his fellow Loremaster.

'Veldan?'

'Elion!' She sounded relieved, and he could understand why. Though there had been no love lost between them since their last disastrous mission, the Shadowleague was a brotherhood, and they were part of that family. Set apart as they were from the rest of the world, Loremasters were accustomed to supporting and helping one another no matter what personal animosity might lie between them, and such bonds were difficult to break.

'Elion? Are you all right? Where are you?'

'Where in perdition do you think I am? On the wrong side of your blasted tree, of course.'

'Damn.' Behind her thoughts he could hear her chagrin. 'Elion, I—'

'It wasn't her fault, you streak of slime.' With a snarl in his voice, Kaz cut in over what was clearly going to be an apology. 'The tree was my idea, I did it to protect myself and my partner, and you'd better believe me when I say that saving *your* miserable hide was the last thing on my mind.'

'Kaz, shut up. Bickering and insults won't help.' Veldan sounded distracted. 'Elion, is there any way you can get through? Do you want us to come back and help?'

'Over my dead body,' the firedrake growled.

Elion ignored him. 'You have Aethon safe?'

'Yes, we've got him. Though at the moment he's trapped within the Hierarch's mind, and the wretched man just won't co-operate.'

'You'd think he'd be more grateful, considering that you saved his life.'

'Wouldn't you, though? Still, there'll be time enough to deal with that problem when we get out of Callisiora and into a place of safety.'

'That's the most important thing,' Elion agreed. 'You carry on, Veldan, and concentrate on getting Aethon back to Gendival. I'll worry about the tree.'

As he spoke, he took one of the small, egg-shaped glims from his pocket and twisted it between his hands. An eerie, greenish glow began to emanate from the artefact, and by its light he began to examine the fallen giant. 'It's all right, Veldan.' He spoke with some relief. 'The situation here isn't as bad as it looks. There's almost a space at the side, where the tree has torn away from the bank. I just have some roots to hack through, then I'll be on your tail before you know it.'

'If only you had Shree there to help, it would take no time.'

'I know, but there's no sign of her. What could have happened? What in the world could harm a Wind Sprite?'

'I can't imagine – but I'm not looking forward to facing the Archimandrite once he knows we've lost her.'

'Thanks for saying "we," Veldan, but ultimately it's my

responsibility. Shree was my partner on this mission, not yours.'

Veldan paused. 'Look here, Elion. Do you want me to tell him for you? I hadn't planned to contact Gendival until dawn, though. At the rate Kaz travels, we should at least have reached the Curtain Walls by then. Cergorn isn't likely to be too happy about anything we have to tell him, but if we're safe in our own lands with Aethon when he hears from us, that would be *some* good news, at any rate.'

Surprised and grateful, Elion could only stammer his thanks.

'And in return,' Veldan went on, 'you'll back me up over Toulac, won't you?'

'You might as well ask me to put my head between a bear's jaws, and have done with it,' Elion complained. 'All right. It's the least I can do. Under the circumstances, I think we're better off sticking together – though I don't know what the fuss is about. What's one old woman more or less? Still, you know her better than I do. If you think she'll make a Loremaster, I'll back you up, and reserve my own judgement until I meet her.'

'What happened to the Godswords?' Veldan changed the subject. 'Since you have the chance to talk to me like this, I presume they're gone. Are we safe from pursuit now?'

'Yes, you don't have to worry any more. Kaz's little stunt certainly solved *that* problem for us.' He went on to tell her about Blade's fall, and how, without their leader to drive them, the Godswords had lost no time in returning to Tiarond.

There was a long moment of silence before Veldan spoke. 'So that's the end of Blade. You know, I can't help but feel there's something amiss somewhere. His death was just too quick and simple. There was such a sense of *power* about the man. Somehow I thought he'd be a lot more difficult to kill.'

'Dropping somebody over a precipice will usually do the job,' Elion replied with forced cheerfulness. He pulled out his sword and began to hack his way through the tangle of roots, deploring the damage he was doing to the weapon in the process. Well, there was no other option. He would just have to get the smith to put an edge back on the blade when he got back to Gendival. And on the subject of blades, he was glad now, that he had not told Veldan that the Godsword Commander *had* survived the fall, and that he had cried out for help. There was no sense in worrying her for nothing, and besides, Blade was as good as dead. It was only a matter of time.

It wasn't Scall's idea of fun to pick his way, for the second time in as many days, along a muddy trail on a cold, damp winter's night. The going was slick and treacherous underfoot, and Tormon, leading the group, had been hard pressed to find his way across the plateau in the dark, with the dim glow of the smouldering bonfires as his only guide.

At least Scall was not alone, as he had been when Smithmaster Agella, to whom he had been apprenticed, had sent him up the trail to Mistress Toulac's house, in hopes of securing him a better future. Where was Agella now? Scall wondered, remembering the massacre in Tiarond, and the dreadful screaming borne on the wind from the Sacred Precincts. Had the Smithmaster survived? What of his parents and his sister? If Felyss still lived, she was a widow. He had glimpsed Ivar's body in Lady Seriema's room, and in shock, had almost given the game away. Luckily, the attack of the skyborne demon and the subsequent escape with Tormon and the others had given him time to work things out. Clearly, the slaughterman had attacked and almost killed the Lady Seriema, but why?

Scall had no idea, but he was sure of one thing. With the future so uncertain, his survival depended on the folk who rode with him tonight. Besides, he owed Tormon debts of gratitude and of guilt, and he respected and pitied the newly-widowed trader. He had never liked his sister's husband, having been on the receiving end of the slaughterman's temper more times than enough, when he had lived beneath his roof. Ivar was no great loss to the world as far as Scall was concerned, and he wasn't about to alienate these new companions by claiming kinship with one who had nearly murdered the Lady Seriema.

In the darkness, the travellers almost missed the guardhouse at the top of the cliff road. A single lantern, veiled by mist and rain, was all that marked the location of the building. Scall waited for the door to open, spilling light across the carved wooden rails of the porch. At any moment he expected a voice to cry, 'Who goes there?' Nothing happened, however. The guardhouse remained shuttered and silent; dark apart from the dim lamp that swung above the door. Beckoning Scall to him, Tormon handed over his sleeping child, who had succumbed to exhaustion long before. Annas stirred and whimpered in the boy's uncertain grasp, but did not wake. The trader dismounted and climbed the porch steps while the others waited, and Scall heard a rattle as he tried the lock.

'Curse it.' After a moment Tormon came back down the steps. 'It's locked. The guards aren't here, though, and that's the main thing. Clearly they went to the ceremony and never came back.'

'That's all very well, but what shall we do now?' Lady Seriema demanded. 'We can't stay out here all night in the rain.'

'We won't have to.' Tormon took back his child from Scall, then turned to lead his horse along the front of the building. 'There's a stable tucked away here, around the side. They won't have bothered to lock that, I hope.'

It was very dark around the corner of the guardhouse. Scall groped his way along, leading his chestnut mare and the tired little donkey. He kept bumping into the others in the darkness, and was nearly knocked sprawling by the Lady Seriema's gelding. Blessedly, there came the rattle and scrape of a latch, and the creak of hinges as a door was dragged open. A moment later a square of yellow light, partially obscured by the backside of Tormon's horse, sprang up in the darkness. Scall's little chestnut, smelling the hay and grain inside the building, jostled eagerly forward for her share.

The stable was roomy and dry, with space for a dozen horses in stalls on either side of a long passage. At the far end a door led to a tackroom with pegs for saddles and harness, and bins of fodder along the wall. Though the place was not what Scall, in better days, would have called warm, it was luxury compared to the chill, wet night outside, and there was even better news to come. Beyond the fireplace was another door which, though locked, yielded when the trader put his shoulder to it. Beyond was the barracks for the resident guards, with bunk beds, another fireplace, and cupboards which held a treasure trove of items for the needy traveller: spare clothing, weapons and, above all, food.

Tormon settled Annas into one of the bunks, and tucked the blankets around her while Scall lit the fire – a task at which, having served his apprenticeship in a blacksmith's forge, he was very proficient. The trader hesitated by his daughter's bed, plainly reluctant to leave her alone while he tended to the horses.

'I'll watch her, if you like.' The young fair-haired girl who had come with Presvel spoke up. Seeing his doubtful look, she added, 'It's all right. I don't know anything about horses, so I won't be much use to you there, but I'm used to children. I had little brothers and sisters of my own before the blacklung took them. Besides, I want to do my share. I don't believe in being a burden on people.' She spoke the last words so defiantly that Tormon looked at her in surprise. Daunted by the cold, closed expression on her face, he did not pursue the subject, but simply nodded. 'Very well – and my thanks to you. What are we to call you?'

'My name is Rochalla.'

'Well, I'm Tormon and this is Scall. And now that we all know one another, let's get ourselves settled down for the night. While we're seeing to the horses, do you think you could get us something to eat, Rochalla?'

'Of course.' For the first time the girl smiled, and Scall suddenly realised how pretty she was beneath the dirt that splattered her face. He wished he could think of an excuse to stay in the barracks and help her, but unfortunately, there was work to be done, and he knew better than to shirk his duties. Already learning Tormon's ways, he settled his mare and the donkey into adjacent stalls, and set about making them comfortable for the night.

'Look at this!' The trader was visible through the tackroom doorway, lifting the lids of the bins and peering inside. 'Thanks be to Myrial, the Godswords actually have grain here for their horses.'

'Blade's horses are more fortunate than the people of the city. *Their* only option is to starve.' The blonde girl had appeared in the doorway of the barracks beyond the tackroom, a scowl on her face. 'Still, who cares if little children die of cold and hunger and disease, so long as the horses are all right?' With that she was gone. Presvel took a hesitant step, as if to follow her. Then, with a helpless shrug, he went back to tending his horse, but Scall noticed that his eyes never strayed far from the doorway through which Rochalla had vanished.

Seriema was staring at her assistant, and her cold, angry countenance made Scall shudder. With her attention fixed on Presvel, she made no effort to care for her horse, and the gelding nosed around its empty manger and began to fidget and stamp. Tormon, returning from the tackroom with fodder for his stallion, frowned. 'We care for our own horses while we travel, my Lady,' he said quietly. 'Avrio has carried you all this way through the rain and mud. The least you can do to repay him is see to his food and comfort now.'

Seriema turned on him, eyes blazing. 'Damn your horse. At least the beast is only tired and hungry. That's just the start of *my* problems. I lost everything today. My home, my livelihood, my place in the world – everything.'

Tormon's expression grew hard and grim. 'Every one of us here has lost both loved ones and our place in the world,' he told her harshly. 'I lost my home and livelihood as you did. I also lost my lifemate, the woman I loved more than life itself. Do you see *me* standing around whining? Is anyone else in this party shirking their responsibilities?'

Seriema flushed an ugly shade of red, and Presvel stepped in to defend her. 'That's not really fair, Tormon. Remember what she went through today. Don't trouble yourself, my Lady. I'll take care of the horse.'

'You'll do nothing of the kind. Your own animal is in need of attention,' the trader said firmly. His expression softened a little. 'I know the Lady had a tough time today, Presvel. But that's why she needs useful occupation, to keep herself from brooding.' He turned back to Seriema. 'It's for your own good. I'm speaking from experience, believe me.'

Judging by Seriema's truculent expression, she hadn't listened to a word. 'It's your horse,' she said. 'You take care of it if you're so concerned. I'm cold and I'm tired, and I ache all over. I'm going to sit by the fire.'

Tormon's mouth tightened. 'Suit yourself, my Lady, but I hope you're good at walking. Because if you don't take care of that horse tonight, you won't be riding it tomorrow.'

For a long moment the two of them locked eyes. Watching the battle of wills, Scall held his breath. At last Seriema, her movements jerky, her body rigid with anger, tore her gaze away and stalked off to the tackroom. *Great Myrial!* the boy thought. *She's still defying him.* He wondered what would happen to her on the morrow. Though he had not known Tormon long, he knew already that the trader was a man of his word.

Suddenly Seriema reappeared in the tackroom doorway, with a bucket in her hand. Without meeting anyone's eyes, she stalked past her companions as though they did not exist, went into the gelding's box, and began to tip feed into his manger.

Scall stared at her, eyes popping – then jumped as Tormon's hand came down on his shoulder. 'Son,' the trader said softly, 'mind your own business. Have you no work of your own to do?' Then the hand was gone. Hastily Scall turned back to his little mare and began to groom her as though his life depended on it.

Seriema stared at the Sefrian gelding and bit her lip. A surreptitious glance around the stable showed her that everyone else was hard at work, though they displayed varying degrees of competence, and Presvel, at least, was tackling the job with distaste written all over his face.

Though her pride would not let her admit it, Seriema was feeling very sorry for herself.

Am I the only one who has never done this before? Is it only me who doesn't have a clue? What do they expect of me? My father had very strong ideas about our station in the world, and I wasn't brought up to do this sort of menial work. The groom brought my horses to the door, all ready to ride, then took them away again when I was finished. I don't know where to start with all this brushing and feeding and stuff.

Across the passageway, Tormon's scruffy young lad was working away with a will on the pretty little chestnut mare. Seriema sneaked a sidelong glance at him, and gritted her teeth.

Am I going to be bested by some common urchin from who knows where? If he can do it, so can I.

Clumsily she began to copy Scall's actions, her aching body protesting every movement, but after a while she wished she had been the one riding the little chestnut. There seemed to be an awful lot of this big black horse to groom.

'You've never done this before, have you?' Tormon had appeared beside her.

Still angry with him, Seriema turned her face away. The trader, who had already finished his own beast, began to complete her inefficient work with swift, sure hands. 'I realise this isn't easy for you, my Lady, but you have to understand that these wet and weary animals are our only way out of here.'

Seriema continued to ignore him, but he went on speaking softly, none the less. 'In these endless days of cold and damp it's hard to keep horses fit and healthy, especially when there's so little fodder around for them. It's vital that we take good care of them, because they are our only lifeline, and if we lose them, we won't find replacements easily.'

Somehow, without her realising, he had taken over Seriema's task completely, letting her lean back against the partition and rest, while she watched and learned from an expert. Because her pride would never allow her to do anything badly, she observed him closely, vowing that next time, she would do better. An essential fairness in her acknowledged that Tormon was right about the horses being a lifeline, and she shivered, suddenly feeling very lost.

It was only just beginning to come home to her that she was now a homeless wanderer in the wilderness, and though the notion seemed too terrible and terrifying to bear, her common sense and the ruthless practicality that she had cultivated over her years as merchant told her she would have to get used to the idea pretty damn quickly. It began to dawn on her that staying alive in this hostile new world would be a lot more complicated than just taking good care of the horses, and if she wanted to survive, she would have to learn a whole new set of skills.

While she had been coming to terms with these harsh realities, Tormon had finished rubbing down the horse. As he left the beast with a final pat he turned to face Seriema and spoke again, continuing where he had left off as though his thoughts had been bridging the long silent pause between them. 'Besides,' he said bitterly, 'these Sefrians belonged to Kanella, my lifemate, and she loved them like children.' The open anguish on his face twisted in Seriema's heart like a knife. He took a deep breath as if to speak again, then shook his head and stumbled out of the stall, his head bowed down as though the burden of his grief were a crushing weight across his shoulders.

Further up the mountain, it was deep into the night before a hand – filthy, broken-nailed and bloody – came groping up over the edge of the cliff. With a last gargantuan effort, Blade pulled himself over the brink of the precipice. Lacking the strength even to get to his hands and knees, he rolled away from the perilous drop and lay under a bush, trying to gasp enough air into his burning lungs while his aching muscles cramped and spasmed, and his body shook with fatigue.

No-one else could have done it. Only Blade's relentless, driving will had brought him safely to the top. For hours he had inched his way up the unyielding cliff face, unable to rest, not daring, even for an instant, to relax his grip, his concentration, or the agonising tension of his muscles. The toes of his boots were worn right through from scraping the rough rock in search of the tiniest foothold to help support his weight while one hand groped desperately for another crack in the weathered stone. His fingertips and nails were torn and bleeding from being jammed into a thousand tiny crevices, and the palms of his hands were blistered and raw.

Even in his exhausted state, Blade burned with the white-hot fury that had driven him for every step of his climb. As he had clung to the perilous rock face, he had used his anger as a spur to drive himself towards his goal. His prey had escaped him. His plan to rid himself of Zavahl had perished. His men had defied his orders, had betrayed him, had deliberately left him to die. Now that the former Commander was safe on level ground, however, he knew he must be calm and calculating; must put his rage aside, lest it cloud his thinking. It took very little reflection to tell him that his alternatives were down to three: one of which, simply leaving this benighted land all together and starting again elsewhere, he did not count as an option at all. That aside, he could either return to Tiarond and try to seize back the reins of power – and there seemed little point in that with his men in a state of open mutiny and the entire surviving population penned like sheep within the temple – or he could follow the trail of the girl and the firedrake, and return to Gendival.

A shiver went through Blade at the very thought: a thrill compounded of pain, excitement and dread at the thought of seeing again the enchanting Valley of the Two Lakes that had once given a lonely wanderer a home. Gendival, a place of beauty and danger, with its memories of ambition and failure, love and loss, had always maintained a special hold on his heart. Blade smiled grimly.

After all these years the exile will return. And if Cergorn gets his hands on me, I've no doubt he'll be only too glad to welcome me with the execution he was forced to postpone for so long.

This was not the return that he had imagined. He had planned to enter Gendival at the head of an army and to strike with the swift, deadly precision of a serpent, for no matter how many soldiers were at his back, the key to conquering the Shadowleague was speed and surprise. Once Cergorn and the most powerful of his supporters were out of the way, the rest would be easy – at least, that had been his original strategy. Now, all alone and with his power base gone, he would have to come up with a new scheme, and to have any hope at all of succeeding, it had better be a damn good one.

Had Blade been a lesser man, he would have huddled beneath his bush on that stark mountainside and wept for the ruination of so many years' hard work, and for the future that had been snatched without warning from his hands. Instead, he turned his mind to his immediate goal: survival. The night was bitterly cold, with the rain turning back to sleet, and he was soaked through and chilled to the bone after his long climb. Also, he was exhausted, on foot and far from help. If he didn't get moving soon and find shelter, there'd be little point in making any plans for the future.

Luckily, the sawmill was within walking distance, and he had no doubt that the handful of troops he had left on watch there would have slunk back home to Tiarond by now with the rest of their treacherous, disloyal brethren. It was unlikely that they would have left any food behind, but he could have a fire at least, and rest in comfort. All he had to do was reach the place.

Slowly, after several attempts, Blade managed to pull himself to his feet. At least I still have my sword, he thought, as the scabbard tangled itself between unsteady legs, almost pitching him back onto his face. Only a few steps away a humped shadow, a blacker clot of darkness in the night, lay on the ground, unmoving. It was the body of his horse. There had been no hope for it – he had heard the snap of its leg breaking even as it went down with him – and clearly one of his men had put the animal out of its pain before they left.

At least they showed the poor beast some mercy, even if they had none for me.

The former Commander knelt beside the horse's body and fleetingly stroked its cold neck in farewell. Though he bore little love for his fellow humans, his fondness for horses was a weakness he had always been careful to conceal from his Godsword soldiers and the world at large, for since Cergorn's victory and Aveole's loss, it had suited his purposes to cultivate the reputation of a cold, stone-hearted monster who inspired fear and awe in the hearts of those he met.

This horse had formerly, in the secrecy of its master's heart, been called Windsong. Now the strong, fleet, spirited creature was nothing more than a lump of dogmeat, and Blade, after one last, regretful farewell, put it out of his mind and turned his thoughts to the future. The Godsword horses never went forth from the Precincts, even on routine patrol, without their saddlebags containing firemaking equipment, a spare knife, a covering of flexible oiled hide, and emergency rations. Having looted his mount's corpse of these valuable items, he cut himself a rough staff from the very tree that had almost ended his life when it fell and, leaning on its flimsy support like an old, old man, he staggered away down the trail.

Three

Sanctuary

The interior of the Basilica resembled a battlefield in the aftermath of a fierce affray. *Well,* Smithmaster Agella thought, *that's not so far from the truth – and a poor showing we made in the fight for our city.* Throughout the immense building, the dispossessed Tiarondians who had been fortunate enough to survive the attack of their winged assailants were encamped on every spare inch of floor. The elderly and the injured sat or lay wherever they could find a space, the lucky ones tended and guarded by friends or family, the other desperate souls in continual danger of dying from shock, neglected wounds, or simply being trampled to death by their heedless fellows. Already some people were quarrelling viciously over a few inches of precious space, and frantic folk pushed between the crowded bodies, searching for loved ones who had been lost in the stampede for safety.

The noise was deafening. The moans of the wounded and the wails of the bereaved echoed beneath the lofty vaulted roof. Many of the Tiarondians were screaming and sobbing in shock and fear, while others cursed aloud. Small children howled, uncomforted, in the arms of stricken parents. From every side, people shouted the names of the lost, hoping against hope that those they sought had survived the bloody onslaught outside.

As far as Agella knew, the only surviving member of her family was Felyss, the daughter of her sister, though hopefully the girl's brother, the Smithmaster's former apprentice, was also still alive.

Thank Myrial I sent him away up the mountain before this disaster happened. If he only reached safety with Toulac, he'll be all right. My old friend will take good care of the boy. There's no-one better in a crisis. I've got to concentrate now on Felyss. I'm all she has left, poor soul.

Agella shuddered as an image flashed into her mind: the girl's parents, torn to pieces by the winged fiends that had laid waste to the city. And if it hadn't been for Galveron, she and Felyss would be lying out there among the carrion, too. They owed him their lives.

Agella's opinion of the young Lieutenant, always high, had soared to a new level today. Throughout the attack he had kept his head, staying outside until the very last minute, fighting a fierce and fearless rearguard action to save as many of the Tiarondians as possible. They had been the very last to make it, she and Felyss, falling through the Temple doors with Galveron on their heels, protecting them to the bitter end. Once they were safe inside, the Lieutenant had actually kept the new Hierarch waiting while he took a moment to find them a quiet corner in a little alcove that had remained unclaimed because of its proximity to the Temple doors. Though they weren't far enough away from the entrance for Agella's peace of mind, the building was so packed with people that it was impossible to get any further inside, and at least here in their little niche, they could keep out from under the feet of the milling throng.

Galveron had brushed off Agella's thanks with his usual diffidence, his eyes going to Felyss, who leaned weakly against the wall with her eyes closed, gasping for breath. She was pale as a corpse and her hair, burnished copper like that of her aunt, was spattered with blood from the fight at the Temple doors, as was her face and clothing. Suddenly he frowned. 'Isn't this the girl who—'

Agella remembered then that he had been the one who'd intervened when Felyss had been set upon and raped outside her own home by a gang of the Lady Seriema's bullies. She held up a hand to forestall him from saying any more, but tempered the gesture with a smile. 'Yes, this is Felyss. I hope you won't have to make a habit of coming to her rescue.'

'So do I.' He addressed Felyss directly, though she seemed to be taking little notice of what was going on around her. 'Right now, things must seem bad beyond imagining, but if you're anything like your aunt Agella, it'll take a lot to daunt you. Just hold on tightly to your courage and dignity and hope, and you'll get through somehow. We all will.'

To Agella's astonishment, the girl opened her eyes, and anger flashed from them as she glared at the Lieutenant. 'Courage, dignity and hope!' she spat. 'And where am I supposed to find them, you idiot? They were torn away from me by Seriema's men. *Let's all be brave and stick together and everything will be all right?* Do you realise what you're saying? Didn't you *see* those things out there, and the corpses and the blood? Everything will be all right, indeed! Get away from me, and take your stupid fairy stories with you!'

'Felyss!' Agella protested.

Galveron smiled. 'See? You've already got your fighting spirit back, and that's the hardest step of all. The dignity and hope, and all the rest will follow.' He inclined his head to Agella. 'I must go now. The Hierarch will be needing me. There's a lot to organise.'

'Well, if I can be of any help, just let me know.' Agella took his arm, looking at him with a slight frown. 'You should really get those bites and scratches seen to first, though. Some of them look nasty.'

'All in good time. You and Felyss take care of one another.' With that, he was gone.

Gilarra was overwhelmed. Now that she had become their leader, it was up to her to act, but what could she possibly do to alleviate such suffering and terror? She herself was still reeling from the events of this dreadful night, and she wanted nothing more than to clamp her hands over her ears and run to the sanctuary of the Hierarch's quarters, far above the pandemonium in the temple. She longed for the comfort of her own little family: her lifemate Bevron, and Aukil, their little son, who were already installed upstairs in safety. Fortunately they had been spared the carnage in the courtyard. She had refused to allow them to witness her conducting Zavahl's sacrifice, and had shamelessly invoked her new authority to excuse them from the ceremony, sending them to the Hierarch's chambers to keep them out of the way and out of sight.

Maybe that's why the Great Sacrifice was such a disaster, prompted an unwelcome, insidious voice at the back of her mind. *Your very first ceremony, and you cheated Myrial by giving special favour to your family. What if this entire tragedy is your fault?* A chill went through her at the thought. For the first time, she truly began to appreciate the burdens of responsibility and conscience that had haunted her predecessor, and driven him so hard. Had Zavahl been right all along? Maybe it was better if the Hierarch remained alone, isolated from the loves and family ties that might conflict with his duty to his God. Gilarra clenched her fists.

No! It can't be true! I can *have both my family and Myrial. I can balance my responsibilities. I must.*

Suddenly, the longing for her loved ones overwhelmed the new Hierarch.

Maybe I could go up to Bevron. Just for a little while. Surely I'll be able to cope much better when I'm rested.

Myrial only knew, she needed the respite. And surely folk would have more confidence in her if she *looked* like a Hierarch, at least. Right now her rich robes of office were ripped and tattered, and plastered with muck and gore. Her face was stiff and sticky with dried blood from the injury she had sustained out in the courtyard, when the platform had collapsed beneath her and she'd been hit by a piece of flying debris. The cut across her forehead was stinging furiously, and her head throbbed from the blow. Gilarra slipped through the shadowed doorway that led to her quarters, and hurried towards the stairs.

I'll just slip upstairs for a few minutes, and sort myself out. After all, it's not as if I'm running away. I'll be right back. In just a little while . . .

'Lady, don't.' Galveron was standing at the bottom of the stairs.

Gilarra felt herself colouring. 'I was only going to change. How can I talk to them looking like this?'

'If you don't mind me saying so, Lady Hierarch, that's exactly how you should look,' the young Godsword officer replied. 'I know these people. Right now, it would be a big mistake on your part to come before them all neat and spotless, and clad in rich, warm robes. When they see you now, hurt and filthy and dishevelled, they'll know that you're one of them. They will understand that you share their suffering, but you're still willing to carry on, and pull yourself together somehow, and keep fighting with all the courage you possess. It's important to them, Lady. They'll respect you all the more for it, I promise.'

'But what can I say, that could possibly help folk in such straits?'

'It'll come to you, of that I'm sure. You have a great deal of compassion in you, Lady Hierarch, and that is what they need right now. Your heart will tell you what to say, and how best to reassure them. Once they know they still have leaders to take responsibility for their well-being, they'll be much happier.' He pulled a rueful face. 'That'll give us a little time to work on the mountains of problems that face us.'

Gilarra looked at his bloodstained clothing, the shadows of tiredness beneath his eyes, the scabbing bites and scratches on his face and arms. She was impressed by the speed with which this young man had pulled himself back from the brink of catastrophe, and was already taking thought and making decisions for the future. She knew that he was right about her own responsibilities. Sternly, she reminded herself that many other families had not been so privileged or so lucky as she had been, to have her family alive and safe, and if she did not act soon, the distress within the Temple would turn to panic, and then, inevitably, to violence. Gilarra sighed. 'You're right,' she told Galveron. 'I'll go at once.'

As she mounted the steep corkscrew of oaken steps that led up to the high pulpit, Gilarra was shaking so hard that she was forced to hold tightly to the curving rail to keep her knees from giving way beneath her. When she reached the top, and looked out over the crowd, her courage faltered. As soon as she began to speak, those hundreds of eyes would turn towards her, for the Temple had been designed with great cunning in ages past, so that even the lowest whisper uttered on the pulpit could be heard quite clearly throughout the massive chamber.

What can I say? Where can I find the right words? Oh Myrial, how can I help them?

'Your heart will tell you,' Galveron had said. It was all right for him, standing safe down there on the ground, waiting for her to begin. As she looked down at him, he caught her eye and made an encouraging gesture. Gilarra, unable to put it off any longer, took a deep breath and began to speak whatever came into her mind, just hoping that the right words would come to her in this time of need.

'My people. My own, dear friends. Listen to me! You are safe now.' She paused deliberately, to let that truth sink in. 'You are safe.' By this time, silence had fallen in the cathedral. A host of faces were turned up towards their new Hierarch, like flowers seeking the sun.

'I promise you that here in the House of Myrial, His children will be succoured and sheltered while we find the answers to this calamity that has beset us.' As she looked down on them, Gilarra found her eyes blurring with tears. Though there would be more than enough to feed and shelter, there were so few of her people down there. Less than two thousand were all that remained of a great and thriving city. There was a catch in her voice as she continued.

'Right now, you are angry, grieving, shocked and deeply afraid. Most of you are missing loved ones and friends. I know it's natural for you to want to search for them among the survivors, but for now, I implore you to stay where you are. Our first thought must be for the hurt and wounded. I want all healers, apothecaries, midwives and herbalists – anyone with any experience of healing whatsoever – to report to the Silver Chapel off the east aisle of the cathedral. As soon as they have been organised, these healers will pass among the crowd to identify and treat those who need their care. The seriously injured will be taken to the quarters of the Priests and Priestesses.'

Gilarra took a deep breath and leaned down towards the listening refugees. 'Due to our foresight and planning in the Sacred Precincts, emergency food supplies are available, and rations will be distributed shortly, as soon as we have some kind of system in place. Also, Priests and Priestesses from the Scriptorium will be sent to take down the names of every one of you. That way, friends and families can be reunited without this endless, hopeless searching through the crowds.'

She could feel the change in atmosphere now. The panic-stricken air of confusion, anger and fear was fading, and they looked to her with trust and dawning hope.

Dear Myrial, so many desperate people are depending on me now. Please don't let me fail them.

'As you can see,' she found her voice again, 'there is much to organise: healing, food, bedding, drinking water – not to mention sanitation. This can't all happen at once, so I beg you to be patient and forbearing.' Her eyes swept the crowd. 'I'm going to need a number of volunteers to help organise these matters. I know that those of you who are lucky enough to be with your families won't want to leave them, but if anyone else would like to help, or if anyone has any special skills they think would be useful in this emergency, please report to Commander Galveron in the Opal Chapel.'

Gilarra stretched forth her hands and made the ritual gestures of Myrial's blessing over the crowd. 'I won't detain you in formal prayers now, my children, because we must tend to our wounded as soon as possible, but my love goes out to you all, and I will pray unceasingly for our safe delivery. May the next few hours bring us comfort and hope renewed.' With that she turned and left the pulpit.

For a moment, the silence stretched out, then from the crowd, a lone voice called out. 'Long live our Lady Hierarch!'

Cheers and cries of approval broke out among the rest of the assembled refugees, and Gilarra could hear relief in their voices.

Galveron was right. They just wanted someone to take charge. But

Myrial help me if I should fail them as Zavahl did. They'll tear me apart.

Now that she no longer needed to show a brave, confident face to her people, the new Hierarch felt weak and giddy with relief. She found her legs starting to tremble beneath her, and stumbled, slithering down the last of the steep pulpit steps. The strong arms of Galveron caught her at the bottom, steadying her. He looked down at her, frowning. '*Commander* Galveron?' he hissed. 'Why, in the name of all that's holy, didn't you warn me that you were about to heap such honours and responsibilities on my head?'

Gilarra pulled away from him, and stood as tall and straight as her scant inches would allow. 'Had I thought of it before I got up to speak, I *would* have warned you, but the idea came to me just now, when I was up there on the pulpit.' For the first time, she noticed that beneath the crust of mud and dried blood on his face, Galveron looked very white, and she realised how terrified he must be feeling. Her own responsibilities were new enough to let her feel nothing but sympathy for the stunned young man. Nevertheless, though she pitied him, she was not about to relent in the matter of his sudden promotion. She needed him too much for that.

The Hierarch turned back to her new Godsword Commander. 'Galveron, I know what an enormous burden I am placing on your shoulders, but I have no choice. Blade is no longer here, and even if he should return, I don't trust him. He works towards his own ends, and I need someone I can rely on to work towards mine. Between the two of us, I'm relieved that he chose to leave when he did, and if he does return, he'll find himself under arrest for treason, and deserting his post in an emergency. Do you understand me?'

The new Commander's eyes widened, and a slow grin broke across his face. 'By Myrial! You're not daft, my Lady Hierarch, are you?'

Gilarra grimaced. 'I should hope not, but sometimes I'm not so sure. I think anyone would have to be daft, as you put it, to attempt to lead in such a desperate crisis. I'm beginning to understand Zavahl a little better now, when it's too late. I can't shake the feeling that I'm just hanging on by my fingernails, and whatever I do, it will never be enough. But the mantle of Hierarch has fallen on my shoulders now, so I'll just have to do the best I can.'

'You'll do a good job. You'll cope much better than Zavahl would have done. Over the last year or so, we could all see him falling apart.'

Gilarra shook her head. 'Myrial help Zavahl, he was such a driven man. I wonder what has become of him.' She shuddered, drawing her mantle more closely round her shoulders. 'Galveron, what could it have been – the dragon-creature that snatched him away? The same beast that the traders found on the mountain?'

'I don't know what else it could have been, unless suddenly there are a whole host of dragons infesting Callisiora in much the same way as those winged horrors have done.' Galveron looked grave. 'I'll tell you one thing, though, my Lady. I would rather have a crack at apprehending the dragon than arresting Lord Blade, should he return.'

'If he tries to return to the city now, our winged attackers are likely to take that worry from your shoulders. Besides, we have more pressing matters to deal with.' Gilarra rubbed a hand across her eyes, her head buzzing with weariness. She felt daunted by all that remained for her to do.

Galveron nodded. 'You're right, and I suppose we'd better make a start. There's so much to do, it's difficult to know where to begin. There's one good thing though, my Lady. At least everyone is safe here, and under shelter.'

Galveron was wrong. Outside the Sacred Precincts and beyond the tunnel, in the wash-house of a wool-merchant's mansion near the Esplanade, something stirred in the shadows. The girl who had taken cover there, cowering terrified behind the copper as the dark shadows of the skyborne menace flickered past the soap-smeared little window, began to move at last. Aliana gasped as the circulation returned, scalding and tingling, to limbs that were numb from being confined for so long in a narrow space. She rubbed frantically, got to her feet too soon, and staggered like a drunk out of her hiding place, colliding with the handle of the mangle in the darkness.

'Ow!' Aliana bit back a curse and rubbed at the painful spot on her hip. Another bruise to add to her colourful array. Oh well, it was all part of a day's work for a thief – though on this particular day, and the night that was now following it, her work had included an unexpected new set of opportunities and dangers.

At the time, her plan had seemed infallible. The gang had only to wait until everyone else went up to the Temple for the Great Sacrifice, then the whole city would be theirs, ripe and ready for the taking. No-one would be around to stop a thief. Even the poxy Godswords would be expected to attend this particular ceremony, right down to the last accursed man. What could possibly go wrong?

The answer to that question had come swarming out of the clouded skies, and had been more horrific than a thief's darkest nightmares. Aliana, frustrated in her original plan of robbing Tiarond's richest merchant by the sound of some kind of commotion going on in Lady Seriema's house, had been sneaking along behind the mansions on the far side of the Esplanade, deciding which to ransack first. A shadow had passed overhead, no more than a flicker of movement at the edge of her vision, but enough to send her diving for cover. Ever since then she had been hiding in the merchant's wash house with the smell of soap tickling her nostrils as she listened, trembling, to the screams that resounded from the nearby Precincts. Every now and then, through the smudged windowpane she had glimpsed the winged shapes that thronged the skies overhead, as the attackers fanned out across the city.

Though Aliana's first, panic-stricken impulse had been to cut and run, to flee for her very life back to the safe refuge of the gang's headquarters, second thoughts had brought her to her senses. To run while there was still light in the skies and those creatures, whatever they were, circling like vultures overhead, would be crazy; would turn her into prey. No, surely it would be better to wait until darkness fell, then she could stay under cover, hiding in the shadows and working her way back across the city house by house, until she finally reached home.

I'll be safe there, and so will the rest of the gang if they can make it back. Those creatures will never find us in the Warrens. All we have to do is get there.

Through the following hours she had tried to cling to those convictions while she huddled and trembled and waited, growing more afraid with every passing moment: not only for herself, but for the other gang members, and in particular her beloved twin brother Alestan. Had he found shelter in time, as she had? Or had one of those voices, frantic and fearful, screaming in agony, belonged to him? Was he lying somewhere dead even now, his body mangled, mauled and savaged beyond all recognition? Would she ever see him again?

Now that night had fallen, she could find out. She must leave her hiding place and risk herself in the open at last. Judging by the horrific screaming, now dwindled to an eerie silence, that had come from the Precincts, the attackers were a lethal adversary, but Aliana had no doubts about her ability to move, unseen and undetected, through the city. Was she not a Grey Ghost? And a leader at that? She was proud of the gang that she and Alestan had created, pulling together the best of the city's thieves, persuading them – by far the most difficult part of the entire operation – to work together for the good of all, and forcing them to live up to her own exacting standards.

The Ghosts must move unseen through the city, must leave no trace of their presence, must never be noticed or caught. Any gang member who was captured would be banished forever from the gang, and from the safe haven of the Warrens, the labyrinth of caverns in the spur of the mountain that formed the eastern boundary of Tiarond. From time immemorial, these caves had been the last refuge for the city's faceless ones: the homeless, the hopeless, the dispossessed and the criminals. So-called 'decent' folk avoided the place, and even the Godswords preferred to behave as though the Warrens had never existed, and none of them would venture within. So far, not a single one of the Grey Ghosts had been taken – and Aliana, the founder, with her brother, of the gang, had no intention of being first.

It was an odd road she had travelled to find herself here. She and Alestan had been the offspring of a merchant, and had once dwelt here, in the upper part of town. Aliana still had vague memories of her life at that time. His wife had died bearing the twins, and he had lavished his love on his children instead. Rich and well educated, they had seemed destined for a successful, happy future, but when they were nine years old, he had died in a burning warehouse down by the docks when a cargo of wool had caught fire. Their uncle took over the business, ostensibly managing it until the children grew up, but he lacked his brother's head for commerce. Within a year he had hung himself to escape his angry creditors, and the children had found themselves in the streets, homeless, penniless and lost. Being accepted into the Warrens had saved their lives, and through a combination of confidence and daring – the hallmark of the merchant classes – and the education given them by their father, they had eventually risen to become leaders of the gang of thieves that supported those members of the community of the dispossessed such as the elderly and infirm, who could not feed themselves.

As leader, Aliana reminded herself, her responsibilities went further than setting an example. Now that they had found the city, those creatures, with their advantage of flight, would be very difficult to dislodge. As far as she could see, they would be around for the foreseeable future, and she must make plans accordingly. Though surely the Warrens would be safe, this situation stood every chance of turning into a siege. The Ghosts would need all the foodstuffs they could lay their hands on to sustain them through the difficult times ahead, especially if it became too dangerous to venture outside. Since she was here anyway, she might as well go into the house, where she could take advantage of whatever pickings there were to be had. She would gather together all she could find on her way home, and pray that the other members of the gang would have the sense to do the same.

Moving stealthily, with one eye on the perilous skies, the thief crept out of the wash house. Keeping to the edges of the courtyard, tucked into the shadows cast by those nice, high walls, she worked her way round to the servants' door of the mansion. Though deploring the extra minutes it cost her, she paused to pick the lock, manipulating the mechanism by touch while her eyes searched above her head for danger. It would have been easier, and quicker, to break the kitchen window, but she was a Grey Ghost, and she had her standards. To the continuing bafflement and frustration of the Godswords, the gang never damaged any property, never left any clues, and always left a house as though no-one had ever been there at all. Besides, the sound of splintering glass or the sight of a broken pane might alert the predators to her presence.

A shadow passed overhead, and she dropped, curling her limbs beneath her to become just another patch of formless shadow by the kitchen door. Aliana was an expert at hiding in plain sight. When the skies were clear again, she went feverishly back to work, and shortly afterwards the back door eased open a crack, just enough to let her enter. She darted inside, closing the door behind her quickly, and leaned against the cool, thick wood. Wiping a mist of sweat from her forehead, she waited until her hammering heart had slowed before bolting and barring the kitchen door. Once all was secure, she turned back to the room and its contents, and began her night's work in earnest.

The kitchen was her first priority. She looted the larder of everything edible, then turned her attention to the food and drink stored in the cool cellar, taking a bottle of spirits (for medicinal use, she told herself) but leaving, with deep regret, the contents of the merchant's extensive wine collection. She noted, with a flash of anger, that the elite of Tiarond found it a lot easier to come by sufficient food than did ordinary folk. Well, it was high time that some of this largesse spilled over into the Warrens. Everything that she took went into the backpack – carefully designed to lie flat beneath a cloak when empty – that strapped across her shoulders and left her arms clear to climb or fight.

From the kitchen she began to go through the house, systematically searching every room for any small valuables that were light to carry, for this was a perfect chance to make the Ghosts wealthy beyond their dreams, if only the Godswords would make themselves useful for once, and restore order to the city.

The Godsword soldiers, left to keep watch in the old woman's house at the sawmill, had deserted their posts, just as Blade had expected, leaving the door swinging open to let in the cold wind and the rain. Though the building, dark and abandoned, had an oddly forlorn look, it seemed none the less to hold out both welcome and hope to a weary wanderer in the night.

Reaching the mill had taken the last dregs of Blade's strength; indeed he had completed the final part of the journey on willpower alone. He staggered up the porch steps on numb legs that would barely support him and collapsed across the threshold, barely able to believe that he was safe at last. After a moment, he pulled himself all the way into the kitchen and kicked the door shut behind him, shutting out the wind and rain, and the cold, dark killer of a night. He had reached shelter not a moment too soon. His head buzzed with exhaustion. Every inch of his body hurt from his fall down the cliff, and that gruelling, terrifying climb back to safety. Icy slush had soaked through the holes in his boots, and his feet and hands were numb with a chill that seemed to be eating into his body, all the way through to his heart.

In the darkness of the kitchen, Blade spotted a faint, red glimmer in the fireplace. The fire his faithless troops had kindled was still alight! On hands and knees he scrambled across the room, and feverishly began to stuff twigs, wood chips and bits of bark from Toulac's kindling box into the grate, almost smothering the feeble glow of the embers in his haste. After an eternity, the fragments smouldered and caught alight, the tiny flame brightening the shadowy room. Blade's world had shrunk to that tiny golden flicker and the need to nurture it and keep it alive. Patiently he built the fire, gaining immense satisfaction from the simple homely task: one that the exalted Godsword Commander had not attempted for many years. Though his fingers were clumsy at first, unresponsive as blocks of wood and shaking from the cold, his touch became more sure as the fire began to grow. The extra heat brought the blood back to his hands and face as he piled the logs high, and the fire grew to a healthy blaze.

Blade could not remember when he had last slept. He had spent most of the previous night chasing around the mountain in pursuit of that accursed firedrake, then during the day that followed he had returned in triumph to the city with the captive Hierarch, only to see Zavahl snatched from his grasp and rescued from the very sacrificial pyre.

The attack of the winged demons, the panic in the crowd, the mad dash up the mountain in pursuit of the fugitives: all of these memories seemed to blur together as his eyes began to close. He managed to stay awake long enough to pull off his boots and stand them on the hearth to dry, then rolling himself in the hearthrug, he lay down in front of the fire, unable to stay awake a moment longer.

As Blade sank into sleep, one last thought nagged at him. He had done something else today: an act of great importance. But what? He was too tired to concentrate, his brain wouldn't focus. It was no good. He felt too drowsy.

Maybe when I've rested, I'll remember . . .

Then, as his consciousness ebbed away, it came back to him. The Wind-Sprite! He had trapped the Elemental, another agent of the Shadowleague, within an object of rare power; an heirloom of the Mageborn race he had left so long ago. The artefact, resembling a pouch formed from some mysterious, silvery material, was a remnant of some former age, before the Magefolk had lost their powers. Perhaps it might even have belonged to the unknown race who had created this world of Myrial. It had the capability to remove its contents a step beyond physical reality, enclosing them in a pocket of *elsewhere* that existed beyond the boundaries of existence as it was normally perceived.

The device was unique and priceless, its Loremaster prisoner even more so, now that Blade would be heading back to Gendival in pursuit of his quarry. Among the Shadowleague he was still a condemned man, and if he must contend once more with the Archimandrite Cergorn, it would be useful to have a hostage. Unfortunately, both the pouch and its captive were exactly where he had left them, in the Commander's chambers, back in the Godsword Citadel – and there was nothing he could do about it. Nothing at all.

The sound of Blade's own curses followed him down into his dreams.

Four

The Grey Ghost

Having gradually worked her way from the bottom to the top of the house, the silent thief emerged from a doorway in the upper storey, and slipped down the hall. She had thoroughly searched the very last bedroom of the wool-merchant's mansion, and could put off the perilous journey through the dark streets no longer. It was time to go.

The snick of the back door latch sounded unbelievably loud in the still night air. Aliana froze in the doorway, then opened the door just a chink: enough to check her surroundings and no more. Having seen nothing to alarm her, she slid through the narrow opening, moving cautiously and with care; sticking to the wall of the house until she had gained the shelter of the alley dividing the high walls of the mansion from those of the next. She threaded her way through the narrow gap, glad of the swags of ivy that overhung the walls on either side. As a thief, she felt better with darkness and secure cover around her.

All too soon, the end of the passage opened out into the wide spaces of the Esplanade. Normally, the square was illuminated at night by many lanterns that hung from walls and buildings all around, and Aliana would not have dreamed of crossing that brightly lit expanse. Tonight, however, there was no-one to kindle the lamps, and beneath clouded skies the open spaces were almost as dark as the alley had been. The only light came from the Precincts, where many torches and lanterns had been kindled for the ceremony. Though their light could not be seen directly beyond the high canyon walls, it shone up out of the great stone bowl to be reflected from the low clouds in a faint, diffuse glow.

Aliana had a choice. Should she take the safe but slower route, working around the edges of the Esplanade from one building to the next, hugging walls and flitting between shadows like the ghost for which she was named? Or for once in her life should she take a calculated risk and make a quick dash across the open space? It would save so much time, and tonight she wanted very badly to be home, to find out whether her beloved brother had survived the winged onslaught, and to see how the rest of her gang had fared.

She hesitated – a rare event indeed. Alestan was usually the careful one, weighing up all the possibilities and risks, while she preferred to act on instinct. The thought of him, however, was enough to spur her to action. Aliana summoned all her courage, hoisted the heavy backpack containing her spoils higher on her shoulders, took a deep breath, and ran. She had only gone a few steps when she sensed rather than saw the first shadow move across the sky. Then the rooftops of the surrounding houses seemed to come alive as countless winged shapes lifted out of the blackness into the faintly glowing clouds.

'Shit!' The thief swerved and doubled back as the first of her attackers folded its wings and plunged towards her. She gained the mouth of the alley with inches to spare: she could feel the wind of its wings even as she made her dive for cover. As she had hoped, those very wings, spread wide to break the speed of its headlong descent, would not fit across the passageway, and the creature was forced to pull up short with a hiss of rage.

Aliana sped along the narrow lane, protected by the constricted space and the overhanging eaves of the houses on either side. She could hear the fiends above her, calling to one another with hisses and harsh, guttural cries as they hunted. She dreaded reaching the end of the sheltering alley, for then she must cross the back yard before she reached the kitchen door, and in that open space she would be at their mercy. When she had left the house, had she locked the back door behind her? She couldn't remember. If she couldn't get inside, she would be finished.

Breathing a frantic prayer, Aliana flung herself across the gap. A screech of triumph came from above, and she glimpsed three dark shapes plummeting towards her. Terror sent ice and fire along her veins. Time seemed to slow to a crawl. Nothing existed beyond herself and the menacing creatures dropping with deadly speed to intersect with her. They were gaining on her; coming closer and closer. She would never make it . . .

A shriek rent the air as two of her attackers, careless in their haste, crashed into one another and fell in a tangle of limbs and leathery wings. The third, already low to the ground and swerving to miss the collision, flew right into the clothesline and was brought up short and hurled to the ground by its own momentum. Those extra few seconds were all Aliana needed. Her fingers closed around the doorknob and, mercifully, the door opened at once. She flung herself inside, slamming the bolts home for the second time that night, and dropping the bar into its socket.

There was no time. As Aliana looked frantically around the room, she saw a dark silhouette in front of the window and heard splintering glass. She didn't wait for them to enter. It was dark in the kitchen, but she remembered from her previous explorations that the cellar door was open to her right. Within an instant she was at the top of the cellar steps, bolting yet another door behind her – for all the good it would do. As she picked her way down the stone steps into that lightless hole, she heard bangs and crashing from above her: the deadly winged horrors wrecking the kitchen as they searched for her.

How did they hunt? By hearing or sight or scent? Aliana wished she knew. She didn't dare light a candle in case the tiny thread of light around the edges of the cellar door should give her away. She had already made one deadly error. The predators had arrived at twilight and she had simply assumed that they were daylight creatures. How could she have known that they were denizens of the night?

That's torn it. I'll have to stay here until morning – if I survive that long.

Above her, she thought she could hear a snuffling and scratching at the cellar door, and a shudder went through her. Her thoughts raced in mindless panic.

They've found me! What shall I do? Where can I hide?

Well, if she had been discovered, there was no point in groping around in the darkness any longer. With unsteady fingers she hunted for the candle stub that she always kept in her pocket, and wasted precious time in trying to strike a spark. By the time she finally got the wick to catch alight, the scratching at the wooden panels had turned to a series of heavy blows that rattled the door in its frame.

Aliana looked wildly round the cellar by the flickering light of her small flame. She remembered from her earlier search that coal and kindling were kept in this first room. Beyond, through the doorway at the far side, there was the wine-cellar and foodstore. Beyond that was nothing but a stairway leading down another level to the family crypt, with its tombs hewn from the rock of the mountain and sealed with great stone slabs. Too late, it dawned on her that in taking refuge down here, she had effectively trapped herself in a dead end.

She ran towards the further doorway, hot wax spilling over her hand with every step. The hammering at the door grew louder. A quick glance over her shoulder showed her the sturdy planks shuddering and bending beneath each impact. All at once, the timbers shattered under one last gargantuan blow, and the creatures were in the room with her.

She didn't stop to count them, but fled into the foodstore. Even though flight seemed hopeless, Aliana was driven by stark terror: the mindless, animal urge to flee from her hunters. She carried no sword – there was little need for such a weapon in her line of work – but she had her long dagger at her belt and small throwing knives in arm sheaths. As she ran, she drew her dagger with her free hand. All she could do now was prolong the final moments of her life, but when they finally cornered her, at least she would go down fighting.

There was no lock on this door. The thought of blocking it with crates and casks flashed through her mind, and was discarded. There was no time. The horrors were already coming through the doorway behind her, their avid eyes glittering red in the candlelight, their lips curling back from jagged fangs, and their talons extended at the end of long fingers, ready to grasp and tear. The foremost leapt towards her, and there was the sound of tearing cloth as its claws caught at her arm, ripping her sleeve and slashing across the flesh beneath. She took a wild swipe with her blade across the creature's face, and it fell back shrieking, its hands clasped over its eyes. The two others fell on it, their snarls echoing through the underground chamber and mingling with the screams of the fallen one. The reek of blood and ordure filled the air as they tore out great lumps of its flesh, swallowing the gobbets whole in their greed.

Aliana, ignoring the pain and the blood that dripped from her savaged arm, backed away from them, terrified that any sudden movement might attract their attention back to herself. Slowly, she edged towards the last set of steps, that led down to the family vaults. Perhaps if she could hide down there, these monstrosities would sate their hunger on their former comrade, and forget about their original prey. It was a slender hope, but it was all she had.

She reached the head of the staircase without being noticed and was creeping carefully down when her foot slipped on the steep stone stairs and she fell, dropping her candle and hitting each step with a bruising impact. The iron-barred grille at the bottom burst open, catapulting her through, and she heard a howl of rage from upstairs as the creatures discovered that their prey had escaped. Acting on instinct, Aliana staggered to her feet and kicked the door shut. As she did so, a dim half-light filtering down the passageway from the tombs picked out the silvery shaft of a key in the lock. Even as the winged horrors came hurtling down the stairs towards her, she reached between the bars and turned the key, then snatched it out of the keyhole and retreated just before they could reach her.

It soon became clear that the iron bars would be sturdy enough to defend her from the predators, and Aliana felt sufficiently confident to retreat down the passageway, out of their sight. She hoped that the corpse of their companion would lure them back upstairs, and maybe if she stayed quiet and hidden, they would forget about her, or get tired of waiting and leave in search of easier prey. She hoped so. Otherwise, she was doomed to starve to death in here. That, however, was the last of her concerns at the moment. Now that there was no longer any need to flee, she was desperately weary, her body one single knot of aches from her fall down the stairs. The wounds in her arm, though not too deep, hurt as though three searing brands had been laid across her skin. Weaving like a drunkard, she staggered away from the door and made her way into the first vault she came to, where she discovered that the faint illumination that had so puzzled her came from small votive lamps that burned on top of the tomb. She was glad of the light, though following her recent experiences, the dead no longer seemed to hold any threat for her.

Stumbling forward. Aliana sank down gratefully onto the smooth, flat marble top of the tomb. She unslung her heavy pack from her shoulders, wincing as the straps slid down her injured arm. Rummaging inside for the brandy, she used it to flush out her wounds, catching her breath and swearing vehemently as the burning liquid stung in the open cuts. With any luck, the strong spirits would help prevent the lacerations from becoming infected, for Myrial only knew what sort of filth those abominations carried on their claws.

Too spent now to worry about her hunger and thirst, she glanced around the dim, bare little chamber, wondering where she could sleep. Somehow, the top of the tomb seemed too exposed, and too disrespectful to the dead, for though she refused to be afraid, a last vestige of awe and superstition made her uneasy in this silent, lifeless place. But sleep she must, for her head was swimming and her eyelids had begun to close of their own accord. Trembling with fatigue, Aliana curled up in a corner and her last thought, before she fell fast asleep, was of the long-dead merchant who occupied this grave of stone. Even though she was a thief and an intruder, she prayed that he would take pity on her, and that his spirit would watch over her for what remained of the long, dark night.

Contained within Blade's relic of the ancient Magefolk was timeless, limitless night, in a region one step removed from the normal, physical world.

She could see nothing.

She could feel nothing.

She could neither hear nor make a single sound.

Thirishri hung suspended in a lightless void, deprived of information from any of her senses, her cries for help stifled by the dead nothingness around her. All she could feel was anger. Anger at the so-called Lord Blade, whom she had discovered to be none other than the renegade Loremaster Amaurn. Anger at his interference in the affairs of Callisiora and the whole of Myrial beyond, for now she had discovered his whereabouts she had begun to suspect that some ancient power lay hidden beneath Tiarond, and that the turncoat was somehow behind the crisis that affected the whole of Myrial. Most of all, however, the Wind-Sprite was angry at her own culpable stupidity, that had allowed Amaurn to trap her so easily and imprison her in this dimension beyond her own, from which she could not escape to share the vital information she had obtained.

Through the crimson shroud of Shree's anger ran a thick black thread of terror. Time had no meaning in this nightmare place; she might have been here for a minute in her own world's measure, or a thousand years. Countless questions circled in her mind. What was happening to her world? What had become of her friends, and fellow Loremasters? What havoc would Amaurn wreak next? If she ever managed to escape from this place, would her former companions still be alive? Would she even recognise the world she had once known?

And how long do I have before my sanity is eroded away completely?

Whenever this last thought overwhelmed her she tried to flee, hurtling blindly through the void trying to escape this terrifying nothingness. But with no sensation of motion, no feeling of speed, and no change in her surroundings, how could she be sure that she had moved at all?

I have to get a grip on myself. If I don't, I'll lose my mind.

The prospect of insanity was enough – at present – to quench the Wind-Sprite's impending hysteria. *Steady, Shree, steady,* she told herself in the recesses of her mind. Fighting for calm, she deliberately distanced herself from the feelings of terror until they were faint and far away. Concentrating hard, she created in her mind a stronghold, impregnable and secure against the empty darkness with which she was surrounded. She formed it from memories of happiness, the contemplation of past triumphs and successes, the warm recollection of love and companionship from the many dear friends she had made along the way. In her mind she built her fortress big and strong and bright, and topped it with a bold, high tower wrought from future plans and dreams, with a shining beacon of hope burning brightly above.

The structure kept the void at bay, and was a refuge from the fear and helplessness of her position. Within her shining walls she could think clearly once more, and keep a rein on her wild imaginings. It ensured her sanity, for a while at least, but it could not help her to escape her prison. Nothing could do that. Thirishri knew she would have to wait until Blade freed her – and how likely was that? – or her friends came to the rescue. And before they could help her, they would have to find out where she was being kept, and wrest her prison from the renegade's hands.

For a while, the dread that she would never be rescued threw her back into doubt and confusion, and all her fear, like dark armies, came crowding back, battering at the walls she had so carefully constructed to be her refuge. Feeling the foundations of her fortress beginning to shudder at the prospect of being trapped here for always, Shree firmly turned her thoughts elsewhere, to memories of light and warmth and love. With nothing else to do, she drifted, secure in the citadel of her own determinedly calm thoughts, keeping her consciousness away from the terrifying, formless void around her, not knowing whether she was actually moving or at rest. Instead she immersed herself in her dream landscape, using the reference points of her imagination to construct an environment that made some kind of sense.

When the light appeared, the Wind-Sprite could not believe it. She emerged from her thoughts to see a faint glow, like distant sunlight, but instead of relief, her initial reaction was one of panic.

It's happened! I've lost my mind! Blade has won, and I've gone mad!

'No you haven't.'

And now I'm hearing voices!

'No you aren't. Well, actually you are, but it's my voice you're hearing, not your own imagination. Did you really think, considering all the years the Magefolk have possessed this device, that you would be the only prisoner in here? Come, Wind-Sprite. Follow the light. You have no idea how good it is to have company after all this time.'

Unsure, untrusting, only half believing that what she'd heard had come from outside herself and terrified of the consequences if it had not, Shree drifted slowly forward, towards the distant glow. Insane or not, she felt weak with relief at the sight of something beyond the endless darkness. As she moved forward, the light brightened around her, and then, without warning, she burst into brilliant sunshine, drifting over a lapis-blue ocean, far below.

What in the name of wonder . . . ?

Then Thirishri was jolted from her speculation by the sight of land. There was an island in the distance, seemingly floating on the tranquil breast of the ocean. It was long, narrow and curved in a sickle shape, with great masses of trees that softened the contours of its slopes like banks of silver-green cloud. Near one end stood a single mountain peak, its harsh crags standing proud from the groves of trees around its feet. In some places, the land was bordered by shining golden beaches, in others by soaring cliffs of the mountain's reddish stone.

The sight of such glorious beauty should have heartened her, but instead, all Thirishri's hopes were crumbling into dust.

I've gone mad after all. I might have known. How else, in the midst of this Magefolk prison, in this other, dark dimension, could I be seeing the birthplace of my people, and my childhood home?

'Because it isn't.' Again, the other voice was in her head, much stronger this time. It was authoritative, soothing – and most definitely female.

What? What do you mean, it isn't?

'Come down to the west coast, the place that's a labyrinth of inlets and bays. You know where. Come down, and shed your fears. Come, Wind-Sprite, and everything will be explained.'

Sane or not, she had no choice other than to go along with this. Shree drifted down, riding the warm winds to the place the other voice had mentioned, the series of headlands beyond headlands and bays within bays that made a fascinating puzzle of the western coast. There, nestled in the curve of an inlet, a big white house had been constructed, surrounded by trees and a glorious garden of vibrant flowers, and fronting onto a wide green lawn that ran right down to the beach.

That's a human dwelling! It was never there before!

Suddenly, Shree began to feel better, her fears of insanity dissipating like smoke. Surely there was no way, even if she'd lost her mind, that she would have imagined such an unlikely building in her childhood home. But as she drifted closer, she began to wonder. Could it really be possible that here, in this formless void, there could really be a woman, sitting on the terrace of a white house that overlooked the ocean? Could that really be a small white table in front of her, and on it, what looked suspiciously like a cup of tea?

At that moment, though Shree was not a creature who existed in a spectrum that could be registered by human eyes, the woman looked up and noticed her. Lifting a slender arm she waved, and beckoned the Wind-Sprite down.

It was still dark when Zavahl awoke from a nightmare of bewilderment and horror, only to find that the reality of his situation was worse than his darkest dreams. He lay bound across the back of some huge, swift-moving creature whose unaccustomed motions jolted his bones with every stride. It was hard to think with his head hanging down, so that the blood pounded in his temples. What had happened? Had he died after all on the sacrificial pyre? Was some demon, even now, bearing him away to some infernal punishment for his failure as Hierarch?

Then, from above him, came a female voice, pitched low. Another woman answered with a quiet laugh, and Zavahl stifled a cry as memory came flooding back. A series of disjointed images flashed through his mind: the canyon of the Sacred Precincts darkening under a clouded sky; the swelling murmur of the crowd as he was led forth from the Temple; all those avid eyes, bright with expectancy, that pierced him as though they would suck out his life before he even reached the pyre. He remembered stumbling on the logs that rolled and shifted underfoot as he was manhandled to the stake by expressionless Godsword guards; the bite of ropes that bound him into place; the night wind and the drizzle striking, clammy and chill, through his thin white robes; Gilarra fidgeting beneath her heavy vestments, looking nervous and distressed; Blade's normally impassive gaze burning with triumph as he looked on. Zavahl's mind tried to slide away from recalling subsequent events: Gilarra, white-faced, moving through the ritual; the flash of fear and uncertainty behind her eyes when the sacrificial fire would not kindle . . .

Then suddenly, chaos as the huge creature burst out of the temple: Zavahl crying out, terror like a bolt of icy lightning through his body as the pyre ignited beneath its fiery breath. Choking, suffocating smoke and the searing heat of the flames against his skin. The monster reaching for him, snatching him safely from the fire, stake and all, and dragging him into the Temple. The two women had been waiting there: the crone from the sawmill and her companion, the younger, scar-faced bitch. Beyond that, his recollections vanished in hazy confusion.

He was uncomfortable, disorientated and afraid. Though they

had wrapped some sort of cloak or blanket over his thin sacrificial robe, it afforded little protection against the piercing cold. The burns on his skin, superficial though they were, stung like perdition, and his arms and legs were cramped into knots of pain from being bound for so long in one position. He was wedged between the two women on the monster's knobbly back, and could see nothing in the darkness. Where were they taking him? What did they intend to do with him? A shiver of fear ran through him. He was completely at their mercy.

Zavahl could have wept. The sacrifice had been his one last chance to redeem himself, to give his life for his people and somehow make good the mistakes that had caused Myrial to turn His face from Callisiora and its Hierarch. He had come so close to escaping all the wretchedness that had beset him: the crushing weight of his responsibilities and the burdens of his failure and guilt, and the perfidious machinations of Lord Blade . . .

And then, just when it seemed that things could get no worse, he heard the Voice again.

'Hold on to hope. All is not lost.'

Zavahl groaned. If he had died on the pyre, as Myrial had clearly intended, he would finally have been rid of this fearsome demon that possessed him. Why had those two accursed harpies interfered?

'Trust the women. They mean you no harm. They saved your life, and mine.'

'I didn't *want* my life saved!' The words burst out of Zavahl.

'Well, of all the damned ingratitude!' It was the rough voice of the older woman. 'Make no mistake, matey, if there had been any choice we'd have let you roast like the pig you are. Shall I hit him again, Veldan? Otherwise he'll be whining all the way to wherever we're going.'

'Just leave him,' the younger woman advised. 'Right now, we don't know if Aethon feels the same pain as his host does, and I don't want to risk hurting him. Besides, we're almost at the Curtain Walls now. After that, it doesn't really matter if Zavahl whines, moans, bitches and complains all the way to Gendival.'

'Myrial's teeth and toenails! You mean we have to put up with this useless lump feeling sorry for himself the whole time?'

'You won't have to put up with him for long. We should arrive early the day after tomorrow – in fact it's almost tomorrow now, because the sun will soon be up, so you'll only be stuck with Zavahl for a little over a day.'

'Thank goodness for that,' Toulac muttered.

Veldan gave a bitter laugh. 'Oh, this is nothing. If you think Zavahl is drowning in self-pity you should try spending some time in Elion's company.'

Zavahl had been about to speak up, to protest at the way he was being treated and ask them what they meant to do with him, but the grim edge to the younger woman's voice was enough to change his mind. No, better to stay silent. If they believed he was asleep once more, or unconscious, they would speak more freely in his hearing, and might give away some information he could use in a later escape. Even though his life had reached its lowest ebb, their mocking talk about his whining had stung, and he was surprised to learn that he did, after all, have some scraps of pride buried deep within.

He tried not to think about what he'd do if he *did* win his way free. Go back to Tiarond and be sacrificed? Now that the Eve of the Dead had passed there was little point in that. It was too late to intercede with Myrial on behalf of his people, and after all his failures, there was no chance that he would be accepted back as Hierarch. Besides, having schemed for so long to get rid of him, the Godsword Commander never would allow him to return. The one enjoyable aspect of his escape had been catching the briefest glimpse of Blade's face, no longer impassive but contorted with shock and rage. No matter what happened, at least he had won free of his most deadly enemy. That thought was a comfort to him as consciousness drifted away once more.

Zavahl had closed his eyes to darkness. He opened them to light, and for a joyous moment it seemed that a miracle had happened. At long last, the sun had risen over the beleaguered land! Then he heard a sound like the thunder and hiss of a thousand waterfalls, and realised that he was not seeing the clean, natural light of dawn, but the flickering, changeful glow of the Curtain Walls. His captors had brought him right to the boundaries of Callisiora.

Suddenly everything became clear. Why, the women and their unnatural companion must be in the pay of the Eastern Reivers! After all, didn't those uncivilised hill-clans still permit female warriors? And surely the old crone from the sawmill had been well known as a mercenary? There was no love lost between the Reivers and the Godswords. Obviously the Easterners had decided to kidnap him, to strike some kind of blow against Blade. The clans were too barbaric and ignorant to understand the ramifications of their deed, and in any case, the hand of Myrial had always lain but lightly on them. He knew perfectly well that in secret they worshipped other, primitive gods of their own devising.

Yes, it all made sense now. He had no doubt that he was right, in fact he felt stupid for not realising much sooner where he was being taken. After all, where else could the women be heading? Once through the Snaketail and down the mountain, the only passable routes wound among the eastern hills – a fact not lost upon those larcenous Reivers. Then, within his head, Zavahl heard the laughter of the demon.

'Wait,' it said. *'Just wait and see.'*

In that moment, Zavahl realised that the women had not turned to take the southbound trail that led beyond the ridge, but had kept going straight ahead, into the steep-sided vale that terminated in the Curtain Walls. His innards clenched into a cold, tight knot of fear. It was many years since he had visited the borders of the world but there seemed to be something different about the barrier. The ever-changing colours had become oddly clouded, with an ugly, curdled look about them, and the roaring sound that he remembered was overlaid with an ear-splitting crackle and hiss. Had the disturbance in the weather affected Myrial's boundaries, or had it been the other way around?

Zavahl was a helpless passenger on the strange creature, which carried him inexorably closer to the vast sheets of energy that cut across earth and sky. As they closed with the barrier, the buzz rose in pitch to an intolerable whine and he felt an unpleasant tingling sensation, as though biting ants were crawling all over his skin. What were the two women playing at? Overwhelmed with panic, he began to struggle violently against his bonds. 'Stop,' he cried. 'For Myrial's sake, please stop! Have you gone mad?'

The monster let out a bellow of protest and stopped abruptly. It swivelled its head on its long, sinuous neck until it was glaring right into Zavahl's face with ominous red eyes. A low snarl rumbled in its throat.

'Kaz says if you don't stop kicking him in the ribs, you're breakfast.' The scar-faced woman – Veldan, he remembered – sounded amused. 'And I think you should be warned that he's a firedrake of his word.'

Zavahl ceased his struggles immediately. Though firedrakes (whatever they were) had not featured in any aspect of his education, he had discovered an instant respect for the size of their teeth.

'Wise decision,' said the woman. After a moment's pause, she spoke again. 'Look, just stop fighting us, will you? It would be easier on everyone, especially yourself. I know you don't understand what's happening yet, but we'll see that you come to no harm.'

When he did not answer she shrugged and spoke again to her companion. 'Are you ready, Toulac?'

The older woman's voice was gruff with excitement. 'I've never been more ready for anything in my life.'

'Then let's get out of this benighted place.'

Suddenly the monster was dashing towards the barrier. Zavahl closed his eyes instinctively but the women's earlier mockery was still fresh in his mind, and he forced them open once more. If he was about to meet his death, at least he would look it in the face. He braced himself for the collision. It never happened. Before his disbelieving eyes, the Curtain Walls parted and a gap appeared. Without hesitation, the firedrake sped through. Beyond Callisiora.

Beyond all that Zavahl had known and trusted and believed in. Beyond everything that had given his life meaning and purpose.

Toulac let out a whoop of triumph that could even be heard above the firedrake's joyful bellow. 'We did it! Myrial in an alehouse, what an adventure!' She reached forward across Zavahl and clapped her companion on the shoulder. 'And I owe it all to you, girlie.' Her voice was soft but brimming with jubilation. 'You've given me a second chance.'

Veldan looked back at the older woman. 'This is only the beginning, Toulac. Just wait till we get to Gendival!'

Zavahl began to shake from head to foot. His heart pounded strangely in his chest. He gritted his teeth and shut his eyes tight.

No! This is impossible! Myrial made our world, and bounded it with light. Beyond that there is nothing. Nothing! This isn't happening. It can't *be happening!*

Then a comforting notion struck him.

Wait. You were moving fast and from this position you could see very little. You can't possibly have passed through the Curtain Walls. You must have been mistaken. Yes, that must be the answer. Somehow, at the last minute, you must have blinked, or briefly lost consciousness. This loathsome creature must have turned aside. Your captors must have climbed the ridge, or taken some little back trail between the hills that you know nothing about. Right now, you're heading into the eastern hills towards the lands of the Reivers, just as you thought. Of course that's what has happened.

And what of the women, and the brief conversation he had overheard? Well, Zavahl must have misheard them, or misunderstood. Or perhaps they weren't quite right in the head. After all, there was a fair likelihood of that. One was practically senile, and the other hideously scarred – yes, it all made perfect sense. He closed his mind to them and shut out the sound of their voices, refusing to listen to their ravings any longer.

Gradually, Zavahl stopped trembling and opened his eyes. Leaving Callisiora? What a fool he had been. The whole business of his kidnapping, following Blade's treachery, must have affected him far more deeply than he had realised. Passing through the Curtain Walls indeed. What absolute nonsense! And when the faint glimmer that preceded dawn appeared in utterly the wrong quarter of the cloudless sky, Zavahl shut his eyes firmly once more, and refused to look.

Five

The Listeners

Veldan lit the fire in the wayshelter and sat back on her heels, letting the welcome light and warmth wash over her scarred face. After a night's hard travel she was aching, cold and hungry, her eyes scratchy with weariness – but oh, it felt good to be back over the border, and safe in Gendival at last! For the first time in months she could truly relax. No need here for the habits of wariness, caution and vigilance that were trained into every member of the Shadowleague until they were second nature.

Careful! Veldan warned herself. *Never let your guard down all the way.* Her eyes strayed to the prisoner who sprawled, apparently sleeping, on the bed at the far side of the shelter. Though they had loosed his bonds, she and Toulac had taken the precaution of securing him to the bed with a short length of chain locked around one ankle: not because they thought he could escape, with Kaz just outside, but in case he found something among the shelter's supplies that he could use to harm himself, for Zavahl had fought her all the way from his native land, despite the fact that she had saved him from a hideous death on a sacrificial pyre.

Rot him! the Loremaster thought. *If only he would co-operate. Surely he can see by this time that we aren't his enemies?* Yet, looking at the former Hierarch, it was impossible not to pity him. His skin was grey with weariness, and disfigured by bruises and a vicious burn. Anger, frustration and bitterness had stamped their mark in each harsh line of his face.

Poor fool. If only he'd let us help him. The thought surprised her. Until now, she'd spared no sympathy for the wretch – not since he had flinched away from her scarred face on the first night of their meeting, refusing to even recognise her as human. As yet, she had scarcely had time to come to terms with her recent disfigurement, and his horrified response had cut deep. She had responded with anger and resentment, and it had been all too easy to see Zavahl as nothing but a burden and a hindrance.

Veldan stared into the fire as her thoughts unwound. For the first time, she considered his predicament, trying to understand a little of his fear and pain, and the dreadful uncertainty of being kidnapped by strangers, and taken, for some unfathomable purpose, to an unknown place. She realised uncomfortably that she was treating him at present no better than he had treated her at the first time of their meeting – indeed, the thought of his suffering had given her an obscure sense of satisfaction.

'Plague on it!' the Loremaster muttered. Though these new insights had not made her like Zavahl any better, she had begun to understand that he could never be brought to co-operate if he was allowed to remain in his current state of fear, distrust and sullen defiance. And co-operate he must. In his hands was the fate of the Dragon Seer, along with all the irreplaceable history and lore of the Dragonfolk spanning uncounted generations. With a shudder Veldan remembered her last view of the dragon's body, as she and her companions had climbed the approaches to the Snaketail pass: the dull skin and sunken flanks, the crumpled wings and one great, jewelled eye with its lustrous sparkle forever dimmed. There could be no going back for Aethon. His body had perished beyond all hope of restoration. All that remained of his mind and spirit were trapped inside the head of a half-crazed man whose beliefs denied his very existence. And the very future and continuation of the world might depend on the dragon's memories.

Somehow, Zavahl must be brought to understand what was at stake. Someone would have to try to retain his trust. Veldan rubbed her forehead. *Why me?* she thought with a weary sigh, but really she – and every Loremaster who had ever lived – knew the answer to that.

At a very early stage of her training, Cergorn himself had spelled it out for her. 'If you want to be a Loremaster, you'd better get used to the idea that you're going to spend a good deal of the rest of your life doing things you'd rather not do. They will range from inconvenient, right through uncomfortable, painful and downright distasteful, but there's no avoiding them. If you can't cope with that, you're not worthy to be a member of the Shadowleague, and you won't be part of it for long. We have to take care of this world as best we know how, and mostly, that involves clearing up other people's messes. If the idea doesn't appeal to you, get out now, and save us all a lot of time and trouble.'

Veldan looked back to the huddled figure on the bed.

I suppose it's worth a try. But frankly, I'd rather face the danger of rescuing the bastard all over again than try to make friends with him now I have him.

She cleared her throat. 'Zavahl,' she began, 'I know you're not asleep, but that's all right. You don't have to speak if you don't want to. Please listen to me, though. Don't shut out what I have to say because you're frightened. It may be difficult to believe me right now, but truly, we mean you no harm. We need your help for a little while, just as you need ours. After that, you'll be free to do whatever you want.' She paused, hoping in vain for some reaction from the unmoving figure on the bed.

When no response was forthcoming, Veldan shrugged and went on, nevertheless. 'You must be wondering why complete strangers would go to the trouble of kidnapping you. How can we possibly expect you to assist us, and what in the world can *we* do to help *you*? I'm sure you must have a lot of questions at this point,' she prompted. 'If you want to ask me, I'll try to answer as best I can.'

More silence. But the Loremaster was almost certain she could see a glitter between Zavahl's closed eyelids, as he watched her covertly through his lashes. Well, at least she had his interest now. It was a start. Quickly, she looked away from him again, staring into the fire as she continued to speak. 'The other night you called me a demon.' It was hard to keep the emotion out of her voice, to retain the same soothing tone. 'I'm nothing of the kind, you know. I'm as human as you. I expect you can see that, now I'm not looming suddenly out of the darkness, scaring you out of your wits. In fact, I probably seem quite normal, now that you've met my friend Kazairl! No-one knows where he came from. He hatched from an egg that my mother found when I was a little girl, and has been my true companion all my life. Of course, he can't be unique. He had to have parents *somewhere*, but his origins are a complete mystery. I know it may be hard for you to accept, but he is an intelligent, thinking being, and he's not a monster. At least,' she added with a wry smile, 'not once you get to know him.'

There was a sharply indrawn breath from Zavahl's corner. Veldan could see the struggle in his face as he forced himself not to speak.

'When I met you that first time,' she continued, 'you said there was something in your head. That must have been terrifying for you. But have you stopped to think that the poor being trapped within your mind must be as scared as you? After all, he doesn't have so many choices. He's just a passenger – a captive, in a way. He's within you because his own body has perished, and he has nowhere else to go. Yet apart from frightening you, he hasn't threatened you in any way, has he? You still have control of your body, and your thoughts are still your own, are they not? But if we hadn't rescued you, if you had died on that pyre, he would have perished too, over something that was none of his affair. You're an intelligent man and, as the Hierarch, surely you're not without compassion.' (Privately, Veldan doubted that, but at any rate, it seemed worthwhile to plant the suggestion.) 'Can you put yourself in his place? Can you imagine how utterly terrified *he* must have been in those last few moments, as they tried to light the fire?'

Again, there was no response from Zavahl, and Veldan decided to quit while she was ahead. Though he had made no sign, she knew he had been listening. 'You get some rest now,' she told her captive. 'There's water in the bucket beside the bed, and a mug to drink from. I've left a couple of cloths in case you want to wash, and there's another bucket at the foot of the bed in case – well, in case you need to go. You must be pretty desperate by now, I should imagine. When it's ready, I'll bring you something hot to eat, and then maybe you'll start to feel better. You've had a rough time this last day or so, and I know we haven't helped. I'm sorry about that, but truly, it was necessary. I hope that in time, you'll understand.'

As Veldan left the shelter, the sun was just rising, and gratefully, she turned her face to the warmth and light. She almost found herself feeling sorry for Zavahl – until the astringent voice of Kazairl broke into her thoughts. 'Save your pity, Boss. That one's a bad lot, Toulac says, and not to be trusted. Personally, I'm prepared to take her word for it.' Though he spoke harshly of Zavahl, there was an undertone of smug satisfaction in the firedrake's voice that clearly had nothing to do with his opinions of the unfortunate captive.

'You're going hunting?' she asked him.

'I certainly am. I'll be back in no time, sweetie, so tell Toulac to get the firepit stoked up. Breakfast is on its way.'

Though Veldan would be glad of some fresh meat for breakfast, she had to shake her head at the firedrake's attempt at subterfuge. To her, he was as transparent as air. He knew full well that she planned to contact the Archimandrite, and was making himself scarce.

Oh well, he wouldn't help in any case. It will be difficult enough to placate Cergorn, without contributions from a tactless, short-tempered firedrake.

With a sigh, she walked away from the camp and headed for the brow of the hill above the wayshelter. She wasn't looking forward to this at all.

The listeners in the Tower of Tidings were all young, even as these matters were reckoned among the oddly varying races of the

Shadowleague, and a strange combination of creatures besides. Nevertheless, they were a well-seasoned team who had been picked out from an early age for their strong telepathic gifts and trained assiduously with other youngsters who boasted the same talent. In the fullness of time they had banded together to form their trio, through friendship and a natural compatibility of skills. They were honoured that Cergorn had set them to listen today, because it showed how much he valued and respected their abilities, but they felt the responsibility keenly. None of them dared to contemplate the wrath of the Archimandrite, if they should miss an all-important communication from the missing Loremasters in Callisiora.

Bailen, a heavyset young man with light brown hair tied back in a long, unbraided tail, sat at the window, his blind eyes unfocussed on the growing daylight outside.

'Is he still down there?' asked Vaure from the fireplace.

'I expect so. He's been pacing around the bottom of the tower for hours.' Bailen shrugged. 'Dessil, may I borrow your eyes for a minute?'

'Surely.' Dessil, though his mouth was not well adapted to reproduce human speech, could communicate clearly, like all Loremasters, from mind to mind. He looked like a large otter, but in fact was one of the Dovruja, or race of river-folk from the wastelands of Liatris. Like the Dobarchu, their sea-dwelling brethren who dwelt among the long peninsula and clustered isles that formed the land of Nemeris, they were bright-eyed, intelligent, and clever, with surprising dexterity in their little webbed paws. He flowed across the room with its customary undulating motion, pushed against Bailen's knee and put his forepaws on the sill, peering out and down. Bailen put a hand on the otter's smooth, flat head and linked minds with his friend. An image came into his mind, seen with Dessil's vision, of the large, dappled grey centaur, seemingly pacing a groove around the tower's base.

'Oh, he's still there all right,' the human reported. 'At this rate he's going to wear away the turf in a ring all round the tower.'

'Well, I wish he'd stop it.' Sitting amid the flames in the fireplace, Vaure the Phoenix ruffled her bright, glowing plumage in irritation, sending a drift of sparks up the chimney. 'He's beginning to get on my nerves. Thank the Lords of Creation he can't climb those stairs!'

'You're right,' Dessil agreed, though he himself was pattering back and forth across the room. 'It's sufficiently off-putting to have him lurking around down there, without having him sitting right on top of us.'

'You can't blame the Archimandrite for being worried, though,' said the reasonable Bailen. 'It bodes ill indeed that those Loremasters in Callisiora haven't reported in yet – especially Thirishri. Such a senior member of the Shadowleague should understand the importance of keeping us well-informed here in Gendival.'

'But they aren't necessarily in trouble,' the Phoenix argued, spreading her glowing wings. 'If anything *had* gone wrong, Thirishri would certainly have reported back to us. So what's there to worry about? After all, what could possibly harm a Wind-Sprite?'

'I agree.' For a moment the otter stilled his quick, restless movements. 'Shree is in no danger, and with her to help them, I doubt the others could have come to much harm. And I must say, this is typical of Cergorn,' he added bitterly. 'All this fuss and commotion over a handful of humans and one accursed Dragon, while my Dobarchu brethren are being slaughtered in their thousands down in Nemeris, and nobody lifts a finger.'

'I'm sure he will send someone,' put in Bailen the peacemaker, 'but these catastrophes are taking place the world over, and the Archimandrite has so few folk to spare . . .'

'Oh, don't give me that old tale!' Vaure snapped. 'He didn't have any difficulty sparing *two* teams of Loremasters to get Aethon here safely.'

'And by the look of things,' Dessil added, 'even those two teams couldn't manage such a simple job. I don't know what the Shadowleague is coming to these days, but if Cergorn doesn't wake up his ideas—'

'Listen!' Bailen held up his hand. 'There's something coming in. It's Veldan.'

One of the advantages of being a Listener was that they always got to hear the news first, though a special oath of loyalty and secrecy was demanded of them, preventing them from repeating what they had heard to the Shadowleague at large. Cergorn kept control of the flow and dissemination of all information that came in, and though Bailen and his companions often agreed that they might handle things differently, they kept their opinions to themselves. And when the tidings were bad, they often got to hear things they would rather have been spared. Bailen, acting as focus and interface for the trio, felt his heart sink as he heard Veldan's burden of news, and when Cergorn remained grimly silent in response, his heart went out to her as she kept talking, in a desperate attempt to fill the void caused by the Archimandrite's pain at the loss of his partner.

'Goodness knows how we're going to get that wretch Zavahl to co-operate with us. He's not reacting well at all, and we've had neither the time nor the opportunity to cosset him. He was bad enough when he just had Aethon and Kaz to deal with. He's convinced that the dragon is a demon trying to possess his mind. The real trouble started, though, when we brought him through the Curtain Walls. He seems to be in a sort of stupor now. I think he can't cope with the disintegration of his beliefs, so he's retreating into himself.

'As for Shree,' she went on, 'I'm sorry, Cergorn, we just don't know what could have happened to her. She went off before dawn yesterday to scout, and we haven't heard from her since. But what could harm a Wind-Sprite? What has enough power? And how could we fight such a thing?'

Cergorn was still stunned by the news of Thirishri, but the Listeners sensed his anger, and felt the strength of his will as he struggled with his grief and pain. At this range there should have been little need of their assistance, but the Archimandrite, in his efforts to control his wrath, was neither sending nor receiving clearly, so they worked together to amplify his reply and send it back.

'Come home immediately. Give the Godswords the slip as fast as you can and get back here. Once you're all back in Gendival, we'll find some way to deal with this mess.'

'Did he hear me properly?' Veldan asked Bailen privately. 'I told him Elion had to give the Godswords the slip, not us. Kaz and I are back through the Curtain Walls already.'

'Never mind,' Bailen told her. 'Cergorn is upset over Thirishri. I don't think he's taking everything in right now. You just carry on with what you have to say, and I'll straighten the details out with him in a little while.'

'Thanks, Bailen. This may not be the best time, but I have some other news to break that might distract him a little from Shree.' Once again, Veldan addressed herself to the Archimandrite. 'All right, Cergorn. I'll see you soon – with company. I've found you a new Loremaster.'

'*What?*' exploded the centaur.

'I think that got his attention all right,' Bailen put in dryly.

'We'll be back as soon as we can,' Veldan put in hastily. 'Though we had to rescue a horse first. But then we decided not to—' She realised that she was babbling, and shut up hastily, before she dug herself in any deeper, but it was too late.

'A *horse?* What the blazes do you think you're playing at, girl? You get back here at once!'

'Now you've done it,' Bailen said. 'I think he misheard that last part too. He thinks you're going chasing off after a horse now. You'd better go, Veldan, before things get any more confused. Leave me to sort this out – and take your time about resting up. Hopefully, by the time you get back, Cergorn will have calmed down. If he hasn't, you might want to start thinking about a new profession.' Though his blindness kept him from travelling beyond the Curtain Walls, and he was greatly respected as a Listener, Bailen could not help but envy, a little, the freedom and adventure of Loremasters' lives. Though he liked Veldan, the temptation to needle her was just too much. 'I'm sure there must be lots of opportunities for an ex-Loremaster.'

'Curse you, Bailen,' Veldan snapped. 'That's not even remotely funny.' Then she was gone.

'Curse you, Tormon! Have you lost your mind? I'm not going down there!' Rochalla stared in horror at the road from the plateau to the lowlands. Born and bred in Tiarond, with the care of her little family taking up all her hours and attention, she'd had neither the time nor the inclination to take an interest in what lay beyond. How she wished she could have remained forever in that blissful state of ignorance.

She had been told that the road left the city, crossed the river, then ran alongside the mountain torrent for a couple of leagues until both vanished over the edge of the plateau. She had not, however, been prepared for the reality. It was difficult to accept the sheer scale of what she was seeing. The cliffs plunged endlessly down, and whatever lay at the bottom was lost in a layer of what she recognised, to her great dismay, as clouds. How in Myrial's name could she be looking down on clouds? It just wasn't natural.

From the position of the guardhouse, which was set some dozen yards back from the brink, the road had seemed to disappear completely in a morass of water and mud that ended abruptly at the edge of the drop. Now, Rochalla discovered that the route ran between two tall pillars, then snaked abruptly left down the cliff face, heading back towards the river and following a natural ledge in the rock. In these rains, it had turned into an additional watercourse that flowed swiftly with brown, turbid water that looked to be a foot or two deep. Her eyes followed the route she was about to take along the side of the cliff, and she received her second shock. The river, engorged after so many months of rain, flung itself over the precipice in a spectacular waterfall. With a sound like thunder, the seething waters leapt out into space, heavy and sleek where they poured over the brink, churning and foaming as they descended and dissipating into fine white spray far, far below. The roar was almost deafening, and the raw elemental force of the plunging water made the ground tremble underfoot.

From Rochalla's clifftop vantage point the road, looking frail and insubstantial as a cobweb that clung to the face of the rock, headed unerringly towards the waterfall and disappeared into that boiling welter of foam. She stepped back hastily, her stomach churning. 'We can't do it. We'll be killed!' She could hear her own voice rising in panic and felt like a fool, but she couldn't help herself.

Tormon gave her a sympathetic look and patted her clumsily on the shoulder. 'Don't fret, lass. This route scares the pants off me every spring, and in normal times, it's not nearly so bad as this. The road doesn't usually go under the falls – it tunnels into the cliff and switchbacks down for a few hundred yards, then it comes out further away from the cataract to pick up a fold in the cliffs where there's a trail, of sorts. There's only one thing to worry about, really: whether we can use the tunnel entrance because the waterfall is so swollen with the rains. Scall and I will go down in a minute to check that out, and if it isn't passable we just can't go this way and that's all there is to it. Come on, Scall, let's take a look. We can't loiter around up here all day.'

He turned to the others, who stood in a forlorn huddle, protected from the drizzle by soldiers' thick and sturdy cloaks, of which they had found a supply in the guardhouse. 'Those accursed creatures are still in the city, remember,' he went on. 'Before they think of hunting further afield, we want to be well gone. Leave the horses inside until we need them. You may as well go back too, for there's no point in everyone standing out here in the rain – only one person needs to stay out here and watch. Keep a good lookout, and if you see anything bigger than a sparrow in the air over Tiarond, get back into the barracks as fast as you can and make sure the windows are shuttered and the doors are all locked. Rochalla, can you take care of Annas until we come back?'

'Of course.' Rochalla, almost swamped by a cloak designed to fit a man half again her size, smiled at the little girl and took her hand. 'I'm sure we can think of a game or two to pass the time.'

Down went Scall and the trader, with the dark, wet cliff rising on their left hand. Unguessable ages ago, the road had actually been carved by hand into the steep rock face, and so a lip of weathered stone overhung the narrow way, partially sheltering them from the miserable drizzle that was growing heavier by the minute. The terrifying drop, mercifully shrouded in clouds and mist, fell away on their right, and on that side, the road was bounded by a shoulder-high wall, which was a comfort until Scall noticed that the crumbling mortar between the stones was steadily being washed away by the relentless floodwaters. He placed little faith in its ability to hold him if he should slip and fall against it, and it seemed a frail and chancy thing to be all that was standing between himself and certain death at the bottom of the precipice. Ahead, filling his entire field of vision, was the waterfall, which seemed bigger, more powerful and more intimidating the further they descended. With every step, the thunder of the plummeting waters grew louder, throbbing and pounding in Scall's head until he felt dizzy.

Though the torrent was not too deep, Scall found it difficult to keep his feet in the swirling floodwaters that ran like a river down the road. He and Tormon slid and slithered down the steep incline, grabbing each other when one of them slipped, and supporting themselves with new staffs that had enjoyed a previous existence as spears. Presvel had found the weapons earlier that morning, propped in a corner of the barracks, and had suggested cutting off the heads to make walking sticks. 'Forget that,' Tormon had growled. 'I'm not going to pass up any weapon we can lay our hands on. They'll do just as well for walking sticks with the business end attached, and we might be glad of those blades before we're through.'

Scall shook his head at the memory. Those bookish folk from the city had no idea. (He conveniently forgot the fact that, until the last few days, he too had spent his life within the walls of Tiarond.) It was a good thing the party had two practical men along, in the shape of Tormon and himself.

The din of the falls was growing too loud for further conversation, which was fine by Scall. He had been thoroughly damp when he started, from the fine, misty drizzle that hung in the air, but as he approached the churning white torrent he found himself dripping, his hair and clothing saturated by heavy spray. A cold wind began to blow, growing stronger and stronger, created by the movement of the tons of water hurtling down.

Scall's heart quailed to be so close to such unfettered power. If he were washed away into the cataract, it would mash him to a pulp just as effortlessly as he would crush an insect.

Just how far are we going, anyway? If we don't reach the tunnel soon, we're going to end up right underneath the falls.

Over recent months, the water draining down from the plateau had increased the volume of the waterfall, widening it until, to Scall's dismay, it extended well beyond the access to the tunnel road. Now that he was only a few yards away, the roar of the cascade had reached a deafening crescendo, and the force of the plunging waters sent tremors through the stone beneath their feet. Tormon jerked at Scall's arm to get his attention and pointed, gesturing towards the road ahead. It was difficult to see through the haze of flying spume that filled the air, but when he looked closely, there seemed to be a darker patch ahead where the road clung tightly to the cliff. Was that the tunnel mouth?

The trader gestured for Scall to stay where he was. Clearly he meant to go ahead by himself, into that welter of frothing water, to investigate. Scall, weak-kneed with fear, would have been more than happy to let him – but suddenly the face of Annas, small and scared, flashed into his mind. Tormon was the only family she had. If the waterfall swept him away, the little girl would be all alone. In a flash, his mind was made up. 'Stay here! I'll go.' Pulling at the older man's arm to hold him back, Scall pushed past Tormon and plunged ahead into the curtain of churning spray.

Gasping and half-blinded, he slowly felt his way along, guiding himself with his left hand on the rough, wet stone of the cliff. He was horribly aware, at all times, of the weight and speed of the falling water on his right. The falls seemed to suck at him, trying to draw him down to be crushed and mangled in their depths. There was so much water in the air that it was difficult to breathe. The tumult was like the stampeding hooves of a thousand giant horses, repeated endlessly and without respite until his head felt as if it must burst. Still he stumbled doggedly forwards, protected from the worst of the deluge by the lip of rock that overhung the road. He constantly tested the broken surface of the road with his staff, and inched his way towards the patch of darkness he had glimpsed from beyond the waterfall.

Suddenly his left hand groped in empty air. The solid wall of rock had vanished and he staggered sideways into a deep, dark void. He had done it! He had conquered his fears and beaten the odds: he'd faced the raw powers of nature and won. It *was* possible to get into the tunnel from the cliff road, despite the peril of the swollen falls – and he had been the one to prove it.

Scall's heart swelled with pride. He was no longer Smithmaster Agella's clumsy, failed apprentice. In Tormon's group he was an important, helpful assistant to the trader; far more useful than that high and mighty merchant woman, or that bookish townie, Presvel. Sternly, he reminded himself not to exult too soon. He had to check that the rest of the way was safe before he could go back in triumph to the others. Sloshing through water that covered his feet, he groped his way into the tunnel for a few yards, to get well clear of the spray from the waterfall outside. From his ex-Godsword backpack he took a torch, also 'borrowed', like so much of the group's new equipment, from the guardpost at the top of the cliff. He wedged the brand upright between his feet to leave his hands free and, after some fumbling in the dark with his tinderbox, he finally managed to get it alight, almost singeing his eyebrows in the process. He had failed to take into account the fact that the sloping tunnel acted like a chimney, and a steady wind, blowing upwards from below, set the torch flames streaming out like banners.

Still coughing and spluttering from the smoke, Scall held up his makeshift light and looked around him. The passage was some ten feet wide, hewn by hand from the rock, with the arching roof about the same height at its apex. The dark stone glistened with moisture, and drops of water falling from the roof glittered like diamonds in the flickering light of the torch. The floor felt rough under his boots – a safer surface for carts and horses, he reckoned, than slippery paving, especially on such a steep slope. As with the open trail above, a river of swift, murky water, almost reaching his boot-tops, ran down the road, the ceaseless liquid babble of the flowing water echoing with a hollow tone in the narrow confines of the tunnel.

Sternly, he reminded himself not to waste time. He had responsibilities now. The others would be waiting for his return, and Tormon would still be shivering on the wet, uncomfortable ledge outside, worrying in case something had gone wrong. Besides, torches didn't last forever.

'Come on,' Scall told himself, speaking aloud to bolster his courage. 'Let's get on with this.' With his heart beating fast with excitement and fear, he lifted his torch high and set off into the dark unknown.

Six

Dark and Grim

Blade woke to daylight, furious that he had given way to his exhaustion. How much time had he lost? A glance at the fire, sunk once more to a dimly glowing bed of ashes, reassured him that only a few hours had been wasted in slumber. Besides, what else could he have done? Despite possessing the robust, quick-healing constitution of the Mageborn, he had pushed his body to the very limit over the last day or two, and there was no way he could have gone any further without rest.

He wasted no time on self-recrimination. What was done was done. It was more important to get the fire going again. Now that it had died away, the temperature in the room was dropping rapidly. With a groan, he rolled over to free himself from the rug that was wound around his body, and struggled to his knees on the cooling hearth to repeat his fire-building task of the previous night.

Though the embers had sunk even lower this time, Blade was not hampered by cold, exhaustion and weakness, and he soon had the first flames crackling up through his newly placed kindling. Only when a blaze roared up the chimney did he pause to assess the damage he had inflicted with that idiotic fall. Though he'd suffered scratches and scrapes, torn clothing, and his body felt as though it had been squeezed in a giant fist, he knew how lucky he had been. Cuts and bruises would heal, but right now, his mangled corpse could be at the bottom of the cliff, a feast for insects and crows. Even worse, he might have been lying down there with broken legs or back, facing a long, slow, agonising death.

Blade was still very much alive however – and ravenously hungry. By the side of the hearth was a soup-pot, its cold contents concealed by a thin scum of fat. He broke the pallid surface rather gingerly with a spoon, not looking forward to what he might find. His men would already have gone through this place like a plague of locusts in search of anything edible. That they had left this behind did not bode well. The soup – he supposed he must call it that – was a thin, greyish slop containing stringy odds and ends of meat and great indigestible-looking chunks of root vegetable. Blade dipped a tentative finger into the mess, tasted and grimaced. Had his men been using the soup kettle as a piss-pot, rather than going out into the cold winter's night? He wouldn't put it past them, and really, the taste was so disgusting that it was impossible to tell. Nevertheless he hung the pot back over the fire, and waited impatiently with growling stomach for the contents to warm through. When it was ready he devoured every mouthful, and wished that there was more.

With great approval he discovered the water supply that was piped into the kitchen. Having drunk deeply, he set about cleaning up his cuts and scrapes as best he could, rummaging through Toulac's belongings until he found a pot of the all-purpose salve used by most ordinary folk. Having tended to his hurts he turned to his clothing, brushing off the mud and cobbling together the biggest rents with a needle and thread. Unfortunately, there was little he could do about his ruined boots, other than stuff the toes with scraps of old leather and rag, and hope for the best.

Now that he had rested and, after a fashion, been fed, Blade's robust constitution was already beginning to recover. Now that he felt better, his mind began to work furiously. There could be no altering the decision he had made last night. Now that his men had revolted, Gilarra would never let him return to Tiarond. He had given her the throne of Callisiora, so he was superfluous to her needs and she – quite rightly, he was forced to admit – would see him as nothing but a threat. The other obstacle in his path was the horde of skyborne abominations which had attacked the city. Though he couldn't remember encountering this particular species during his Loremaster days, it was clear that the invaders would spread far and fast through Callisiora, and nothing would stand in their way. What was worse, while the swarms of voracious predators held Tiarond, he couldn't even sneak or bribe his way back into the Godsword Citadel to collect the captive Wind-Sprite, who had figured so prominently as a hostage in his plans.

No, he must abandon his schemes for Callisiora for the present, at least, and return to Gendival. Hopefully he would be able to lie low, undiscovered by Cergorn, until he found some aspect of the current crisis that would work to his advantage. Something would turn up, he knew. It always did. Besides, there were other reasons to go back. He still had some unfinished business with Zavahl, and most important of all, there was the mysterious female Loremaster. Blade told himself that he wanted to pay her back for wrecking all his plans, but in his heart, he knew that his motives were far more complex. Ever since he had first set eyes on her, her face had haunted him with its resemblance to Aveole, his lost love. For once, he didn't want to think about the implications of that. Not yet. He would wait until he found her again.

It was all very well to think of finding her, how could he catch her? He knew all too well how swiftly the firedrake could travel. In no time they would be back in Gendival with Zavahl, while Blade, formerly the hunter, had turned into a fugitive. He must cross the intervening miles on foot: friendless, foodless, ill-equipped and poorly clad for such a venture. He would succeed eventually, he had no doubt of that, but the journey would be difficult, slow, and unpleasant. Surely there must be a better way? If only his poor horse had not perished! Frowning, he gazed into the fire, ransacking his brains for a solution.

Blade had been wishing so hard for a mount that when first he heard the whinny of a horse, he was sure he must be dreaming. Or was someone coming? He leapt to his feet in alarm, but there was no sound of approaching hoofbeats. No, the animal was nearby, stationary by the sound of it, and almost certainly in some kind of distress. Suddenly, he remembered Toulac's warhorse, which had been quartered in the kitchen when first he had come here with his men and the captive Hierarch. In a flash he was out of the door, running across the yard to the rickety barn.

The horse was tied up in the draughty wooden building. When it saw him it laid its ears back and plunged, fighting as hard as a hooked salmon to break its tether. On close inspection, Blade was delighted with his discovery. When he had been here the first time, he had been too preoccupied with other matters to pay much attention to the beast, and because its owner had been long in the tooth, he had assumed that her mount would be the same. In reality, however, the warhorse was not so far past his prime, and given the circumstances of the last lean year, it had been kept in excellent condition. Like the best of its kind it was graceful and strong, clean-limbed but very powerful, regal with a stallion's bearing and pride. Its large dark eyes, filled with intelligence and fire, were well set in a shapely head, and its pale coat was beautifully marked with darker dapples that clouded its quarters. Its mane and tail, if the tangles and mud were combed out, would be cascades of shimmering white. For the first time in a long while, Blade found that he still could smile, and mean it.

This was a stallion and a warhorse and must therefore be treated with caution. Usually such animals were trained to allow strangers close enough to tend them, for how else could their owners put up at inns? Any attempt to ride one, however, would result in a display of violence that would end with the would-be horse thief, more often than not, killed or crippled by those formidable teeth and hooves. Trained fighting horses were a very valuable commodity, and it was only common sense on the part of the owners to make their property as unstealable as possible.

The animal, tied in one place for so long, was suffering through thirst and hunger. While it drank deeply from a bucket that Blade had cautiously placed within its reach, he searched the place for fodder. Finally, when he had just about given up hope, he found a good supply of hay and corn in the house, where they could be kept dry more easily. The old woman must have been more wealthy than he had guessed to be able to stockpile these amounts in times of shortage. It was also plain that she must care a very great deal for the horse.

Once the grey had been made comfortable, Blade embarked on the next step. Though he knew subtle techniques to train the horse to accept him, he lacked the time for them. He had lingered long enough here already. No, this occasion called for the skills of a Loremaster and telepath, rather than those of a horseman. Reaching into the animal's mind, he found the simple image of Toulac; the sight, the scent and the sound of her as a horse would perceive her. He then located the image of himself, recent and superficial, but present all the same. Gradually and skilfully, he manipulated the thoughts of the simpler beast, merging the two images until he was linked in its mind with the same bonds of affection and trust that it shared with its owner.

Blade spent a little time – as much as he dared afford – in grooming and handling the warhorse, staying close and talking softly all the time to let it grow accustomed to his smell and his voice. He found its tack, again stored in the house for safekeeping, and readied the animal for the road. It took far less time to pack for himself, as his possessions were few, but he filled his water bottle, and took some woollen socks and a pair of worn leather gloves from the old woman's chest. A couple of thick, warm blankets from her bed completed the equipment for his journey. He pocketed the pot of salve, and filled a small sack with grain for the horse. Food for himself, unfortunately, would just have to wait. Well, he would manage. He had gone hungry before, and taken no lasting harm.

Once he had strapped his scanty belongings behind the saddle, Blade led the horse from the barn. Outside in the yard he mounted cautiously, taking his time and waiting until the animal was ready to accept him. Though deep within he wanted to howl with frustration at all these additional delays, he knew that they were necessary, and was very careful not to betray his irritation to the sensitive warhorse.

When he finally hoisted himself into the saddle, with much

protesting from his stiff, bruised body, the beast stood tense for a moment, its ears laid back, Toulac's training at war with the new instinct to trust Blade that he had placed so carefully in its mind. He waited patiently, again reaching into its simple thoughts to reinforce the new bond he had created. After a moment it shook its mane and relaxed its rigid stance, and he knew that he had won.

'All right, my boy. Let's go.' He urged the warhorse out of the yard and up the trail towards the pass, his spirits rising with every step. It felt good to be in pursuit of his quarry once more, and to have such a magnificent animal underneath him. The irony was not lost on him, that he was using Toulac's own horse to catch her. 'This makes us even, you old baggage,' he muttered. 'You and your companion robbed me of Zavahl, and I've stolen your precious horse.' Already, he had decided to keep the beast. There would be plenty of time to tinker further with its mind before he caught up with the women, and soon he would be the only master it would accept.

As he continued to make his way up the trail, Blade reached the place of the mudslide, where the body of the dragon still sprawled beside the track. The sight of it turned his thoughts, once again, to the former Hierarch.

I'm on your trail, Zavahl. I'll find you soon, and when I do . . .

But he was surprised how little venom he could summon. Following the events of the previous night, Zavahl had slipped a long way down Blade's list of priorities. Now his thoughts were all turned towards Gendival, and the leadership of the Shadowleague.

As Blade passed the narrow side-canyon that had been filled with detritus from the mudslide, he glanced down through the gap at the river which, in this particular spot, raced through a narrow defile, far below. With an exclamation he checked the grey warhorse and stood up in his stirrups, craning to see a little further. Trees, boulders, silt and rubble from the landslip had partially blocked the flow of water, and these had clearly been supplemented by fallen timber and other debris that had been washed down the flooded river, until a tangled pile of flotsam lay athwart the flow, reducing it from a torrent to a trickle. The natural dam must have been building up since the landslide, Blade thought with some surprise. Certainly, the flow of the river hadn't been so badly affected yesterday. But now . . . He looked above the obstruction at the amount of water that churned and swirled behind the barrier. Eventually, the increasing pressure would burst the barrier apart, and when that happened, the entire bulk of the pent-up torrent would come smashing downriver in a single, monumental wave.

Blade glanced up at the sky. The clouds were dark and lowering, carrying a heavy burden. Already the drizzling rain had turned into a harder, thicker downpour, and the wind was beginning to gust, driving the black cloud before it, over the top of the pass, promising much worse to come. He imagined the waters spreading out across the plateau and slamming into the walls and bridges of Tiarond. That ought to be interesting. He was almost sorry he wouldn't be there to see it. With a smile, he urged the horse forward and went on his way, leaving the thrashing turmoil of water behind, and consigning the city to its fate.

As he rode towards Gendival, Blade found himself whistling, despite the merciless rain that blew into his face. These last few years had been too easy. It would be most enjoyable to face a real challenge again. Yes, even though the odds were currently stacked against him, today he had taken the first steps on the long climb back to power. And best of all, there were certain people, even here in Callisiora, who would support him every inch of the way.

Like all the lands of Myrial, Callisiora had its own resident Loremasters, and Blade could not have kept his identity secret from the Shadowleague all these many years if he had not managed to get his own supporters into these critical positions. It had taken some skilful manoeuvring in the beginning: so many agents had met with fatal accidents in the first few years that Blade was astounded that Cergorn hadn't become suspicious and made a thorough investigation of the matter. Complacent fool! He didn't deserve to be Archimandrite. Well, it was the centaur's loss.

Blade felt a surge of excitement. At long last, his time had come.

He considered the Loremasters – *my* Loremasters, he thought – in the south and east of Callisiora, one who dwelt near the warm sea coast, and the other among the eastern Reivers. (The third, who had dwelt in Tiarond itself, had died recently of the blacklung fever.) His southern agent was too far away to be of much immediate use, but the Reivers were conveniently close to the Curtain Walls, some little distance to the south on the other side of the Snaketail Pass. As soon as he was over the mountains, he would send his thoughts out on a tight beam, and make contact with Grim.

They were hardy folk, the Eastern Reivers. *We have to be,* Dark thought ruefully, *considering the conditions under which we live.* The thick, sucking mud clung to his feet as he tramped along the track to the little settlement with its scattering of primitive homes: low stone dwellings that were half-sunk into the ground, and roofed with sods. The sharp smell of smoking turf fires and breakfast bacon frying mingled unhappily with the reek of excrement, both animal and human. Muck-plastered pigs roamed loose between the houses, and chickens and mongrel dogs scurried here, there and everywhere. Children darted about, playing some complicated chasing game, their exuberance unhampered by the misty grey drizzle – until Dark and Grim, his master, approached. As the two black-cloaked Summoners drew near, their faces hidden by the gruesome masks made from real human skulls, the youngsters scattered, their shrieks now of genuine terror, and vanished into the low, turf-roofed homes like rabbits into burrows.

'Their mothers say that if they are bad, the Summoners will get them,' commented Dark's master, with a wry twist to his mouth. 'Did you know that?' He was using mental speech, a talent that set himself and his assistant apart from their fellow Reivers, and even, to the best of Grim's knowledge, their fellow Summoners from the other clans.

Dark shrugged, and replied in equal silence. 'Of course I do. My mother used to tell me exactly the same thing. When you picked me out to be your successor, I just about died from sheer terror on the spot.'

'And after all this time? Knowing what you know now, are you sorry I chose you?'

'Ask me again in an hour or two.' A shiver ran through the young man.

'I understand.' There was sympathy in Grim's eyes, seen through the dark holes of the bony mask. 'You've been dreading this day for long enough, and no doubt you've spent sleepless nights agonising over the morality of this blackest aspect of a Summoner's life. When it's all over, though, I hope you'll feel somewhat differently. It doesn't get easier with time, but after a while you'll learn to detach yourself a little and see the necessity, and indeed the mercy, in what you do.'

'And you've known of my doubts all the time.' Dark thought he had done a good job of concealing his dread, but as usual, his perceptive mentor had seen right through his hard-earned professional façade.

'My dear boy, every Summoner worth the name since the start of time has felt the way you feel. But the only way to truly understand is to go through the experience yourself. Today is your greatest test, and will prove once and for all whether I was correct – or otherwise – in my choice of my successor.'

'I'll do my best, Grim.' The younger man took a deep breath. 'Come on. Let's get it over with.'

The long, low dwelling was indistinguishable from any of the others in the settlement. The Summoners pushed back the coverings from the doorway: first the flap of thick, stiffened hide, then the heavy inner curtain of felted wool. Once inside, Dark paused to let his eyes adjust to the gloom, for the narrow slits of window let in little light, and the fire was smouldering dully in the fireplace, as though it had been affected by the atmosphere of sorrow and despair that pervaded the room.

A woman awaited them, her back bent through long years of labour, her hair streaked with grey. Dark saw her flinch away in terror as they entered, and in a flash of understanding, saw himself and his master through her eyes. She only saw the ghastly skulls that masked the two men, giving them an air of anonymity, of mystery and menace. She did not see Grim's shrewd but kindly glance. To her, there was no sign of his seamed face, like hewn granite, and the profile resembling that of a bird of prey, and she had no knowledge of the lines carved by humour on either side of his mouth, and the compassionate nature the old man so carefully hid. In his own face, Dark knew she would not see the beginnings of those chiselled, ascetic features, and the same stern expression that he seemed to have absorbed, through the years, from his master. She would not see his comparative youth and, thank all that was sacred, she would see no sign of his fear.

Despite her own fear of their forbidding aspect, she kept her feelings under control, inclining her head deferentially to the two Summoners. 'My grandson is yonder, in the next room, good sirs.' She gestured for them to precede her. As he entered the cramped little bedchamber, it took all of Dark's self control not to run in the opposite direction, out of this house and far, far away across the hills.

The child had been ill for some time. Beneath the rumpled blankets of the bed, the silhouette of the little body with its wasted, stick-like limbs could barely be seen. The face was hollow-cheeked and bloodless. Dark already knew it was hopeless, but none the less he looked at his mentor, reluctant to admit defeat. Grim gave a barely perceptible shake of his head, before turning to the anxious parents who kept vigil at the boy's bedside. The mother, her face pale beneath a straggle of unravelling dark braids, looked barely out of childhood herself, though her boy must have been about five or six years old. The father, little older but already showing the lean, weatherbeaten aspect of a seasoned warrior, looked at the old Summoner with a naked plea in his eyes. Both had been weeping. Both were clearly afraid of the two grisly figures in the cloaks and masks.

From his bed, the boy whimpered and moaned, breaking the

silent tableau. His eyes were dark and wide with agony, his little body twisted and tense. His hair clung in spikes to his sweat-slick face. Grim beckoned to the two young parents. 'Come,' he said gently. 'Say your farewells and come away. The boy is in great pain now. Let him go. It is time for him to sleep.'

With one last, desperate look at his son, the father left the room obediently, but the young mother let out a single, choking sob. 'No!' she cried fiercely.

Grim's voice grew stern. 'You must,' he replied. 'Can you not see how cruel it is, to let him linger thus?'

The woman bit her lip and nodded. 'I understand that,' she whispered. 'But I want to stay with him. He'll be afraid of you. I won't let him go with only strangers – such terrifying strangers – to send him on his journey.'

The old Summoner looked at her steadily. 'Are you sure you can bear it? All your strength will be needed, for you must not give way to your grief in the presence of the boy. That would only make his passing harder.'

The girl straightened her thin shoulders. 'I am a daughter of warriors. I am strong enough. He is my only child, and I will bear it for his sake.'

Grim nodded. 'So be it.' He placed the mother at one side of the child's bed, and beckoned his assistant forward to the other.

Dark swallowed hard. For the first time, he must conduct a Passing on his own, and the circumstances were not at all as he had imagined they would be. It was one thing to assist an elderly person, their enfeebled body weary after so many long years of toil, to lay down their burdens and go to a well-deserved rest. He had expected that to be hard enough. But it was another matter entirely to snuff out the life of a little boy who should be outside running and playing, with all his life before him. And to make matters worse, he had the grieving mother at the bedside, looking on.

'Have you lost your mind?' Again, he used mental speech. 'Why did you say she could stay? This is all I need.'

'Would it be fair to deny her?' His mentor's voice sounded serenely in his mind, its gruff intonations exactly the same as when he spoke aloud. 'What are you worrying about, Dark? You know you're more than capable of conducting this Passing. But get a move on, my young friend. This delay only creates further torment for everyone concerned.'

Dark stepped up to the bedside and saw the child gasp and flinch away from the black cloak, the necklace of bone – and worst of all, the mask made from a human skull.

Damn. This is ridiculous. Just this once, for a little boy, we can bend the rules. He reached up behind his head to unfasten the mask, but was forestalled by a thought from Grim as forceful as a hammer-blow. 'Stop that! Leave the mask alone!'

'But surely for a child . . .'

'Never, under any circumstances. We'll talk about this later, Dark. Now get on, and do what you must do.'

His mentor was right, Dark knew. His own reluctance was making him postpone the inevitable, but all this delay would only serve to increase the child's distress.

'It's all right,' he said softly to the boy. 'Don't be frightened. It's only a disguise, like a masquerade. If you think this is ugly, you should see what I look like underneath!' Thankfully the youngster responded to the jest, and the ghost of a smile crossed the thin little face. 'Now,' Dark continued, 'I'm going to make the pain stop, all right?' He kept his voice low and soothing. 'I'm going to touch you gently, right there—' he laid his fingers on the little boy's fore-head, 'and soon the pain will leave you. You'd like that, wouldn't you?'

As he spoke, the young Summoner's mind was probing the child's brain, locating and blocking the centres of pain. All at once the child relaxed, an incredulous smile flooding his face. 'There,' murmured Dark. 'That's better, isn't it?' He took a deep breath, fighting to keep his voice steady. He could feel his hand trembling against the youngster's skin.

'Thank you.' The little boy's voice was a faint, scratchy whisper.

Dark blinked back tears, thankful that the mask hid his face. 'Sleep,' he murmured. Swiftly, he located the deep centres that controlled heartbeat and breathing. The boy was already so weak that there was little left to do. His eyes closed as Dark sent sleep to him. Then slowly, gently, the Summoner stilled his breathing, and stopped his heart.

Dark got up from the bedside. 'It's done,' he said, his voice harsh with the strain of keeping back his unshed tears. 'He is at peace now.'

Sobbing wildly, the mother flung herself on her son and took him in her arms. Grim touched his assistant's arm and motioned for them to leave the room.

In the outer chamber, the father sat at the table, hunched over an ale cup. Tears were streaming down his face. The old grandmother sat by the fire, plainly disapproving but not daring to speak.

'Beware.' Grim's warning echoed in Dark's mind.

Suddenly the man flung himself away from the table, overturning his chair and spilling his ale as he lurched towards them. 'Monsters!' he roared. 'You murdered him!'

Grim raised his hand and the distraught man stopped dead, straining against an invisible barrier. Dark looked at his mentor with new respect. Planting the illusion of an unseen wall in a non-telepath's mind was far more difficult and complex than the mind-speech the Summoners used between themselves.

'For shame.' Grim spoke sternly. 'Do you think we would have let him go if there had been any alternative? You know full well that there is no cure for the wasting sickness. Your son is free from pain now, and has gone to join the Guardian Spirits. Is that not better than suffering, day upon day without respite, agony beyond all comprehension?'

The man's eyes dropped. Then the words burst out of him in a flood. 'But he was so little – so young. Why should he be taken?'

Grim sighed. 'I know,' he said softly. 'Truly, I understand your anger. There is no justice in such a tragedy. But go to your wife now. You must comfort each other through the difficult days ahead.'

With that, he turned in a swirl of black cloak and left the little house, hastily followed by Dark.

When they were out in the clean fresh air, the young Summoner took several deep breaths, trying to steady himself. But the ordeal was not over yet. Outside the door stood a knot of waiting villagers, clearly neighbours of the tragic family, standing silent in the rain. They fell back respectfully as the Summoners left the dwelling, but Dark could feel the hostility in the air like blades of steel aimed at his heart. It took all his courage to walk away, his unprotected back towards the danger. The skin between his shoulders crawled, expecting at any minute to feel the impact of a missile, or worse still, a knife. Behind the Summoners a low swell of sullen muttering broke the silence. Dark made out the words 'murderers,' and 'ghouls,' among other epithets.

The two men walked back up the narrow vale, blown along by the gusting wind at their backs. The high, steep slopes on either side were a soft mix of purple, amber and green, the same shades as the multi-hued cloaks the Reivers wore – at least, they did if they weren't Summoners, Dark thought ruefully, condemned to their eternal black. Unlike the thick Reiver cloaks, however, the mantles of the hills were thin and threadbare, allowing the raw bones of the earth, the outcroppings and crags of pale limestone, to show through in places. Sheep grazed here and there, wet and depressed-looking amid the swatches of heather and bracken on the steep fellsides, their thickening winter fleeces dark and heavy with the rain.

The shaggy white cattle, mainstay of the Reivers, grazed the valley floor, guarded at all times by watchful riders whose job was to protect the valuable animals, to keep them out of the well-fenced pockets of crops – mostly barley, roots and hardy winter greens – that grew in every sheltered pocket of land, and not least, Dark thought wryly, to protect the human settlers from the beasts. The cattle were of a wild, ancient, barely domesticated breed, known for their uncertain temper and their tendency to attack without provocation. They would encircle the unwary victim, then all point themselves towards the intruder and charge. Even the wolves who roamed the fells in winter treated them with caution, giving them a wide berth when possible, and concentrating on the more vulnerable sheep.

Once the Summoners had left the settlement behind them, Dark struck away from the main track, wanting to be alone for a while with his turbulent thoughts. He had only gone a few steps when his mentor called him back, aloud this time, his rough old voice carried on the wind. 'Best stay together for now, my young friend. You can weep when we get home. Though we're usually held in sufficient awe and fear to protect us, the father of that boy was wild with grief, and there's no saying that we might not be followed. I don't want you meeting with an accident in a lonely place.'

Dark was horrified. 'But surely they wouldn't dare . . .' None the less, he fell quickly back into step beside the older man.

'Time was when they wouldn't dare,' replied Grim, 'but anyone who claims their authority through the supernatural, be they Summoner, Seer, or the Hierarch himself, will find their authority waning in times of natural disaster.' He raised his eyes towards the rainy heavens. 'It was ever thus.'

'But I thought it would be the opposite,' Dark protested, 'that the people would turn to their spiritual leaders in the hopes of some divine intercession.'

'Oh, they do, lad. They do – at first. But when the disaster goes on as long as this one has without respite, they start to lose respect for us, and from there it's only a short step to being blamed. I hear that the Hierarch in Tiarond has already fallen foul of the wrath of his god-fearing congregation. They planned to sacrifice him last night, I heard.'

'But that's terrible!' Dark was genuinely shocked. 'And they have the gall to call *us* barbarians.'

The older man shrugged. 'You live by the gods, you die by the gods. There's a lesson in that for you, my young friend, even though our own Guardian Spirits are nothing like their Myrial that they keep trying to foist upon us. The gods may differ, but people are the same the world over. In bad times like these, stay on the main trails, don't wander alone – and watch your back.'

As the Summoners trudged back up the valley, Grim couldn't keep from looking at his student with a series of surreptitious, anxious glances.

Dark is taking this badly. Of course, we all do, the first time we have to end a life, but then most Summoners do not have the abilities – and burdens – that have been given to the two of us.

He remembered how pleased he had been to discover Dark, a lad with rare telepathic abilities similar to his own.

Before that, I always thought that I would be forced to train an ordinary lad, as the other Summoners do, in the uses of herbs and potions, both for healing and for imposing our will – ostensibly the will of the Guardians – on others, in the misdirection and sleight of hand that makes the majority of my kind appear to possess such arcane and mystic powers. At the time, I thought it was a miracle to find Dark, as though the fates had sent me my true successor. I never stopped to consider whether this was the best future for him. It was different for me. Much easier. I was discovered by the Loremasters all those years ago, and became one of the Shadowleague. After I'd been to Gendival, the world became a different place.

Grim sighed, losing himself in memories, recalling the excitement and the frustrations of his Loremaster training. He had learned so much in Gendival – most of which he was not permitted to take out into the world and use. Dissatisfaction with this state of affairs had led to his association with the brilliant, charismatic Amaurn. Lacking the courage to stand up and be counted, he had become one of the renegade's many covert supporters.

Which was just as well, in the end. If I had been brave enough to declare myself openly, I would never have become Loremaster for eastern Callisiora, and Blade wouldn't have a secret supporter among the Reivers.

Over the years, Grim had been impressed by the determination with which the former Amaurn, now calling himself Lord Blade, had managed to work himself into such a position of power. And though he was forced to move very slowly and carefully, lest Cergorn's suspicions be aroused, he had recently begun to release information to the Tiarondians; the most notable of these little gifts being blasting powder, an innovation which the miners had welcomed with open arms. He had also managed to insinuate his own people into all three of the Shadowleague posts in Callisiora: in the east, in the south and even in Tiarond itself, although the old woman – ostensibly a priestess at the Temple – who had filled the pivotal post in the city had recently died, and due to the current crisis in the world, had not yet been replaced by Cergorn. Grim himself, using his own private and most unusual messengers, had been sending word out to Amaurn's supporters in Gendival, encouraging one of them to volunteer for the post.

But I wish he'd make his move soon. What can be holding Blade up now? Surely things can't get much worse – not unless the Curtain Walls collapse entirely. If only Cergorn could be forced to release some of the knowledge that he guards like a dog with a bone, so much suffering could be avoided.

Once again, Grim looked across at his companion, who trudged along, his head down, his gaze turned inward. Anguish and turmoil showed clearly on his face. Bitterly, the Summoner thought of all the medical lore collected at Gendival, much of it unexamined and unstudied for years beyond counting, because the Shadowleague had decreed that it could never be taken out into the world and used.

Was there something in all that vast treasure house of information which might have saved that little boy's life, instead of saving him from further suffering? Dark is a good man, talented and sensitive. Why can't I give him useful knowledge, to preserve lives instead of ending them? Why can't we put our unusual abilities to better use? Instead we conceal them by taking ridiculous names like Grim and Dark to disguise our humanity, we hide behind these outrageous death's-head masks, and we must bury the true nature of the power we possess amid all these ridiculous arcane ceremonies and mystic rites, to hide our true nature from a bunch of ignorant and superstitious people.

Again, Grim looked at his assistant's anguished face, and shook his head. It wasn't fair that Dark should have to suffer such needless pain. He deserved so much better than this. The Summoner shook his head.

Blade had better make his move soon. I'm not sure how much longer we can go on like this.

Seven

The Dreamer

'What's wrong, Boss?' The mental voice of Kazairl followed close upon the end of Veldan's communication with the Listeners. 'Did old horse-arse give you trouble?'

'Not half as much as I gave him, apparently,' Veldan said ruefully. 'The news that Shree was missing hit him hard. He was so angry, I don't think he heard half of what I said after that.' Quickly, she changed the subject. 'You weren't away long. I take it the hunt went well?'

'Naturally.' He even sounded as though he was smirking. 'Breakfast is on its way, sweetie. Toulac is starting it roasting in the outside firepit even as we speak.'

'Thanks, Kaz. What a change it will make from travel rations! It seems like forever since we had anything decent to eat. There certainly wasn't anything to be had in Callisiora.' The firedrake deserved his breakfast, Veldan thought, as she started back down the hill. He had brought herself and the others all the way from Tiarond to the haven of this wayshelter. And though he was as weary as any of them, he had hunted for them all. As she directed her thoughts to him, her mouth filled with a fleeting taste of fresh blood and greasy fleece. 'Ugh!' She spat on the ground. 'Sheep.'

'I know,' Kaz said ruefully. 'Stupid creatures! I'll be picking wool out from between my teeth for days. But there's not much else out here for me, Boss. Cute little bunnies aren't much use to someone my size.'

'Just so long as you don't start coughing up furballs all over Cergorn, like you did last time,' Veldan warned him. 'I don't think our glorious leader ever got over the affront to his dignity.'

Kaz snickered. 'How can somebody with a horse's backside worry about his dignity?'

Somehow, the Loremaster managed to smother her laughter. Kaz had little regard for authority – even that of the centaur who led the Shadowleague, and who was therefore one of the most important people in the world of Myrial. 'You behave yourself with Cergorn,' she told her partner sternly. 'He *is* Archimandrite after all, and we'll be in quite enough trouble when we get back, without you stirring up more.'

'Me?' Kaz was all injured innocence. 'You wound me, Boss. As if I didn't always treat old horse-arse with the utmost respect.'

Veldan sighed, and decided not to pursue the conversation any further. It would only encourage him. Luckily, she was saved from having to reply by a call from Toulac outside. 'There's someone coming, girlie. I think it must be that friend of yours.'

Almost in the same instant, there came a low growl from Kaz. 'It's Elion, all right. And the day I sprout wings is the day I'll call *him* friend.'

Elion came slowly over the rise on his tired horse, following the scent of roasting mutton that threaded the breeze. Below him he saw Veldan, on her way down the hill towards the wayshelter, and her broader, grey-haired companion, sitting close to the smoking firepit looking after the food. Nearby, Kaz lay dozing in a patch of sunlight by the warm shelter wall. He lifted his head as the newcomer rode up, and Elion caught the flash and glitter of his eyes.

Veldan looked up at her fellow Loremaster's approach. 'You're a bit early, I'm afraid. Breakfast isn't ready yet. But I'm sure when it's done, we'll let you have some.'

The firedrake gave Elion a dirty look. 'Personally, I'd let him starve.'

'Oh, shut up, Kaz,' sighed Veldan. 'Can't we have a little peace for once?'

'I suppose so,' her partner conceded. 'If you insist. You've had a hard enough morning already. And just for you, I'll even let slime-bag there have some of *my* sheep.'

'Don't put yourself out on my account, you overgrown reptile,' Elion snapped.

Veldan's companion, who had been turning the mutton, leapt to her feet, interrupting the unpleasantness before it escalated any further. Wiping her greasy hand on the leg of her pants, she held it out to Elion. 'I'm Toulac.' She spoke aloud, and he remembered that she could hear thoughts very well, but did not know how to broad-cast yet. 'It's good to meet you face to face at last,' she went on. 'Here, sonny, give me that horse of yours, and I'll see to him while you sit down and rest yourself. You look like death warmed over.'

'He looks like vomit warmed over,' muttered Kaz.

Veldan cast her eyes to the heavens. 'One big, happy family – that's us. For goodness' sake sit down, Elion, and stop hovering like that. I presume you *are* staying?'

Elion didn't need telling a third time. Mumbling his thanks, he pushed the reins of his horse into Toulac's hand and simply let his knees buckle. It felt wonderful to sink down onto the soft, fragrant turf. He was so hungry that it was all he could do to keep himself from tearing bloody chunks off from the underdone roast, and gulping the meat down like a starving dog. To take his mind off his stomach, he got Veldan to tell him of her recent conversation with the Archimandrite. Her account of Cergorn's reaction filled him with dismay.

'I don't know what you expected,' the firedrake said. 'You lost his partner. He was hardly going to be pleased, was he?'

'I did *not* lose her!' Elion shouted. 'She damn well lost herself, and I don't see why I should take the blame for it.'

'*And* you seem to have mislaid that favourite little chestnut mare of his,' the firedrake went on, undeterred. 'He's not going to like that.'

Elion scowled. 'Then he'll just have to lump it. This horse might not be so fast or so good-looking, but at least it's placid, and doesn't roll, kick and bite.'

Kaz snickered. 'That won't cut much ice with Cergorn. You've probably given away one of his girlfriends.'

At this, Veldan finally intervened. 'Kazairl! That's enough. It's bad enough to joke about the Archimandrite, but to accuse him of unnatural practices is going much too far. You're never careful enough, and who knows when you might be overheard?'

'Ah, come on, sweetie . . .'

'I don't want to hear it!'

The meal was a good one, with Kaz's mutton, potatoes from the wayshelter's stores baked in the ashes of the firepit, and apples to follow. Eventually Toulac stretched her legs out in front of her, sighing with contentment. 'I suppose someone had better take some food in to Zavahl,' she said. 'After we went to all that trouble rescuing him, there's no point in starving him to death now.'

'If he'll eat it,' Veldan said sourly. She half-rose, but Elion waved her back down again. He was very curious about the man who had been partially responsible for the murder of Tormon's wife. 'Stay where you are,' he said. 'I'll take care of it.' Seeing her surprised look, he added, 'it's the least I can do, after you ladies and Kaz provided such a good meal.'

'You know, that might not be a bad idea,' Toulac said thoughtfully. 'He seems to think we're a couple of harpies, and I don't think he likes women much in general right now. Maybe if we keep on taking a tough approach, you can be the Kind One. If we can get him to make friends with even one of us, we'll have made an enormous breakthrough. You're still wearing a Godsword uniform, too. It might make him trust you more than he trusts us.'

'I wouldn't be at all surprised,' Kaz muttered. 'It's already clear that the human is a complete and utter imbecile.'

Zavahl had fallen asleep at last, and the Dragon Aethon seized his chance. Any attempts to address his troubled host directly resulted in panic. It was imperative that he find a more subtle way to communicate, so that he could help them both. Now, if he could only insinuate himself into the human's dreaming mind, it might somehow be possible to gain his trust.

It was not an encouraging beginning. Aethon had expected to find himself in a symbolic landscape of thought while he tried to merge with the unconscious mind of his sleeping host. This was quite normal in making the adjustment to an alien species. The symbols, however, would be a true reflection of Zavahl's waking mentality, and the dragon was far from encouraged to find that the hinterland of his mind took the form of a lake of turbulent dark water, hemmed in by obdurate mountains. A tempest whipped the surface of the tarn into a froth of waves.

Well, what did I expect? I should know by now what kind of character I'm dealing with. But if I'd known it was going to be like this, I wouldn't have been quite so impatient for the human to fall asleep.

But Aethon knew that there was no alternative. With a shudder, he stepped into the turbid, lightless mere, and sank beneath the surface.

Zavahl was dreaming. The dragon hovered, an invisible presence, waiting for events to unfold. Perhaps this way he might find a key to unlock the cage of fear, mistrust and superstition in which the former Hierarch had isolated himself.

The dream itself seemed fairly straightforward and predictable. Wearing the rough garments of a servant, Zavahl was scrubbing the broad, stone steps of the Basilica of Myrial. Gilarra, resplendent in the Hierarch's formal robes, stood over him at the top of the steps, obstructing the way into the building. She was talking to the renegade Amaurn, now wearing a Godsword uniform and calling himself Lord Blade. As he looked on, Aethon's hopes kindled. He had simply hoped to enter Zavahl's dream and speak to him in some appropriate guise, to help the troubled human to accept his altered circumstances a little more readily, and to put his trust in his new companions. But if the former Hierarch was dreaming of the Temple, this would be an incredible opportunity to find out more about the secret access to the core of Myrial that must lie beneath.

Carefully, the Dragon introduced his presence, slipping into the fabric of the dream. He appeared as a tall, magnificent human figure who glowed with a shimmering aura of refulgent light that obscured any features which might clash with Zavahl's own image of his God. As he approached, he just had time to glimpse the terror and awe on the former Hierarch's face before the wretch prostrated himself on the ground, crying, 'Myrial, have mercy! Forgive me for failing you.'

This is going to be more difficult than I imagined, Aethon thought. *I've never been forced to impersonate a deity before.* He was about to step forward when he realised, to his dismay, that he was not too clear about the articulation and positioning of his human limbs when they moved.

Very clever, Aethon. Now what?

In the end, he settled for hovering an inch or two above the ground, his long, flowing robes covering any mistakes that might betray him. 'Be at peace, Zavahl. Come, cease this unseemly grovelling and look at me.'

Slowly, as if he scarcely dared to believe what he had heard, Zavahl lifted his face out of the dust and raised his eyes to the vision of splendour. 'O Great One . . .'

'Speak, my faithful servant, and do not be afraid.'

'All powerful Myrial, if you are not displeased with me, why are my people suffering? Why are you punishing them and me?'

You would ask that.

'You are not being punished, Zavahl.'

'But what of this endless rain? Is it not a result of my mistakes? My failure?'

Had it been possible, the Dragon would have shaken his head. It was difficult to be patient with a man who was suffering from his own inflated ideas of self-importance. When an individual assumed such power, there came an equivalent amount of guilt when things went wrong. 'Your mistake lay in trusting Lord Blade,' he told the former Hierarch. 'While you were preoccupied with self-centred concerns about your own purity and piety, you handed him power on a plate.'

'Great Myrial, I am unworthy . . .'

'Oh, shut up.' Aethon finally lost patience. 'In the course of their lives, Zavahl, everyone is guilty of a certain amount of folly. So long as you don't make a habit of it, the results can usually be rectified, given time.'

'Merciful One, how may I atone . . .'

At last! 'Walk with me into the Temple, Zavahl, and we will continue our talk.'

The woman in the rich robes, who had assumed the Hierarch's place, had vanished from the top of the Temple steps, and Zavahl and the Dragon masquerading as a god could now pass unhindered. Curious to see the inside of this elaborate human edifice, Aethon followed the dreaming consciousness of his host through the great doorway and into the shadowed gloom beyond – to discover a lavishly jewelled interior which filled him with incredulous delight.

The Dragonfolk, whose actual language was made up of music and patterns of pure, coloured radiance, loved jewels, which transformed light into such lovely colours and made it shift and shimmer like a living thing. Deep in Aethon's accumulated racial memories were recollections of Dhiammara, a glorious city carved out of colossal gems, set in the midst of a dazzling jewelled desert. It was the original dwelling place of the Dragons on their homeworld, the place whence all Dragonkind had originally sprung.

Aethon was staggered by the opulence of the Basilica's interior, and a little surprised that humans could have produced such a wealth of rich beauty. Intriguing jewelled mosaics encrusted the double row of massive pillars that marched down the centre of the massive building, and tapestries embroidered in gold and dazzling with gems hung at intervals along the cold stone walls, turning them into a blaze of colour in the light from the many lamps of silver that were suspended above the echoing vault like a galaxy of stars.

The Dragon had never suspected that humans could be capable of creating so much beauty, but there was more to the fascination that the place exerted on him than mere aesthetic appreciation. The sparkle and glow of coloured radiance seemed to form an evocative pattern that was trying to speak to him in his own language of light, delivering a message that was just beyond his comprehension.

'Holy Myrial?' The former Hierarch was standing beside a beautiful screen made of filigree silver. It must conceal something of great importance, judging by Zavahl's restless, shifting stance and the nervousness and tension that showed clearly in every line of his face and body.

Aethon swallowed his irritation at being distracted from the cryptic message of the gems. 'You have something to ask me, my servant?'

Zavahl looked down. When he spoke his voice was shaking but defiant. 'Why did you stop communicating with me? Why did you turn your face away? Why did your Eye become dark and silent?' Now that he had screwed up enough courage to ask them, the questions came blurting out of him all in a rush.

The Dragon, out of his depth, felt a twinge of panic. Suddenly his impersonation of Myrial, which had seemed such a good idea at the time, stood in danger of being unmasked.

Communicating? Eye? What in all creation is the crazy human talking about?

Then he remembered Zavahl's earlier dream, which had given him his first inkling that a secret lay beneath the Temple. There had been something about an eye then too, but the details had been vague and misty, obscured by a dreamscape of confusion and pain. He was gripped by excitement. If something had really been communicating with Zavahl, something that he looked upon as a manifestation of his God, then surely he must, without realising it, have found a way to tap into the artificial intelligence that kept this world in balance?

Belatedly, he turned his attention back to the human, while his brain raced to come up with plausible answers that might also lead the former Hierarch into revealing the information that he so desperately needed. 'A God may sometimes test the faith of his servant,' he said cautiously. 'Let us go to the Eye, Zavahl. Take me there and in its presence, let us discuss this matter further.'

Zavahl gave him a puzzled look, but nodded in acquiescence. Aethon felt a shiver of excitement as the human pushed back the delicate screen to reveal a doorway that contained only blackness, like the entry to an endless void. Darkness swallowed up the former Hierarch, and the Dragon followed.

It's only a dream. I can't come to any harm, and I can leave at any time I like.

He repeated the words over and over as though they were a charm that would protect him from whatever nightmares inhabited this sinister, daunting place. Doubt began to assail him. How did he know this place existed in reality, and not just in the human's troubled mind?

I'll just have to take it on trust. It feels so real, I'm sure it's coming from his memory, not his imagination. Besides, what sort of ridiculous coincidence would it be if Zavahl had invented the very thing we've all been seeking for so long? No, it's far more likely that this dream, or at least the landscape of it, is true.

He remembered the mysterious message that the jewels had been trying to convey. Was there a connection? Surely there must be!

They passed over the black abyss, though Aethon only knew it was there because he picked up the thought from his human companion's mind. He stopped when he felt Zavahl stop, wondering what was going to happen next. He heard a click that broke the profound silence like the crack of a whip. Then a sound, like the sigh of a great wind in treetops, set the air vibrating all around. Then, as if awakening out of nothingness, a vast red circle appeared, set on its edge, with the black void still in its centre. As it grew brighter, Aethon glanced across at Zavahl's face, which had the stillness of intense concentration. In front of the former Hierarch was a plinth, with a depression at the centre, into which he had fitted the great red stone of a ring.

Ha! That stone must be the key.

As the circle grew in brightness, the Dragon was just leaning forward for a closer look at the crimson stone when suddenly a voice was heard across the void.

'Sir? Wake up. I've brought you something to eat.'

The chamber collapsed and vanished as Zavahl was pulled back to wakefulness by the intruding voice. Once more, Aethon found himself a helpless passenger in the human's mind.

I don't believe this! Why did you have to come in just then, you stupid man? I was so close to finding some real answers!

Whoever the intruder was, the Dragon cursed the day he had been born. Now he would have to bide his time, helpless and hidden in Zavahl's mind, until the tortured former Hierarch dreamed again.

'Cergorn, calm down.' Syvilda threw up her hands in exasperation. 'You've got to be patient. You don't know half the story yet.'

'I know that my so-called Loremasters have made an appalling mess of their mission. And to think I trusted them. I can't believe this of Veldan. Has she gone mad? What in the name of all creation does she think she's playing at? She *knows* that it's against our strictest laws to bring strangers here.'

Syvilda gave a worried glance around the lakeside on which they stood. No-one seemed to be nearby, but with the Shadowleague, you never knew for sure who might be listening. 'Look, don't you think we'd better discuss this behind closed doors?'

The Archimandrite, as was his wont when he was angry or worried, was pacing up and down, digging up clods of turf with his hooves. 'I don't want to discuss it at all. You're the one who's discussing it.'

'Oh, for goodness' sake, Cergorn! I don't understand why you're being so childish. Why, we practically raised Veldan. You know very well that she wouldn't be bringing those people here without a very good reason. She's always respected our laws. Why else would she want to break them, unless she had to?'

Cergorn stopped and looked at her, and when Syvilda saw the expression on his face, a shiver ran along her spine. 'What about her father? He was an expert at breaking our laws, and her mother broke quite a few of them too, before her death. Maybe blood will out, Syvilda. That's what worries me.'

Now Syvilda was both worried and alarmed. 'Have you actually *listened* to what you're saying? That is the biggest load of nonsense I ever heard!'

Cergorn shook his head. To her dismay, he was wearing what she always thought of as his mulish expression. 'And what about the firedrake? You know very well he doesn't give two pins for the law when Veldan's welfare and wishes are at stake. I can't take the risk, Syvilda. Everything is breaking down around us. Not just Shadowleague edicts, but all rules, all reason, and I can't seem to stop the rot. I can't have my Loremasters adding to the chaos, and if I don't make an example of these three, the others will start to think that *they* can take shortcuts and put their own interpretation on our laws.'

Syvilda sighed. She had tried suggesting to Cergorn that, in the face of this crisis, greater flexibility might be the answer. It was certainly what many of the other members of the Shadowleague were saying behind his back, but dared not tell him to his face. Unfortunately, the Archimandrite was under tremendous pressure, and his reaction to the current instability was to try to regain lost ground by clamping down as hard as he could on anyone who tried to deviate from the letter of the law. Remonstrating with him seemed only to make him more firmly entrenched in his position, but she supposed she'd have to keep trying. In his current mood, no-one else dared to disagree with him – at least not aloud.

'But Cergorn, if Aethon really transferred his mind into this other man's body, what else could Veldan do but bring him?'

'Don't be ridiculous,' Cergorn snorted. 'Whoever heard of such a thing?'

Syvilda took a deep breath. 'I did, as a matter of fact. Isn't that exactly what the Dragon Seers do when one of them dies? Transfer everything to their successor?'

The Archimandrite sighed, and rolled his eyes in exasperation.

'Of course they don't. How could they? Think how many generations of Seers there must have been and just imagine what a crowd of individuals would all be trying to share one body. No-one could tolerate those conditions for endless centuries, and stay sane. It's the *memories* that get transferred. The actual spirit and personality of the Seer passes on the way we all do.'

Syvilda stared at him. 'Are you trying to say that Veldan is lying? Because I refuse to believe it.'

'I'm saying that she's mistaken. I think she's so distressed at having lost the Seer that she has misinterpreted the ravings of a madman into the biggest case of wishful thinking I ever heard. And if she believes, that will be good enough for Kazairl.'

'And what about Elion? Is he mistaken too?' As soon as the words left her mouth, Syvilda wished that she could take them back.

'*Elion*? Since Melnyth was killed, Elion has turned into a walking, talking mistake. To think I actually sent that imbecile to help the others. And now look what he's done to my partner . . .'

'Cer, you're raving. As far as I can tell, Elion didn't do anything to Shree. I don't see how you can blame him if she went off on her own. What was the poor boy supposed to do? Sprout wings?'

'He shouldn't have let her go.'

'She's a Senior Loremaster. Elion didn't have the authority to stop her doing anything she wanted. And you know what she's like. She always suits herself, no matter what.'

'You've never liked my partner, have you? You were always jealous of her. I suppose you're glad to see the back of her.'

Syvilda threw up her hands in despair. 'I'm going. There's no talking to you when you're like this. But I warn you, Cergorn, the last time I saw you in this mood was when we had that challenge from Amaurn – and look what happened then. Frankly, you were lucky to retain control of the Shadowleague, and you can't count on it happening again. Unless you ease up on everyone, you're going to find yourself with no supporters at all.'

Cergorn glared at her. 'Don't be ridiculous. Stability is all that can hold the Shadowleague together in the face of this crisis, and the Loremasters – apart from the inevitable few malcontents – have the sense to realise that.'

'You're fooling yourself,' Syvilda said sadly, as she turned away. 'I only hope you come to realise that, before it's too late.'

Up in the Tower of Tidings, there was a moment of stunned silence among the three Listeners. Then the uproar broke out.

'Did you *hear* that?'

'Can you *believe* the things he said?'

'I feel sorry for poor Veldan and the others. Little do they know what's waiting for them.'

'Do you think we should warn them?'

Vaure the phoenix took charge. 'No. Sadly, we can't warn them. It'll alert Cergorn that we're spying on him. Are you sure you got everything, Bailen?'

The blind man nodded. 'One of the few advantages of not having eyes is that you really learn to develop your hearing.'

The Dovruja, Dessil, sat up on his hind legs, looking more otter-like than ever. 'I don't like this. Whatever you might say about Cergorn, he always used to be just. Maybe part of this behaviour is his anger at losing his partner, but that's not the point. If he's starting to pick on Veldan, of all people, then any of us could be next.'

Vaure flew out of the fireplace, trailing a tail of sparks behind her like a comet, and scattering ashes in her wake. 'Maskulu had better hear about this at once,' she said. 'It may be that the time for a change of leadership is coming sooner than we thought.'

'Vaure, are you sure?' Bailen was always the cautious member of the trio. 'The Moldan can be such a hothead. With the world falling into chaos just now, will the upheaval and strife within the Shadowleague not do more harm than good?'

The phoenix, perched on the windowsill, shook her golden feathers. 'Dessil, what do you say?'

'I say go. What's the good of us possessing all this ancient knowledge if Cergorn is determined to keep suppressing it? We've tried his way. It doesn't work. Things can't get any worse for my people with a new Archimandrite, and they might just get some effective help for a change – while some of them still survive.'

Vaure turned back to the human. 'Well, Bailen?'

He sighed. 'All right.'

'Good. Cover for me while I'm gone.' With a flip of her wings, the phoenix was out of the window and away.

Eight

Dead Meat

After Tormon and Scall had vanished down the cliff path, Rochalla started back towards the guardhouse, but was pulled up short by the child dragging at her arm. Annas was standing still, her little feet planted firmly in the mud, her face flushed and mutinous.

'I'm not coming.' The child glared defiantly at the older girl. 'I'm staying here to wait for my Dad.'

Rochalla sighed. 'But lovey, we're getting wet. Your Dad won't thank you for catching cold, you know. Now that would be silly, wouldn't it?'

'Don't care.' With her little boot, Annas kicked at the mud.

'Come back by the fire where it's warm,' Rochalla coaxed, 'and let's see if the guards have hidden any sweets somewhere amongst their stores. I'm sure they have some squirreled away that we never found.'

Annas never wavered. 'I can't,' she said stubbornly. 'I've got to stay here.'

'But he'll be back soon.' With an effort Rochalla managed to keep the impatience from her voice. 'Why do you have to wait right here?'

The child bit her lip and looked at the ground. 'So he doesn't get lost,' she said in a tiny voice. 'When he went away before, he got lost and the bad man put his hands around Mama's neck. She fell down and I never saw her anymore . . .'

So he doesn't get lost. The words went right to Rochalla's heart. She knew that Tormon's wife had been killed within the last few days, in circumstances so dreadful that no-one had dared discuss them. But she'd had no idea that this poor child had undergone such horrors.

'Please let me go down,' Annas whimpered. 'I've got to find Dad.'

Rochalla gave up the argument. She could see that the little girl was genuinely in distress. 'All right,' she sighed. 'I'll tell you what. We'll wait right here at the top and watch for him coming back. Is that good enough for you?'

'Oh, thank you!' Annas hugged her.

Presvel had returned to the warmth and shelter of the guardhouse, but Seriema, who had accompanied him, came back to fetch the others, sloshing determinedly through the mud, clearly irritated that Rochalla and the girl had not followed Tormon's instructions, and had forced her to make this unnecessary trip. She shivered, pulling the folds of her hood further up over her damp hair. 'I don't know why you're letting her get away with this. For Myrial's sake, bring the wretched child inside. Don't you realise that if any of those winged fiends come out of the city, you're making targets of us all, standing there in the open like that?'

Rochalla felt herself flushing. Her attention had been so focussed on the child that she had never considered the possible danger of their position. Seriema had made her feel like a fool, and she burned with resentment. 'Why don't you mind your own business,' she snapped. 'Can't you see that Annas is worried about her father? You power-crazed old maid! Are you so dried up and callous that you can't understand simple human emotions like love and fear?'

Seriema's lips tightened, but she did not lose her temper. Even in the heat of the moment, Rochalla had to admire her control. 'I understand a good deal more than an ignorant girl who'll never be anything more than a nursemaid,' she said coldly. 'I know that the child will catch a chill by staying out in this weather. And it's about to get worse. Look over there.' She gestured towards the mountain, its top hidden in low, black cloud. Rochalla saw her face change. One hand went to her mouth, and her eyes widened with horror. 'All that rain on the mountain,' she breathed. 'The river – can you hear it?'

In the distance there was a low, roaring sound, growing louder like a great gale blowing. Was it Rochalla's imagination, or was there a tremor in the earth beneath her feet?

Seriema was quicker on the uptake. 'Get the child into the barracks. Quick!' Seizing the arm of the protesting Annas, she yanked the wailing little girl across the mud and all but threw her bodily into the building.

'Leave her alone, you bully!' Rochalla flew at her like a fury, to be stopped in her tracks by a resounding slap.

'Look over there. See that water spreading this way? The river has burst its banks. Get inside. Now!' Pushing Rochalla towards the open doorway, she picked up her skirts and began to run in the opposite direction.

'But where are you going?' Rochalla called after her. 'Come back!'

'Tormon and the boy. Somebody's got to warn them.' Seriema flung the words over her shoulder. Then she was gone, scrambling down the treacherous, slippery path as it dropped away over the cliff.

The wave had come racing down out of the narrow valley of the Snaketail pass, a great upswelling of water as high as a man. When it reached the level plateau the water spread out rapidly, its terrifying pace slowing somewhat, but the forward momentum of the current carrying on. A great wave smashed into the city walls, and spray flew high into the air. One section of the wall, its foundations already undermined by months of ceaseless rain, collapsed with a splash into the swirling, muddy waters that were already flooding the riverside warehouses and carrying away the flimsy, wooden slum dwellings. One by one, the smouldering funeral pyres on the plateau were extinguished, and faggots of wood and decaying, part-burned corpses were borne away on the flood that spread further and further outwards, heading inexorably towards the cliffs at the plateau's edge.

Rochalla, hypnotised by the power and destruction, suddenly realised that the waters would soon be at the guardhouse, and came out of her trance with a jerk. She darted inside, slamming the door behind her, just as Presvel, with Annas tugging him by the hand, emerged from the stables. 'What's going on?' he asked.

'The river!' Rochalla gasped. 'A flood . . .'

'Where's Seriema?'

'Gone. She went to warn Tormon. I couldn't stop her!' Guiltily, she realised that she had never tried.

Presvel turned pale. 'She'll be killed!' He ran to open the door, but Rochalla stepped in front of it, barring his way. 'Let me out!' He tried to push her aside, and they struggled. 'I must help her!'

'No, don't open the door! It's too late . . .'

With a crash, the wall of water hit the guardhouse. Rochalla winced as the impact made the whole building shake. Annas clung to her skirts, mute and white with terror, while in the stables, the horses whinnied and stamped uneasily. Presvel, shaking visibly, turned to her, moving with the slowness of shock, his eyes dark and wide. 'My Lady,' he whispered. 'She'll be . . .'

'Shut up,' Rochalla hissed, gesturing to the child who still clutched her in a terrified grasp. Through the window, she could see the water pouring over the edge of the cliff. The trail would be deluged, the tunnel filled with water. Tormon, Seriema and Scall would be swept to their deaths – how could it be otherwise? Poor little Annas was truly an orphan now. A pang of grief went through Rochalla. Lately she had suffered so many losses. Why should these near-strangers, these people she had known for less than a day, affect her so strongly? Yet they did. Adversity had forged a bond between them, making them almost as much her family as the children she had buried in the graveyard.

For a moment, Rochalla's eyes blurred with grief for her lost companions. Then another thought struck her, adding dismay to her horror. Only Tormon, Seriema and Scall could control the horses. Presvel was an indifferent rider at best, and before yesterday, she had never been in the saddle in her life. The two of them had just gone along with the others, mainly trusting their horse to stay with its companions, and hoping for the best. They had never even been off the plateau, and had no knowledge of the wider world beyond their city. Only Tormon had any idea where they were heading. He was the only one who had ever travelled far beyond the boundaries of Tiarond.

Rochalla looked at Presvel, who slumped against the wall, his face in his hands, still reeling from the sudden loss of Seriema. He was clearly adrift in this perilous situation. It was no use looking to him for help. She yelped, looking down as freezing water poured into her shoes.

'Rochalla?' Annas tugged at her skirt. 'My feet are all wet.'

The floods were in the room with them, creeping under the door and rising rapidly. A shudder ran through Rochalla as she hoisted the child into her arms. Already, the dirty water was lapping round her ankles, and rising rapidly. *What will become of us?* she thought despairingly. *Where will we go now? What shall we do?*

Tormon, with all his attention fixed on the tunnel beyond the waterfall, had no idea of Seriema's approach until he felt her hand upon his arm. The roar of the descending waters seemed to be growing louder, so deafening that he almost had to read her lips, but the expression on her face told him all he needed to know. They were in bad trouble. Rain in the mountains. The river in spate. *Annas!* Tormon's blood turned to ice. He made as if to start back up the path, but realised that it would already be too late. In a dozen places along the cliff face, the water was already coming down in filthy brown torrents. At any moment, it would pour down across the trail, and a part of its volume would be diverted by the path, into the tunnel.

Tormon grabbed Seriema's hand. 'Run!' But no-one could run behind the waterfall. Despite the need for haste, they were forced to sidle along, pressed tight against the cliff. Tormon, flinching back from the raw power of that inexorable curtain of water, realised that since Scall had gone through here the torrent had grown considerably, increasing in force.

As they burst into the dark and cavernous tunnel, Tormon tugged on Seriema's hand. 'Up there,' he shouted. 'Climb!' In the faint light that filtered through the entrance a rusted ladder could be seen on the right-hand wall, leading to a metal walkway near the curved ceiling. Without hesitation, the woman bundled up her skirts and began her ascent. Already the water in the tunnel was deepening, swirling around Tormon's knees, the strength of the current threatening to pull his legs out from underneath him. He knew with a sinking certainty that this was only the beginning. He took a deep breath. Cupping his hands to his mouth, he shouted: 'SCALL!'

As he had hoped, the tunnel magnified his voice and carried it downwards. Faint and far away, he heard a voice. 'Tormon?'

'Floods! Climb, boy! Climb up to the walkway.' Without waiting for a reply, he followed Seriema up the ladder as fast as he could.

Not a moment too soon. The floodwater had reached the edge of the plateau, and came deluging down from above. Though most fell harmlessly down the cliff, some – enough – was caught by the jutting cliff path and funnelled down into the mouth of the steeply-sloping tunnel which acted like a drain, sending the water rushing downwards with alarming speed.

The torrent came spurting in with a sound like the ending of the world, a rumbling roar that reverberated through the tunnel, magnified over and over by the curving roof. Brown, churning water snatched at Tormon's heels as he scrambled up the ladder. Gasping for breath, he hauled himself up onto the rusting walkway beside Seriema, who sat with her legs curled up beneath her, her hands clenched tightly round the iron railings, peering down through the half-light at the dizzying flow of water that hurtled past, not far below her.

'Are you all right?' he shouted, noting the pallor of her face.

She nodded. 'I'm fine. My knees just went a little weak, that's all. It was such a shock when all that water came bursting in. Even though I was expecting it, I didn't anticipate anything like *that*.'

He was surprised that she'd admitted to her fear.

She was looking down at the water once more, with horrified fascination. 'Will it reach us, do you think?'

'We'd better pray it doesn't,' Tormon replied grimly, 'because there's nowhere left to go from here. Sweet Myrial, I hope that poor lad managed to get to safety in time.'

Seriema did not reply, but the way she refused to meet his eyes was enough to tell him that she held out little hope of Scall's survival.

They had been here. Aliana looked round the devastated Warrens, and felt herself begin to shake. She had been wrong about the thieves' lair being safe. The winged ones, those foul abominations of the night, had found her home. As she roamed through the silent passages and caves, scene after scene of horror met her eyes. The awnings and crude partitions that had been the fragile homes of so many desperate people had been torn down and trampled. The pitiful belongings of the inhabitants were everywhere: cooking pots with their contents spilled and congealed on the ground, broken mugs and plates with their fragments strewn underfoot, patched clothes and threadbare blankets in discarded, tangled piles. Everything was spattered with blood.

The narrow, labyrinthine tunnels, painstakingly carved into the spur of the mountain by generations of Tiarond's impoverished, forgotten and dispossessed, had turned from a sanctuary into a trap. The remains of the inhabitants were scattered among their broken possessions. The bodies, male and female, young and old, were torn, mangled and dismembered. Limbs were gnawed or missing, and guts ripped out. Many had been reduced from human beings to dismembered lumps of meat, but there were others that she recognised, from clothing, or some cheap trinket of personal adornment, or worst of all from a familiar and well-loved face.

And nowhere was there any sign of Alestan.

Aliana jolted awake, calling out her brother's name, tears streaming down her face. For a moment she could not remember where she was, and the terrifying experiences of the night before, when she'd been pursued by those demonic creatures and finally found sanctuary in this cold, lonely crypt, all became mixed up with the images from her nightmare until she hardly knew where the dreaming left off and the reality began. Everything coalesced into a single thought: she knew, with absolute certainty, that she must get back to her home and her brother as soon as possible.

In the minds of Tiarond's prosperous folk, the Warrens were a disgrace and a blemish on the reputation of the Holy City. The place and its inhabitants were never discussed without curses and complaints, and preferably, they were never to be thought of at all. But to the wretched beings struggling to survive with no work, no homes and no future, the caves in the massive spur of rock that was the city's eastern boundary were a refuge sent by Myrial Himself, the slender thread on which their survival hung. To the city's thieves, the Warrens held a slightly different set of opportunities. The labyrinth of caverns and tunnels extending far back into the mountain, part natural and part chipped painstakingly out by hand over many generations, were a hideout and a conundrum to baffle the most astute of Godswords, and a perfect place to stash all kinds of loot.

To Aliana, on that dreadful morning after terror had come hurtling from the skies, the Warrens were a distant dream to which she despaired of returning. She had awakened, thirsty, stiff, unrested, and with a pounding headache and an arm that stung and burned. On the positive side, however, there was no sign of her attackers save for the torn and mangled body of the one that had been set upon by its companions, at the top of the mausoleum steps. Aliana stepped over it with a shudder of distaste, irrationally and childishly scared that it might somehow come back to life and snatch at her as she passed.

The rest of the house was similarly deserted, though the thief had to make a painstaking search of the building from bottom to top and back again before she could feel sure enough to let herself relax, even a little. Though the place seemed safe enough now, when she returned to the kitchen she was all too aware of the hole that gaped in the shattered window, where the winged fiends had come bursting through. A shiver, from more than just the cold rain that was driving through the window, went through Aliana, a cold prickling along all her nerves as though someone had just walked on her grave. *What are those creatures?* she thought. *How can we ever hope to survive them?* In that instant, she was certain that Tiarond was doomed.

If the situation was so desperate, it was even more important that she find her twin and the gang of thieves who were all the family she possessed. But Aliana knew better than to rush off without making careful preparations. She knew all too well that the more dangerous the situation, the more likely it was that haste would get her killed. In the kitchen she ate whatever she could scrounge, determined, almost as an act of faith, to take the best of what she had found back to the Warrens. She drank draught after draught of clean, cold water, and poured an extra supply into a stoppered flask. After last night, she wasn't going to take the risk again of being trapped somewhere with nothing to drink. *Thank Myrial I had the sense not to start on the brandy,* she thought. *I feel bad enough this morning without that.* She found the cook's supply of willowbark, but decided there was no time to infuse it properly now. Her assorted aches and pains, and the slight shivery touch of fever from those burning scratches in her arm would have to wait. She packed the willowbark in her backpack, though. It would be needed in the Warrens – if the Warrens were still there.

Now that she had taken care of herself as best she could, she was ready to go, but it took more courage than she knew she possessed to leave the dubious sanctuary of the merchant's house. Assuring herself she was not putting off her departure, that it was only wise to make one final check before venturing out, Aliana turned away from the door and ran back upstairs for one last look out over the route she would soon be taking.

The wool-merchant's house looked down over the city, and from the upper windows she made a nervous scan of the rooftops and the skies. There was nothing to be seen: no winged shapes crouching like gargoyles on chimneys, or wheeling through the air like sinister carrion-birds. It must be near noon, Aliana decided, accustomed, like all Tiarondians these days, to judging the hour by the ambient light of a shrouded sun. Today the clouds were low, the surging grey vapour driven down from the mountain by a gusting wind. The rain was coming down harder by the minute, leaving water pooling on the ground and the roof tiles dark and streaming. Would the downpour be enough to keep at bay the fell creatures that had invaded the city? Their absence was unnerving. Though she could not see them, she had a very bad feeling that they weren't too far away. Perhaps they were primarily creatures of the night, only hunting in the hours of darkness, like bats or owls. If so, it should be safe to move about during the daylight. But it could get pretty gloomy through the day right now, she reminded herself – especially when the clouds came down low. She didn't dare stake her life on the invaders sleeping through the day. None the less, the seeming absence of the predators would give her a chance, at least, of getting home in safety.

So what are you standing around for? Let's get going, while the daylight lasts!

As she left the house, her eyes were everywhere, her nerves stretched to breaking point, expecting, at any moment, that death would strike her from the skies. At the mouth of the alley, the esplanade stretched out before her, a lethal open space to be avoided at all costs. Aliana swallowed hard, groping for her courage. Ducking low and sticking as close as she could to the outer wall of the mansion, she moved to her right and scuttled along the edge of the square, hunched to make herself as small as possible, and running for cover like a terrified animal. Never before had she felt so small, so vulnerable, and so alone. By comparison to the vast open space, the wide thoroughfare that led from the square seemed secure and almost cosy, but still she stayed close to the right hand wall, her eyes busy all the time, and her muscles tensed for flight.

'Hssst! Aliana!' The voice was so unexpected that she instinctively ducked and rolled, coming up with a knife in her hand, before she realised that the winged hunters couldn't possibly know her name. Feeling angry and foolish she glared around her – and saw a dirty hand beckoning from the shadows of a narrow alleyway on the opposite side of the street. Aliana ran, her heart leaping with a hope that she dared not even name. Ever since her nightmare of the devastated Warrens, she had been convinced, deep down, that her brother must be dead. But Alestan was alive! For an instant she cared for nothing else. Then her eyes became accustomed to the gloom within the narrow passage, and she faltered, arms still outstretched, her cry of greeting freezing on her lips.

Alestan was filthy and dishevelled, his face and hands and clothing smeared with mud. There was a dirty bandage bound around his forehead, and his curling hair, sandy where his twin's was tawny, was darkened and matted with dried blood. But it was his eyes that told the true tale of suffering and catastrophe. Looking into her face, Aliana knew that she must somehow, with some uncanny connection between their twin minds, have picked up her nightmare from his mind. It had all been true. Her eyes strayed beyond him to the huddle of weary, drooping figures, and she knew without having to be told that this pitiful handful were the only survivors: all he had been able to bring out of the Warrens alive.

But he was safe! She saw her relief mirrored in her brother's eyes. Laughing and crying, the two of them embraced, oblivious of the pouring rain, only caring, in that instant, that the other was alive, and only conscious of a vast relief that it was so.

Eventually they pulled apart. 'What happened to you?' Alestan asked her. 'I didn't think you could be dead – not at first, at any rate. But when you were gone all night, and you didn't come back, I thought . . .'

'I got trapped in a house by those awful creatures.' Aliana shuddered at the memory. 'But what happened to you, Alestan? What happened in the Warrens? Why are you all here?' Her gaze went from him to the others, a small, exhausted, woeful-looking group.

Gelina was the oldest ('When I hit thirty I stopped counting.'), a confidence trickster supreme, who could become any character from a Priestess to a whore, could break men's hearts at fifty paces, and charm the gold from the pocket of the most flint-hearted merchant (except, of course, for Lady Seriema). Today, for the first time, she looked her age to Aliana, with her shoulders drooping, her face grey and drawn with weariness and grief, her rainbow gypsy skirts soaking, tattered and daubed with mud and blood, and her wealth of dark hair hanging in tousled strings. Tag and Erla, expert pickpockets aged eight and ten respectively, clustered round her, clinging to her hands. Tosel, fifteen years old, slight, towheaded and the finest cat burglar in the city, had lost his normal air of cocky ebullience, and huddled, red-eyed and shaking, close to the wall.

The only one who seemed unmarked by the events of the previous night was Packrat, whose thin, sneering countenance looked just the same as ever. Aliana would have laid money on his surviving, though there were faces she would much rather have seen in his place. His age was indeterminate, anywhere between Aliana and Gelina. He described himself as a plain, jobbing thief ('If it's not nailed down, I'll have it.'). Anything was grist to his mill: food, money, clothing or anything else he could find that was unwanted or unwatched. He would steal a farthing from a blind old woman as readily as he'd take a fat purse from a merchant, and for profit he would slit a throat or stick a knife in a back without blinking an eye. Even among thieves, his methods drew comment and disapproval. He was unshaven as always, and his face had its usual, unhealthy pallor. His clothes and hair were slovenly and unkempt, and Aliana had once commented that he only washed occasionally so that his victims would not be able to smell him coming.

Packrat, as she might have guessed, was the first to speak. 'We got slaughtered, that's what happened. And before we go any further with this touching little reunion, we should get off the street – that is, if you don't want to be next.'

Aliana found herself shaking. Though she had known in her heart that the others must be dead, it was still a devastating blow. And to be told in such a brutal manner! She looked at Packrat with more than the usual dislike. 'Pick a house, then. You're the expert at breaking and entering.'

He shrugged. 'The way those flying bastards smash through doors and windows, I don't have to be.'

They took refuge in a house nearby, ransacking the kitchen, and then taking the food upstairs, where they could keep a lookout. The house, though not as opulent as that of Aliana's wool merchant, was large, beautifully furnished, and solidly constructed, with good, thick walls that kept out the worst of the damp and chill. They did not dare light a fire, lest some watchful predator should see or smell the smoke. They made a rough camp in the master bedroom, with a lookout constantly at the window to scan the skies and the neighbouring rooftops, and another stationed in the smaller room next door, which looked out on the rear of the house.

The thieves took turns to wash, and to doctor one another's wounds as best they could before they ate, despite the fact that all of them were ravenous. It was as though they needed first to cleanse themselves, not only of the muck and the blood, but also of the horrors and violence they had witnessed during the hours of darkness. *Some chance,* Aliana thought bitterly – but when it was her turn at the basin, she found herself scrubbing at her skin just as hard as the others had done. Even the scruffy Packrat, for once, seemed to feel the need of soap and water.

The others would tell Aliana very little about the loss of the Warrens. They had only survived because they had still been out in the streets when the creatures attacked. None of them wanted to say much about the destruction they had witnessed on their return, and Aliana felt guilty but relieved that she didn't know the details.

Alestan laid aside the food that he had barely tasted, and rubbed his weary eyes. 'Of course, we can't be sure that everyone is dead. Others may have been like you, Aliana, and found shelter somewhere in the city. Maybe they'll—'

'Maybe nothing,' Packrat snarled. 'Even if they did make it, do you think they'll survive another night on the streets with those vicious sons of bitches on the prowl? Do you think we will? Don't be stupid!'

Aliana glared at him. 'They may. I did. I know it's possible. After all, it's a big city. There's food around for the looting if they look hard, and there are lots of places to hide. Why, with care it should be possible to survive indefinitely—'

'Don't fool yourself.' Packrat treated her to a look of utter contempt. 'Face it – the rest of the Ghosts are dead. And so are we. It's only a matter of time.'

'There's something else you haven't considered, Aliana.' Gelina came in from the other room, where Tosel had just taken her place. 'Right now those killers are well-fed. They don't really need to put much effort into hunting down strays. But there seems to be an awful lot of them. What happens when their supplies start to run short? They'll make short work of any wandering survivors then, you mark my words.'

'And in case you hadn't noticed, that means us,' said Packrat. 'Unless we can think of something really clever before nightfall, we're just so much dead meat.'

When Zavahl opened his eyes and saw a Godsword standing in front of him, his heart leapt. Rescue! One of his own people had come to save him from these madwomen with the monster, and take him home. Then he woke up properly, and remembered that he didn't have a home, and the Godswords were his troops no longer. His belly clenched with fear. Blade had come for him! Knowledge of his desperate predicament came crashing down on him once more. He could not go back to Tiarond; even in the unlikely event that Gilarra and the ruthless Godsword Commander let him live, his own people would most likely tear him to pieces.

The stranger in the black cloak was watching him closely. 'You've missed the right time for the Sacrifice,' he said softly. 'It won't come round again for another year. If you went back now, it would do no good.'

Zavahl sat bolt upright. 'Who *are* you?'

The other put down the plate he was carrying, and sat himself on the edge of the bed. 'I'm Elion,' he said. 'I hope I'm going to be a friend, though I'm afraid you might have different ideas about that.'

'Are you in league with those accursed women?'

'Well, I'm not a Godsword.' The young man smiled. 'I just needed to borrow a uniform for a while. You know how it is.'

Guilt scorched Zavahl, who remembered one night long ago, when he had abandoned the lonely asceticism of his life and gone down into the city with his face and identity concealed by a mask, to sample the alehouses and whores.

Don't think about that.

'Are you in league with the women?' he persisted.

The young man shrugged. 'Well, there's no sense in denying it. We come from the same place – apart from the old battleaxe – and we have the same goals.' He leaned forward confidingly, and spoke in a low voice. 'It's no bloody picnic for me, let me tell you. You've already found out how pigheaded, disagreeable, and downright difficult they can be. But these are inauspicious times, as you've seen for yourself. The world is falling apart around us, and it's our task to try and stop it.'

Zavahl frowned. '*Our* task? How can that be? Surely the fate of the world is in the hands of Myrial?'

Elion started to say something, thought better of it, and started again. 'Even if that's true, don't you think that matters have reached a point where Myrial needs a little help?'

'*What?*' Then suddenly the former Hierarch, on the verge of raging at the young man's heresy, remembered his dream, in which Myrial had spoken to him, and told him that he was not being punished, he was being tested.

Could it really be true? Could this be the test? Did Myrial want him to denounce this heretic? Or help him save the world?

If I had only been allowed to sleep, and dream a little longer!

'But – but how could I possibly help a God?' he said doubtfully.

Elion leaned forward. 'Before we say anything more, will you answer me one question? Are you willing to do *anything* to save your people?'

This was not what Zavahl had expected, but he recovered swiftly. 'If I allowed myself to be tied to a stake and burned alive, I should think that answers your question.'

The stranger's grey eyes never left his own. 'Yes or no?' he persisted. 'Think carefully before you answer.'

Zavahl was the first to look away. 'I don't know,' he whispered.

The young man only waited.

'I had always told myself I would willingly die for my people,' Zavahl went on bitterly, 'but when the time came to stand by my vows and become the sacrifice, I was so terrified that I would have done anything in my power to escape my fate, even if it meant condemning my own people to endless suffering.' He dropped his face into his hands and began to weep.

'And then you did escape,' Elion said softly, 'but since Veldan rescued you, you've been racked with guilt about not going through with the sacrifice.' He hesitated. 'You *can* atone for that, you know. You can help your people, I promise. It won't be easy, that's all. Your whole life will be turned upside down, and your most cherished illusions will be shattered. You'll see things you'd rather not see, and be taken where you'd rather not go. It'll be tough and unpleasant and frightening. It'll hurt you, and make you question yourself in ways you can't even imagine.'

Elion gripped Zavahl's shoulder. 'But you won't have to go through it alone. I'll help you all I can, and so will my companions. If you really want to make amends, then here's your chance, and if it involves some suffering along the way – well, surely that's all to the good. This is your one chance to make your peace, Zavahl: with your God, with your people, and with yourself. And in the process, you'll be doing something a damn sight more useful and effective than letting yourself be burned at the stake. Besides, it's possible that a great deal of good may come out of this situation. You might make new friends, or find a new life for yourself, or grow in ways that you can't even imagine.'

The former Hierarch shook his head. 'I just don't know . . .'

'Come on,' Elion coaxed. 'Zavahl, your life is at its lowest ebb.

What have you got to lose by helping us?'

My integrity? My immortal soul? My misconceptions? Or just my sanity?

Zavahl hesitated. In a way this strange young man, holding out hope in one hand, and friendship in the other, frightened him more than Blade had ever done. All his life, his path, clear and straight, had been marked out for him. Now that path had been washed away by a river, flowing fast and wide, and Elion was asking him to take a deep breath and jump right in, abandoning himself to be whirled away by the current.

What if I drown?

What have I got to lose? And what if this is *my chance to save my people?*

All his life, Zavahl had been alone. He didn't think he could bear it any longer. 'All right,' he said at last. 'You have my word that I'll co-operate – at least for now.'

Elion grinned, and clapped him on the back. 'Good man! Now, I know you must have a thousand questions, but truly, it's best that you save them until we reach our destination.'

'When will that be?'

'We're going to rest here for a few hours, then carry on through most of the night. We'll get there tomorrow morning.'

That news that their destination was so close cheered Zavahl immensely. Maybe he had been mistaken after all, about passing beyond the Curtain Walls. He was longing to ask his new companion, but did not dare. So long as he said nothing, he could convince himself that he was still in Callisiora.

'Pox on it!' Elion broke into his thoughts at a very timely moment. 'I brought you some food, and then I clean forgot about it.' Retrieving the plate, he held it out to Zavahl. 'I'm sorry, it'll be freezing by now. It should still taste all right, though.'

It did. Suddenly, Zavahl discovered that he was starving.

Nine

The Otherplace

Within the timeless void of the Otherplace in which she had been trapped, the Wind-Sprite was discovering that she was no longer alone. Calm and serene, the woman smiled up at a very baffled Shree. 'Welcome, my dear. How good it is to have company after all this time. What a pity you don't drink tea. I've spent an eternity getting the taste just right.'

Thirishri observed her with growing incredulity. She did not appear to be young, as humans reckoned these matters, but her face, with its aquiline nose and high, sharp cheekbones, held a harsh, imperious beauty that was unblurred by the ravages of time. Her abundant hair, hanging straight down her back without a trace of curl or wave, was black streaked with glints of luminous silver, though when she moved her head, Shree could discern the gleam of iridescent colours, like the rainbow sheen on a raven's wing. Her eyes were gentian blue, the most deep and vivid shade the Wind-Sprite had ever seen, and their colour exactly matched the robes that draped and flowed in soft folds over a long and bony frame.

Never mind the tea. Her reply was brusque to the point of rudeness – a sure sign that she was feeling unnerved by this apparition. *Who are you, and what are you doing here?*

'As you must already have guessed, I am a captive like yourself.'

But where did all this landscape come from? The ocean and the island and the sun?

The woman smiled again; that same, beatific smile as before, with a hint of condescension that was beginning to set Thirishri's nerves on edge. 'Why, I made it, of course. I created it all, from memory and imagination, from desperation and from loneliness and longing. You know yourself how terrible the void is . . .' Her voice had taken on a brittle edge, and the Wind-Sprite saw her bony fingers tighten around the thin white porcelain of the cup. Her eyes, when she glanced up again from her knotted fingers, held a flash of something very close to insanity. 'To make my existence bearable, I needed some kind of structure around me, so I remembered my favourite place, somewhere full of warmth and light and colour, and "built" myself a house. I've been here so long – so very, very long – that my imaginings have become real. At least, as real as anything can ever hope to be in this evil place.'

Thirishri understood completely. Had she not done something very similar, when she'd found herself and her thoughts at the mercy of the terrifying void? But this poor woman must have been a captive for a staggering amount of time, for her visualisations to have taken on such a substantial and consistent form! Following her train of thought to its obvious conclusion, she asked: *But what if . . . ?*

'What if I should die? Would my little realm survive without me? Who can say? But that won't happen.' For an unguarded instant her face fell into lines of terrible weariness, and her eyes held pain as bright and sharp and naked as an unsheathed sword. 'No-one dies in here, my friend. We just go on and on, unchanging for eternity. There is no easy escape route for us, no welcome journey to oblivion and rest. In their great wisdom,' she spat the word out bitterly, 'my people have created the ultimate prison.'

Shree froze as she floated in mid-air. **Your* people?*

Again, the smile with its chilling hint of madness. 'Oh yes, my dear. Do you not know the identity of your cellmate? I'm a little hurt that my notoriety did not withstand the test of time. I am Helverien, despised betrayer of my people, and I was assured that my name would be cursed and reviled through all the generations of the Magefolk, to the end of history itself.'

In a swift change of mood she smiled mischievously at the Wind-

Sprite, and her blue eyes twinkled. 'At least I certainly hope so,' she added wryly. 'I should hate to have gone to all that trouble and inconvenience, only to be stuffed in here, out of sight and out of mind, and be consigned to obscurity.'

All what trouble? Shree asked, puzzled. *What did you do, to deserve such a cruel fate?*

Helverien shrugged. 'Well, the way things turned out, maybe it wasn't so very dreadful, when all is said and done. It all depends on your point of view. You see, in order to save the inhabitants of this incredible world of ours – at least, that was my reasoning at the time – I handed over all the deepest secrets of the Magefolk power to the Creators. And as you probably know, they used this knowledge to strip us of our magic, and imprison us forever.'

Thirishri was stunned. She had only half-believed in the legends of the Mages, an imperious and often merciless race possessed of incredible arcane powers. Every child of every race had heard the tale in one form or another, changed and distorted over the years by endless retelling, describing the fall of the Wizards: how in their arrogance they had dared to challenge the Gods themselves, and had been reft of their powers and exiled behind an impervious barrier, so that they could no longer interfere in the affairs of the world. Since most of Myrial's inhabitants were ignorant of the extent and composition of their world, the stories all took place 'far away, in a land beyond our own,' and most ordinary folk did not believe them. But most ordinary folk, and indeed most of the Shadowleague, had not witnessed what Shree had seen, far across the sea to the east: an impenetrable grey barrier in the shape of a dome, covering a vast area. What was beneath it? Land or ocean? No-one knew. But through the aeons it had endured; the only barrier that the Loremasters were unable to penetrate, so impervious and adamant that it made the other Curtain Walls seem like fragile gauze.

What had the Magefolk done to deserve such dreadful isolation? Were they really so very dangerous? Avid for more information, Thirishri turned back to Helverien, brimming over with a thousand questions that tumbled over one another in an incomprehensible gabble of mind speech.

The woman laughed. 'Patience, my friend. I will do my best to explain what happened. It was our pride, of course, that was our undoing. You see, the Magefolk always tended to fall into two categories: the meddlers and the conquerors. The meddlers *meant* well. They wished to use their power and knowledge to help more primitive races to advance – without ever considering that the Wizardly notions of advancement might wreak more harm than good among folk with a different background. The conquerors were much more single-minded. Clearly, the lesser beings had been created to serve them, and so must be enslaved.'

She spread her thin arms in a helpless gesture. 'The consequences were inevitable. When we came here, with so many other races in such close proximity, the temptation for both groups was overwhelming.'

But how did they know? Shree interrupted. *As far as the Shadowleague researches can discover, the races who came here had no idea of their true origins. It was almost as though their memories had been tampered with, somehow.*

Helverien nodded. 'In most cases they were. The Creators wanted their little breeding colonies to be happy in their new enclosures, not hankering after influence, or conquest, or in some cases a few additions to their diet. There are some pretty belligerent species on Myrial, as you know; Magefolk and Humans included.'

But they aren't the worst. The Wind-Sprite was thinking of the Ak'Zahar. *Not by a long way.*

'Maybe not, but apart from those who created this whole world, the Wizards were probably the most powerful and definitely the most cunning. Because of their powers, they found they could shield their minds from the memory-wipe that had erased the collective pasts of other species. Because of their magic, they were well able to conceal all their schemes and activities from the Creators. They carried out their research in secret and in stealth, and in no time they had worked out a way to penetrate the Curtain Walls. That was when I got to know your lovely island, my friend. As Recorder to my people, I had to witness their progress very closely, and some of my happiest memories are of the times when we'd make surreptitious visits to the other realms, to find out about our neighbours.'

She sighed. 'If only we had been content just to satisfy our curiosity. Up to that point, the meddlers and the conquerors had been in complete accord. Their one goal was to break through the barriers that kept them isolated and curbed their ambitions. Once that had been achieved, however, the two factions began to disagree over the use to which the new knowledge would be put. That was just as well for the rest of the world,' she added wryly. 'The fighting amongst themselves delayed their plans to invade the other realms, and for that we can be thankful. Had their schemes succeeded, they would have been like a fox in a hen house.'

Helverien stopped speaking, seemingly lost in her own dark memories, and Thirishri, moved by the sadness on her face, respected her silence. At last, however, curiosity won out. *So what happened?* She had a sinking feeling that she already knew the answer.

The Magewoman looked up at her, almost as if she had forgotten that Shree was there. 'It couldn't be allowed to continue,' she said flatly. 'Or so I thought at the time. I was the Chief Recorder and Archivist to the Magefolk. My whole life's work had been filled with lessons from the mistakes of the past. The discord between the meddlers and the conquerors was escalating towards full blown warfare, and a war between Wizards is an appalling thing. When I realised that we might destroy ourselves as well as the other races, I could make no other choice. I went to the Creators.'

She leapt to her feet and turned her back on the Wind-Sprite, gazing out across the sparkling blue ocean that she had created from memory and longing. 'I truly believed it was for the best. If I had only known what the consequences would be! We Wizards had forgotten, in our arrogance, that the powers of the Creators made our own look like the fumblings of small children. In our pride, we didn't want to believe it could be so.' She took a deep breath. 'Retribution was swift and terrible. They isolated our entire realm behind a barrier far, far stronger and more dangerous than the Curtain Walls. If they had only gone so far, I believe I could have lived with what I had done – but the Creators took our punishment one cruel step further. The barrier was not a simple energy field, as were the others in this world. It also acted as a thaumaturgic damper, absorbing and negating our powers of magic. Without warning, the most important part of our existence was torn away from us, and we were condemned to spend an eternity living purposeless, powerless, and devoid of hope.'

Helverien turned back to Shree, her eyes burning like blue fire with the intensity of her emotion. 'I don't know what I thought would happen to me, but somehow I had believed that the Creators would shield me from the consequences of my deed.' She gave a short and bitter laugh. 'How wrong I was! But I only discovered that when it was far too late. The Creators, builders of entire worlds, did not care about the fate of one small individual. They left me with the people I had betrayed, and you know the rest. Many of the Magefolk wanted to kill me for what I had done, but in the end, they decided to condemn me to a far worse fate.'

And if you could go back and do it all again? Thirishri asked her softly. *Would you?*

'What do you think?' The Magewoman's expression grew bleak, and she turned her face to the ocean.

I'd like to think you would.

'Well, you'd be wrong! Knowing what I know now, I would let well alone, and the other races of the world would have to take their chances. If the Creators had simply been content to imprison my people I could possibly have lived with the consequences of my deeds, notwithstanding the terrible fate that awaited me. But our magic was as essential to our well-being as food, or love, or the air we breathed. Without it we are doomed to live in a constant agony of spirit, and our lives are meaningless, joyless and bleak. Truly, I wish the Creators had slaughtered every last one of us, had wiped out our race completely. It would have been a far kinder act than condemning us to this eternal suffering.'

The Wind-Sprite gave her a few minutes to compose herself before speaking. *Why do you think they acted so harshly?*

'Because we dared to challenge them. Because we were the only race who could. You see, they were so much more powerful than the species with which they peopled this world. They thought of us very much as we would think of animals. Before we came to Myrial, each one of our races was under threat in some way on our original worlds, through war or pestilence, or the destruction of our environment through overpopulation, or thoughtlessness, or greed. The Creators brought us here to save us. In return, we were expected to believe that our enclosures, the little realms within the Curtain Walls, constituted the entire world. They didn't expect a race with sufficient power of its own to escape their memory-wipe, and they were astonished and angered by our temerity and ambition.' A wry smile crossed her face. 'After all, you don't expect the chickens to start plotting to take over the farm, now do you?'

I thought you compared the Magefolk to the foxes.

'So I did. You have a good memory, Wind-Sprite. But a farm is a bad analogy, for it implies that the Creators wanted to use us in some way, whereas in truth, we were simply specimens to them: a collection of rare and curious creatures who were in danger of extinction. So they put us where we would be protected from ourselves, from our own destructive impulses – and from each other.'

It's hard to imagine such power, Shree said thoughtfully. *What did they look like?*

The woman shrugged. 'Whatever they wanted, is the short answer. Such was their power. If they wished, they could take on the forms of any of the creatures on Myrial, and a whole host of other strange and wonderful beings besides. Sometimes they would appear as great globes of blazing light, though I'm pretty sure that wasn't their original form, either. I don't believe we ever saw the true face of the Creators. Sometimes I wonder if they even remembered what it was.'

I wonder what happened to them? Thirishri mused.

'What do you mean?' Helverien asked sharply.

Well, powerful or not, they're gone. I don't know how unimaginably long you've been trapped in here, but there has been no sign of the Creators in our entire recorded history.

'What?' The Mage's reaction was an odd mixture of dismay and hope. 'But what could have happened to them? And if they are truly gone, who is taking care of Myrial? This is an artificial world, and because it contains so many differing environments, all separated by the Curtain Walls, it must maintain a difficult and delicate balance. With no custodians, the systems will eventually start breaking down!'

Tell me about it, Shree said wryly. *The disaster you describe is already happening, even as we speak, and our world is descending into chaos. Even the Shadowleague is powerless—*

'Wait a minute. What is the Shadowleague?'

Thirishri was startled. *You've never heard of us? I'd no idea that you had *that* much catching up to do.*

To her surprise, the Magewoman returned to her chair on the terrace, seated herself comfortably, and poured another cup of the illusory tea that seemed to be forever hot and fresh. Once she was settled, she looked up at the Wind-Sprite. 'Well? Don't just hover around up there wasting time,' she snapped. 'Bring me up to date.'

But that will take ages, Shree protested.

Helverien shrugged. 'You had something else to do?'

The journey through the tunnel had proved to be a lot less frightening than Scall had expected. In fact, he was quite proud of his first small adventure on his own. At first he had inclined to be jumpy when his torch flame wavered in the draught, sending shadows dancing and leaping up the wall, but it didn't take him long to realise, rather sheepishly, that all those furtive movements glimpsed from the corner of his eye were just his imagination combining with the continuous flicker of light and shade.

The tunnel, sloping steeply downwards and hewn in a curving

path through the cliff, was ankle-deep in running water, but so far his boots seemed to be holding out. The biggest irritant was being hit on the head so often by the freezing cold drops of water that kept dripping from the roof. The strong draught that blew up the passage into his face held the dank smell of damp stone, and the place was alive with echoes that repeated the high, chuckling sound of the running stream on the tunnel floor, Scall's breathing, and the sloshing of his feet in the water.

High on the wall on his right-hand side, Scall saw a rusting metal walkway, seemingly bolted into the stone, with iron ladders leading up to it at intervals. A vantage point for the tunnel guards, he supposed, and wondered if it would be a better idea to climb up there and walk along the tunnel that way, to keep out of the water. It looked pretty rickety, though, and he didn't much like the look of all that rust. No, better stay down here on the ground. After all, the horses would have to come down here, and *they* couldn't climb up on a walkway. He needed to check that the floor was safe for them all the way down, in case there were any obstructions or unevenness that could make them trip or slip.

How much longer was this tunnel, anyway? Scall felt that he had been walking for a long time already, but in the cold, and the flickering torchlight and shadow, it was easy to lose track. Certainly there seemed to be a good deal of light left in his torch, and that was the main thing. Even though he knew there was nothing down here that could really hurt him, he didn't much fancy groping his way back up the tunnel in the dark. As he went further, he noticed that the passageway had gradually been growing narrower. At the top, where he had started, the tunnel had been wide enough for two wagons to pass abreast. Down here, though he knew it must really be wide enough, it looked as though there was barely space for a single cart to scrape through. Scall wondered why.

Maybe they just got sick of chipping away at this endless stone. There's an awful lot of work gone into this tunnel as it is. Or maybe it was all narrow, and they started to widen it at the top and something happened to stop them. I suppose I'll never . . .

At that moment, his thoughts were rudely interrupted.

'Floods! Climb, boy! Climb up to the walkway!' Tormon's voice came, faint and distant, from a long way up the passage. For an instant, Scall was paralysed by an ice-cold surge of panic. Then he heard a distant rumbling, as though the tunnel was the throat of a wild beast that had been awakened to sudden anger. With a gasp he took to his heels, his feet kicking up great sprays of water, his torch, held high to look for the next ladder to the walkway, streaming smoke and flame behind him.

It was impossible to wade quickly, but Scall did his best, ploughing as fast as he could through a deepening stream of water whose quickening current snatched at his ankles, then rose to pull at his knees. It was growing more difficult to keep his footing on the slippery tunnel floor, and that reduced his speed still further. What had happened to the next accursed ladder? Where in perdition had it gone? The distant rumble had grown into a roar, and the entire tunnel was shaking all around him. Suddenly, to his incredulous relief, the torchlight caught the dull red of rusted metal rungs that led up to safety. But it was too late. Even as his reaching fingers groped for the ladder, the torrent came crashing down on him.

Everything happened at once. As the wall of water smashed into him his legs went out from underneath him and his torch flew from his hand to be extinguished and lost. His scream of terror was choked off as water filled his throat. Disorientated in the darkness and tumult he flailed wildly, and suddenly he felt cold metal beneath his fingers as his hand caught hold of a rough iron bar that almost tore the skin from his palm. Scall's fingers locked around it. Sheer desperation gave him the strength to bring his other arm around against the ferocious tug of the current, and gain a stronger, two-handed hold that would keep his head above the water. He hung there spluttering, wondering how far up the ladder the flood had lifted him, and how close he was to the walkway. Not far, he would wager. A tremendous amount of water had come down all at once, and it must have lifted him pretty high. If only he could climb up to safety – but he dared not loosen his grip from the rung he was holding, even for the instant it would take to reach up to the next.

Time lost all meaning. Scall's universe had shrunk to that rusting metal bar and his two hands clamped around it. He clung on for his very life as the current tugged and battered at him, twisting his body so that time and again he almost lost his grip, trying to snatch him back into its deadly embrace. There, amid cold and dark and terror and confusion, he discovered strength and determination he had never before possessed.

But human endurance could only go so far. As Scall's hands grew numb with cold, he felt his grasp beginning to weaken. A powerful surge of the current took him unawares, and his grip slackened and shifted. His fingers were slipping, slipping . . . Then the waters took him and whirled him away.

In that moment, Scall realised that the flood wasn't going to subside in time to save his life. Here, where the tunnel was narrower, it was lifting him even higher. Several times it threw him up against the roof, scraping his face and arms against the rough wet stone. Painful though it was, at least it gave him the chance to snatch a breath or two. The walkway that had been his only hope wouldn't be much good to him now. It must be submerged for sure.

This is it. I'm going to die.

Scall's head was spinning from lack of air. He couldn't hold his breath much longer. Though it made no difference in the darkness, he closed his eyes. As the current tumbled him over and over, he waited for the end.

It didn't come – but something else did. Something hard and narrow, that slammed into his body with bruising force, halting his headlong descent of the tunnel. He found his face pressed up against the ceiling, where there were a few inches of breathing space between the water and the roof.

What in Myrial's name has happened?

Scall took a grateful gulp of air. As far as he could tell in the darkness, he seemed to be wedged in the narrow space between the curving apex of the tunnel and a horizontal iron strut, some kind of cross-brace that ran from wall to wall. The current was pushing him against it, keeping him in place, at least for now. Carefully, inch by fearful inch, he moved into a more secure position, straddling the narrow metal pole with his legs while clasping his arms around it in a grip that would have throttled it for sure, had it been flesh and blood. It said a lot for his predicament that he found his position almost comfortable, compared to what he had just been through. For an instant his mind flashed back to his apprenticeship in the Precincts with Smithmaster Agella, and he wondered what, in those halcyon days, he had ever found to complain about.

Then he realised that the water was still rising, presenting him with a dilemma. Should he continue to cling to his perch, and hope that the flood wouldn't reach the ceiling and drown him, or should he let go, and risk being carried out of the tunnel and, in all probability, straight over the edge of the cliff? Not bloody likely! Scall decided to stay exactly where he was. He would just have to hold his breath, and pray.

Another surge smacked into him, loosening his hold and almost knocking him from his perch. Scall grabbed at the strut, kicking out frantically to get himself back into a secure position. The sudden movement was a mistake. The pole shifted beneath him, turning on its axis and almost tipping him off. From above him came a strange and ominous grinding noise, like stone scraping against stone. Scall, still hanging on with desperate determination, froze in terror. Had the flood done more damage than he'd thought? Was the tunnel about to cave in and bury him?

Then all at once, he realised that he could see. Below him, the waters raced by in a giddy whirl, and he looked away hastily. Where was the light coming from? With difficulty, Scall craned his neck around so that he could look above him.

'Holy Myrial!'

A hole had opened in the ceiling above him, round as the pupil of an eye, its perfect curves cleaving cleanly and smoothly through the stone to form a tube that led up into the cliff. A faint, misty light filtered down the new tunnel, subdued as moonlight, but changing in hue all the time so that at any moment it might be blue or red, yellow, green, violet or pearly white. If any sound came from up there, it was drowned in the hollow rushing of the slowly rising waters below. A warm breeze blew steadily down from above, carrying a strange, fresh smell, partly spicy and partly chemical, like the acrid odours of the acids and the caustics that Smithmaster Agella sometimes used for etching. It made his nostrils tingle and, with difficulty, he suppressed the urge to sneeze.

So what do we do now?

Scall looked at the flood that washed around his body, threatening, at any minute, to drag him from his perch. He looked up again. In the tube a sturdy ladder, made from some dark, shining material that showed no sign of rust, vanished into the misty light above. His stomach clenched into a knot at the thought of climbing up into the unknown – but he liked the alternative a whole lot less. Moving with painstaking care, he reached for the lowest rung of the ladder, getting one hand round it then the other, then pulling his shivering body right up out of the water. For a little while he clung there at the bottom of the tube, resting his weary body and marshalling his courage to venture further. If he stayed here too long, he wouldn't have any strength left to climb at all. In a little while he moved on again, heading cautiously up into the light, unsure of what might lie ahead of him, but determined to find out.

After climbing for a short distance, Scall ran out of ladder, as his mysterious new tunnel made a sharply angled bend to become almost horizontal, leading back into the mountain.

Back towards Tiarond? There's no way I want to go in that direction!

But he clambered up anyway, and flopped down gratefully on the smooth, dry surface. He did need a place to rest, if only for a little while. Besides, what if the water didn't subside in the tunnel below? What if he was cut off forever from his friends? What if Tormon had been washed away in the flood and drowned?

'Dear Myrial, no!' Scall whispered. This was the first time, since the torrent had come thundering down, that he'd been able to think beyond his immediate survival, and a chill of fear ran through him as he realised that he could well be on his own. He sank down on the floor of this strange new passageway and buried his face in his hands, fighting the urge to wail like an abandoned child. His parents, his sister and Agella might be dead, Tormon might be dead – would this nightmare never end?

'It will if you keep on sitting here feeling sorry for yourself, you idiot,' he pulled himself up sharply, speaking aloud in an attempt to bolster his courage. 'It'll end in no time, with you starving to death. Is that what you want? Come on, Scall, you don't know for sure if any of them are dead. They might all be perfectly fine. You survived those winged fiends, didn't you? You survived the flood. Well, your family and Tormon might have survived too. And what would Tormon think of you now? He lost his poor lifemate for sure, but he didn't give up, did he?'

Feeling a little better for having given himself a good talking-to, Scall got to his feet once more. Facing back the way he had come, he leaned over the edge of the passage where the tube had come up, to check whether the waters had receded in the tunnel below. Judging from the sound of the running water, they had not. 'All right, then.' Scall straightened his shoulders. 'We'll go the other way. At least it's dry up here.'

The new tunnel was high enough for him to walk upright, though its sides and roof still curved round to form a perfect circle. Only the floor was flat, as though a small section of the circle had been flattened out at the bottom, to make for easier walking. The walls were lined with some kind of soft, elastic material that gave slightly to his touch before springing back into shape. It felt oddly warm beneath his fingers, like something alive, he thought with a shudder. It seemed to be the source of the changeful, misty radiance that suffused the tunnel and coloured the walls in a series of different hues, one after the other. The faint breeze still blew into his face, carrying that odd, tantalising scent, partly spicy, partly sharp, that tickled his nostrils. Wondering what lay ahead, and what would become of him, Scall set off into the unknown.

Ten

The World in His Hand

The floods in the tunnel showed no signs of going down, and every moment was an agony to Tormon. Seeing the savage power of the water as it rushed by below the walkway, he feared that there was little chance that Scall could have survived, and felt heartsick at the thought that he had sent the poor, inexperienced lad down into the tunnel alone, to die.

How many more of the people he cared about would perish? An image of Kanella, his beloved lifemate, came into his mind, and Tormon buried his face in his hands. He had let her down too, had failed to take care of her, had abandoned her in the Godsword Citadel, alone and unprotected, to be murdered. Now his negligence had killed the boy. And what of Annas, up at the top of the cliff? The floods would also be bad up there, and he had left her in the dubious care of Presvel, a bookish, hopelessly impractical city dweller, and Rochalla who, though she seemed to possess more than a grain of common sense, was none the less a slip of a girl, young enough to be a sister to his daughter despite her air of maturity. Were they still alive? Or had they already been swept over the precipice by the raging waters? It was torture to sit here: helpless, trapped, not knowing.

A touch on his shoulder made him turn. Seriema put her face close to his ear, to make herself heard above the sound of the rushing waters. 'There will be time enough for despair if we find out that they have perished. Until then, there's always hope.'

'Hope? What chance does poor Scall have, in these floods?' Tormon snapped.

Seriema remained calm in the face of his bitterness. 'You succeeded in warning him, at any rate. He had a chance to get up on the walkway, just as we did. He's probably sitting there now, as hungry as a wolf, waiting for the floods to go down and worrying in case *we* drowned.'

'I should never have sent him down there on his own, and—'

'By Myrial's mighty muscles, what idiots we are!' Seriema leapt to her feet, dragging the astonished trader with her. 'The walkway! It goes right along, surely?'

Understanding dawned for Tormon, and an unexpected surge of hope. 'We can use it to look for him right now. Come on, what are you waiting for?'

'You, to light another torch.' Seriema's lips twitched in amusement. 'Unless you can see in the dark like a bat. We'll soon lose the light from the tunnel entrance.'

'You're right.' Tormon shrugged out of his backpack and fumbled inside. 'Great Myrial, I feel so stupid. There I was, worrying about Scall, and sitting on the answer all the time.'

'Well, it's scarcely surprising that our brains are a bit slow. After the fright we got we needed a little time to collect ourselves. Besides, we've been through such a lot this last couple of days, we can be forgiven for not thinking like our usual, efficient selves.'

Tormon scowled. He couldn't get the last few days out of his mind as it was. He didn't need Seriema reminding him how terrible they had been. Catching sight of his expression, she looked away, biting her lip. 'I'm sorry. I didn't mean to remind you.'

The trader concentrated on striking a spark, and lighting the torch with a bit of smouldering tinder. 'It's not your fault,' he said gruffly. 'Everything reminds me.' To his relief, she didn't tell him that things would get better, or that time healed all hurts. She squeezed his hand gently as she took the torch from him, and made it almost seem accidental. 'Come on, let's find that dratted boy,' she said over her shoulder, and led the way into the darkness, her small, brave light held high.

Tormon glanced up at the torch to see how far it had burned

down, then looked down again at the broken walkway in front of him. Here where the tunnel narrowed, the flood must have risen higher in a great, violent surge, and the platform had been sheared loose from the wall and twisted into a useless lump of metal by the sheer force of water.

'Damn! How *could* this happen!' Seriema sounded as if the disaster was a personal affront. 'The merchants pay good money to have this tunnel maintained!'

Never mind your bloody money! What about Scall?

The words had been hovering on Tormon's lips, but just then he caught a glimpse of Seriema's face, and swallowed them unsaid. In a split-second of clear insight, he saw the little twist of a worried frown across her brow, and realised that she didn't know how to express her concern for the boy, and was hiding it as best she could.

And now they were stuck and helpless. They could go no further. 'Scall?' Again and again Tormon bellowed into the darkness, hoping for a reply. *'Scall!'* But no answer came from the depths of the tunnel, above the noise of the flood as it swept past them, and away. Seriema sat down on the walkway, regardless of the damp, resting her back against the tunnel wall. 'That's it, then,' she sighed. 'All we can do now is wait.'

The chamber came as a complete surprise. The circular passageway had been so smooth, so featureless, that it had lulled Scall's senses almost into a doze as he walked along. The changing colours and the ambient, misty light had a soothing, hypnotic effect, as though he was passing through the landscape of a dream. Then suddenly, without warning, he stumbled out of the secure confines and into a cavern so immense that he had difficulty recognising it for what it was.

He came to an abrupt halt. 'Holy Myrial!' he gasped, but his words were swallowed up by the vast spaces that stretched on and on, in front, to the sides, and even above him, until eventually the details were lost in shadow. Scall blinked, and a shiver went through him, though the air was just as warm as it had been before. Gone was the soft, confusing haze with its changeful colours. Gone was the security of the enclosing tunnel. The cavern was shrouded in eerie gloom, but on every side streaks and rivers of light in ruby, amethyst, emerald, sapphire and gold crawled and writhed across the blackness of the walls like snakes. High above his head, cutting through the air to bridge the cavern like spider webs were more of the narrow beams, illuminating the darkness with their vibrant hues. The faint whisper of the breeze had been replaced by a low thrumming that seemed to go right up through the soles of Scall's feet, and sometimes the incandescent bolts sizzled and hissed like lightning as they darted across the walls and leapt the void above. Occasionally clouds of glittering particles would detach themselves from one area and drift through the air to another location, where they would settle like a swarm of scintillating bees.

Even more wondrous were the structures that covered the floor of the cavern, some as big as houses, some as small as footstools, and others that were every size between. They came in a bewildering variety of shapes: blocks, pyramids, pillars, cones, spheres, and some that seemed to be formed from a translucent, gelatinous substance that could change its form completely, from one moment to the next. Some were outlined in the same brilliant light that roamed across the walls, others were suffused with softer shades. Some shimmered with the iridescence of a pearl, while others sparkled as though they were covered in flowing streams of jewels.

Scall had no idea what he was looking at, but it was very beautiful. He had no sense of fear. All this strange sound and light and motion seemed to have a purpose all its own that had nothing to do with him, but nothing he could see or hear carried any feeling of menace. Lost in amazement, he wandered through the cavern between rows of the shining structures, at first forgetting his weariness and hunger in the weird, scintillating loveliness that surrounded him.

After a time, however, the wonder and the proud feeling that he was the first to venture where no Tiarondian had ever trod, began to pall. He was footsore, hungry and thirsty, and there seemed little chance of finding anything to eat or drink in here. These glowing forms were all very pretty but he couldn't eat them, and he didn't understand them. Even such incredible sights as this eventually got to be boring when there was nothing else to look at.

I've got to go back. This isn't getting me anywhere. Maybe the floods are going down in the tunnel by now. Maybe Tormon and the others will come by, and I'll miss them!

The thought alarmed him so much that he set off at a run, back in the direction he thought he had come. But either his wanderings had confused him, or his haste had led him astray, because soon he realised that he was out of sight of the cavern walls, and hopelessly lost, with no idea how to locate, in the midst of all this immensity with its bewildering array of structures and lights, the one small aperture that would lead him out.

He began to panic, running on and on through the maze of glowing forms that covered the cavern floor, searching desperately for the way out. If he kept on going straight, surely he must come to the cavern walls sooner or later. Then he'd only need to work his way round and eventually he would come to the exit, no matter how long it took. But it was impossible to keep in a straight line, and to his dismay, it soon became clear that he must have been running in circles. He charged out from between two rows of the weird structures, into an area that was quite obviously the very centre of the cavern.

Scall doubled over, gasping for breath and clutching at the stitch in his side. He felt like bursting into tears. Maybe the useless blacksmith's apprentice wasn't so far away after all. He had messed up again, but this time there was no-one to help him in his plight. But finding himself so badly astray was the jolt he needed to calm him. He took deep breaths, and felt the racing panic beginning to subside.

At least I know where I am now. Surely from here I should be able to make my way back to the edge, and find my way out from there.

While he got his breath back, he looked curiously around him. In the centre of the cavern there was a dip, with a bright, mirrored surface like a large, smooth silver bowl set into the cavern floor. Spaced at equal distances around the rim were six great beams of light, each thicker than Scall's body, that shone up into the air from openings in the ground. Each of them was angled gently towards the centre, so that eventually they must meet somewhere in the air, impossibly high above his head. The lights were the same pure colours that Scall had been seeing throughout this weird journey: red, yellow, white, green, blue, and deepest violet like the sky at dusk. The colours changed frequently in a regular pattern, as though each vivid hue was moving round the circle in turn, so that the effect was one of sweeping waves of colour that travelled endlessly round the circle. It looked to Scall like some kind of vast edifice: a gigantic, spinning tower formed completely from rays of light that soared into the air and vanished high above, through an aperture in the cavern roof.

Scall followed it up with his eyes until he felt dizzy. Hastily he looked down again into the circle, and noticed for the first time that in the centre, at the bottom of the bowl that formed the light-tower's base, was a structure that looked like an enormous bubble. Its translucent walls were covered in streaks and swirls of shining rainbow colours that were constantly in motion, obscuring then revealing vague, tantalising glimpses of the interior. It was, Scall estimated, easily big enough for three or four people to climb inside – if such a thing were possible.

I wonder if it is?

The thought was in his mind before he could stop it.

No! You don't want to have anything to do with that. Just turn around and go back to the edge, as you planned, and forget all about it.

But he had come so far, almost to the very heart of this mysterious cavern, that it seemed a pity not to investigate the very centre, now that he was here. Surely it couldn't hurt to have one tiny peep at that strange bubble? He sighed. Part of him was getting all too carried away, allowing him to imagine himself as a bold adventurer. 'It'll all end in tears,' he told himself, quoting Viora, his mother, but he found himself creeping forward, none the less, as though an invisible thread was reeling him in towards the mysterious structure in the centre of the dip.

Scall's first concern was getting into the silver circle itself. The rays of coloured light were well spaced apart, but would it harm him to pass between them? He found a space equidistant between two of the beams and looked around for something to throw. In the end he settled for his belt. Unbuckling it hastily, before he changed his mind, he threw it, with a flick of his wrist, between the two pillars of light, turning in the same instant to run and dive for cover. After a moment, when there was no explosion, and indeed no sign of anything untoward happening at all, he picked himself up, feeling highly embarrassed, and glad that there had been no-one around to see him. Well, it seemed to be safe enough. He took a deep breath and marched determinedly between the two light rays, and down the shallow slope into the bottom of the featureless bowl, sliding a little on the glassy silver surface. Picking up his belt from where it had fallen, he buckled it back round his waist, then crept up to the gleaming bubble.

As he made his cautious approach, the colours swirled even faster, the rainbow hues forming strange, unfathomable patterns on the curving surface. Scall stretched out a hand, then paused. What would happen if he touched this thing? What would it feel like? Would it burst, like an ordinary bubble? Would it hurt him somehow?

Be reasonable. Nothing in this place has hurt you yet, has it?

That doesn't mean it can't start now.

Nevertheless, greatly daring, he reached out again, and touched the wall of the glimmering sphere. There was an odd, cool tingling sensation in his arm as his hand penetrated the surface – and disappeared as though it had been cut right off. With an oath, Scall sprang backwards. His feet slipped on the smooth surface of the silver bowl, and he ended up flat on his back.

Oh, for goodness' sake!

He sat up, hardly daring to look at his arm, but it felt all right, and didn't hurt.

Just look at the bloody thing, and get it over with!

On close examination, the limb appeared to be perfectly normal, unchanged and unscathed in any way. Weak with relief, he scrambled to his feet and went back to scrutinise the bubble, wondering whether his interference had affected it in any way. The colours were more intense where he'd inserted his arm, radiating away from the place in a starburst pattern that focussed on his point of entry.

Point of entry? Could this be the way to get inside? Just walk straight through the wall? Could it really be that simple? The notion made as much sense as anything else did in this weird place. Without giving himself any time to chicken out, he closed his eyes, took a deep breath, and stepped right through the thin wall of the glistening orb.

Scall opened his eyes.

Great Myrial, what have I done?

The bubble had vanished. He must have burst it, when he came blundering through – but just what had he wrecked? He was sure that, like everything else in this place, it had been here for a special reason. How much harm had he done? What would be the consequences of his rash act? He glanced furtively behind him, imagining that some mysterious inhabitant of this place might leap out and punish him, but the cavern remained as lonely and deserted as before. After a little while, his curiosity got the better of his guilt and he turned his eyes back to the centre, to see what the now-vanished bubble had concealed.

In the very centre of the silver bowl was a slender pillar that looked as though it was made from the same material. It came up more or less to Scall's waist. Lying in its flat top were two items: what looked like a thin, silver mirror about a foot across with a narrow band of gold around the edge; and a small silver sphere about the size of a walnut. Curious, he picked it up, cradling it in the palm of his hand – and almost dropped it as it suddenly began to glow. Above the device, hovering in the air over his outstretched hand, a large, solid-looking image formed: a slowly revolving ball, coloured in irregular shapes of green, blue, brown and gold. It was veined all over its surface with a peculiar network of shining, blue-white lines. Scall didn't know what the image was supposed to represent, but it was very pretty. It vanished as soon as he closed his fingers over the silver sphere, and when he opened his hand again, a new picture appeared in the air. With a start, he recognised his own city of Tiarond, nestled between the arms of the mountain, with its plateau, the muddy expanse over which he'd ridden only last night, spreading beyond to end in the steep cliff with the river making its waterfall over the edge.

Scall gasped at the realism of the picture, which was viewed from above, as though he were an eagle flying over the tiny city, far below. In his surprise, he accidentally closed his fingers once again, and a new image appeared: a broad, blue expanse, studded with irregular shapes of brown and green. Remembering childhood tales of voyagers who had explored Callisiora's southern coastline, he guessed that he was looking at the ocean, with islands scattered here and there. Again, he closed his hand over the sphere, and the image disappeared.

'Great Myrial,' Scall breathed. He dropped the fascinating thing into his pocket, for further investigation later, and turned his attention to the other item on the plinth, the one that resembled a silver mirror. This time, he picked up the object with more caution, not knowing what to expect. Unlike the little sphere, that lit up in his hand, the surface of this new device seemed to darken when he picked it up, becoming featureless and black, and useless as a mirror. As he watched, strange lines of bright, strongly coloured light appeared, forming patterns that appeared at the bottom and moved slowly up the face of the object to vanish at the top. Scall had a feeling that it might be writing, though it was like no writing he had ever seen.

As if you would know.

When he was younger, his mother, ever ambitious, had had the local scribe teach him his letters, but he had never progressed much further than that. Unable to make head or tail of what he was seeing, he put the mirror-thing down. Its surface reverted to blank silver once more.

Oh, well. These two weird objects, the mirror-thing and the little silver nutshell, were the only things Scall had discovered that he could carry away with him from this place. At least they would bear out his improbable story, and maybe he could find some use for them in time. He unslung the compact, lightweight soldiers' backpack that he had taken from the guardhouse, and reached for the mirror. As soon as he touched it the surface darkened again, as the coloured patterns began to form. 'Oh, stop that!' he muttered, and dropped it into the pack, fastening it tightly inside. It was just the same as everything else in this peculiar cavern: beautiful but incomprehensible and, as far as Scall could see, completely useless. Feeling let down and faintly disappointed, he turned to leave. He'd had enough of this place. If he could get past the floods he was going back to the world he knew. And not before time.

He scrambled up the slippery sides of the bowl, rushing at the slope and using his momentum to take him up. When he had reached the top, and the level ground of the cavern floor, he glanced back for one last time – and let out his breath in a low whistle. The bubble had reappeared. It was right there, back in place, just as it had been before. Scall stared at it in amazement, as the truth slowly dawned on him. It must have been there all the time, yet while he had been inside it, he had not been able to see it. It was only visible from the outside, where it concealed the very items that he had so carelessly pilfered. For a moment he felt his face go warm with guilt, then he scowled. 'Well, sod it. I'm not putting them back now. There's no-one here in any case.' Turning his back on the circle, he marched determinedly away.

By the time Scall had, by trial and error and a good deal of hunting, managed to find the exit passage, he was miserable and exhausted. In a weary daze he stumbled along the tube-like tunnel, but when he reached the point where the ladder went down into the normal route, he could go no further. Unslinging his pack from his shoulders, he used it as a pillow and curled up on the warm, spongy floor of the passageway. As he drifted into oblivion he was flooded by an obscure feeling of relief that, for a while at least, he could forget his troubles in sleep.

Back in the beleaguered city of Tiarond, Kaita wished she could escape her troubles so easily. Sleep, however, was a luxury that she could not afford. There was just too much to be done. Among the fortunate townsfolk who had found sanctuary in the Basilica of Myrial, she had been horrified to discover that she was the most senior of the surviving physicians. Such responsibility was a burden she could well have done without. Since the horrific death of her friend Evelinden, two nights past, she had found it difficult enough to keep herself going from one hour to the next, without having to worry about a multitude of shocked, stricken, injured strangers, though their grief was as her grief, and their loss was similar to her own.

Again and again the memories overwhelmed her. Before dawn yesterday morning she had been brought to the Hall of Healing to identify the rags of clothing and remaining pieces of Evvie's hideously mangled body, which had been discovered in the Precincts by a white-faced Godsword guard. Afterwards, crushed by grief and horror beyond bearing, she had accepted her colleagues' offer of a bed, rather than return to the lonely, empty home that she had shared with her companion. Willingly, she had swallowed a bitter sleeping draught. As a physician, she knew her friend had not died easily, and the thought of Evvie's agony and terror was beyond all bearing. She would have done anything to escape the pain of mind and spirit; to obliterate, for as long as possible, the images of Evvie's gruesome remains. Anything to put off the future, if only for a little while.

They had awakened her in time to attend the sacrifice. Under normal circumstances, she would have been furious to find that even the poor patients from the Hall of Healing were to be dragged outside in the damp and cold for an empty, pointless ritual – as if burning that poor useless fool of a Hierarch was going to make the slightest difference to the plight of Callisiora! The irony that Zavahl was the chief proponent of the religion that was killing him was not lost on her. Kaita had stopped believing in Myrial long ago, but even if she had not, the ghastly fate of Evelinden, a woman who had done nothing but good all her life, would have destroyed her faith forever. Uncharacteristically, however, she kept her opinions to herself. Still stunned by her loss, she had meekly donned her white healer's mantle and followed the others outside without a murmur.

She had her colleagues to thank for her survival. Distancing herself from the whole fiasco, she had simply gone where she was taken, and they had kindly stationed her in the shelter of the Basilica wall, to one side of the sacrificial pyre. Because her position gave her such a poor view of the proceedings – no loss as far as Kaita was concerned – there were few people where she stood. Sunk deep in her own misery, and still hazy with the after-effects of the sleeping drug, she had barely registered all the commotion when the Hierarch had been stolen away, and when death had come hurtling down out of the skies, the Godsword soldier who stood beside her had saved her life by seizing her arm and almost hurling her through the Basilica doors.

Since then, Kaita had not been given a moment in which to worry about her own griefs and troubles. The wounded had come thick and fast, along with those who, though suffering no physical injuries, had undergone experiences of such dread and terror that their minds would bear the scars for the remainder of their lives.

The Healer was hampered in her work by the lack of medical equipment – antiseptics for wounds, pain-killing medications, sleeping draughts and even such basic items as bandages and the wherewithal for stitching wounds – all were in desperately short supply. Vestments, bed linen and even curtains from the adjoining priests' quarters were torn up to make bandages, but the other items were much more difficult to improvise, though healers carried a basic medical kit with them at all times in a sturdy leather bag which either slung over a shoulder or clipped to a belt. Out of sheer habit, Kaita had picked hers up when she had left the Hall of Healing to attend the sacrifice, and even though the contents were woefully inadequate given the sheer numbers of wounded, she was glad that such an ingrained habit had stood her in good stead.

Coupled with the scarcity of supplies was the lack of expert help. To Kaita's horror only three physicians, all less experienced than herself, and two students remained from the Hall of Healing. Eventually she managed to round up a motley assortment of others who ministered, in a less official capacity, to the poor of the town: midwives who had picked up a knowledge of basic medicine and crude surgery along the way; apothecaries and herbalists with an astonishingly extensive pharmacopoeia that could be derived from among the basic supplies in the tithe caves; and lastly, those ordinary men and women with the gift of knowing how to care for others. Every neighbourhood had one – the person to whom everyone turned in times of crisis, illness or death. Kaita had seen them time and time again and admired their empathy, their reassuring capability and their practical good sense, as they watched over sickbeds with tireless concern, laid out the dead for their final journey, and comforted worried or grieving families.

Though she knew better than to underestimate the value of the others' contribution, the brunt of the work still fell on her shoulders. When the less experienced physicians were in doubt, or met with a patient with injuries beyond their experience, it was to Kaita that they came, and she found herself pulled hither and thither, with so many conflicting demands made on her that she scarcely knew where to turn. All the time she was forced into making choices: treating one person so that they might live invariably meant neglecting another who would very probably die as a result. As the hours passed, a small but damning row of corpses lay covered at the back of the Temple, and with her vision distorted by grief and exhaustion, the Healer saw each one as a testament to her failure. It was as well that there was no time for her thoughts to stray too far in that direction.

While the healers had laboured on through the hours of darkness and the day that followed, many others, directed by the new Hierarch and Commander Galveron, were also hard at work to make the refugees more comfortable. As she worked, Kaita noticed, at the edge of her attention, that people were busy all around her, doing their own part.

The heavy bowl of water that she was carrying slopped over Kaita's hands as she tried to pick her way through the crowds of folk encamped all over the floor, heading for the guardroom at the rear of the building, where an emergency water supply, drawn from the Temple's own water system, had been set up. The journey seemed to grow longer and more fraught with obstacles every time she made it, and she could swear that this wretched bowl grew heavier every time.

'Look out!' The warning came too late. The Healer collided head-on with a hurrying tall figure in a Godsword uniform, and cold, bloodstained water went over them both in a drenching cascade. The priceless gold bowl with intricate chasing, part of the Temple paraphernalia that had been pressed into useful service went clattering to the floor, masking the startled oaths that came from both partners in the collision. The taller, heavier man knocked Kaita off her feet, and she cried out as her shoulder banged against the door frame. She would have gone down entirely, but her protagonist caught her, steadied her, and set her back on her feet. He turned out to be none other than Commander Galveron.

'Why don't you watch where you're going?'

'Why, you great, lumbering oaf . . .'

They spoke simultaneously, in the heat of the moment, and bit off their hasty words at the same time, both of them having the sense to realise that they were frustrated, overextended, and overtired.

'I'm sorry.'

'It was my fault.'

Again, the words came out at exactly the same time. The tall man in the Godsword uniform gave her a tired smile and picked up her bowl for her. 'Come into the guardroom and dry out by the fire, Healer Kaita. You're half-drowned.'

'But I have to get back. There's so much to do.'

Galveron's expression hardened. 'It can wait a few minutes.' It was an order. 'Apart from the Godsword Citadel, the Basilica is the coldest, draughtiest building I know. You're the most experienced healer we have left. It won't do anybody any good if *you* get sick on us.' Taking her arm, he steered her firmly inside and planted her next to the fireplace, peering intently into her face as he did so. 'When did you last have any rest. Or something to eat?'

Kaita returned his close scrutiny in kind, noting his pallor, the bluish shadows beneath his eyes and at the corners of his mouth, the weary slump of his broad shoulders, and the bloody, untended lacerations on his hands and face, now scabbing over with dirt and Myrial knew what else still inside the wounds. The worst part of it was, she knew that she must look just as ghastly herself. She planted her hands on her hips, and returned his stern look with a steely one of her own. 'And when did you?' she countered.

'Ah, you have me there.' His attempt at a light-hearted tone ended in a weary sigh, and in a flash of clear-headed honesty, Kaita realised that he was right, with regard to both of them. Neither of them would be able to function efficiently if they didn't remember to take a little more care of themselves. Instinctively the Healer in her rose up to take charge. 'I'll take a break if you will,' she bargained.

Galveron began to protest, just as she had expected. She tilted her head to one side and fixed him with the basilisk stare that usually quelled the most recalcitrant of patients. After a moment, the Godsword's blustering ran down into silence. He shrugged, and gave her a sheepish grin. 'Very well, Commander Kaita. You win. We'll *both* rest – and eat something.'

'And while I have you here, I'll also treat those wounds of yours,' Kaita told him firmly.

'Not fair. You're supposed to be resting.'

'Unless you really *want* to die of blood poisoning, of course.' That shut him up, just as she had known it would. Or so she thought.

'I bet you say that to all the boys.'

'Just go and make yourself useful, and fetch me some water.' Kaita thrust her bowl into his hands. As he crossed the room, she watched him with a smile – and suddenly became aware that this was the first time she had smiled since they had brought her word of Evvie's death. *Thank you, Commander*, she thought. *You make a damn good leader*. She was glad that there was a sensible man in charge. It would make her own work so much easier.

Eleven

A vulnerable place

'Thank providence, she's finally asleep.' Rochalla took one last look at Annas, who was curled up in her nest of blankets and pillows like a forest creature in its den. Her round little face was flushed, and streaked with grime and damp smears that gleamed faintly in the lamplight, from the prolonged session of tears and tantrums when her companions would not let her go to look for her father in the flooded area outside the guardhouse. Annas was too young to understand about the deadly power of such a volume of water, or to consider the dangers of floating debris, treacherous footing, unpredictable freak currents and the proximity of the cliff edge. She only saw that the water, about thigh-deep on an adult, was shallow enough to be waded through. 'And I'm a good swimmer,' she had assured Rochalla, with an earnestness that had almost broken the older girl's heart.

It had taken an age to soothe the frantic child, and even so, Rochalla knew she hadn't really succeeded. Eventually, Annas had argued, yelled and wept herself into a state of exhaustion, and had fallen asleep. 'No doubt she's recouping her strength so that she can start again tomorrow,' Rochalla told herself wearily. 'And how am I going to cope with her then?'

She didn't realise that she had spoken aloud until Presvel replied. 'Dropping the little horror off the edge of the cliff is always an option,' he muttered with feeling. 'My poor damned ears are still ringing.'

Rochalla, standing balanced precariously on one of the lower beds, so that she could check on Annas asleep in the upper bunk, glared down at the man who was perched cross-legged like a tailor on the barrackroom table. She opened her mouth for a blistering retort, then thought better of it.

Presvel is grieving too. He and Lady Seriema have been close for many years, and her loss is affecting him far more than he's willing to admit, even to himself.

'You know,' she said carefully, 'Annas is going to need all the kindness and understanding we can give her, in the days to come. I don't see how Tormon could have possibly survived that flood.'

'And neither could Seriema. That's what you're saying, isn't it? From here, we're on our own.'

With one last look at the child, Rochalla let go of the edge of the upper bunk, and dropped down into a foot and a half of dirty water. 'Ugh!' The guardhouse, with its high veranda, had been built slightly above the level of the surrounding plain, but its position had not been high enough to spare them completely. They had spent a frantic half hour when the floods struck, scrambling to gather together such basic necessities as food, drinking water, dry clothing and blankets, lamp oil, fodder for the horses and – as a lucky afterthought – some dry kindling and firewood. They had stored these essentials in the upper bunks, hurrying to complete the task, racing the water which had crept beneath the barrack-room door and was rising inexorably higher with every passing minute.

Now darkness had fallen, and the level of the flood was beginning to drop. In the flickering lamplight, Rochalla could see a filthy tide mark, two or three inches above the murky water that lapped against the walls. 'At least it's going down now.' She was glad of an excuse to change the subject. 'Maybe in a few hours' time we'll be able to light a fire, and start drying things out a little.' She climbed up on the long table beside Seriema's assistant, leaning over the edge to wring out her sodden skirt.

Presvel looked up with eyes dull and sunken with despair and weariness. Every line of his hunched form spoke of defeat. 'And then what?' he snapped. 'When the floods go down, just what do we do next? Where do we go, and how? Because if you think that either of us knows enough about horsemanship to control those hulking great monsters in the stable next door, you're sadly mistaken. We've never been far beyond the city, we don't know—'

'Myrial's teeth and toenails!' Rochalla was so angry that only the presence of the sleeping child stopped her from screaming at him. Instead, the words came out in a hissing whisper. 'Why in perdition are you asking *me*? Are you expecting me – a girl only half your age – to take care of you, as well as Annas?' She regretted the words as soon as they were out of her mouth, but it was too late to take them back.

Presvel flinched as though she had struck him, and his defeated pose sagged a little further. 'I suppose I asked for that,' he said quietly. 'When I brought you to Seriema's house I wanted to spare you any more toil and hardship. I had such plans to take care of you. How could I have guessed what was going to happen? You put me to shame, Rochalla. I keep forgetting you're so young, because you always seem so capable.' He sighed. 'I always led such a soft, sheltered life, I see that now. You've already been through so much more than I have, and the plain truth is, you're far better equipped to survive this disaster than I am.'

'But that doesn't excuse you from trying,' Rochalla interrupted. She accepted that there was truth in what he was saying, but was still impatient with his spineless attitude of defeat. 'I had a pretty soft life too, until my parents died. After that it was learn or go under. I chose to learn, and so must you. I was the eldest in my family. I had to take care of the younger ones because there was no-one else to do the job. You're the oldest here, Presvel, though admittedly we're in a worse mess now than I ever was, back in the city. But in a way, you're also better off than I was. At least you have me to help you, and I can take care of myself. I'm not about to go belly-up now, even though things look so black, and I'm not letting you do it, either. Back in the city, I did whatever I had to in order to survive. Now you'll have to learn to do the same. You can, you know. It's amazing what a person is capable of, when they find themselves in a corner.'

Presvel raised his eyes to her with a grateful smile. 'Rochalla, you're incredible. Do you know that?' He put an arm around her shoulders and pulled her close. She wanted to stiffen, wanted to pull away, wanted to shout, 'You promised you wouldn't make me do this any more!' But the survivor in her knew all too well that this was no time to bring any kind of discord between them. The old, practical Rochalla reminded her that right now, and for the foreseeable future, they only had each other. Besides, what could it hurt? He could hardly take things too far with Annas in the same room, and liable to wake at any moment.

All of this went through Rochalla's mind in a single flash of indecision – then despite all the promises she had made to herself about starting a new and different life, she let herself relax into his embrace. As she did so, her own words came back into her mind like a mocking echo.

It's amazing what a person is capable of, when they find themselves in a corner.

In the Basilica, Kaita was thinking very much the same thing. It had seemed to take forever, but as the long hours passed, the healer had gradually succeeded in establishing some order among the masses of injured Tiarondians. The quarters of the Priesthood, which occupied the lower levels of the Temple beneath the Hierarch's lofty suite of rooms, were pressed into service for those most seriously injured. The skilled physicians and students laboured here. One of the smaller chapels had been put aside for those whose hurts were more superficial, who were cared for by their families and by the lesser healers of the town – apart from a select group of apothecaries and herbalists who had been sent by Kaita to ransack the tithe caves for whatever they could find. Their sole task was to produce whatever simple medications they could concoct from the materials at hand. The upper guardroom had been commandeered to give them their own clean, private space in which to work, away from the crowds and commotion in the Temple below. Having no idea that two women and a firedrake had spent the previous night there, they were puzzled by the fresh ashes in the fireplace and the gaping hole where the door had once stood, but they were so pressed by the growing needs of the injured that they had little time for speculation as to the cause.

Through the day, the Healer had caught glimpses of Gilarra scurrying about from task to task, and several of the other surviving artisans and craftsmen from the Precincts, all hard at work arranging for food, drink, and lighting, grappling with the difficult and unpleasant problems of waste disposal, and improvising screens, hangings and pallets to make the vast, echoing space of the Temple a little more comfortable, safe and secure for the refugees who sheltered within. Agella, the practical, inventive Smithmaster, seemed to be needed in at least as many places as Kaita herself, and Galveron's reassuring presence seemed to be everywhere at once, helping, settling disputes and smoothing difficulties that only moments before had seemed insurmountable.

At last, when night had fallen once more, the Hierarch called a meeting of her chief helpers, to assess the progress made. When she received her summons, Kaita was tending to the broken arm of a bruised and battered child who had stumbled in the crowd's panic-stricken stampede towards safety, and who had come very close to being trampled. Her first sensation was one of irritation. 'I don't have time for that nonsense,' she told Smithmaster Agella, who had brought her the message. 'Tell the Hierarch I'm much too busy.'

The tall, sturdy woman pushed back her shock of red hair and shrugged. 'You and me both. I'm trying to organise a clean water supply and waste disposal for those helpless sheep down there, before you physicians have an epidemic on your hands on top of everything else. But the Hierarch feels that we'll all be the better for taking an hour or so out from our tasks to assess how we're all managing, and to get an idea of the bigger picture.' She sighed. 'I dare say she's right. It makes sense to co-ordinate our efforts instead of running around at cross-purposes like a bunch of chickens. I'm only afraid that if I stop now, I'll never be able to get myself started again.'

Alerted by a rough catch in the other woman's voice, Kaita took her attention away from the patient she was attending and looked properly at the Smith. Agella's face was pale and haggard with weariness, but beyond that, the physician saw the grief that shadowed her expression, and remembered that almost everyone in the Basilica had lost someone dear to them. She took a deep breath and rubbed her eyes, trying to dispel the ache of fatigue that was beginning to overshadow and blur her thinking. When she replied, her voice was much more gentle. 'All right, I'll come with you now. The sooner we have this meeting, the sooner we can get back to our real work.'

When Kaita and Agella arrived in the Hierarch's quarters, somewhat out of breath from having dragged their weary bones up the endless stairs, the Physician saw that she was not alone in her concern. Most of the dozen or so faces around the great council table betrayed the same hollow-eyed exhaustion and, judging from their scowls and fidgets, none of them wanted to be there. Suddenly, Kaita began to feel sorry for the new Hierarch. *It's hard enough, just taking responsibility for the sick and injured,* she thought. *What must it be like to be ultimately in charge? How can she bear such a burden?*

In front of each place round the table was a cup of the strong black soldiers' tea that was also much favoured by healers who kept long, late hours with the sick. Gratefully, Kaita wrapped her stiff, cold fingers around the hot mug and took a cautious sip of the scalding liquid that had been sweetened with a spoonful of honey. She watched as everyone sorted themselves and took a seat around the table, placing themselves more or less at random, except that Commander Galveron sat at the Hierarch's right hand.

As soon as everyone was settled, Gilarra spoke. 'Firstly, thank you all for coming. I appreciate that this meeting has dragged you away from urgent tasks, but at this point it's important that we gather together all our information and expertise, so that we can work as efficiently and effectively as possible.' She looked gravely around at them all. 'Make no mistake. Those of us sitting around this table hold the future of the Tiarondian survivors in our hands.'

Kaita looked from one face to another as the Hierarch introduced each of her helpers. Beside Commander Galveron was a blunt-faced man of middle years, with blue eyes and sandy hair turning grey. This was Sergeant Ewald of the Godswords. On Gilarra's left sat Custodian Maravis, keeper of the priesthood's extensive library, an elegant woman with silver hair and a face of sweet, serene beauty that belied her advancing years. Beside her was a tall, stick-thin woman with a sour expression and a tight little mouth beneath a mass of grey hair piled on top of her head. Kaita's heart sank to find her at the meeting, for this was Bergamia, self-elected spokeswoman for Tiarond's apothecaries and herbalists. Though admittedly she was very skilled, she held an unfortunate, unshakeable conviction that she knew just as much, if not more, than any physician. The Healer had crossed swords with her on several occasions during the day and the thought of another tussle with this stubborn, self-important old harridan filled her with dismay.

The Healer already knew Smithmaster Agella, with her sturdy build and short-cropped hair of flaming red, and Stablemaster Fergist, tall and bony with an iron-grey thatch. The big, fat, bald man with one arm was Flint, the Godsword Quartermaster, and keeping a wary distance from him, were two plump little men of about Kaita's age, with golden curls clipped short like fleece and identical features. These inseparable twins, Telimon and Quiller, were the Head Cooks at the Godsword Citadel. When Kaita and Agella had entered, the general discussion around the table had concerned food, and Gilarra nodded to Flint to finish what he had been saying.

The Godsword Quartermaster spoke of the stocks of provisions in the storage caves, and the need for careful inventories and rationing. He had been invalided out of active soldiering when he'd lost his arm in a skirmish with the Eastern Reivers. Not wanting to leave the Godswords, he had taken the post of Assistant

Quartermaster, and all the old passion he had reserved for the warrior's life, he had poured into the organisation of the Citadel's storerooms and supplies. After a remarkably short time he had replaced his lazy superior, seemingly gaining weight with his promotion until he had metamorphosed into the big, bald, hefty Quartermaster of today. Though his manner was genial, his mind was precise, and he had no use for inefficiency or disorder of any kind. It seemed to Kaita that he was looking on this catastrophe as a personal affront as he discussed with Telimon and Quiller the provision of communal meals for the refugees, and a place in which to cook and eat them.

Luckily, the Temple had its own water supply. Near the bottom of the stairs that led up to the Hierarch's quarters, another staircase went downwards, beneath and behind the Temple. It led to an underground lake, the wellspring for the entire city's water supply. From there, the water ran down through an intricate network of pipes, and though only the richest folk in the upper levels of the city had their own private supplies piped into their houses, there were pumps on every street corner, so not even the poorest folk had very far to go for fresh water, and any excess just drained away into the river at the bottom of the slope. Now the lake would be used to provide fresh water for the refugees. Waste was another problem, though there were caves beyond the great lake cavern containing deep crevices and potholes, down which the ordure could be dumped, and washed away.

Flint spread his hands. 'It's not ideal, but it's the best solution we've come up with for the present,' he said. 'After all, we can't have them crapping all over the Temple.'

Kaita had no argument with that. The situation looked like continuing indefinitely, and hard as she tried to concentrate, she found that her tired mind kept straying. The talk was mostly between Flint, Telimon and Quiller, and concerned the provision of a communal kitchen down near the lake, and the organisation of teams of volunteer cooks. She let the discussion slide over her, until an interruption from Galveron brought her back once more.

'If you'll excuse me,' he interrupted, 'I believe we can leave the details of provisioning in your capable hands. If the Hierarch will permit, we must turn instead to matters of defence.'

As Gilarra nodded to him to continue, Commander Galveron continued with an assessment of their current position. 'The good news is that we occupy a very defensible place,' he said. 'It's as though the folk who built the Basilica deliberately constructed it as a refuge. Because we're set into the cliff, the Temple has only one external wall, and those few high windows are all too narrow to admit an invader – even one as spindly as those flying freaks. They are, however, ideal for my men to shoot through, and I have archers stationed all along the catwalks beside them.' He gave a tired grin. 'If the arrows hold out, maybe we can teach the enemy to avoid this area.'

'So we should be safe – at least for the time being,' Gilarra said.

Galveron's smile faded. 'The Basilica itself is secure, but there is one vulnerable place in our defences that troubles me.'

The Hierarch leaned forward in her chair. 'And that is?'

'You're not going to like this,' he warned her. 'We're extremely fortunate in that the Basilica is so old. I imagine they made the windows so small in those days, because there was no glass to fill the gaps, but it works to our advantage now. The only other chambers with external windows were constructed more recently, above the Temple itself: the Priests' quarters on the level beneath this, and here in the Hierarch's suite, on the upper floor. Those openings are certainly large enough to admit those creatures. With your permission, Hierarch, now that it's dark once more, I want to position warriors and archers up here and on the floor below. It does no harm to err on the safe side.'

'What? In my private quarters?'

'To protect you and your family, Lady Hierarch,' Galveron told her patiently.

Gilarra rubbed her tired eyes. 'Of course. You're right, Galveron. You must do as you think best.'

'I haven't finished. Archers or no, this area is open to attack, and that puts us all in danger. I feel that the risk is unacceptable and unnecessary. We ought to abandon these two upper floors and pull down the ceiling to block the stairwell . . .'

'*What?*' The Hierarch leapt to her feet. 'You can't start pulling the Basilica of Myrial to pieces! I have a duty to conserve this place for future generations.'

Galveron shrugged. 'May I remind you, Lady, that if those monstrosities break through into the Temple itself, it's unlikely that there'll be any future generations. Not from Tiarond, at any rate, and Myrial only knows what will become of the rest of Callisiora if they gain a foothold and start to breed.'

Gilarra bit her lip. 'But surely, if you put warriors in this room, that will be sufficient defence.'

'You'd be staking your life – and the lives of everyone in the Basilica – on that assumption. Why take the chance? It's only lifeless stone, when all is said and done. When this crisis is over, there'll be plenty of time to rebuild.'

'When this is all over, we'll have years' worth of rebuilding in every respect,' Fergist the Stablemaster put in quietly. Kaita realised that he was thinking not only of the Precincts, and the streets and houses of the town, but also of his carefully nurtured studs and bloodlines, bred over generations and now, presumably, gone.

And what of ourselves? she thought. *All those sundered families, those broken hearts and shattered lives; all the widows, widowers and orphans left alone. All those hopes and dreams and future plans, blown away like leaves in the wind. So much talent and potential, so much knowledge and skill – all gone. It will take a long time to put our city to rights, but how much longer it will take to repair the fabric of our society! Will we ever truly recover from this blow?*

In that moment her thoughts turned to Evelinden, and Kaita was smitten by a grief so profound that she could feel the pain right through her body, deep within her bones. Tears pricked behind her eyes, and she wiped at them hastily, pretending that she was simply rubbing her tired eyes, and hoping that no-one would notice.

A loud crash jolted her out of her thoughts. An icy wind blew through the chamber, blowing out the lamps and plunging the room into darkness. For a moment, all was confusion, a nightmare filled with shadows and running figures, backlit by the flickering flames in the fireplace. There were screeches as chairs were scraped back, loud clatters as they overturned. People were colliding, tripping, falling. There were screams and curses, and the ringing scrape of steel as a sword was drawn. Kaita saw Sergeant Ewald, who had been sitting closest to the window, launch himself at the attackers.

'Ewald, wait!' The Commander's warning came too late. Three of the winged fiends were already in the room, and another was just climbing through the window. The foremost attackers converged on the Sergeant, and with a howl of agony, he went down.

In the corner, someone was screaming, loud and shrill. *That stupid Bergamia. Useless cow,* Kaita thought. Automatically, she had started towards the injured Ewald, her healer's instincts overriding her sense of danger, but with a vicious hiss, a winged shape loomed up in front of her, its clawed fingers snatching at her eyes. Almost too late, she leapt back, and the talons scored lightly down her cheek and tore into her robes at the shoulder, tangling in the loose fabric. Kaita looked up into its ghastly face, and felt her blood congeal. The warped features were twisted with rage. Fangs gleamed white in a lipless, bloodstained mouth as the creature snarled. Then above the din, cutting through the panic and confusion, came Galveron's voice, loud and strong. 'Flint, Agella, Fergist! To me! You others, *get out!* Kaita, run. Fetch help. *Move*!'

The voice broke the spell of frozen horror, and the creature, startled, hesitated for one split second. The instant of doubt was just enough to free her. Tearing herself loose from the clutching talons, Kaita ran.

Pushing past Telimon or Quiller, she wasn't sure which, Agella barged her way towards Galveron. Though there had seemed to be little need in the Basilica, she had been wearing a sword ever since her narrow escape from death on the Temple steps, and she had persuaded Fergist to do the same. Somehow, the proximity of cold steel had proved to be far more reassuring than the thick stone walls of the building that sheltered her, and this attack proved that her gut feeling had been right. Quartermaster Flint, ex-soldier that he was, carried a weapon as a matter of course. As those with no skill at fighting cleared the room, the four defenders converged on the winged shapes, beating them back towards the window so that they were impeding the entry of their foul brethren outside.

One of the creatures screamed as Galveron's sword pierced it. It went down in a welter of thrashing limbs and flailing wings. A clumsy two-handed swing from Agella beheaded another of the abominations, and very nearly did the same for Flint, such was the momentum of her blade, wielded with the strength of pure panic.

'Watch out, missus,' roared the Quartermaster as he ducked. As he dropped he thrust his short sword up into the belly of another foe. The creature let out a dreadful shriek as blood sprayed and guts slithered down onto the floor. Flint was grinning as he came up, his teeth gleaming white in a crimson mask of blood. 'By gum, it's just like the old days.' He turned to help Fergist, who had not touched a weapon in years, and was being driven back by a red-eyed, leather-winged demon armed with vicious fangs and lethal talons. Flint's sword drove into its back, and rammed home with such force that the point grated against the narrow ribs. But unlike Fergist, not everyone had escaped the onslaught. One of the corpses on the floor was human. Blood matted the short-cropped fair curls. One of the twins, then: the Smithmaster had no idea which. The throat had been torn out, and a pool of sticky blood was spreading out from beneath the body.

As soon as one of the winged abominations fell, another clambered through the window to replace it. Agella, fighting beside Galveron as they tried to carve a way through to Sergeant Ewald, felt that they were making little progress at first, but when Flint came to their side, the three of them managed to hold the invading creatures at bay while Fergist darted in and pulled the fallen man out of the chamber. They heard his voice calling urgently from the landing. 'For Myrial's sake, hurry. They're in downstairs rooms, too. I can hear the fighting.'

'Retreat!' shouted Galveron. Moving with care to avoid tripping over the limp-winged corpses or slipping on the blood that slicked the floor, they backed towards the door – and not before time, Agella thought. Unused to fighting, she was tiring fast, for her technique tended to rely on brute force and a dollop of luck, rather than the skill that Galveron and even the one-armed Flint displayed. 'If I get out of here in one piece, I'll damn well learn to do this properly,' she muttered.

'You're doing fine,' said Galveron. 'Get ready to dash out. We're getting close. I'll slam the door behind us.'

It was in that instant, just as Agella thought they were going to get away with it, that they heard the Hierarch scream.

Twelve

Choices

When the winged predators attacked, the Hierarch had not obeyed Galveron's order, and fled with the others. Aukil was asleep in the adjacent bedchamber, with Bevron watching over him, and her first thought was not for her own safety, but for that of her lifemate and their child. The bedroom had no windows, so it would be safe from outside attack, but the only way out was the way that she had come: through the Council Chamber that swarmed with the winged monstrosities. Unless she was quick, Bevron and Aukil would be trapped.

Leaving Galveron and his fellow fighters to deal with the invaders, Gilarra, her heart beating wildly, slipped out of the other doorway, running down the passage and up the short flight of stairs to the bedchamber. She dared not call out, for fear of attracting the predators' attention, but she soon discovered that Bevron had already heard the commotion that was taking place in the other room. As she burst through the door a chair came smashing down scant inches from her head, and splintered against the wall.

'Gilarra!' Bevron sounded distraught. 'I didn't know it was you.'

'I should hope not.' There was no time for unnecessary talk. 'Where's Aukil? We're under attack. We've got to get you out of here.'

'Mummy?' The little boy came out from under the bed, dust-smeared and with his jerkin and trousers pulled on haphazardly over his nightshirt. His mother ran to pick him up, and he laughed. 'We're playing hide and seek,' he told her happily. 'Do you want to play too?'

'Not just now, lovey.' Gilarra held him close. 'We have to go.'

Dreading the horrors that might be waiting to greet them, they hurried back down the stairs and the corridor, with Bevron, armed with the fireplace poker, in the lead, and Gilarra following with their son in her arms. *It will be all right,* she kept telling herself. *Galveron will get us out.* But when they reached the doorway of the lower chamber, her lifemate gave a low cry of horror and stopped abruptly, so that she almost fell over him. Looking over his shoulder, she saw the big red-haired Smithmaster vanishing through the doorway with Galveron right on her heels. Everyone else had fled the Hierarch's quarters, which now seethed with the sinister winged shapes of the predators. Unable to stop herself in her panic, she screamed. Immediately, the narrow, bony heads turned in her direction, and gleaming red eyes fastened hungrily on this new and helpless prey.

Gilarra was paralysed with terror, trapped in a body that seemed disconnected from her brain. Bevron was tugging urgently at her arm, shouting at the top of his voice, but she seemed incapable of movement, as though her feet had been nailed to the floor. Aukil struggled in her tightening grasp, wailing in fear and pain.

Galveron swung round and she heard him curse. Yelling loudly to attract their attention, he launched himself at the winged invaders, just as Agella burst back into the room with a bloodcurdling yell, magnificent as an avenging goddess as she bore down, sword in hand, upon the enemy. The one-armed Flint, looking more capable but less enthusiastic, was right behind her. Beckoning to Agella to follow, he slipped between the Hierarch's family and their attackers, while Galveron seemed to be everywhere at once, his sword a silver blur as he clove a path through the hideous creatures, leaving carnage in his wake.

'Come on!' the Smithmaster yelled at Gilarra. 'Move your arse, you silly bitch!'

It was the verbal equivalent of a bucket of cold water, or a slap in the face. Suddenly able to move once more, the Hierarch, with Bevron still hanging on to her arm, scuttled around the edge of the room, staying close to the wall, trying to be inconspicuous and keeping as far away as possible from the enemy.

They almost made it. Only two of the foe remained, the others were either dead or had fled, frightened off by the fury of Galveron's attack. But just when Bevron had almost reached the door, one of the predators broke through the Commander's guard, raking its claws left and right in a lightning movement across his face, going for his eyes. Crying out, he doubled over, clutching at his face, his sword dropping from his hand. Both Agella and Flint were distracted by his plight, and before they could gather themselves, the foul creature had dodged past them, snatched the child from Gilarra's arms and bounded back towards the window, while its companion, with a blood-freezing snarl, converged on the wounded man.

'Help Galveron!' Agella shrieked at Flint. The other predator had reached the window before she could catch up with it, and was balanced precariously on the sill preparatory to launching itself out into the night, the howling child clasped tightly in its arms. If she used her sword and wounded or killed it, it could drop the boy or fall from its perch, killing both of them. Gilarra held her breath. The Smithmaster launched herself forward in a desperate dive, her hand closing on the ankle of her quarry, even as it tensed itself to spring aloft.

Yanked abruptly off balance, the creature fell backwards into the room, on top of Agella. With a shriek of fury it twisted violently and turned on her, casting the child away from it to free its deadly claws for use. Aukil's head hit the corner of the hearthstone with a crack that was clearly audible across the room, and Gilarra screamed. Bevron was already moving. Darting across the room, he sidestepped the struggling combatants on the floor and snatched up the still form of his son. As he dashed back, Gilarra saw that Aukil's face was very white, his head dropping limply over his father's arm. Was the boy alive or dead? For an instant, the room darkened around her and she felt that she must faint, but she took a deep breath, willing the giddiness to pass, and followed her lifemate and his precious burden out of the chamber.

Echoing up the stairwell came the sound of more fighting on the floor below. On the landing, the Stablemaster stood helplessly over the unmoving form of Sergeant Ewald. His expression was a mixture of relief and, on seeing the injured boy in Bevron's arms, dismay. 'Is he . . . ?'

Bevron shook his head. 'I think he's breathing, but we need to get help for him, and fast.'

Fergist nodded. 'That goes for the Sergeant, too. Lady, if you could carry your boy, then Bevron here can give me a hand to get Ewald downstairs.'

'Of course.' Quickly, Gilarra took her child. He felt so cold and heavy in her arms.

He'll be all right. He will. Dear Myrial, let Aukil be all right.

At that moment the others came bursting out of the chamber, with Flint leading a stumbling Galveron, whose hands were clamped tightly over his face. Blood leaked out between his fingers. Agella was right behind them, guarding their backs, brandishing a sword that dripped with gore. The Smithmaster slammed the door behind them and leant her back against it, wishing she could have a moment, just to catch her breath.

Some chance.

'Do you have a key?' she asked the Hierarch. 'It won't delay them long, but every minute helps.'

With difficulty, Gilarra shifted the heavy burden of her son to one arm, and fished in her pocket for the large ornate key. She handed it to Agella, who fitted it into the sturdy lock, turning it with a decisive click. The Smithmaster turned to Galveron. 'Can you see at all?' she asked him urgently. He shook his head. 'My eyes are full of blood.' He seemed dazed, and was trembling. *Shock,* Agella thought. 'I'll help you,' she told him, and taking his arm, led him down the stairs. Gilarra followed with the unmoving child in her arms, and Bevron and Fergist brought up the rear, carrying Ewald between them.

One flight down, there was pandemonium. There were several exits from the Priest quarters leading onto this landing, and it had proved impossible to defend them all. Winged figures had broken through in several places, and a cluster of Godsword soldiers, aided by civilians armed with whatever they had found to hand, were defending the top of the stairs, in a desperate attempt to prevent the invaders from gaining access to the crowded Basilica below. Agella's heart sank. The foul invaders were clustered at the top of the staircase in a seething knot, cutting her little group off from any assistance, and blocking their escape route completely.

The Smithmaster's thoughts were racing. *We're desperately short of fighters, and those that we have are hampered by our wounded. We're not going to battle our way out of this. So how in the world can we possibly get out of this?* Out of ideas, she found herself wishing instead that she were safely back in her forge, hammering out a sword blade that glowed white-hot from the fierce heart of the fire . . . And just like that, she had the answer.

She turned back to the others, who were clustering uncertainly behind her. 'When I say run,' she told them, 'you run – no matter what is happening around you. Don't hesitate, don't freeze, even you're terrified. You'll only get one chance at this, and if you hesitate even for an instant, you'll be dead. Galveron, you hang on to me, and I'll take you through. Now, are you ready?' Without waiting for an answer, she lifted the nearest lantern from its hook on the wall, and hurled it with all the strength of her brawny arm, right into the centre of the mass of predators.

The fragile lantern shattered and exploded into flame, spraying burning oil in every direction. Shrieking, the winged ones scattered, beating frantically at the fire that clung to their skin and flared in their stringy hair.

'Run!' Agella yelled at the top of her voice, and taking a deep breath, plunged into the middle of the fire, dragging Galveron after her, and praying that the others had the sense and nerve to follow. Flames leapt up around her, and the heat was terrific. She dared not breathe the scorching air. Blinded by smoke, she kept bumping into screaming predators, crazed with terror, who scuttled mindlessly here and there. The biggest risk from them, in that moment, was being clawed by mistake. Ignoring them, Agella ploughed right on through, and kept moving no matter what. Everything depended on getting through at speed. Had she done the right thing? Or had she killed them all?

Suddenly there was cooler air around her, and she could breathe again. Willing hands beat at her smoking clothes and the smouldering ends of her hair. They pulled her through the crowd of defenders and guided her stumbling steps to a safe place further down the broad stone staircase. Someone took Galveron from her, and led him away downstairs. The Smithmaster sank down gratefully on the edge of a step, ignoring all the commotion and activity behind her. The exposed skin on her hands and face was stinging, every muscle in her body was aching from the exertions of the fight upstairs, and she spluttered and wheezed as she gasped in lungfuls of blessed cool, fresh air. It had never felt so good to be alive.

In a moment, Gilarra appeared, her face black with smoke and her hair frizzled as Agella knew her own must be, though the Hierarch, with far longer hair, had fared much worse. She coughed rackingly, and sagged under the weight of her son, but clutched him tightly to her nevertheless, steadfastly resisting any attempts to take him from her. She faced Agella, her eyes alight with anger. 'Of all the stupid . . .' Then she seemed to collect herself. 'Stupid and brave. You saved us all. I never would have dared do what you did.'

Behind her Bevron and Fergist came staggering through the crowd, bearing the unconscious form of Ewald between them. They laid him down and straightened their backs gratefully. Bevron went straight to his wife, and they made their way downstairs to seek help for their son. Two Godsword soldiers took up the burden of the Sergeant, and followed them. Fergist, his face and bald head smeared heavily with soot, came and sat down heavily beside the Smithmaster, putting an arm around her shoulders and hugging her close. 'Bloody maniac,' he said gruffly. 'Agella, you're amazing. You have more in the way of balls than any man I know.'

'I'll try to work that out and see if it comes to a compliment.'

A soldier, unrecognisable in his helmet and with his face smeared with blood and smoke, almost tripped over them as he came clattering past. A cluster of lanterns swung by their hooks from his hand, obviously, judging from the shadows below them, pinched from brackets all down the staircase. 'Clear the stairs, you people,' he ordered. 'We're going to burn those bastards out and we'll need a fast retreat. We don't need civilians getting in the way.'

'Well of all the bloody cheek!' Agella muttered. 'Whose idea was it to use the lamps in the first place, I'd like to know?'

'Best to let them get on with it,' Fergist told her. 'We've done quite enough for one day in any case. It's time we got some rest.'

'Too true.' She leaned against him, letting her weary body relax for a moment, then heaved herself reluctantly to her feet. Together, hand in hand, they began to grope their way down the shadowy staircase. Behind them they heard the crash of shattering glass, and the whoosh of exploding flame. A blast of heat followed them down the staircase and from behind them came a ragged cheer. 'Just listen to those idiots,' the Smithmaster said. 'I hope somebody's already thinking of a back-up plan, because we can't use up all the lamps in the Basilica, and the fear of fire is only going to keep those critters off the landing for so long. I wonder if we could . . .'

'Oh no you don't, Agella,' Fergist interrupted. 'Let somebody else come up with a good idea for a change. It's not going to be your problem – at least not until after you've rested.'

'You could be right,' Agella conceded. 'By Myrial, but I'm beat! What about poor Ewald? Is he still alive?'

The Stablemaster shrugged. 'He was before we took him through the fire – I think. They ripped his belly open, though, and he looks in a bad way. We can only keep our fingers crossed. He's a tough old sod, when all's said and done. What about the kiddie?'

'Who knows? His mother wouldn't let go of him long enough to let anyone take a look.'

The Stablemaster shook his head. 'It didn't sound too good when his little head hit the corner of that hearth. Still, if there's any kind of a chance for him, I'm sure Healer Kaita will pull him through. She's damn good, that woman.'

'She'd better be. She'll certainly have her work cut out today. There's poor Galveron, wounded too – and we *need* him, more than anyone else. He's such a natural leader. Goodness only knows what damage has been done to that left eye. He wouldn't take his hand away to let me see.'

The reached the bottom of the steps and, pushing their way through the anxious crowd that thronged the doorway, came gratefully out into the light and space of the Basilica. They had scarcely moved forward a step or two, when they were pounced on by a distraught Telimon.

'Quiller – is he with you?' he demanded, grabbing hold of Fergist's arm. 'He *is* with you, isn't he?'

The Stablemaster shook his head. 'I'm sorry, Telimon. More sorry than I can say. They got your brother, I'm afraid. We saw him. There can be no doubt.'

The little man's round face crumpled. ''I thought he was right behind me,' he whispered. 'I was so *sure* he was right on my heels. There was such a rush and such confusion, and we had to run so fast when those creatures started appearing on the lower landing.' He choked on a sob. 'I panicked I suppose, but if I'd thought for an *instant* that he wasn't following, I'd have gone straight back, winged monstrosities or no. But I got down here, and the Godswords wouldn't let me go back up the stairs to look for him, and now you say he's gone.'

'I'm sorry,' Fergist repeated helplessly. 'If there was anything we could have done . . .' But Telimon was no longer listening. He stumbled blindly away through the crowd, shaking with sobs, and people fell back respectfully to let him pass.

Agella took a deep breath to quell the tremor in her own throat. There wasn't time for tears now; not even tears of sympathy. They wouldn't help Telimon anyway. He would have to find his own way through this. 'Where did they take the wounded?' she asked a woman, anxious to take her mind off the grieving little man by doing something useful.

'To the lower guardroom.' The woman was staring in astonishment at the Smithmaster's singed and blackened appearance.

Ignoring her, Agella went back to Fergist's side. She looked across at the guardroom door and shook her head. 'I only wish we had more experienced Healers, for poor Kaita's sake if nothing else.'

He nodded gravely. 'Aye. She can only be in one place at a time, and with three of them badly hurt all at once, she'll have to be making some tough decisions now.'

Kaita was in a desperate quandary. If only more experienced Healers had survived! She needed to be everywhere at once. She looked at the mess the predators had made of Sergeant Ewald's belly, and shook her head. He had lost a tremendous amount of blood, she was certain that his guts had been perforated, and Myrial only knew what manner of filth had been on the creatures' talons. She beckoned Shelon, a very bright young man and in her opinion the best of the less experienced physicians, to her side. He looked down at Ewald's injuries and gave a low whistle. 'Holy Myrial, what a shambles! Do you really think you can get him through?'

'I don't know, but I'm going to have a damn good try.' Kaita was sick of death taking her patients from her. It had happened all too many times in the first terrible hours of the siege. Besides, she liked the Sergeant. He was a good man: kind, straightforward and brave. Just the kind of man they so desperately needed in this crisis. He had been the one who'd come and told her about Evvie's death, and she had never forgotten his sympathy and kindness on that dreadful night. 'Keep an eye on his heart and breathing, and keep mopping the blood out of the wound while I stitch,' she told her assistant.

'He's unconscious now, but do you want to give him anything to make sure he stays that way?' Shelon asked.

She shook her head. 'I daren't. He's having enough of a struggle to keep going as it is.'

The Sergeant had been laid on a well-scrubbed table in the guard-room, and the young Commander sat beside it, holding a pad of cloth to his forehead. He'd refused to let Kaita attend to him until she had cared for his friend. Ewald was the one in desperate danger, and to have any hope at all of saving his life, it was imperative that she tend to him at once. She couldn't disagree with that, but she'd insisted very firmly that Shelon check the extent of his injuries at once. It turned out that his eyes appeared to be undamaged but, with one hand, the creature had clawed the right side of his face, tearing the skin along his cheekbone, and with the other, it had caught the skin of his forehead, ripping it open to the bone just above his eyes. The wounds hurt like perdition, but he was so relieved to still have his sight that it seemed a small price to pay. Kaita would stitch him up when she had time, but at the moment his worries were more for his old friend, who was barely clinging on to life.

'Can you do anything for him?' Galveron sounded anxious.

Kaita looked at him squarely. 'I'll clean the wound and patch him up as best I can.' Her hands were already busy as she spoke, flushing out the dreadful injuries. 'But you must have seen soldiers hurt as badly as this before. You know what the real chances are of him surviving.'

Galveron swallowed hard. 'I owe him such a lot,' he said softly. 'He's been better than a father to me, ever since I joined the Godswords.'

'Then you'd better pray,' Kaita told him. 'Goodness knows if it'll do any good, but right now, he needs all the help he can get.'

'I will,' Galveron promised, 'but when all's said and done, I would rather put my faith in your skills.'

At that moment, Gilarra, with Bevron beside her, rushed up to Kaita, clasping her son in her arms. 'It's Aukil. He hit his head, and he won't wake up. Please, you must look at him at once.'

The Healer shook her head. She was already beginning to stitch the perforated length of gut, and dared not even look up from the finicky task. 'I'm sorry,' she said, 'but this man is barely clinging on to life as it is. I can't leave him now, or he'll die for sure. One of my assistants will look at your boy, and I'll be with you as soon as I can.'

'But Aukil could be dying too! You *must* examine him at once!'

Kaita could not take her eyes from what she was doing to look at Gilarra's face, but the woman sounded on the thin knife edge of hysteria.

Wonderful. This is just what I need.

'I'm very sorry,' she repeated gently, 'but I can't right now. Surely you can see how it is.' All the time she was speaking her nimble fingers were at work, patching together the Sergeant's dreadful injuries with an increasing sense of hopelessness. He had lost so much blood already, and despite her best efforts, she had no doubt that there must be all sorts of muck and foreign substances inside the wound.

Come on, prompted an insidious little voice at the back of her mind, *you know it's hopeless. Where's the sense in drawing this out? He hasn't got a chance. Why not spare him the suffering? You can end it painlessly for him, right here and now, and attend to Galveron and the Hierarch's child.*

As if in echo of her thoughts, she heard Gilarra's voice again. 'This is ridiculous! That man is going to die in any case!'

Kaita had had enough. 'And so will that poor child, very probably,' she snapped, 'unless you stop hauling him around like a parcel, and let someone tend to him.'

'How *dare* you!' This time it was Bevron.

Oh go away, Kaita prayed. *I understand exactly why you're doing this, and I can sympathise, but please leave me alone.*

Galveron came to her rescue. 'Lady, I know you wouldn't say such things if you weren't out of your mind with anxiety,' he said gently. 'You know you don't want Ewald's life on your hands. Healer Kaita will be with you just as soon as ever she can. She won't let you down.'

The reproof was very subtle, but clearly, it had hit home. Out of the corner of her eye, Kaita saw Gilarra turn away, and heard the sound of her muffled sobbing. Her heart went out to the distraught woman, and she regretted that she'd let herself be goaded into losing her temper. She raised her voice over the general commotion in the guardroom. 'Ameris, please tend to the Hierarch at once, please. I'll be there just as soon as I can.'

Then she glanced up and saw Galveron, sitting patiently beside his friend, holding tightly to the pale, limp hand with his free hand, while the other still held the pad to his lacerated forehead. He nodded to her. 'Thank you,' he said softly.

'Thank *you*,' she answered.

At last it was done. Kaita, shaking with exhaustion, washed the blood from her hands. Ewald, still clinging on to life against all the odds, had been moved to one of the guardroom beds, and Galveron sat beside him, still holding his hand, his lips moving as he spoke softly. At first, she thought he was praying, but when she grew closer, she realised that he was talking to his unconscious friend, telling him how the fight had gone, what a good job Kaita had done in patching him up, and how he would soon be on his feet again. As the Healer approached, he looked up guiltily. 'Am I doing the right thing in talking to him?' he asked her. 'Should I be letting him rest?'

'I should say you're doing exactly the right thing,' she told him. 'Right now, he needs anything that will help him hold on to life.'

Galveron looked away from her. 'You don't really hold out much hope, do you?'

'No,' Kaita told him honestly. 'On the other hand, I'm not letting him go without a fight. Now, let me see that eye of yours.'

'Not yet,' Galveron told her. 'Go and see the Hierarch's boy first. We both promised her you would.'

It turned out, however, that Ameris, the other assistant Healer, had the situation well under control. 'He should be all right,' she assured Kaita. 'It doesn't feel as though he cracked his skull, though he's going to have a grandmother of a headache for a few days. He was conscious a little while ago, and he's sleeping naturally now.'

'Thank Providence for that.' Her decision to stay with Ewald had been the right one. And surely his mother would see now that she had been overreacting. But when she went to speak to Gilarra, the Hierarch did not speak but simply looked at her coldly, and walked away.

Hoping that matters would sort themselves out when the child was running around again, Kaita returned to Galveron, trying hard to put the unpleasantness out of her mind. 'Now,' she said firmly, 'let me see to that face of yours. If you want to save your good looks, you can't put this off any longer.'

Thirteen

Homecoming

When the Loremasters and their companions came home at last, the Valley of Two Lakes was bathed in the delicate shimmer of early morning sunlight. Because the hill country around Gendival was at a much lower elevation than the mountains of Callisiora, and the climate seemed, so far at least, to have been less disturbed, the trees here were just turning to the russets and golds of autumn, which the slanting light kindled to a blaze of bronze and gold. The sky was the cool, pale blue of an aquamarine, and the morning breeze was fresh, with an autumnal bite to it. The scents of the countryside were an evocative mixture of smoke, musk, and spice; so different from the sappy, green, flower-scented fragrances of summer. Birds were everywhere, making the most of the fruits, seeds and nuts that were autumn's bounty, before the coming of lean wintertime.

Toulac, riding on the firedrake behind Veldan, stretched her arms out wide and took enormous breaths of crisp, aromatic air. Oh, to feel the sun on her face again! She felt as though she was twenty again, strong and energetic and hopeful. Only now did she realise how greatly the endless dark and clouded days in Callisiora had contributed to her sense of depression, uselessness and age. It was as though the bleak, grim conditions had imprisoned her in a heavy carapace of iron that the sun had finally shattered, allowing her to move and breathe once more. Despite lingering worry over Mazal, and her sorrow at having to leave her beloved horse behind, she felt as if she had been released from prison, or awakened from a long night of evil dreams to face a new and glorious day.

She looked across at Zavahl, who was riding in front of Elion. Was he feeling this same euphoria? Though he still wasn't smiling, it seemed to Toulac that the grim lines around his mouth and eyes had relaxed a little, and he was no longer confronting the world with a scowl on his face. Idly, she wondered what Elion had said to him in the wayshelter. Whatever it was, it seemed to have worked – and that young puppy had been insufferably smug about the whole business ever since. He had even taken the chain off the former Hierarch and let him have the freedom of the wayshelter while they slept, though Kaz had prudently taken his nap sprawled right across the doorway, just in case. So far, though, there had been no trouble, and before they had left to continue their journey, he had even come out to eat with them (while keeping a very wary eye on the fire-drake). Though he was still not happy and could, or would, not hide his resentment of Veldan and Toulac, Zavahl had dropped his unco-operative attitude, and seemed to be less terrified of the situation in which he found himself, though the veteran wondered what would happen when he came to the lakeside settlement of the Loremasters. Veldan had warned her that she would encounter beings who were extraordinary enough to make Kaz look very commonplace indeed.

It seemed that the Loremasters were having similar thoughts to her own. While she had been far away in thought, they had clearly been conferring amongst themselves. As they progressed further up the lovely valley, they came to an area where the lush bottom lands had been ploughed and cultivated in places. Horses, sheep and glossy cattle grazed the fields beside the river, so that Kaz hardly knew where to look. His hungry thoughts were leaking into the warrior's mind, making her own stomach rumble.

Veldan and Elion looked at one another, and a message passed between them so quickly that Toulac missed it. Elion pulled up his horse, while Kaz kept going until he was out of earshot. Veldan turned to talk to her companion. 'We decided it would be best if Zavahl went in blindfolded. That way, we can introduce him gradually to the weird and wonderful inhabitants of Gendival. His beliefs are firmly entrenched, and he hasn't coped very well so far with having them threatened. I think his sanity will be at risk if we push him too far too fast, and goodness knows what will happen to Aethon if he loses his mind.' She made a wry face. 'Now Elion has just got to persuade him that it's a good idea.'

'Thank goodness for Elion,' Toulac said. 'At least he's someone Zavahl half-trusts, and that makes life a lot easier for everyone. He never would have let *us* blindfold him.'

Veldan grimaced again. 'I hate to admit it, but you're right.'

'At least old misery-guts is good for something,' muttered Kaz.

To Toulac's surprise, it didn't take Elion long to talk Zavahl into binding a length of thick cloth across his eyes. 'Well, may I be dipped in dog's dung,' she muttered to Veldan. 'I get the feeling that he doesn't *want* to know what's up ahead.' She couldn't understand it. To ride helpless, defenceless and blind into a strange new situation would rank among her worst nightmares. As it was, she had worries of her own to occupy her. Would they really accept her in Gendival? Or would they dismiss her as being too old?

The village was the home of the workers, mostly human, who cared for and maintained the Shadowleague. As Toulac and the others rode down the single street, people paused in their work to wave, or call out a cheery greeting. Seeing their smiles of welcome, the ageing warrior, who had grown increasingly nervous the closer they came to their destination, began to feel more cheerful and at ease.

'That's better.' The voice of Kaz came into her head. 'You've got nothing to worry about, you know. You belong here, and myself and Veldan will make sure old horse-arse knows that too.'

Veldan was obviously listening in on the conversation too: she forbore to comment, but gave the firedrake a furious scowl for using Archimandrite's disrespectful nickname so close to the settlement itself.

Toulac scowled at him too, annoyed that he had seen so clearly through her outward show of bravado. 'What makes you think I'm worried?' she demanded, as usual speaking aloud.

Kaz snickered. 'You may not be able to broadcast your thoughts in mindspeech yet, but you're certainly improving. Ever since we set out today, your feelings have been hitting me between the ears like hailstones.'

'Now look here, you smart-mouthed, scaly bugger – I'm not taking any impudence from you! You're not so big that I can't—'

'Can't what?' Kaz drawled. 'I'd like to see you try.'

'Why you—' She thumped the firedrake with her fist, but it had no effect.

Chuckling, Veldan intervened. 'Well done, Kaz.' Turning to the fuming veteran, she added, 'He fished for you and caught you that time, Toulac. Don't you see? He was only trying to distract you from being nervous. Perhaps it worked too well. But he's right, you know. We could feel your emotions very strongly, and that's a great sign for your learning mindspeech. All you have to do now is learn focus and control, and you'll be able to turn those feelings into words, and be every bit as much a Loremaster as the rest of us.'

'Do you really think so?' Toulac's irritation – also born of nerves, she admitted to herself – dissolved in delight.

'I know so,' said Veldan firmly. 'Look, here we are at last.'

At the bottom of the village street, the narrow lane curved round and went over a small, arched bridge that spanned a narrow, lively river, stained the colour of whiskey by the peaty moorland soil. A short distance upstream, a mill with a tall, turning wheel stood at the water's edge. On the other side of the bridge was a crumbling old wall of grey stone, furred with mosses and gilded with lichen: a tiny world in itself, with the delicate little purple snapdragons of toadflax cascading down, and the round, waxy leaves of pennywort clustering between the stones like a treasure-trove of verdant coins. Dark green ivy and the delicate spears of hart's tongue fern had taken root in every chink and crevice. Piercing the venerable wall was a narrow entry, a lane with walls on either side. Clearly this had been a tunnel once. Looking up at the remains of the construction, Toulac suspected that there had once been some kind of gatehouse built over the top, and wondered why her new hosts had let it fall into such disrepair.

To her surprise, Kaz veered away from the entrance, turning to the left. After a few yards, the wall curved, but when they turned the corner Toulac gasped in surprise. Here the fortifications plunged into a small copse of trees, and vanished. The veteran couldn't believe it, but the walls had been allowed to crumble away to nothing, leaving only scattered stones amid the grasses, nettles, and bramble trailers that grew in profusion around the roots of the trees. 'What in the world happened here?' she gasped.

Veldan shrugged. 'It's been like that for centuries. Apparently there was a schism among the Shadowleague, and a group split away and formed a settlement further up the valley.' She shuddered. 'They must have been a hardy lot. It's incredibly desolate and bleak up there. Anyway, the situation escalated until there was open warfare, which was when these walls were built. Eventually, when the new group looked like winning, and this settlement was cut off and under siege, the Archimandrite of that time used a weapon of such dreadful power and destructiveness that it should never have seen the light of day. The attackers here were wiped out, and then their settlement, which included old folk, mothers with young children, and the eggs of some of the more extraordinary races we have here, was levelled.' She shuddered. 'I hate to go up there now. The place is full of ghosts, and the memories of pain and terror seem to ooze out of every stone.'

'Bollocks! I don't believe in ghosts,' lied Toulac stoutly. Nevertheless, she felt the skin crawl between her shoulderblades. In a sense, though, Veldan's words bolstered her courage a little. She had been very much in awe of coming among these mighty folk, but clearly, they weren't above making the occasional mistake. And in her opinion, letting these perfectly good fortifications go to ruin was sheer stupidity.

If you ask me, the high and mighty Shadowleague may not be as clever as they think.

'No, but they are telepaths.' Kaz's voice, intruding into what she had assumed was a private thought. 'If I were you, I'd be careful about those sort of opinions, at least until Veldan teaches you how to shield.'

'But Kaz, don't you see what this means?' Veldan sounded very excited. 'She projected! Not very far, which is just as well in the circumstances, but enough for us to hear. Well done, Toulac!' Twisting around on the firedrake's back, she clapped her friend on the shoulder. 'Now we know that you truly belong here.'

As she spoke, they rounded the cluster of oaks, and an incredible scene opened out before Toulac's eyes. The settlement spread out before her, set in emerald lawns that stretched down to the shore of the lake. The buildings were all crafted from a weathered, light grey stone, its soft tones blending gently with the landscape. Apart from the soaring tower down by the lake, they tended to be only a single storey in height, though several of them covered a fairly large area. 'Why are they all so low?' she wondered aloud.

'Quite a few of them have additional levels built down into the ground,' Elion told her. 'When this place was built, they didn't want to mar the natural beauty of the site. Besides, it makes the races who dwell underground feel more at home.'

Scattered further back from the lake, or built unobtrusively into the wooded hillside above, were smaller dwellings of different styles and sizes. She wondered why, until she took a good look at some of the inhabitants of this place. Some of them were very strange indeed.

It was a good thing that Toulac had already seen Kazairl. Being friendly with one strange being of alien appearance took the edge off her shock when she saw some of the other fearsome looking creatures: something that looked like a gigantic green insect emerging from the trees at the bottom of the hillside; a long-necked monster poking a curious head out of the waters of the lake; a creature, just emerging from a doorway, that looked like a sleek brown otter – except that it was about the size of an eight-year-old child when it stood on its hind legs in order to use its dextrous, stubby-fingered little hands to close the door behind it. Calling a greeting to Veldan, a bird flew overhead on wings of flame, trailing a long comet-tail of sparks. It was the most beautiful creature that Toulac had ever seen, but bearing down on them, in contrast, there was also a gigantic, bristly centipede-like monster with fearsome jaws, which was without a doubt the most hideous.

'Look at that!' she gasped to Veldan. 'What the bloody blazes *is* that nightmare?'

'It's a Moldan,' her companion told her. 'They live underground, usually. Watch out for him, he's got a very short temper.'

'Don't worry. I'm not about to go anywhere near him,' retorted Toulac. She looked again at the powerful, complex mandibles that glittered in the sunlight, and shuddered. 'If you ask me, underground is where he belongs, with a face like that.'

'Look out.' Elion's mental voice was a whisper. 'Here comes Cergorn.'

Galloping across the grass towards her, Toulac saw a being whose magnificent, dapple-grey horse's body reminded her so strongly of her lost Mazal that a knife twisted in her heart. But rising from the powerful forequarters of the beast was the torso of a man, with broad shoulders and powerful muscularity that contrasted markedly with the age shown on his face, and the short grey hair that fringed a balding head. Behind him came a female, a little more delicately formed than her partner, the pelt on her lower body a burnished black with a scattering of white stars sprinkled across her quarters.

How unusual. I'd love to own a horse like that.

Horrified, the veteran stifled the thought quickly, hoping she hadn't been able to broadcast *that* one! She was going to have to get Veldan to teach her this business of control and shielding as a matter of urgency. To steer her wayward mind back to a safe path, she concentrated instead on the human part of the . . . woman? Female? Desperately, Toulac wondered what would be the proper word to use.

Myrial in a slop-pail! I hope I don't make too many mistakes.

Whatever she should be called, the female, though no longer young, was beautiful. Her long, silver hair, twisted up into an elaborate knot, her luminous complexion, and her delicate, refined bone structure would look superb no matter how old she grew. Toulac thought of her own face, seamed and weatherbeaten after a lifetime spent outside in all weathers, and clenched her teeth.

I'd like to see her *deal with a seven-foot berserker wielding a battle axe.*

The thought restored her faltering confidence.

The Archimandrite stopped at the base of the tall tower and let them approach him. *Clever bugger*, thought Toulac sourly. In her long career as a mercenary she had seen leaders play these little power games many times, and it never failed to get right under her skin. As she drew closer, she studied the lines on Cergorn's face, trying to gain an insight into his character, and made a guess at wisdom, wit and an enormous amount of willpower.

I wouldn't like to cross him, that's for sure. And he may have the body of a horse, but I'll wager he's as stubborn as a mule.

A waiting stillness had fallen over the entire settlement, the only sounds the hum of insects and the shrilling of birdsong. All eyes were turned towards the meeting that was taking place beneath the tower. Then Cergorn spread his arms out as if to embrace them all, and broke the silence, speaking both aloud and with his mind. 'Veldan, Elion, Kazairl,' he called. 'Welcome back.' The coldness of his tone belied the words.

In front of her, Toulac saw her friend's rigid shoulders tense.

'And a welcome to you also, strangers,' said the female centaur. Her voice was musical, low, and well modulated.

Wouldn't you just know she'd sound like that.

Toulac gritted her teeth, and inclined her head respectfully. 'Thank you for your gracious welcome,' she said. 'I am honoured to be here.'

The Archimandrite looked across at her. She could see his eyes, shrewd and calculating, weighing her up. 'Indeed,' he said shortly. 'Syvilda will take you to rest and refresh yourselves, while I speak with my Loremasters.' Abruptly, he turned his attention back to Veldan and her companions, dismissing the newcomers out of hand,

and once again, the veteran found herself gritting her teeth. As she struggled to keep a lid on her boiling thoughts, Veldan reached back surreptitiously and grasped her hand. 'Make the most of a chance to relax,' she said, and didn't bother to keep her mindspeech private. 'I'll come and get you as soon as I've spoken with the Archimandrite.'

'I'll see you soon then, girlie.' Toulac tried her hardest to broadcast the words from her mind, as well as speaking aloud. 'I could do with putting my feet up for a bit.' As she slid down from the firedrake's back, Kaz turned his head, and she thought she saw a glitter of amusement in his eyes.

As the female centaur – Syvilda, she reminded herself – came forward, Toulac caught the edge of Elion's thought. 'This other human is Zavahl, the former Hierarch of Callisiora. If I were you, Syvilda, I wouldn't let him take off his blindfold until you've put him where he can't see outside. And I definitely wouldn't let anyone but humans near him for a while. We need to break him in gently, I'm afraid. He's probably going to have considerable difficulty coping with Gendival.'

'And please take good care that he doesn't escape,' Veldan put in. 'He's very unstable and unpredictable at present, but unfortunately, he's very important to us.'

The centaur nodded. 'Thanks for the warning. I'll see that he stays safe. It will be best to keep them both in the village for the time being.'

Oh it will, will it? I'd like to see you try keeping me somewhere I don't want to be kept!

Syvilda turned to the fuming warrior with a smile. 'My word, Veldan was right. You *are* talented, aren't you?'

Toulac grinned, deciding to brazen it out. 'You'd better believe it, sister.' From behind her, there came an appreciative snicker from Kaz.

'Then that makes you doubly welcome,' the centaur said firmly in mindspeech, ignoring both the firedrake and her frowning mate. 'We can always find room for another sensible female around here.

Now, let's get you settled. According to Elion and Veldan, I had better not get too close to your companion at present. Would you like to guide him to the village?'

'*Like* is not exactly a word I'd use,' growled Toulac. Nevertheless, she helped the former Hierarch to dismount, and took his arm. 'Come on then, sonny. I'm taking you to hot water, food, and a comfortable bed. Don't worry. I won't let you fall.'

'Where is Elion?' Zavahl demanded. 'Can't I take off this damned blindfold yet?'

Toulac shrugged. 'As far as I'm concerned, you can do what you like, but I really wouldn't advise it. Elion and Veldan have to speak with their equivalent of a Hierarch, but we'll see them again in a little while.'

At least I hope we will.

The centaur led Toulac away from the settlement and out through the roofless tunnel that she had seen earlier, crossing the bridge to go back into the village. The houses, situated on both sides of the street and built from the same mellow grey stone as the settlement, were solid and spacious, and the inhabitants had an air of prosperity, purposeful industry, and contentment. Every single house in the street looked well-maintained and clean. Bright curtains hung at the windows, and window boxes were packed with late summer and early autumn blooms, in a riot of crimson, purple and gold.

The inn, the largest and most imposing building, was at the opposite end of the village to the smithy, near the bridge. *The Griffin,* said the sign that swung above the door, and below it was a vivid painting of a golden creature with the front half of its body like an eagle, and the back half like a lion.

Myrial up a drainpipe! Just look at that for an amazing critter.

She nudged Syvilda. 'Excuse me? Does that thing really exist?'

'Of course.' The centaur smiled. 'Maybe you'll get the chance to meet one soon.'

What a place! Oh, thank you, Veldan, for bringing me here.

The doorway was surprisingly large, Toulac thought as she went through, but a glance at the centaur beside her made her realise that not all of the customers would necessarily be human. Inside was a stone-flagged passageway, also of generous dimensions, with plain whitewashed walls. It seemed to go all the way through to the rear of the inn. Part of the way along was a staircase of dark, polished wood, and doors led off on either side, the doorway to the right being high and broad again, while the one on the left conformed to the usual human dimensions.

Syvilda looked through the larger of the doorways. 'Ailie? Olsam?' she called. 'Are you there?'

A man emerged, small and spry, with twinkling eyes that peeped out from beneath a fringe of silver-shot brown hair. 'Syvilda! How good to see you.'

'And you, Olsam. Where's that daughter of yours?'

'Ailie is in the yard, hanging out the laundry.' He grimaced. 'She seems bent on washing every scrap of bedding in the inn, while the good weather lasts. Says it'll no doubt be a long, cold winter, and this is the time to get ahead.' He sighed theatrically. 'A few days ago it was bottling and pickling, now it's laundry – what's a fellow to do? I've just about forgotten what our kitchen normally looks like.'

The centaur laughed. 'You're only complaining because Ailie works so hard, she makes you feel guilty.'

'Too true,' the little man said feelingly. 'I can't keep up with her any more. I'm not as young as I used to be. I keep telling her to slow down, but she says there'll be time enough for that when the snows come. Anyway, what can I do for you, Syvilda?' His eyes went to Toulac and her companion, widening a little as they took in the blindfold over Zavahl's eyes. 'Are these new guests for me?' he asked.

'Meet Toulac and Zavahl,' replied Syvilda, 'and yes, they will be your guests for a little while.' There was never any question, Toulac noted, that Olsam might object. 'Let's get them settled, shall we?' the centaur went on. 'Toulac can have one of those nice chambers at the front if she likes, but I want Zavahl overlooking the yard. Once you've seen them to their rooms, I'll need a quiet word with you.'

Toulac's room was clean and homely, with floor and furniture of dark, polished wood, walls painted the colour of heavy cream, red curtains, a thick patchwork quilt on the generous bed, a red wool mat in front of the fireplace and a big basket containing logs and blocks of peat to one side. Olsam knelt down stiffly and lit the kindling in the hearth. 'There you are, Mistress, the place should soon warm up.' He hauled himself creakily to his feet, and wiped his hands on his trousers. 'You make yourself comfortable now, and Ailie will be up with a meal for you as soon as may be.'

'Would there be any chance of a bath first?' Toulac asked him hopefully.

She might have been imagining it, but she got the distinct impression that Olsam was very relieved at her question. 'Why yes, Mistress, of course. You settle yourself in, and I'll have Ailie arrange it at once.'

When he had gone, Toulac built up the fire, then hung out of the window and took in the scene, feeling as excited as a child on her first outing. At the far end of the village was a smithy, set a little apart to stop the noises, smokes and smells from disturbing the neighbours. Beyond were a cluster of workshops and open fronted sheds. Avidly, she watched the people going in and out, noting what they carried, and discovered tanners, dyers and weavers, coopers and carpenters, potters and masons. Through the doorways of houses, left open to catch the last sunshine before winter, she could see other craftsmen, such as cobblers, chandlers and tailors. *They seem to have everything they need here,* she thought, remembering the mill, and the pleasant little farms further down the valley.

Though it could not be seen, she caught the pungent waft of mingled malt and herbs that revealed a brewhouse nearby, and smells of good food seemed to be everywhere. Fish was cooking in one house, someone was baking bread and pies nearby, and judging from the savoury aroma, someone else was planning to have stew for their midday meal. Toulac, so accustomed to the short rations and rotten food of stricken Callisiora, heard her belly rumble in anticipation.

Again, in contrast to the wretched folk of her homeland, the people here looked healthy, carefree and clean. Cheery greetings were exchanged as people went about their business. Small children, lively and carefree, darted here and there with the abundant energy of youth, playing their private, complex games with their playmates and with the village dogs, who joined in with noisy exuberance.

Toulac's spirits were going up in leaps and bounds. She was too familiar with the vagaries of human nature to believe that everyone in this place could be happy all the time, or get along without dispute. She knew that behind the cheerful façade would be the rivalry, gossip, squabbles and bitching that was an integral part of any small community. But though she was well aware that her perceptions of the village must be coloured by the misery she had left behind her, she didn't give a damn. Life was so much better here, and she had every intention of enjoying her altered circumstances.

The door opened, and Toulac turned swiftly to see a woman enter. Her age must have been somewhere about the far side of thirty, and she was big, blonde and buxom, with a pleasant, beaming pink face. She held out her hand. 'It's good to meet you. I'm Ailie.'

When the introductions were over, she took Toulac along to a room at the end of the corridor. Much smaller than her own bedchamber, it contained little more than a fire stoked to a healthy blaze, a chair and table, and a large tub of steaming water. 'There you are,' she said briskly. 'Take as long as you need, and when you're ready, just come to the top of the stairs and shout for me. I'll bring your meal up directly.'

She gestured at a pile of folded garments on the table, beside the towels and soap. 'Dad said you came without even a saddlebag to your name, so I scrounged around for some clean clothes for you. I know how horrible it feels to put dirty stuff back on when you've just had a bath. There's a fair selection, so you'll probably find something to fit.'

'Why, thank you.' Toulac was touched by such kindness and consideration. 'You really believe in looking after your guests.'

Ailie's pink face blushed to a deeper shade. 'I like folk to be comfortable.'

'Will I be able to get my own clothes washed?'

'Of course,' Ailie said brightly. She managed to hide her dismay *fairly* well, Toulac thought. 'Just leave them outside the door and I'll pick them up.'

'In a pair of tongs, no doubt,' said the warrior with a laugh. Even before she had set out on her journey, her clothes had been far from clean. Because it was so difficult to get things dry in Callisiora's rainy climate, she had tended to neglect her laundry. Living alone as she had done, she had more important things to worry about, and had got into the habit of accepting a certain amount of dirt as part of life. But staying in such a neat, clean place with this well-scrubbed hostess, she looked down at her grimy, ragged outfit, and felt embarrassed. 'Unfortunately, we had to leave rather suddenly, so these are all I have with me,' she apologised, 'so you can't chuck them on a bonfire, which is what they deserve, until I've arranged for new ones.'

Though goodness knows how I'm going to pay for them. Maybe Veldan will help me out.

'Don't worry, I'll see that they get a good scrubbing.' Ailie smiled. 'In the meantime, the sooner we get you some new ones, the better. I'll also get the tailor and the cobbler to come up and take your measure later. All part of the service.'

'That's all right,' Toulac said carefully, 'I wouldn't want to put them to all that trouble. If you tell me where to find them, I can visit them after I've eaten.'

Now we'll see if Syvilda's orders included me, as well as Zavahl.

Ailie blushed again, and looked down at her shoes. 'I wouldn't . . . I mean, don't bother . . . I mean, that is, perhaps you ought to rest . . .'

Ah. Just as I thought.

'It's all right,' the veteran said kindly. 'We're strangers here, and it's reasonable for Syvilda to be a bit cautious. Your village looks so lovely, I can't wait to explore it, but to tell you the truth, my bed looks pretty damn appealing too. Kicking my heels in idleness for a while will do me the world of good.'

Ailie hesitated for a moment. 'The other guest – the young man,' she blurted. 'Is he all right? I know Syvilda told me not to ask or answer any questions, but he looks so ill and unhappy. Is there something wrong with him? Is there anything I can do?'

Well, well! So that's the way the wind is blowing.

Toulac smiled at the woman. 'Zavahl isn't ill as such, but he's had a rougher time, these last few days, than you could possibly imagine. I think part of the problem is that he's very lonely,' she added with a wink.

'Do you really think so?' Ailie's grin was conspiratorial, and growing broader by the minute.

'I know so,' Toulac said firmly. In her opinion, celibacy was highly overrated, and the Hierarch had been denying himself for far too long. Now that his life was in such crisis, an encounter with this pleasant, pretty, kind and (by the look of her) lusty innkeeper was exactly what he needed. 'He may seem a bit reluctant at first,' she warned Ailie, trying to choose her words carefully. 'He was brought up to believe that having a bit of a romp with a willing young woman is wrong.'

'Wrong? Whatever for?'

'Your guess is as good as mine. Anyway, I'm sure *you* can change his mind,' Toulac said slyly. 'It's worth a try. I never saw anyone so badly in need of a friend.'

Myrial in a muck-heap! I hope I'm doing the right thing, here. But if somebody doesn't get that poor idiot to loosen up, he's never going to help Veldan. Besides, I haven't lied to her. He doesn't know it, but Ailie is exactly what he needs.

The woman gave her a grateful smile, looking positively girlish for a moment. 'You're right. It's worth a try. I'm glad you understand. Now, I'll let you get on with it, before the bathwater gets cold. If you want anything, just yell.'

'Thanks. By the way,' she called, as the woman left the room, 'what's for dinner?'

'Bean soup, hotpot and cherry pie,' said Ailie, as she closed the door behind her.

'Yum,' said Toulac to herself, as she started to shed her filthy clothes. 'You've fallen on your feet this time, old girl. This is without a doubt the best prison you've ever been in.' She grinned. Maybe, in a little while, Zavahl would be able to say the same thing.

FOURTEEN

A VOICE FROM AFAR

Dark leaned his elbows on the windowsill and cupped his aching head in his hands. After ending the little boy's life the previous day, he had not closed his eyes all night. Though he longed desperately for the oblivion of sleep, he was afraid to dream; afraid to face once again the angry father and the heart-broken mother, to stand again in that awful sickroom, to look into those dark, pain-filled eyes, and feel the child's heartbeat falter and grow still beneath his hand. Intellectually, he knew that he had done a *good* thing, saving the child from dreadful suffering and an agonising, drawn-out death. There had been no better option, but no matter how many times he told that to himself, he could not escape the knowledge that he had deliberately ended a life, and the certainty that there must be a better alternative.

He had never been so glad to see the dawn. With eyes that burned from fatigue, he looked out of the window at the stark but magnificent landscape, blurred and softened by the drifting veils of sleet. At the head of the valley one great hill rose higher than its brethren, the upper reaches of its steep slopes barren with rock and scree. Atop the hill, as harsh and threatening as its surroundings on this cold, grey morning, stood the fortress of the clan-chieftain and his retainers: a central structure with a blocky wing on either side sitting foursquare and obdurate as it looked down over the valley that was the clan's territory and Arcan's realm. A little way beyond, in a slight hollow, was a small tarn like a sheet of black glass. At the edge of the dark and icy lake, situated on a rocky outcrop, was the squat, square tower that for time immemorial had been the dwelling and sanctuary of the Summoners.

Like all Reiver strongholds, the structure had no windows on the ground floor and only arrow-slits in the next. Only the top two stories were actually living accommodation with proper windows, though even these were small and sparse, thanks to the cold, bleak weather conditions that were prevalent in this high moorland region, piercing sturdy stone walls the thickness of a spear-length. The ground floor was designed to accommodate and shelter livestock – an essential safeguard in a land where raiding and marauding between clans was an everyday part of life.

Because of their status, Grim and Dark were permitted to run their handful of tithed sheep and cattle with those of Arcan, the clan-chieftain. Thus the only occupants of the ground floor were a pig who ate any household leavings, a few chickens, a pair of the swift, sturdy, shaggy moorland ponies beloved of the Reivers, and a white cow, who was so tame and petted that she went off with the chieftain's herd each morning and brought herself back in the evening to be milked, and spend the night in comfort. Though people attributed this to the mysterious supernatural powers of her owners, in truth it was simply due to an overabundance of pampering and titbits on the part of the Summoners.

Dark sighed. He had always found peace and contentment here, and learning enough to satisfy his hungry mind. But today the tower had never felt less like home.

Do I really belong here anymore?

What alternative is there? No matter what has happened, this is my home, and Grim is like a father to me.

He looked out at the tarn. The obsidian waters; fathomless, brooding, smooth as glass, looked capable of absorbing all the secrets and grief in the world. Suddenly Dark felt a great need to immerse himself, to cleanse himself, to wash away the memories and the insidious sense of guilt. Acting on the urgent impulse he left his chamber, and knocked on the door of Grim's room. His mentor looked bleary-eyed and dishevelled. 'Dark? Are you all right?'

'I couldn't sleep.'

'Evidently. And you were worried that I was missing out on all this wakefulness? How very generous,' Grim said dryly, but there was a twinkle in his sleepy eye.

'Sorry.' Dark felt appropriately guilty. 'I'm going for a swim,' he explained. 'I just came to tell you that I won't be long.'

Grim's eyebrow lifted. 'You most certainly won't. Even in summer that lake is pure ice-water. What it must be like now doesn't bear contemplation.' But his eyes were understanding and kind. 'Breakfast will be ready as soon as you get back, and I'll get Izobia to stoke up the fire.'

Dark swallowed hard, trying to get the image of the little boy's pain-filled eyes out of his mind. 'I don't think I want any breakfast this morning.'

'You will,' Grim assured him, 'once you've dunked yourself in that oversized vat of liquid ice.'

Despite his troubles, Dark found himself smiling. 'How can there be such a thing as liquid ice?'

'I think you're about to experience that for yourself. Don't let me spoil the surprise. If you're not back soon, I'll come down and chip you out.' With that, he went back into his room, presumably to snatch a few more minutes in his nice, warm bed.

Dark made his way down to the bleak and wintry tarn, thanking providence that Izobia was still asleep. No doubt she would have something to say about this. She had something to say about everything, and while he appreciated the wonderful way in which she looked after himself and Grim, he wished she wouldn't consider everything they did to be her business. Still, he supposed he ought to feel sorry for her. She was the daughter of Arcan's sister, and four years ago had been one of the wildest and most headstrong of the young girls, confident that her beauty and her ability to charm the menfolk would get her out of any difficulty. Unfortunately, she had encountered a handsome young warrior from an enemy clan, who had come scouting in preparation for a raid. Besotted with his good looks and greatly thrilled by her own daring, she hid him, fed him, and eventually ran away with him, to the horror of both his clan and her own.

Izobia's happiness lasted just long enough to bear a child, before her young man was killed during a raid. Her adopted clan cast her and the little one out immediately, but when she tried to return home, she found that because she had borne the son of a foeman, she was no longer welcome. Her lot might have been hard indeed, had Grim not offered her sanctuary with her child, in return for cooking, cleaning and washing for himself and Dark: a duty that no other woman in the clan would undertake, for none dared to enter a Summoner tower.

One of the storerooms had been turned into comfortable living quarters for herself and the baby, and Izobia soon got over her fears, and settled in. She had been pathetically grateful, and worked so hard that life had never been so comfortable for the two men. Unfortunately for Dark, however, she was still a lusty young woman, and she was determined to extend her role with regard to himself – right into his bed. Though he was flattered, he had decided, to her dismay, that such a complication in his life was the last thing he needed at this time, especially since they were practically living on top of one another in the tower. Dismayed Izobia might be, however, but deterred she was not. He was wondering just how much longer he would be able to dodge her advances.

Below the tower was a tiny half-moon bay with a pebbly shingle shore fringed, but for the narrow path cleared by animals going down to drink, by a low, vicious scrub of blackthorn, bramble and gorse. On the right hand side of the inlet, where a tumble of grey boulders had trapped pockets of fertile soil, stood a cluster of weather-stunted rowans, like bent old women huddled against the wind.

Scrunching his way down across the pebbles into the minimal shelter of the winter-bare trees, Dark shed his clothing quickly, gasping as the wind bit into his goose-pimpled flesh, and icy sleet peppered his skin. He knew this was insane, but after the scenes he had witnessed yesterday, and the part he had played in the death of the child, he felt the need to make atonement somehow with pain and discomfort, and to purify himself – to wash away the black thoughts that filled his mind. Only then, he felt, could he begin to assimilate what he had done. And prepare himself, somehow, for the next time. Shivering violently, he picked his way out to the end of the little promontory where the boulders jutted out into the bay. The water was deep here. Taking a deep breath, he plunged into the lake.

It was like being flayed alive. The cold was so intense that it stopped his breathing, and he felt his heart labour and stutter in his chest. Weed and submerged branches tore at him like living fingers trying to snatch him and hold him down until he drowned. Blind panic filled him, giving Dark the strength to somehow claw his way to the surface. He managed to snatch a desperate breath before going down again.

Under the water it was dark as the tomb. Dark's head spun. His lungs were burning and his limbs felt numb and feeble in the merciless cold. He could hear his heartbeat pounding, racing, booming in his ears, and it was harder now to concentrate, to move, to struggle for his life. Once again, the face of the little boy flashed clearly into his mind. Was this what dying felt like? Was this pain, this panic, this bewildering blurring of the senses inevitable as life slipped away?

I won't die! Frantically, the Summoner forced his weakening body into one last, desperate attempt to survive. Desperation lent strength to his stiffening limbs as he floundered and fought his way forward and up, striving towards the light.

Dark's feet struck yielding, slippery mud and shingle. The bottom of the lake! Simultaneously, his head broke the surface of the icy black tarn. He had managed to claw his way into the shallows. Hardly daring to believe that he was safe, he staggered forward into the shallows of the little shingled bay and dropped to his hands and knees on the uneven pebbled surface, oblivious to the sharp stones digging into his hands. He was alive! He coughed and wheezed and retched for what seemed an age, spitting out water and trying to clear the residue from his lungs. Though he only had himself to blame, he would never be able to look at these waters again without a shudder. They had very nearly become his grave.

For a moment he thought of Grim, and felt a prickle of irritation. Surely his mentor must have known he would get into trouble, going into the lake on a day like this? Why, his struggles must have been visible from the tower windows, if the other man had only bothered to look. Gradually, Dark became aware of the sleet-laden wind chilling his wet skin, and realised that he was not out of danger yet. If he didn't put on some clothes and get back to the warmth and shelter of the tower quickly, he could still die of exposure in this freezing, windswept place.

Growing colder and weaker by the moment, Dark staggered towards the little clump of rowans where he had left his clothes. To his dismay, he found that his hands were already too numb to dress himself. Clumsily, he threw his cloak around his shoulders, wrapping the warm folds gratefully around himself, then swept up the remainder of his clothing into a rough bundle. Clasping it in his arms, he made his unsteady, stumbling way back to the tower.

Above the ground floor animal shelter, the next floor of the building was a store for food, fuel and equipment, with living chambers and bedrooms on the floors above. Almost crawling, Dark made his way up the first staircase. As he passed the storeroom, a noise from within made him stop and look through the doorway. Catching sight of a shapely backside clad in a dark green skirt, he ducked out hastily – but too late. As he had found out to his cost before now, Izobia had ears like a bat. She straightened up from the box in which she had been rummaging, pushed her long red curls out of her eyes, and turned to display a great deal of bosom in a low-cut blouse. '*Dark!* What in the name of all creation have you been doing?'

'Swimming.' He turned away to hurry up the stairs, but she called him back.

'At this time of year? You'll catch your death!'

'So will you, the way you're hanging out of that blouse,' Dark said rudely, and made his escape while she was still spluttering – or so he thought.

'Pig!' she screeched. A jar came whizzing through the air and shattered off the wall close to his ear, releasing a cloud of pepper into the air. What they said about red hair and temper was true, he reflected ruefully. Sneezing violently and mopping ineffectually at his streaming eyes, he made his escape as fast as his frozen limbs could hobble.

When Dark climbed the second narrow staircase, he found a haven of comfort awaiting, completely at odds with the bleak exterior of the tower and its surrounding lands. In the main living area, two deep chairs, padded with sheepskins, were pulled up one on either side of a roaring turf fire. The table, set further back from the blaze, was laid with cups and plates, with butter, bread, cheese and a crock of the precious honey from the south that had been procured from trader Tormon and his family when their gaudy wagon had passed through some days before.

The thick woven wall-hangings, so necessary in these draughty stone buildings, looked bright and cosy in the flickering firelight. The wooden shelves at the back of the room and the big storage chest beneath the window were polished and dust free – almost an impossibility in a room with a peat fire, for the fine, feather-light ashes lifted themselves into the air in the slightest of draughts and spread themselves generously over every surface. The windows were shuttered against the damp chill outside, but the room was lit by the bright, dancing flames in the hearth, the candles on the mantel and the lamp on the table were ready to be lit. A large pot of porridge bubbled softly to itself at the edge of the fire, and in the warm ashes a kettle purred and steamed.

Grim looked up and beamed as his pupil entered. 'Thank the Guardians for the excellent Izobia,' he said blandly. 'Did you enjoy your swim?'

His pupil said nothing. He was staring at the older man's boots: his heavy outdoor boots, not the soft, hide shoes that both men habitually wore within the tower. They were wet, and smeared with mud. Grit from the beach was embedded in the soles. Dark felt his freezing face grow hot. His eyes rose from the boots to meet those of his mentor. 'I didn't see you,' he said.

'I was among the trees, and you *did* have one or two other things to occupy your attention.' There was sympathy and understanding on Grim's craggy face. 'You didn't really think I'd let you drown?'

Dark stood there dripping, conflicting emotions robbing him of speech. He felt squirming embarrassment that his mentor had been there to witness his desperate act of folly, amazement that he could even have contemplated such madness, relief that he had survived, and gratitude to Grim, for being there to watch over him. 'You let me cut it pretty fine,' he said in an unsteady voice, remembering again the terror he'd felt as he fought to reach the surface, his numbed and weakened limbs, his bursting lungs, and the icy water filling his nose and mouth.

Grim got up and handed him a towel that had been warming in front of the fire. 'Here. Now give me that wet cloak.' As Dark's knees began to buckle, he steered him towards the fireside chair, and sat him down. 'I had to let you do what you needed to do,' he said, as he rubbed his pupil's chilled flesh vigorously with the towel. 'You went into that lake today for a whole tangle of reasons. You wanted to cleanse yourself of yesterday's events, you wanted somehow to atone, and—' he leaned forward, his eyes burning into Dark's own, 'you wanted to look Death in the eye again. You felt that you must confront him, and win this time. Only by doing that would you be able to live with your special abilities, and your role as a Summoner. Only then could you feel that you, and not Death, were in control.'

Dark's mouth fell open. 'You knew,' he whispered.

His mentor took warm garments from a pile by the fire, and helped him put them on. 'Son, we've all been through this, to a greater or lesser extent. Those of us it hits hardest, as it did with you, tend to make the best Summoners in the end.' His mouth twisted wryly. 'In my case, I jumped off a cliff.'

'You *what?*'

Grim shrugged. Was his face red from his proximity to the fire, or could it possibly be embarrassment? 'It wasn't all that big a cliff, but it was big enough. It took months for all the broken bones to heal. Fortunately, there were some bushes at the bottom to break my fall. *Un*fortunately, they were brambles.' He grinned sheepishly at Dark, and thrust a mug of hot tea into his hands. 'So you'll see that by comparison, your little jaunt in the lake today was almost sensible.'

Ironically, now that he was warmer, Dark had started to shiver violently. His teeth chattered against the rim of the mug. Grim wrapped a thick quilt around his shoulders and across his knees, and held the cup steady so that he could drink again. 'You may not believe it, but this is a good sign. It means you're warming up.' He ladled some porridge from the pot into a bowl, added some honey, and gave it to his pupil.

As he felt each mouthful go scalding down, Dark actually began to believe that a time might come when he would be warm again. And you could say what you liked about Izobia, but she could certainly cook. At that moment the woman herself entered, carrying two plates of sausage, bacon, and fried eggs. With a dirty look for Dark, she set them down with a bang in the middle of the table and flounced out without a word – but not before he had noticed that she'd changed her low-cut blouse for a more decorous garment.

Still cocooned in the quilt, he tried to struggle to the table, but Grim pushed him back down into his chair. 'Stay where you are. Don't leave the fire. I'll bring the food over here.'

Breakfast had never tasted so good. Dark finished up with more tea, to which Grim added a generous dollop of the powerful moonshine that they brewed up at the Chieftain's stronghold. 'Now that you've warmed up a bit, this should do you good,' he said as, to Dark's surprise, he poured out a generous glass for himself. Only then did the young man truly understand just how much anxiety he had caused his mentor.

Barely giving him time to finish his tea, Grim hurried him off to bed. As he lay there, with a hot stone for his feet and a bright blaze crackling in the fireplace, Dark felt truly warm at last. He also felt at peace now, and very glad to be alive. This time, he managed to fall asleep with no difficulty at all.

After chasing his pupil back to bed, Grim sat brooding by the fire for a time, staring into the flames, his mind far away. Izobia, who had a healthy respect for the Summoner, came in, saw him preoccupied, cleared the table very quietly, and went in silence. He scarcely noticed. He was thinking of his pupil, and of a time in his own life long ago, when he had gone through a similar ordeal.

If only there was something more we could do. If only we had the power to deal in life, instead of death.

'Maybe you can.'

'*Amaurn?*' Swiftly, fiercely, Grim concentrated his wandering thoughts. No communication save in an emergency; that was the rule. 'What's happening? Where are you?' He broadcast the mind-speech on the tightest possible focus, to minimise the risk of being overheard by other members of the Shadowleague.

'I'm in Gendival.' There was quiet triumph in his leader's tone. 'Back from exile at last – no matter how surreptitiously.' Grim wondered at the wry amusement in his mental voice. 'At present I'm near that wayshelter on the moors between the valley and the Curtain Walls. Not too far away from you as the crow flies – if it's a pretty fast crow.'

The Summoner frowned. This did not sound like the cold, calculating Lord Blade that he had known for so long. 'But what in the world has happened? Surely it's too soon to take on Cergorn.' This sudden turnaround of events had taken him completely by surprise.

'What hasn't happened! All manner of havoc has broken loose in Tiarond. I was forgetting you'd have no way of knowing. Suffragan Gilarra, with the backing of the people, decided that Zavahl had failed as Hierarch, and must become the Great Sacrifice . . .'

'Helped by you, no doubt.'

'I do my best. In any case, the Sacrifice never happened. The rule of Callisiora was almost within my grasp when a blasted Loremaster, of all unlikely people, turned up out of nowhere and snatched our hapless Hierarch from the very sacrificial pyre. That was when the real disaster happened. The northern curtain wall has collapsed, my friend. Tiarond has been attacked by a horde of Ak'Zahar.'

'*What?*' Grim's blood turned to ice. 'But this is a catastrophe! The whole of Callisiora will be decimated, when those abominations start to spread!'

'You never said a truer word. You'd better warn the Reivers as soon as possible, Grim. Make sure the warning is broadcast throughout the clans, too, and into the lands beyond, if the messengers can be spared. This is too serious a matter for the usual petty enmities and squabbles. They'll have to start their defensive preparations now, if any of them are to survive, just as we must put our own plans into action, though it's sooner than I wished.'

'Of course.' Despite the gravity of Amaurn's tidings, hope and excitement were rising in the Summoner's breast. 'Can I help you in any other ways?'

'For certain. Can you send one of your little creatures to Gendival? Let our allies there know what is happening, and tell them to be ready.'

'Of course.' Though he was using mental communication, Grim took a deep breath. 'Amaurn? Can I join you? Don't leave me here in this backwater while history is being made.'

'Of course you can, my friend. I'll need all the allies I can get. Just hold on a little longer, until I've had a chance to assess the situation. I'll send you word to follow me in a day or two, I promise.' And with that he was gone.

Grim leaned back in his chair and let out a long slow breath. At last it was happening. Maybe now the world could be freed from the primitive ignorance into which it had been allowed to sink. How long he had waited for this day!

Hastily he got to his feet and ran upstairs to the topmost floor of the tower, almost tripping on the worn stone steps in his haste. At the top was a single wooden door, preventing further access. On the other side he could hear soft scritching, fluttering sounds which Dark and Izobia, who had never been allowed inside, attributed to pigeons.

Pigeons indeed! Well, I suppose it's one way of sending messages. Unless you have a better alternative.

Grim fished out a key that hung round his neck on a gold chain, turned it in the lock, and went inside. This was his workroom, a spacious chamber that took up the entire top floor of the tower. On the right-hand wall was a fireplace, with large, lockable cabinets on either side. Opposite the door a long table stood beneath the window, bearing a number of projects in which Grim was currently immersed. Samples of the local vegetation, carefully pressed flat and glued to bits of paper, were scattered round a plant press that had been roughly made from two blocks of wood and a heavy stone. A mortar and pestle stood beside various jars of dried and pulverised herbs. A wooden box, divided into compartments, held samples of assorted rock, all neatly labelled. Nuggets of copper pyrites glittered like false gold, alongside samples of powdery red earth. (Grim's discovery of the local copper deposits and the subsequent opening of a mine had greatly enhanced the wealth of the clan, and increased his standing in the eyes of chieftain Arcan, if not those poor unfortunates whose heads had been broken in order to persuade them that mining *was* a respectable occupation for a warrior.) Ink and writing materials, some used, some not, were stacked neatly at the other end of the table, opposite a tangle of sticks and string like the remains of a child's game of jackstraws, which bore witness to his failed attempts – so far – to construct a new kind of bridge.

The left-hand wall of the chamber was lined with bookcases, holding volumes of lore collected from many of the lands beyond the curtain walls. Some were handwritten on bound pages, others on parchment scrolls. Some were etched on metal, scratched on clay, or chipped painstakingly into thin slabs of stone. Grim even had precious printed books from Gendival, borrowed unofficially from the great library there, and never returned.

In the angle of the walls between the bookcases and the table was a large cage, like a gigantic birdcage, built into the corner from floor to ceiling. As the Summoner approached it, the inhabitants set up a chorus of animated jabbering and squeaking. Smiling, he took a tiny silver key from a wooden box on the windowsill, and unlocked the door.

Out they came, all five of them swooping around his head and clinging to his shoulders and hair, all the while keeping up their excited, non-stop chatter. They were small, the largest not quite six inches in height, and their bodies were covered in sparse black fur over leathery black skin. On the rare occasions when they chose their feet in preference to their wings, they walked upright. The wings themselves were soft black membrane ribbed with delicate bone, exactly like those of a bat. Their eyes were twin red sparks that glowed and glittered with mischief, set in wrinkled faces, also batlike, that were full of ugly charm. Their tiny hands were quick and clever, with long, hooked, pointed nails for fighting or clinging, that could be retracted like those of a cat. Their long, hairless, prehensile tails ended in wicked barbs that could do just as much damage as their sharp little teeth.

Grim laughed out loud as his creatures zipped and swooped exuberantly around the room, swinging from the lamp brackets, dislodging a shower of books from the highest shelves, and creating general havoc on his table. That was the reason the imps were normally caged; they were more than happy to stay with him and would not stray, but their insatiable curiosity and their habit of testing everything to destruction meant that he dared not leave them unsupervised in his workroom.

Though at first sight they looked very similar, Grim had lived with them long enough to be able to tell them apart quite easily. Gar was the biggest of the imps, and the leader. Slant-eyed Iss had insatiable curiosity and an uncertain temper, Bir of the spiky fur was a clown and a master of mischief. Of the females, Ell, rather chubby and extremely affectionate, was Grim's particular pet, and livewire Vai had enormous eyes set in a charming little face.

The imps were not native to Callisiora, and under Cergorn's rules, Grim should not be keeping them at all. He had discovered them many years before, when he was still a wandering Loremaster. He had been returning overland from the realm of the Dragonfolk, when he had stumbled across a small colony deep in the rainforests of Rakha. Charmed by the strange little creatures, he had made camp for a few days to investigate them further. They were curious, sociable and easily tamed, and when he had left, these five had chosen to accompany him. Knowing that the Archimandrite would not allow him to have them, he had decided to keep their existence a secret – not the easiest of tasks, given their mischievous and inquisitive natures. They had lived for an inordinately long time for such small creatures and showed no sign of ageing but, to his disappointment, they had never bred. He suspected that the climate of these northern latitudes was just too cold for them.

They were, however, very intelligent, and good at carrying messages to the handful of Blade's supporters who knew of their existence. Each of these Loremasters would supply the imps with a different delicacy on their arrival, and so when Grim showed them a certain type of food, they knew exactly where and to whom they must go to in order to find it. Sitting down at his worktable, Grim scribbled a quick message on a piece of paper. He rolled the note into a tight tube, wrapped it in a scrap of oiled silk, and strapped it to Gar's back, taking care not to foul the delicate wings. With the imp perched on his shoulder, chattering excitedly, he opened one of his cabinets and took down a jar of dried cherries. Gar took the wizened fruit delicately, turning it round and round in his delicate hands as he ate. When he had finished, the Summoner took him on his hand and looked deep into his eyes. 'Good. Now you know where to go.'

The imp chattered, for all the world as though he was answering. Was he? Or was it just wishful thinking? Grim suspected that he would never really know just how much the little creature understood. It flew from his hand to the window and waited impatiently on the sill for him. When he opened the shutters, it gave a farewell chirrup and swooped away into the veils of sleety rain, heading in the general direction of Gendival.

Grim closed the window with a sigh. 'Safe journey, little one,' he said softly. 'I wish I was coming with you.'

Fifteen

Conflicts

Scall was awakened by the sound of voices, calling his name with increasing urgency. It was the most wonderful sound he had heard in his entire life. 'Tormon!' He scrambled to his feet. 'I'm here! I'm up here!'

A moment later a welcome blaze of torchlight came round the curve of the lower tunnel. Clumsy with excitement, Scall scrambled down the ladder and back onto the treacherous metal strut that ran from wall to wall. As he did so, he noticed that the floodwater had gone down while he had slept.

'Scall? Scall, is that you?' The trader and Lady Seriema appeared, their eyes widening as they looked up and saw him clinging to his precarious perch. 'How in Myrial's name did you get up there?' Tormon gasped. Then suddenly, he burst out laughing. 'Bless me, but it's good to see you, lad. I thought you were gone for sure.'

Lady Seriema, looking much less distant and more friendly than usual, nodded agreement. 'When we didn't see you anywhere on the walkway, I wouldn't have given a brass farthing for your chances. I'm very glad that I was wrong.'

To his horror, Scall found his throat going tight. Never before had anyone been so glad to see him. He was suddenly warmed by a glow of belonging that made him forget his damp clothes, his shivering body, and his ravenous hunger.

'Come on, lad,' Tormon said. 'Time you came back down to earth.' Handing his torch to Seriema, he lifted his arms to help Scall down.

Scall unlocked his death grip around the uncomfortable strut, and the trader helped steady him as he dropped. 'Right,' he said. 'Let's get moving. You can walk off your stiffness as we go, but we can't afford to loiter around in here. We should have started sooner, but I must confess we fell asleep while we were waiting for the waters to go down.'

'Tormon?' Seriema's voice came from the shadows behind them. 'I think you'd better have a look at this.' She was standing below the circular aperture in the ceiling, looking up by the light of a torch held high.

Tormon gaped at the opening. 'If I had a gold piece for every time I've been through this tunnel, I'd be as rich as you are – and I'd swear on my life that *this* was never here before!'

'It's a perfect curve,' Seriema marvelled, 'and the inside is perfectly smooth. How ever did they make it like that?'

'I've been up there,' Scall told them proudly. 'Tormon, it's like nothing you've ever seen! It goes right into the mountain, and there's this great big chamber, full of the most unbelievably weird stuff. You ought to see it, you really should.'

For a moment the trader hesitated, torn between curiosity and common sense. Then he shook his head. 'We have enough to worry about, without mysteries,' he said. 'Leave it, Scall.'

'But you might find something up there that will help us, something that I missed . . .'

'Look,' said Tormon flatly, 'you saw what happened yesterday. If we don't get through this tunnel before it rains again, we're dead. I would love to take a look up there . . .' His voice tailed away wistfully, then he squared his shoulders and turned his back on the enticing portal. 'But we just daren't take the risk. Now I don't want to hear another word about it. We've got to collect the others and be on our way.' He turned to go – but Scall noticed him glance once more, over his shoulder, at the mysterious opening, with a look of regret and disappointment.

Tormon would love to go up there, but he's thinking of our safety instead. Maybe there's a lot more to being the leader than I realised.

Obediently, they followed the trader up the tunnel, and it seemed no time before Scall could see the wonderful sight of daylight from the tunnel mouth, and felt the booming thunder of the waterfall vibrating through the stones beneath his feet. One by one, he and his companions ducked quickly out from behind the curtain of plunging water, heedless now of the deafening roar and drenching spray that had seemed so frightening yesterday, when they were facing the unknown. Since then they had faced far worse, and had lived to tell the tale.

When Scall came out onto the narrow roadway and saw that it was still in place all the way to the top, he could have wept with relief. The force of the flood might so easily have sent a portion of it crumbling away, stranding the others and cutting Tormon's party off from their horses. (Afterwards, Tormon told him that he had been worrying about the very same thing, and the young man felt a glow of pride because he'd been thinking like a seasoned traveller.)

It was good to be out in the open again, though the wind was very cold. The day was brighter and clearer than the previous one, and though the sky was still grey, the cloud cover was much higher and lighter. From his vantage point, Scall could see showers like dark smudges drifting across the sky, and falling on the misty lands below.

The three climbed as fast as they could up the slippery path, and were greeted at the top by the glorious sight of the guardhouse, a stalwart island amid a sea of muck and devastation. The unexpected arrival of Tormon's missing party caused a sensation. The horses went wild at the sound of their master's voice, and could be heard whinnying and kicking at their partitions as they tried to pull loose their tethers. With a squeal of joy, little Annas launched herself right out of her upper bunk and into her father's arms.

Rochalla, trying to coax a sulky, smoking fire into flame, spun round with a yell and, to Scall's complete astonishment, flung her arms around his neck and kissed him soundly. Blushing furiously, he felt his neck and face glowing hotter than the coals in the fireplace. He very nearly ruined the whole thing by pulling away in embarrassment then, realising all in a flash that though he had never kissed a girl before, now might be an excellent moment to get in some practice, he kissed her back. To his surprise, when they broke apart, Rochalla's pretty face was as pink as his own must be. Her eyes met his, then shyly looked away. Suddenly, he was very conscious of being watched. Over her shoulder, he saw Presvel standing in the doorway, his eyes narrowed with hatred, an expression of black murder on his face. A sudden chill ran through Scall, as though someone had just walked over his grave.

Presvel's hands were shaking as he crammed the salvaged clothing, provisions and weapons into a backpack. Close by, Rochalla was also packing, with Annas trying (with varying amounts of success) to help her. Now that Tormon had returned, the happy child was chattering loudly and brightly without, it seemed, even pausing to take a breath. Her voice was beginning to grate on Presvel's nerves.

'You've never been down the cliff before, have you Rochalla? *I* have. We used to go in the wagon, but now we don't have it any more. I liked the wagon. I had a bed with my own pillow and a patchwork quilt and everything, and I had a red dress and a doll called Betsy and a picture book, and I could lean out of the back of the wagon and feed Esmeralda . . . I like Esmeralda, don't you, Rochalla? She has such soft, furry ears.'

On and on and on. Presvel gritted his teeth. How could Rochalla stand it? How could she reply so patiently to all that rubbish? Why did she have to sound so bloody *cheerful*? Over and over he saw her face in his mind's eye, as it had been when she'd kissed that gangling oaf. She had looked so happy and so young – as young as that damned boy. He had never thought much about her age when she'd been walking the streets. 'If they're big enough, they're old enough' – wasn't that how the saying went? And she had always seemed so mature . . .

Damn her. Damn them both. Why couldn't things have stayed the way they were?

Trying unsuccessfully to shut out his unhappy thoughts, he turned his attention to making a last-minute check of the items in his pack. How had that dagger come to be there? He didn't remember putting it in. Oh, never mind. Might as well hang on to it in any case. It was a good blade: long, keen-edged, and pointed. It was bound to come in useful.

'Are you done in there?' Seriema, who had been helping Scall and the trader to tack up their mounts, stuck her head around the door. 'The horses are ready. Tormon says it's time we went.'

'Tormon says entirely too much, considering that he voted himself into the position of leader,' Presvel snapped. 'Tell the miserable slave-driver we're coming.' He didn't bother to look round as he spoke, but even with his back to her, he could sense Seriema's disapproval. He knew that her eyes were on him. He could almost feel them, boring into the back of his neck.

Why does she have to keep doing that? She's always looking at me, watching me, spying on me . . .

He crammed the dagger back into his pack, and pulled the buckles tight.

When they finally got moving, things were just as bad. Presvel had been looking forward to riding double with Rochalla again; to feel her warm, slight body pressing close to him, her arms around him, clinging tightly to his waist. But Tormon had decreed that they must walk down the steep and slippery cliff road, and lead the horses. Rochalla wasn't even near him as they set out down the narrow path in single file. She was up near the head of the line, right behind Tormon, because again she was looking after Annas, and the child refused to be parted from her father. Seriema, leading her big, black gelding, was between Presvel and the girl, a tall, rather gawky figure in the man's trousers and tunic that she'd appropriated from the stores in the guardhouse. There was nothing left of the elegant, richly-dressed lady, but she seemed completely unconcerned, insisting that the new outfit was warmer, more comfortable, and far easier to move about in. Much to Presvel's irritation, Rochalla had followed her lead, and the smaller girl looked quite ridiculous in his opinion, with her pants hacked off at the bottom and ballooning round her legs. Her tunic, reaching almost to her knees, was belted in tight folds around her slender waist. When he had told her that she was a laughingstock, she had simply shrugged. 'Nobody seems to mind but you,' she'd told him.

Once the travellers were on their way, however, Presvel soon discovered that he had more to worry about than jealousy. The state of the roadway had not been improved by yesterday's flooding, which had gouged out great ruts and potholes, and even cracked the surface in places before disguising the worst of the damage beneath a coating of slippery silt. Given the conditions, the gradient was frighteningly steep, and the low retaining wall at the edge had been battered away in many places, to leave nothing between the travellers and the mist-filled void below.

The horses, too fresh after being cooped up all day yesterday, were nervous, balky, and plainly reluctant to attempt the road at all. Presvel's ex-Godsword mount, aware, as horses always are, that it had an amateur in charge, played him up continually. Had it not been for that wretched boy, who was bringing up the rear with his own neat-footed little chestnut *and* the donkey, and therefore blocking the trail, the blasted animal would have been away back up the cliff in a flash. What was worse, he thought, as he wrestled grimly with the bridle and freely damned the animal to perdition, Scall was in the ideal position to see him struggling, and to laugh at his mistakes.

Worse was to come. When it came to taking the horses behind the waterfall, the animals decided that enough was enough. Tormon's stallion planted his feet and whinnied, nervously rolling his eyes. The trader remained calm and unperturbed, soothing and petting him as if they had all the time in the world, and after a little persuasion, Rutska followed him trustingly, his ears pricked forward to hear Tormon's voice, which was pitched to be heard above the roaring of the falls. Seriema, learning from their example, had less trouble with her quieter gelding, who had travelled this road so many times, albeit in better conditions. After a little encouragement he went with her quietly, following his stablemate, and vanishing into the passage behind the curtain of water.

Then it was Presvel's turn. His was a fairly young beast, and it had never been this way before. To his horror it went berserk, its screams drowning even the thunder of the water as it reared and plunged, snapping at Presvel with its teeth and kicking out at Scall's chestnut mare as she came up behind. Faint with terror, Presvel wrestled with the bridle, trying to keep himself from being dragged right off his feet, knowing that the horse was out of his control, and all too aware that at any moment it would go over the edge of the cliff, and send him plunging with it.

Then Tormon was there. He ripped off his tunic and put it over the horse's eyes, tying it in place with the flapping sleeves. It stood there trembling violently, its neck streaked dark with sweat. 'Daft old thing,' he crooned. 'Were you scared then? It's all right now.' The panic-stricken animal calmed as he stroked it, then he turned to Presvel. 'Go on, then. What are you waiting for?'

Scowling, Seriema's assistant scurried into the tunnel, barely noticing the drenching he received from the waterfall. When the trader handed back the reins of his horse, he lifted his arm to punish the stupid beast, but Tormon grabbed him before he could strike. 'Leave him alone, you idiot. That's not the way to handle him. He's young. He's scared. He'll learn – and so will you, or you'll have *me* to deal with.' There was a grim finality to his tone. 'While you're travelling with me, you'll never strike an animal in temper.'

Rochalla's anxious eyes were fixed on the pair, and as Presvel, cursing, wrenched himself out of the trader's grasp, she came up between them and laid a hand on his arm. 'Please,' she whispered, 'don't antagonise Tormon. Without his knowledge and his horses, we'd be dead.'

He knew that she was right. 'I'm sorry,' he mumbled to Tormon, but as he turned away he was trembling with anger.

You wait. We may need you now, but some day you'll be the one who is sorry.

As soon as Scall had brought the last two animals through, torches were lit, and they continued down the trail. The atmosphere in the group should have been more cheerful, for the horses were less skittish in the tunnel, and there was no longer a lethal drop on one side to worry about. They dared not relax their vigilance, however. None of them had forgotten the terror and destruction of yesterday's flash flood, and how swiftly and unexpectedly it had struck. They walked along with every nerve at snapping point, straining their ears for the rush of distant water. When they reached Scall's mysterious tunnel, nobody was tempted to linger for a closer look. They would be in constant danger until they could get right off this cliff road, and no-one could forget it for an instant.

The tunnel turned back on itself, zigzagging on downwards. Not long afterwards they saw daylight up ahead, and then they were out once more on the open cliff face, on a narrow road with a heart-stopping chasm on one side. They had travelled down into the mist layer, and could only see for a dozen yards ahead. The hoofbeats of the horses, the creak of leather and the sound of each snorting breath was oddly muffled, lending the journey an air of dreamlike unreality. Silver droplets netted Seriema's black hair, making her look old before her time. Presvel craned his neck to look past her, but Rochalla was invisible, vanished in the eerie haze.

The mist grew thick and thicker as they descended further. Tormon ordered the torches to be re-lit, though they were reluctant to burn, and of little real use when they did. Presvel began to despair of ever reaching the bottom. Would they be condemned to spend eternity shuffling down this endless, sloping road? At last, to his relief, he heard Tormon's voice from up ahead. The words were oddly distorted by the moisture in the air, but they couldn't have been more welcome. 'We've made it, everybody! We're down at last!'

Gilarra found Galveron still sitting beside the empty bed. 'I'm sorry about your friend,' she said softly.

Somehow, the Commander had created a little island of stillness around himself in the busy guardroom, with everyone respecting his right to grieve in private.

Everyone but me.

For a moment, she thought that he wasn't going to answer. Then he spoke. 'Kaita did her best.' He shook his head, masked like a bandit with bandages above and below his eyes. 'Poor Ewald never woke up. I wish he had come round for a little while – just long enough for me to say goodbye.' He swallowed hard. 'I'm going to miss him. He used to joke that he was my right hand, but he wasn't far off the mark.' After a pause, he spoke again. 'You know, a soldier is forced to get used to his comrades dying. In a very real sense, death is all part of the job, and we learn to deal with it. We have to, but—'

'But you're only human, and some deaths are bound to be more of a blow than others,' Gilarra said.

'Exactly. It's the same with Kaita. If she let herself go to pieces every time she lost a patient, she wouldn't be a physician very long. But she's so overstretched just now, and so many of our injured have died already. She fought so hard for Ewald, and in the end it was all for nothing. This has hit her hard.' He looked up at the Hierarch, and though only his eyes and mouth were uncovered in his bandaged face, his pain was clear. 'So you were right, when you said she ought to treat your son. Ewald didn't have a chance.'

His bitterness was like a blow; in fact Gilarra caught her breath, as though he had really hit her. 'Galveron, please don't remind me of that. It was unforgivable. But Aukil wouldn't wake up, and I was in such a panic—'

'Hush, Lady,' Galveron said. 'It wasn't fair of me to bring it up. I understand how you must have felt.'

'None the less, I had no right to make that kind of judgement on the value of someone else's life, and I'm very sorry.'

He looked her in the eye. 'Don't you think that maybe you should be apologising to Kaita, not to me?'

Gilarra didn't answer. To avoid his eyes, she turned away to pull up a chair for herself. She wasn't going to forget what the Healer had said and done with regard to her precious child, and she wasn't about to forgive it, either. Galveron didn't need to know that, though.

I'm sick of him sticking up for Kaita!

'Why not come away from there?' she coaxed, anxious to talk about something – anything – else. 'You're exhausted. You should be lying down.'

'So should you,' Galveron replied. 'You didn't get any sleep last night either, and you've been worried sick about Aukil. Now he's come round, and seems to be all right, you should take the opportunity to get some rest.'

'Don't change the subject, Galveron. We're talking about *you*. You were in a fight, you were wounded, and you lost a fair amount of blood. How much longer do you think you can go on?'

He shrugged. 'I can rest later, when this place is more secure. Right now, those winged fiends have too many points of ingress upstairs. We can't keep on defending the stairway with fire as we've been doing. We don't have the fuel to spare. So it comes back down to men and swords.' He shook his head. 'Gilarra, you've seen those things. They're *fast*. How many more Ewalds do there have to be? How long do you think we can last out? Right now, the creatures have stopped attacking because its daylight, but I guarantee you that after dark, they'll be back in force. If we don't do something about it, I daren't think what will happen tonight.'

Gilarra narrowed her eyes at him. 'All right, Galveron. You might as well tell me and get it over. What exactly are you planning, that I'm not going to like?'

He tried to grin at her, and winced as the movement pulled the lacerated skin of his face beneath the precariously secured pads of bandage. Though Healer Kaita had done a painstaking job of stitching the jagged wounds, Galveron's good looks would never be the same again. Gilarra tapped her foot. 'Well?'

The Commander got to his feet, and began to pace back and forth. 'You're right. You aren't going to like it, but it's the only safe way.

We need to cut off those upper chambers completely, Gilarra. I want to bring the ceiling down in the stairwell.'

The Hierarch gasped. 'Mutilate part of the Temple? It's unthinkable! Haven't the events of this last year taught you anything? Myrial is already displeased with us. To anger Him still further would be disastrous for our people.'

Galveron sat down again. 'Gilarra,' he said quietly, 'that's a risk we have to take. If we don't, there won't *be* any of our people left to anger Myrial.'

Gilarra looked down at her fingers, twisting in the heavy fabric of her robes.

Why me? How can I possibly make such a decision?

Because there's no-one else. Like it or not, I'm Hierarch now. I always used to believe I could do a better job than Zavahl, but when my chance came along, I never realised the stakes would be so high.

She looked up at the Godsword Commander. He seemed so young.

How does he do it? How does he *cope with the burdens of responsibility?*

'All right.' She took a deep breath. 'Go ahead. But how will you do it?'

There was a sparkle of mischief in Galveron's tired eyes. 'I'm going to blow it up.'

'What?' Gilarra didn't even notice that she had leapt to her feet.

'I'm going to blow up the stairwell with that new blasting powder that the miners are using.'

Gilarra stared at him. He sounded calm and reasonable, but surely the wounds and the lack of sleep had affected his mind. He was rambling – wasn't he? 'But Galveron,' she said gently, 'just think for a moment. You can't go blowing up our only refuge.'

'That won't happen,' he assured her, with an airy confidence that made her shudder. 'I haven't been sitting here brooding *all* the time. I've been talking to some of the miners, and they tell me that a small, controlled explosion in the right place will do the job. The stairwell is a confined space. We won't damage the rest of the Temple.'

'But can you be *sure* of that?' She was grasping at straws now, and she knew it.

'As sure as I can be. Don't forget, the miners have families sheltering here too. They wouldn't advise me to endanger their loved ones.' He took a deep breath. 'Lady, one of the most important parts of being a Commander is weighing up the risks, and the way things stand at the moment, blowing up that stairwell is the lesser danger to our people.'

Gilarra sat very still, trying to project an image of outward calm, though her thoughts were churning wildly.

Damned if we do, damned if we don't. Why me? Why me?

Because I'm the Hierarch.

'All right,' she said. 'Do it.'

'Thank you, Lady.' She could hear the relief in his voice. 'You've made the right decision.' He hesitated. 'Er . . . There's only one more thing. We don't have any blasting powder with us.'

Gilarra felt a weight lift from her shoulders. Myrial had taken pity on her, and had taken the decision out of her hands. There was only one problem . . . 'But if you don't have the stuff, why did you bring the matter up in the first place?'

Again, that mischievous twinkle. 'Because we can get some. Under Lord Blade's orders, our siege engineers have been experimenting with its use as some kind of a weapon. There's a good supply of it in the armoury of the Citadel.' Seeing the horrified look on her face, he went on quickly. 'Think about it for a minute. We also need more weapons, especially arrows, and extra bows and crossbows. And Kaita says that there's a whole lot of medicines and bandages and whatnot in the Hall of Healing that would make a huge difference to us here.' He lowered his voice persuasively. 'Come on, Gilarra. One quick foray in the daylight, when those creatures are quiet, would make all the difference to our chances.'

So that was what he had been leading up to all along! Gilarra leapt to her feet. 'No,' she shouted, regardless of the curious stares from the folk at work around her. 'No, no, no and no!'

But she could tell by the set of his shoulders and the stubborn jut of his jaw that one way or another, he would do it anyway. If she didn't want to risk an outright challenge to her authority, she would have to let him go.

Sixteen

Food for Thought

Cergorn interviewed his errant Loremasters in the Meeting House, a large building of elegant proportions near the Tower of Tidings. Though it had the same low, inconspicuous profile as the other parts of the settlement, the floor inside was sunk well below the level of the ground to create a single, spacious, airy chamber with a soaring, vaulted ceiling. The doors had also been made very high and wide, so that the larger members of the Shadowleague could be accommodated inside.

The Archimandrite looked at the newly returned wanderers, and suppressed the urge to shake his head. They were not a prepossessing sight. Elion wore the wrinkled, grimy and ill-fitting uniform of a Callisioran Godsword soldier, while Veldan looked like something off a rag-picker's cart. Even Kaz looked exhausted, with a greyish tinge to the colour of his hide. Elion, slumped in his chair, looked weary and dejected. Veldan's jagged scar stood out cruel and livid on a face as white as chalk. Her own journey had been much longer and more arduous than Elion's brief mission, for she had come all the way from Zaltaigla, the land of the Dragonfolk, bringing Aethon the seer to Gendival. At least, that was what she *should* have done, the Archimandrite thought.

Merciful Providence! How can I tell the Dragons that we've lost their Seer? This will be an incalculable blow to them.

It was impossible not to be angry with the Loremasters. Veldan had made a complete shambles of her mission by losing Aethon, and then had compounded her sins by breaking one of the

Shadowleague's strictest rules and bringing an outsider through the Curtain Walls to Gendival. Kazairl had managed to get himself seen by a couple of thousand people who had, up to that point, existed in the innocent and happy certainty that monsters like the firedrake did not exist. And Elion . . . That damned fool Elion had managed to lose Shree. Cergorn's common sense could tell him a thousand times that the loss of his beloved partner was not the Loremaster's fault, but his heart could not forgive.

As for Veldan's conviction that Aethon was trapped in the body of the former Callisioran Hierarch – well, whoever heard of anything so ridiculous? How could it be possible? The Loremaster had no real proof to back her tale. Why, by all accounts, the man wasn't even a telepath! To make matters worse, unlike the ageing mercenary, who was at least here voluntarily, they had kidnapped Zavahl who, by their own admission, was a highly unstable character with a deep-seated religious faith that precluded what was happening to him now, and who might well be tipped over the edge into insanity when he saw some of the beings who awaited him in Gendival.

'I don't know what came over you,' Cergorn raged at the culprits. 'What's the point of all your training if you just ignore it when a crisis comes along? What's the point of us having rules if you're going to break them left, right and centre at the slightest provocation?'

Veldan leapt to her feet. 'But it wasn't *like* that,' she protested. 'Toulac is a telepath, and highly skilled in her profession. She may not be young any more, but she has a tremendous amount of experience to contribute. She deserves to be here. She belongs here. And if your mind wasn't so tightly closed against anything new, you would examine Zavahl and check the facts before you start ranting about what's possible and what's not.' She was trembling with pent-up anger. 'And as for Shree – how dare you blame poor Elion for that? Just how the bloody blazes is it his fault? You talk about sticking to the rules? Well, your partner went off by herself, didn't maintain contact, and mucked up all on her own. That's the truth, but you can't face it, so you try to put the blame on us instead.'

'BE SILENT!' Cergorn exploded. 'How *dare* you speak to me like that! Why, you're no more fit to be a Loremaster—'

Kaz, who had been sitting in a half crouch with his tail flicking back and forth, for all the world like an irritated cat, erupted into motion, putting himself between Veldan and the Archimandrite. Turning his head to glare at Cergorn through slitted, glittering eyes, he bared his teeth and gave a blood-freezing snarl. 'Leave her alone, you brain-dead lump of horsemeat. You're talking through your backside. Veldan is right. Toulac does belong here, and she'll make a damn sight better Loremaster than half the complacent idiots in this place. Aethon *is* trapped in the body of the Hierarch, and Thirishri did leave Elion and get lost of her own accord, without any help from him. We've done our best to handle this situation so far. Just because *you* can't cope, you've no right to take it out on us.'

Cergorn was stunned by such insubordination, and so enraged that he could barely speak. 'Get out, the three of you,' he spluttered. 'Just get out of my sight. Take yourself back to your quarters. I don't want you talking to other people right now. I'll deal with you later, when I've worked out how to undo the mess you've made.'

The three Loremasters walked out into the sunlight. The peace of the valley seemed unreal, after the stormy scenes that had taken place in the Meeting House.

Kaz was the first to break the silence. 'That went moderately well, I thought.'

Veldan gaped at Elion, then both of them burst out laughing. Even though the laughter was a little shaky, it helped to ease the tension.

They walked around the outside of the settlement, not really wanting to talk to anyone just then, and not permitted to in any case. But word spread fast in Gendival, and it soon became clear that the other Loremasters were giving them a wide berth. 'They don't want to be tainted with our disgrace – it might be catching,' Kaz muttered bitterly, quite forgetting that only a few moments ago, he hadn't wanted to speak to *them.*

The trio reached the river that flowed out of the Lower Lake and ran down the valley near the foot of the wooded hillside. They crossed the sturdy wooden bridge and halted prior to seeking their own homes, set high up the slope amid the trees: Elion's little house that overlooked the settlement, and specially-designed quarters shared by the other two, which were further up the valley, overlooking the lake.

'Well,' said Elion reluctantly, 'I suppose I had better be going.' The hostile edge that was usually in his voice whenever he spoke to Kaz and Veldan had vanished, and the firedrake, in astonishment, realised that the enmity that had existed between them for so long seemed petty and unimportant now, compared to their need to stick together in the face of Cergorn's wrath.

Elion turned off to the left, in the direction of his own dwelling, a small and lonely figure on the shadowed forest path. Veldan looked at Kaz. 'What do you think?'

The firedrake sighed. 'Dammit, I was really looking forward to some peace and quiet,' he grumbled. 'Just the two of us. But yes, you're right. Tell old slime-bag he can come.' All the usual venom had gone out of the insult.

'Elion?' Veldan called, and the other Loremaster turned back almost too readily. 'Would you like to come back with us for a while?'

He frowned. 'But surely you and Kaz would rather be on your own? I don't want to intrude . . .' He sounded almost painfully polite.

Kaz cocked his head, his tongue flicking over his jaws in the firedrake version of a grin. 'Oh, I dare say we can put up with you for a while. After all, we're all up to our necks together in this crap.'

Elion broke into one of his rare smiles. 'We're way over our heads in it, if you ask me. My thanks to you both. I would love to come. To tell you the truth, I was dreading the thought of going back to that cold, empty house alone. The way things stand right now, some company would be very welcome.'

'Even ours?' Veldan raised an eyebrow.

'I can put up with it if you can. I'll just go and pick up some clean clothes, and then I'll be right with you.'

Toulac would have been very surprised to learn that Zavahl's assessment of his prison was similar to her own, despite the fact that there was a guard in the corridor outside his door, and another in the yard below his window, presumably in case he decided to risk the jump. He might be a captive, but captivity had its compensations. He felt immeasurably better for a bath, and the clean clothes that had been provided for him by a pretty, smiling young woman. Later, she had brought him a robust midday meal, and he had tackled it with tremendous appetite, finishing every bite of the homely fare. It had been so long since he had last enjoyed any of his food, and none of the elaborate dishes cooked especially for the Hierarch had ever held such savour for him.

Now he was sitting looking out of the window of his room, sipping at a mug of ale, and basking like a cat in the bright autumn sunlight that shone through the glass. Ah, the sun! Maybe his dream was true, and Myrial was not angry with him, if he had been guided to this lovely place. His window, at the back of The Griffin, looked out onto a neat, cobbled yard surrounded by stables and outbuildings of the same mellow stone as the inn itself. On the opposite side a gap between the buildings led to a garden: he could glimpse the corner of a bed of cabbages, and a washing line laden with white sheets that flapped noisily in the wind. It was a far cry from the soulless stone of his barren mountain city. The air was fresh and crisp, so different from the raw, bone-chilling, endless damp of Callisiora. He could smell clean straw and horses, and the earthy musk of the nearby autumn woods.

Leaving the window, Zavahl looked again at his cosy room. The walls were panelled in warm wood, with brightness and colour provided by the embroidered cloth on the table, the gay patchwork quilt on the bed, the red and blue cushions on the fireside chair, and the multicoloured rag rug on the floor. A brass pitcher on the table held a bunch of autumn flowers that blazed with the colours of the fire, and on the wall hung a large brass plate engraved and enamelled with the picture of a peacock, that glowed bright as a sun against the darker background of the wood.

Draining the last of his ale, he lay down on the comfortable bed. To his amazement, Zavahl felt a curious lightness of heart. So many dreadful things had happened recently that it felt good just to be still for a little while, and rest. For days, it seemed, he had been torn apart by violent feelings: anger and terror, bitterness, misery and dread. No-one could sustain such strong emotions indefinitely. It seemed to him that on reaching this peaceful place – wherever it might be – his mind and body had consented to accept his fate, to stop fretting and fighting for a while, and to let him rest. Even the demon seemed to have left him; or at least he hoped so. He had not heard or felt the intruder in his mind since he had spoken with Elion yesterday. Had it really been there at all? Had he imagined it? No, Veldan mentioned it when she had spoken to him in the shelter. According to her, it could not leave.

Should I try to talk to it?

He didn't want to. The whole idea of having another being in his mind still filled him with fear and dread. As long as the interloper remained quiet, he could pretend to himself that it was not there.

I'll wait until Elion comes. I can't deal with this alone.

Right now, Zavahl wanted nothing to shatter the fragile little shell of calm that surrounded him. He was still a prisoner of course, and Myrial only knew what horrors awaited him in this place. Why else would Elion have wanted to blindfold him? But though he knew in his heart that he ought to be more afraid of what was going to happen to him, he felt detached and unreal, and unable to care. In a strange way, he felt as if he had truly died on that sacrificial pyre, and had been reborn to a new, and very different life.

Suddenly there was a brisk knock on the door, which opened to reveal the smiling woman who had brought him the clothing and the food. She was carrying a tray. 'I've just come for your dishes,' she said brightly. 'No, don't bother to get up, dear. I can manage.'

Dear? No-one had ever addressed the Hierarch of Callisiora with such kindly, brusque familiarity, yet coming from her, it felt absolutely right. To his increasing astonishment, she left the dirty plates where they were, and came over to sit down on the bed. 'You look better than you did before, at any rate,' she said. 'When they brought you here, you looked like one of those limp little critters the cat leaves on the doorstep. Some good, hot food has put a bit of colour into your face.' Lightly but deliberately, she ran a thumb along the edge of his jaw. Zavahl's eyes opened wide. A shiver of pleasure ran through him. She leaned down towards him and he could see the swell of her breasts straining against her dress. She kissed him very gently, her mouth soft and sweet on his own. Her hair fell around his face, with a faint scent of flowers and sunshine.

Zavahl's first instinct was to push her away, to tell her that all his devotion must go to Myrial – but somehow it didn't happen. With increasing fervour he returned her kisses, and felt her fingers moving deftly on the fastenings of his borrowed clothes. His breath catching in his throat, he undid the row of tiny buttons down the front of her dress, to reveal flesh as golden as a peach. She straddled him, too impatient to wait until they could undress completely, and as he entered her, Zavahl's head spun in a flood of glorious sensations. Poised above him, seen through a glow of mounting desire, she looked like one of the Reivers' pagan goddesses. For a fleeting instant he felt a pang of guilt, one final vestige of the old Zavahl.

I can't do this! I dedicated my life to Myrial!

Then she smiled at him, and he looked up into her dazzling eyes, and the old Zavahl was lost.

To blazes with Myrial! What has he ever done for me?

When finally they were sated, and she lay curled beside him in a tangle of bedclothes, Zavahl had braced himself, wondering when the guilt would strike. So far, however, there was little sign of it: in fact, he was amazed at how delighted he felt, with himself and with this generous and lovely woman. How different it had been from that other time when he had gone disguised into Tiarond, driven by a body whose urges would no longer be denied. That time, he had felt remorseful and unclean, and had suffered agonies of conscience ever since. So why did this time feel so very different? In part, it must be due to the change in his circumstances: now that Zavahl the Hierarch no longer existed, Zavahl the man could have a chance at last. There was no doubt, however, that most of the credit must go to the woman who lay content and sleepy by his side, tracing the flesh of his chest and neck with an idle finger.

Ailie – her name had emerged at some time during the course of their lovemaking – was open, warm-hearted and generous; honest, loving and kind. She had changed everything, and had made him feel wanted as no-one had ever done in his entire, lonely life.

Into his mind came disconnected flashes of Elion's words, when they had talked back in the wayshelter: 'It won't be easy . . . Your whole life will be turned upside down. It'll make you question yourself in ways you can't even imagine . . . You won't have to go through it alone . . . It's possible that a great deal of good may come out of this situation. You might make new friends, or find a new life for yourself, or grow in ways that you can't even imagine.'

How right he had been.

If only this moment could last forever! If only I could stay here, poised right on the crest of this wave of happiness.

But already she was stretching against him, emerging from the contented half-doze in which they had both been wrapped. 'Mmmm . . .' She sighed. It sounded like the contented purring of a drowsy cat. 'That was nice.' She leaned over and kissed him on the lips. 'I'm tempted to stay here for the rest of the day, but I've got a heap of stuff to do, and Olsam will be wondering what's become of me.'

'Olsam?'

'Yes. My father. He—'

But Zavahl was no longer listening. It had suddenly hit home to him that he was a prisoner here, under guard, and therefore completely at the mercy of an irate father.

Ailie dissolved into laughter. 'Gracious, if you could see your face! It's all right, love. I'm old enough to go my own way, and Olsam respects that.'

Zavahl's eyes widened. 'But doesn't he mind?'

'Oh, he'd love me to settle down and get wed, and bear him a litter of grandchildren. But he's a bit torn, you see. He loved my mother very much, so he doesn't want me to settle for anything less than they had.' She shrugged. 'So in the meantime, he minds his own business and I mind mine if he should happen to get lonely – though in truth, there's usually precious little business for either of us to mind. He can't find anyone who could hold a candle to my mother, and I'll have you know I'm very, very choosy.'

'So why in the world did you pick me?'

Propping herself up on one elbow, she looked down on him with eyes that had suddenly turned serious. 'I chose you because I fancied the look of you,' she said with devastating honesty. 'And you seemed so lonely and sad that I wanted to hold you and take care of you.' She gave him an evil grin. 'And now I've lured you into my wicked clutches, I would like to stay here and make love to you until we both collapse from exhaustion – but I really don't have time.' As his face fell with disappointment, she added, 'I can come back tonight, though.'

Suddenly Zavahl remembered his precarious circumstances, and the delight in his heart died away. 'I don't even know if I'll be here tonight.'

'Oh, you will,' Ailie said. 'Trust me.'

'Right now, you're about the only one I *can* trust.'

She looked puzzled. 'But what about Elion and Veldan? They brought you here, didn't they?'

'They kidnapped me,' Zavahl said grimly. 'Or at least, Veldan did, with the help of her pet monstrosity.'

'They *did*?' Ailie frowned. 'Is the gossip wrong, then? They didn't rescue you right off a sacrificial pyre?'

Suddenly Zavahl felt himself blushing. 'Well . . . Well yes, they did as a matter of fact,' he admitted sheepishly.

'But wasn't that a good idea, love? Or am I missing something here?'

'I . . .' He threw up his hands helplessly. 'I suppose I felt it was my duty to go through with the sacrifice. It was supposed to help my people.' Though it had sounded very brave and noble in the privacy of his mind, he was forced to admit that when he said it out loud to someone else, it *did* sound a bit silly.

'And you didn't think that maybe you could help them better if you were actually still around to *do* something?' Ailie smiled and hugged him. 'Well I, for one, am very glad that Veldan intervened when she did. What kind of idiots go around burning folk alive? At least she's given the rest of us a chance to talk some sense into you.'

She sat up with her arms wrapped round her knees and looked down at him, her face very serious. 'You know,' she said, 'I grew up with Elion and Veldan – and the firedrake too, for that matter. I would trust them with my life. Elion's family were just ordinary folk from here in the village. Veldan's mother, Aveole, was a Loremaster across at the settlement, and her father was a bit of a mystery, although there *was* some talk . . . Anyway, Aveole died when Veldan was very little, and the only legacy she left her daughter was Kaz's egg. They grew up together, both of them orphans, and . . .'

'Why are you telling me all this?' Zavahl interrupted.

'Because when people are strangers, it's easy enough to look on them as monsters. When we get to know them, we see them in a different way, and sometimes we realise that just maybe they had a good reason for their actions, all along. If Veldan gave you a hard time, it's just that she's had it pretty rough herself, lately. She got that scar on her face fighting some monsters that damn nearly killed her – in fact, they *did* kill Elion's partner. Poor Veldan was badly wounded, and she's been in a lot of pain for quite a while. That's why Kaz gets so protective. Did you know that until lately, she insisted in wearing a mask all the time? That's how bad she felt about that scar. She—'

But Zavahl was no longer listening. He was thinking about the first time he had encountered Veldan, and his reaction to her scarred face. He cringed inside. No wonder she had treated him so unkindly!

'Ailie? Ailie? Where are you?' Olsam's voice came faintly from downstairs.

Ailie leapt to her feet. 'I'm sorry, but I've really got to go. I'll be back later.' She kissed him swiftly, and was gone.

Seventeen

High and Low

The small group of surviving Grey Ghosts had made their cautious way back to the Esplanade, and spent the night in the safest place they could think of: the crypt of Aliana's wool merchant. Now they were skulking in the garden behind Lady Seriema's house, down at the far end where a collection of dead brown sticks in the muddy ground marked the place where a shrubbery had once flourished.

'I can't believe I'm back here again,' muttered Aliana. 'Am I destined to spend the rest of my life hiding among these wretched mansions?'

'Yes,' her brother replied in a whisper, 'if you don't get a move on. And the rest of your life will last exactly until one of those damnable creatures spots us.'

Aliana set her jaw. 'I still think this plan is a crazy idea.'

'Well, you couldn't come up with anything better,' Alestan snapped, 'so it's the only plan we've got.'

'But taking refuge in the Temple! What's going to happen if we manage to make it that far? What if there's nobody left alive? What if they won't let us in?'

'Well, it can only be one or the other,' he pointed out reasonably.

Aliana ignored him. She was in no mood for reason. 'And what do you suppose we're going to tell them? How can we explain to the accursed Godswords why we weren't at the Sacrifice?'

'We'll think of something.' Alestan's expression was lightened by a wry and fleeting grin. 'You never know, those fiends might have done us all a favour, and eaten Lord Blade.'

Packrat pushed his way between them, glaring. 'If you keep us standing out here much longer while you squabble, there won't be anything to fight over,' he hissed. 'Those flying bastards will settle matters for you.'

Aliana felt her usual flare of temper at the attitude of this unsavoury sneak, but Alestan, as usual, remained unruffled. 'Did you check the tunnel?' he asked patiently.

Packrat shuddered. 'Yeah – and you were right. That's where the buggers are hiding out. There's not much stirring right now, so it looks as though they do sleep in daylight. I could hear them breathing though, and a sort of rustling that I suppose was their wings. And the stench! You could smell them a mile off.'

You'd have to, thought Aliana, wrinkling her nose at Packrat's own unsavoury odour.

Alestan was frowning, deep in thought. He was always the steady one, the planner, while his mercurial twin sister tended to act on impulse, though her instincts and common sense usually saved her from making too many mistakes. 'It looks as though we were right, then,' he said at last. 'They don't like the daylight. If they're crowding into the tunnel like that, they probably live in caves. That would explain why they were so attracted to our Warrens.'

'It also means that your plan is no good,' Aliana pointed out. 'We can't get to the Temple now.'

'Oh yes we can,' her brother argued. 'We'll climb into the Precincts – go over the canyon wall, right over the top of those predators in the tunnel.'

Aliana stared at him, speechless at such audacity. Not everyone was so restrained, however. '*What?* Are you *crazy*? I can't climb up there!' Gelina was white with horror.

Alestan patted her gently on the shoulder. 'I know climbing's not your game,' he told her patiently, 'but right now it's our only chance. It'll be all right, Gelina. We'll take it nice and slowly, and I'll be there to help you over any difficult bits.'

The woman shook her head slowly. 'You must be mad.'

A short while later, Aliana was tempted to agree with her, as she clung to a rock face with very little in the way of discernible holds. Time was pressing, for the climb, up one side of the canyon wall and down the other, must be completed during the daylight hours. They had been forced to make a rapid choice of location, picking the best place they could find in a hurry, and trusting to skill and luck to get them over the most difficult parts. They had chosen a place at the far left of the Esplanade, beyond Lady Seriema's house, where the high ridge on the eastern side of the city curved round to join the cliffs that guarded the Sacred Precincts. Tosel, the best climber of the party, had pointed out that the weathering of the stone was most advanced in this corner, due to the swirling action of the wind and the rain.

So here they were, strung out on the cliff face, with Tosel going ahead to find the best way up. Tag and Erla came next, with Aliana following to assist the children over any difficult parts, though she was beginning to think she need not have worried. The pair climbed like little squirrels, far better than herself. Packrat came behind her and Aliana wished that he were anywhere else, for his comments, ranging from the lewd to the obscene, about the view he was getting, soon began to grate on her nerves. Eventually she was lucky enough to find a nice bit of loose rock on a ledge, and kicked it down into his face as he followed her. That put paid to Packrat and his filthy mouth for a while, though she had a bad feeling that he was lurking behind her, plotting his revenge.

Gelina and Alestan brought up the rear, moving much more slowly than the others. Aliana could hear her brother's voice, calm and encouraging, as he guided the frightened woman up the cliff, pointing out the best places to put hands and feet. She hoped that the two of them would make the climb in safety – or that Alestan would, at any rate. She was aware that her attitude seemed heartless, but she couldn't help it. Earlier that day, and all through the previous night, she'd been convinced that he must be dead. To her relief, the fates had proved her wrong, and it would be too cruel if she were to lose him now. 'Get a move on, Gelina,' she muttered under her breath. 'Come on, you stupid woman! It isn't *that* hard.'

Not *that* hard perhaps, but hard enough. Though she would never admit it, Aliana's injured arm was giving her trouble, hampering her movements and preventing her from stretching fully out for holds. Like everyone else she was weary and distracted, constantly taking her concentration away from what she was doing to make a nervous scan of the surrounding skies. Rain dripped constantly into her eyes, and trickled in icy rivulets down her neck and inside her sleeves. Worse still, the moisture darkened the surface of the cliff, making it more difficult to see what lay ahead, and laid a slick and slippery sheen on the crumbling stone. Before long, not only Packrat was cursing. They all were doing it – even Tag and Erla, who had grown up hearing strong language all around them. Hearing the coarse words uttered in their piping, childish voices, Aliana began to wonder, as she had never wondered before, whether the Warrens had really been a good place for a child to grow up. But for all its faults, she reminded herself, the rough-and-ready community had presented a far better alternative than starving on the streets.

Abruptly, Aliana's straying thoughts were jerked back to attention as a chunk of rock broke off in her hand, leaving her dangling by her wounded arm. Her feet slipped and she scrabbled for a hold, kicking a shower of loose stone down over the unfortunate Packrat. 'Watch what you're doing, you clumsy cow!' he snarled, but in another instant she was grateful to feel him guiding her flailing feet back to safe niches, so she could regain her grip and her balance. She called out shaky thanks through gritted teeth and stretched her aching arm up to the next safe hold, hauling her weary body after.

Suddenly, she was at the top. First Tosel vanished from sight, followed by Tag and Erla, then Aliana was hauling herself over the edge onto a blessed level surface with Tosel, who didn't even have the decency to be out of breath, reaching down to give her a hand. He flashed her a grin as she flopped down to rest her aching limbs.

'That was a nice little climb. And just think, you'll get the fun of doing it all again when we go down the other side.'

I'll strangle him – when I get my strength back.

Galveron's little band of foragers assembled by the Temple door. They were eleven in all: eight hand-picked Godsword warriors, chosen for their intelligence, level-headedness and combat skills; Shelon, Kaita's assistant, who was needed to identify the medicines and equipment that the Healer had listed, a miner named Areom, who was coming to select the blasting powder, fuses, and any other paraphernalia that might be needed for bringing down the ceiling in the stairwell. In addition, there was Galveron himself.

The Commander's decision to select himself had been universally unpopular, and his exchange of opinions with the Hierarch on the subject had been as explosive as the powder he was going to find. Amid the stink, the overcrowding and the background of constant noise within the Temple, it was easy for tempers to flare. Kaita, on the other hand, though as furious as her counterpart, had been contemptuous of his folly, pointing out that he was injured, probably still in shock – which might explain why he was acting like such a fool – and far too indispensable in his role of Commander to be risking himself on such a dangerous venture, which one of his men could lead just as well. To give additional weight to her warnings, she had reminded him that she also wanted to go along, but had enough sense to accept the fact that, as the most experienced Healer, she had no right to put herself at risk.

In his heart, Galveron knew she was right. 'But it's different for me,' he had told her. 'I need to get out there, and assess the situation for myself. I must try to get an idea of the numbers of these creatures, and find out where they're spending the daylight hours. I've got to get into the Citadel armoury, and see exactly what weapons and equipment we have at our disposal. Gilarra isn't thinking far enough ahead. We can't stay penned up in here forever. If we can't find a way of taking the fight to the enemy, we're finished.'

Kaita folded her arms and cocked her head to one side. 'And that's the real reason, is it?'

'I told you it was.'

'So it's nothing to do with Sergeant Ewald's death? You've no ideas about avenging him, or expiating some kind of guilt that you survived and he did not? Or feeling so bloody angry at the needless death of a good man that you must act somehow, or explode?'

The indignant denial died on his lips.

What's the point in pretending it's not true? I'll only look like even more of a fool. Clearly she knows me better than I know myself.

Kaita patted him on the arm. 'I don't mind if you lie to me about your motives, but you'll be much more effective if you are honest with yourself. Just be careful out there, that's all. Make sure you're thinking clearly. We need you, Galveron. You're the real leader here.' At that moment, someone called her away, and before he could answer, she was gone.

When Galveron opened the door of the Temple, there was a great rush of wind and a sound like muted thunder, as the sky filled with a whirl of black wings. With a curse he leapt back, ready to slam the door, but then his brain caught up with his reflexes, and he realised that the air was full of birds: dozens and dozens of great black carrion crows, who had come to feast on the dead.

'Myrial blind me! I thought we was goners, there,' someone muttered behind him, and he recognised the voice of Areom the miner, a stocky little man with hair cropped to a short black stubble, and an ebullient nature that, so far, seemed to have weathered all the vicissitudes of the siege. Glancing back, Galveron saw the ashen faces of the rest of his party, and knew that, with their nerves already stretched to breaking point, they had made the same mistake as him. 'Well,' he said ruefully, 'now we know there's nothing wrong with our reflexes, at any rate. Let's get on with it before the real ones wake up.'

Once outside the great doors of the Basilica, Galveron felt horribly exposed at the top of the broad staircase. On first sight, nothing seemed to be stirring between the buildings of the Precincts or in the skies above, but his heart was pounding hard, his body poised to fight or flee, and the skin between his shoulders crawled as though he was the target of unfriendly eyes.

The courtyard outside the Temple was a scene of horror far beyond Galveron's darkest imaginings. Everywhere he looked there were bloated, decomposing corpses, their eyes eaten out by rats and ravens, their bodies eviscerated and butchered, their limbs and faces gnawed. The stench, which had already begun to infiltrate the sanctuary of the surviving Tiarondians, was overpowering out here. Already the crows were settling, resuming their interrupted feast. Everywhere there were scamperings and furtive flickers of movement. The vermin of the city had suffered as lean a time as the human inhabitants over the last few months. Now every rat in Tiarond had converged upon the Precincts to take advantage of this unexpected bounty.

'This is the best thing that could happen,' said a cool voice from behind Galveron's shoulder. He glanced around to see Shelon, Kaita's studious young assistant, calmly appraising the macabre scene. 'Right now, the dead are a real danger to the living,' the Healer continued. 'With so much decomposition taking place, the threat of disease is growing every hour. We should be thankful it's winter, so we haven't got the flies and maggots, but the sooner the scavengers can clean up these corpses, the better it'll be for us all.'

He was right, of course, but that didn't make it any easier. By the time they had picked their way through the slough of decaying bodies in the courtyard, every one of the Godswords, seasoned warriors all, had vomited themselves empty. Areom the miner, grey-faced and trembling, looked ready to pass out at any moment. Only Shelon seemed comparatively unaffected, though Galveron, noticing the young man's clenched jaw and the sheen of perspiration on his brow, guessed that he was not quite so detached as he would wish to appear.

The Hall of Healing was a shambles, with smashed doors and shattered windows. Beds and other furnishings were overturned, and sheets and blankets shredded, and scattered far and wide. For the first time, Shelon looked distressed. 'Let's hope they haven't managed to get at our medicines,' he muttered. As it turned out, however, he need not have worried. The ointments, herbs and potions were always locked in a strong-room for safety, for many of the ingredients were very dangerous, or difficult to make or obtain. The reinforced doors and barred windows had withstood the onslaught of the winged invaders and soon Shelon had found the keys, right where Kaita had told him they would be, and was filling two sacks and a large backpack, carefully ticking off items on the list in his hand. Most of the Godswords had been stationed by Galveron at various points in the building, so that they could keep a lookout in all directions, while Areom and the two remaining warriors carefully packed up bandages, dressings, and surgical supplies. The work was completed with speed and efficiency. No-one wanted to loiter here, expecting at every moment to be attacked.

So far, Galveron's plan seemed to be working. The clouds were fairly high, the light was good, and there had been no sign of the winged aggressors. *Dear Myrial, let our good luck last,* Galveron prayed, as he led his little band back across the slimy charnel-house of a courtyard. They had to pass the Basilica to head for the Citadel on the other side of the Precincts, and Galveron made Shelon scurry back inside to safety, taking all of the priceless items recovered from the Hall of Healing back to Kaita. The Commander did not intend to risk one of his precious Healers any more than was absolutely necessary, and certainly Shelon raised no objections to leaving their party.

The Temple doors opened a narrow crack to Shelon's coded knock, and he slipped quickly inside, laden down with all his finds. When he had seen the Healer back into the Temple, Galveron hurried the rest of his companions onwards, towards the dark, looming walls of the Citadel. Time was wearing away, leaving only a couple of hours until sunset. Still, if they didn't waste any time, they should have long enough to do what they needed, and get safely back. Though there was always the possibility of spending the night within the Godsword Citadel, so long as the building was secure, Galveron would use this option only as a very last resort, for it would mean that Gilarra and her people in the Temple must survive another night of repeated onslaughts from the winged abominations, as they poured in through the shattered windows upstairs.

Hurrying through the archway and into the Citadel courtyard, the Commander and his companions found, to everyone's relief, that there were few bodies there. Probably due to the tightly packed crowds attending the sacrifice, and the panic caused by the initial attack, not many people had managed to get this far. When he realised how much darker it was within the high enclosing walls, Galveron reminded himself to be doubly wary. He had never really noticed before, just how much darker it was in here than in the broad open space before the Temple. Until now, it had never been important. To make matters worse, a glance at the sky showed that a new lot of thick, low cloud was coming in fast from the north, already obscuring the peak of Mount Chaikar. He muttered a warning to his men. 'So stay alert,' he finished. 'Keep your eyes peeled for any movements or unexpected shadows. Stay in pairs or larger groups at all times, and choose one person to be the lookout. That's his *only* job, so don't distract him.'

One or two of the Godswords were looking at him oddly, and he suddenly realised he was keeping them waiting around in the open while he gave them instructions, not only distracting them but putting them in danger.

Was Kaita right all along? Am I unfit to be in command?

Well, it was too late to worry about that now.

Because everyone was required to attend the great Sacrifice, the Citadel had been left empty and unmanned; a state of affairs that normally would have been unthinkable. Was the fortress still secure? Had those accursed creatures managed to get inside? He discovered that he need not have worried. Blade, as always, had been nothing if not thorough. The main doors, great slabs of iron, had been barred from the inside.

Galveron ran along the side of the building until he reached a small, unobtrusive postern, set deep into the thick wall, in a shadowy corner. It too was locked – and Blade must have the key.

Blade locked us out of our own fortress? I don't believe this.

To his horror, there was no time for him to consider his next move. From the skies came the rapid drumming of wings, in the courtyard there was the sound of racing feet. A number of raga-muffin figures were pelting towards him at full tilt, trying desperately to outrun the menacing shadows that dropped swiftly from above.

Aliana discovered that the top of the canyon wall was much broader than she had expected: a plateau of weathered rock some thirty yards wide. She had never set foot in the Sacred Precincts in her life for, to a thief, the environs of the Godsword Citadel were the most dangerous place in the city, and the canyon, with its single exit, was nothing but a trap. Somehow, she had always imagined the great stone barrier as being little thicker than one of the substantial walls of the merchant mansions, and because she had never been through the entrance tunnel to see for herself how long it was, she'd had no idea of her mistake.

Tosel and the two younger children were already heading across towards the far side of the plateau, in a hurry to look over the edge and assess the downward part of the climb. Packrat, wheezing and cursing, was just pulling himself onto the top of the cliff, and Gelina and Alestan had not appeared yet. While she waited for them, and took the chance to catch her breath, Aliana struggled to her feet and looked around her. To her great surprise, the broad expanse of rock was not flat, as she had expected, but had been carved into weirdly-shaped hummocks and hollows by centuries of rain and wind. Many of the protuberances were as high as her head, and had holes in them that looked deep enough to swallow an arm up to the shoulder. The thief in Aliana took appreciative note of so many wonderful hiding places for loot, but right now, she had other concerns.

It was absolutely freezing up here. There was no shelter from the bitter wind, which seemed much stronger than it had been on the ground. Sharp as a blade, it sliced across the expanse of stone, wailing and screaming like a tormented soul. There was no way to escape its blast. Aliana felt horribly exposed, silhouetted against the skyline, with no decent cover anywhere in sight. A shiver ran through her that had nothing to do with the icy wind. If those fiends should come, there would be nowhere to run and nowhere to hide.

Where were the others? She turned back to the cliff they had just climbed, to see a very white-faced Gelina collapse in a panting heap near the brink of the plateau, while beyond her, Alestan was just scrambling over the edge. Looking around for Packrat, she discovered him some distance away, poking around a nub of weathered, wind-sculpted stone that looked to Aliana just like a kneeling figure. There were several deep holes in the rock, and he was testing them one after the other, groping around inside to see if anything happened to be hidden there.

Aliana sighed. *He never gives up, does he? What could he possibly hope to find, all the way up here?*

At that moment, Packrat gave a whoop of triumph. The others all came running. 'What the bloody blazes do you think you're doing?' hissed Alestan. 'You'll have those accursed creatures right down on top of us!'

Packrat, in the meantime, had both hands behind his back, and was looking even more shifty than usual. 'Nothing,' he said. 'I didn't do nothing at all. I thought there was something in there, so I shouted out, but I was wrong. I'm sorry I made a noise.'

The apology was enough to excite Aliana's suspicions right away. Packrat *never* showed the slightest hint of contrition for any of his dreadful deeds. Alestan, however, had other things on his mind. 'Come on,' he said. 'Let's get moving right now. It's too dangerous up here, and we daren't hang around a moment longer than we have to.'

Aliana was about to protest, but the others – led, she noticed, by a suddenly enthusiastic Packrat, who was now jamming his hands into his pockets – were already hurrying towards the far side of the plateau, picking their way as quickly as they could over the uneven surface. They were right, she knew. Her curiosity would have to wait.

When she joined Tosel and the little ones on the other side of the plateau, she knew at once that there was something wrong. The children were whimpering, and Tosel's face was grey, and set like stone. 'Look,' he whispered. 'Just look.'

For a moment, Aliana didn't know what she was supposed to be looking at. A glance down into the Precincts showed her that there were many more buildings in the canyon than she had expected: a whole cluster of surprisingly ordinary little houses near at hand, close to the entrance tunnel. Further away was the dividing wall, with its great golden gates, beyond which she could see the sinister looming bulk of the Godsword Citadel, and the Temple itself, with its fascia carved in relief from the very cliff itself. When seen from this height it was a truly awe-inspiring structure, overwhelming in size, its every line and carving showing the consummate craftsmanship with which it was built.

Then her eyes followed the line of the building down, and she saw what was in the courtyard. Behind her, she heard her brother's gasp, and Gelina's stifled sob. At her shoulder, Packrat was cursing with steady, uninterrupted venom. For a moment it was impossible to take in the sheer horror of the situation, to believe the evidence of her own eyes. But Aliana saw the crows flapping and fighting over the piles of corpses and, now that she was aware of the source, she realised that ever since they had reached the top of the canyon wall, the north wind had been carrying traces of corruption and decay. What the smell must be like down there didn't bear thinking about.

'Dear Myrial,' Gelina murmured. 'It looks as though everyone in the entire city is down there. Could anybody have survived? Are we the only ones alive?'

'Look at the Temple doors,' Alestan told her. 'Tight shut. There must be survivors sheltering inside, and for once we'll stand a better chance if we're with everyone else.'

Aliana said nothing. She just continued to stare, in frozen shock, at the carnage down below. 'Get a move on, you silly bitch!' Packrat gave her a hard dig in the ribs. 'It looks as though we've got to go down, no matter what. Are you going to stand there gawping all day?'

Aliana couldn't think of a sufficiently unpleasant retort. The scene below her had left her bereft of words. Besides, the little swine was right and he knew it, and so did she. Flipping her finger at him, she turned away and eased herself cautiously over the edge of the cliff.

The descent of the canyon wall was even more of a nightmare than the climb up had been. Though in one way, it was less of a strain because it lacked the effort needed to haul her body upwards, in other ways it was worse, as Aliana soon discovered. It required strength and great precision to let herself down slowly, one foothold at a time. Soon the muscles in her hands and calves burned fiercely, and kept going into spasm from the sheer effort needed to cling to the rock face, and lower herself down in a controlled and careful fashion. To make matters worse, it soon became clear that Alestan had been right about the need to hurry. Thicker clouds, low and dark, were scudding in fast on that freezing wind from the north.

It'll probably snow again tonight – supposing we live that long.

Bracing herself carefully against the rock, Aliana glanced over her shoulder again at the racing clouds. Already, about a third of the sky had been covered by their lowering masses. Already the light was beginning to dim. It wouldn't take long for them to come right over, and then . . .

And then those foul abominations in the tunnel will be on us in a flash.

She remembered how fast they could move; what fierce and voracious killers they were. The thought of them caused her to tremble, made her hold on the rock face shaky, gnawed at her concentration just when she needed it most. Cold sweat ran down between her shoulderblades. With an effort, she did her best to pull herself together.

For pity's sake, just concentrate on getting down off this bloody cliff, or it won't matter a damn whether those blasted creatures wake up or not!

One thing at a time – or one problem at a time, more like. This side of the canyon wall was a much more difficult proposition. The rock was smoother, and there were fewer decent holds. It was more sheltered here, she supposed, and less exposure to the elements meant less weathering. A glance down showed her that Tosel and the children seemed to be making good time below her, while above her she could hear Packrat puffing and swearing. Somewhere beyond him, she could hear Alestan's voice, patiently coaxing, encouraging and instructing, and knew that Gelina was having difficulties again. Damn the woman! They should really have sent her down first, and let her take her chance. If she fell now, she could take the rest of them to the bottom with her.

'We're down, Aliana. Look out for the—' She didn't hear the rest. Erla's piping voice broke into her concentration so unexpectedly that she slipped in the middle of reaching for a new hold, and came down the last three or four yards the fast way. To her surprise, she hit the sloping roof of a building, invisible from higher up. She rolled and slithered, clawing vainly at the tiles, and felt empty air below her as she dropped over the edge.

Quick as a flash, Tosel was at the bottom to break her fall. He caught her just in time and they went down in a heap together. She heard him grunt as the air was knocked out of his lungs.

'Thanks,' Aliana said shakily, as they picked themselves up and disentangled their limbs. 'I owe you one.' An older man, she knew, would probably have made a joke about it being a pleasure, but Tosel, with all the gawky self-consciousness of a boy on the threshold of manhood, was crimson-faced, and could scarcely meet her eye. He covered his embarrassment by turning to the unfortunate Erla and giving her a slap. 'You stupid little idiot!' he snapped. 'Don't you know better than to call out like that when somebody's climbing? If she'd broken an arm or a leg, where would we be?'

The blow was a mistake. The child let out a piercing wail, loud enough to awaken every winged fiend in the city. Packrat, who was just lowering himself from the roof, hit the ground running, clamping poor Erla under one arm and covering her mouth with his other hand. 'Oh, very clever,' he snarled at Tosel. 'Now look what you've done, you mucking fool!'

Alestan and Gelina came slithering down behind him, hanging by their hands from the guttering and dropping neatly to the ground. Even in that moment of crisis, Aliana felt a flash of irritation that the clumsy older woman had made a better descent than she had. Then, looking round for the first time, she realised just how close they were to the mouth of the tunnel. On their descent, the available holds must have led them across as well as down: sure enough, when she looked up she saw a slanting fault across the face of the rock that they must unwittingly have followed.

From the black maw of the tunnel came a scratching, scrabbling noise, and soft, hissing whispers that sounded like some unknown tongue. The creatures were waking!

Above, the sky was growing darker and darker. Any moment now . . .

'Come on.' Alestan grabbed her arm. 'Don't just stand there. Run!'

In a bunch they pelted through the Outer Precincts, passing workshops and neat little homes, and leaving tracks across a muddy village green. No-one suggested sheltering in any of the houses. There was no point. Everyone had seen the creatures come bursting through windows in the city. They had no option other than to keep running, hope that the Temple or the Citadel would provide them with a haven, and pray that they would reach it in time.

Soon they had almost reached the great gates of the Inner Sanctum, but the clouds were right across the sky now. The skin between her shoulders crawled, as in her mind's eye, Aliana saw hundreds of winged shapes come boiling out of the tunnel like bats out of a roost. Was it true? Were they coming? There was no time to look back. Driven by fear, she discovered that she could run faster than she had ever run before. With the others, she pounded through the imposing golden gateway, and into the Inner Sanctum.

Here they encountered a new challenge. How could they run across the Temple courtyard, with hundreds of decomposing corpses piled up everywhere? The doors of the Basilica, lying opposite them across that broad expanse, might as well have been beyond the Snaketail Pass. To make matters worse, some of the others were showing signs of distress. Gelina, never the most athletic of people, was gasping for breath, and the children were stumbling with exhaustion. Aliana glanced back over her shoulder, and found that for once, her imagination had fallen short of the truth. The creatures were emerging from the dark mouth of the tunnel. Soon the sky would be black with wings.

If we don't do something, we'll be ghosts indeed.

In one of those rare flashes of twin-like accord, Alestan and Aliana came to the same conclusion. Rather than attempting to cross to the Temple, they set off to the left and, keeping to the edges of the courtyard, made for the Godsword Citadel. At least here, in the lee of the high wall, there was marginally better cover. And the Citadel entrance was a great deal closer than the Temple doors. Nevertheless, by the time the Grey Ghosts had reached the archway, a dozen or more of the creatures were above them, circling in the sky like vultures. As Aliana and her companions burst through into the courtyard, her heart sank as she saw the massive doors of iron tightly shut. Then, to her astonishment, she noticed a knot of black-cloaked figures clustered around a small doorway near the larger entrance.

I never thought I'd be so glad to see the Godswords! But why don't they get that door open?

Even as Aliana and her companions raced towards the strangers, she knew it was too late. Triumphant shrieks came from above her, as the fiends came plunging from the skies.

Eighteen

The Citadel

Galveron could scarcely believe his eyes when he saw the strangers, but he was more concerned with what pursued them. 'Archers!' he bellowed. The three crack bowmen he had brought with him unslung their weapons from their backs, and the other Godswords, drawing their swords, grouped around them and miner Areom in a protective formation.

'Fire!' shouted Galveron. Three arrows flew upwards. With a dreadful screech, one of the creatures plummeted from the sky. Another faltered in its flight but stayed up there. It veered away back towards the tunnel, skimming low, a trail of dark blood dripping down behind it. Behind him, Galveron could hear his bowmen making wagers amongst themselves and, in spite of the danger, he smiled.

The running figures were close now, but even as they approached, a dark shape swooped like a striking hawk, and struck one of them down. The creature landed, leapt towards its prey – and crumpled, a black-feathered Godsword arrow sticking out of its bony chest. The victim of the attack didn't get up again. To Galveron's dismay, one of the runners doubled back, hoisted the fallen one over his shoulder with a strength that belied his wiry frame, and came staggering after his friends.

One of the Godswords cursed. 'He'll never make it!'

'Corvin – you cover him,' Galveron told one of his archers. 'You other two, protect the rest of us. Keep picking them off. We want to discourage any more of them from coming down.'

The rest of the fugitives, including two children, came staggering up and were pulled into the midst of the defensive knot – apart from one of them, a girl who, when she had seen her friends to safety, tried to double back. Galveron caught her arm and pulled her to safety. 'What do you think you're doing?'

'Alestan!' She was fighting him like a fury. 'My brother!'

Galveron swore. Pushing her into the unready arms of Areom, he darted forward and helped the young man over the last few yards, partly hauling him, partly helping to steady the dead weight of his burden. He could see instantly that the man was dead, his neck broken, his head at an impossible angle. 'Put him down!' he shouted. 'It's too late!'

The other took no notice. Another winged shape and another came in low over their heads, and were both brought down by the keen-eyed archers. Galveron pushed the man and his grisly burden among the others, and turned to face the foe again. Behind him, he could hear the children weeping, a sound like a knife twisting in his heart. 'Tosel,' they were crying, 'Tosel, wake up!'

More and more of the winged abominations were arriving now, circling overhead, keeping the Godswords and their companions pinned down where they were. The creatures were sitting targets, but the arrows were running out, and Galveron had to order his men not to fire until a fiend was actually swooping down to attack. He knew they were only waiting for the last of the arrows to be fired, then they would all come at once, and that would be the end.

Well, we tried. I'm sorry, Gilarra, I failed you. Kaita, you were right. I wasn't fit to command, and now I've led these men to their deaths.

Then from behind him came a sharp click, and the creak of an opening door. The miner gave a cheer. Galveron spun round in astonishment to see a pinch-faced ragbag of a figure brandishing a lockpick and grinning evilly from ear to ear.

'Get inside!' yelled the Commander, but no-one needed telling. With great restraint, the Godswords maintained their defensive positions until the others had gone through, with Areom helping to carry the body of the fallen one.

'Leave him behind! He's slowing us up,' Galveron shouted desperately. 'He's dead, you fools.' They took no notice.

Bloody civilians!

Seeing their prey escaping, the predators attacked. Suddenly Galveron found himself at the centre of a conspiracy as his men seized him and bundled him through the door ahead of them, and into the narrow corridor beyond. An instant later there was a choking carrion stench, and the air was full of wings as the creatures struck. There was a dreadful scream, but the knot of struggling soldiers blocked his view. After a moment, all light was extinguished as the door was pushed shut, with considerable difficulty, against the press of bodies trying to break through from the outside. He heard the slam of heavy bars dropping into sockets. In the pitch darkness further up the passageway, someone struck a spark, and lit a stub of candle, which they held up in a wavering hand. In the growing light, Galveron saw that two of his Godswords were gone.

With bitterness in his heart, he looked at the ragged little group who clustered, weeping, around the body on the floor. Scum from the Warrens: there was no mistaking them. But where in Myrial's name had they been hiding until now? Not that it was important. What mattered was that they had cost two good men their lives. 'You fools,' he snarled. 'If you hadn't held us up with that accursed corpse, my troops might still be alive.'

The young man who'd brought in the body leapt to his feet, tears streaking his face. 'So there are two Godswords less?' he snarled. 'So what? Suddenly the world's a better place.'

Galveron's fist flashed out so fast that he had acted before he even realised what he was doing. The other, catching the blow right in his face, staggered backwards, tripped over the body of his friend, and slid down the wall, blood pouring from his nose and a cut mouth. Then, with an acrobat's grace, he was back on his feet, advancing on Galveron with murder in his eyes. Out of nowhere, a knife had appeared in his hand. Corvin the bowman, who had lost a good friend today, put one of his last arrows to the string in one smooth motion. The other soldiers drew their swords.

'Stop!' The younger of the two women thrust herself between the protagonists. 'Alestan, put that blasted knife away. *Put it away.*' They stood eye to eye for a long moment, and Galveron could almost feel the tension in the air between them as will vied with will. Then, after what seemed an eternity, the young man looked away from her, and sheathed his weapon. The soldiers surged forward.

'Leave my brother alone!' the girl shouted.

Myrial, is she *going to draw a knife now?*

Galveron put out an arm and stopped his men. 'This has gone far enough.'

She looked at him and nodded coolly. He couldn't exactly call it thanks, but at least it was acknowledgement. Her hand dropped back to her side, but he saw the wary tension in her stance, and knew that she was still ready to fight, if need be. 'I'm sorry about your men,' she said in a clear voice.

'You're *what?*' her brother spluttered. Without looking at him, she held up a hand for silence. 'Alestan, let me handle this.' To Galveron's surprise, he subsided.

She continued speaking, addressing the Godsword Commander. 'I understand why you're angry. But don't you see? *We* have nothing but each other.' Her sweeping gesture included all of her companions. 'We're family now. We have to be. Everyone else, everyone we know, is dead. Tosel—' there was a catch in her voice. 'He was just fifteen. In the heat of the moment, Alestan felt he couldn't just leave him to be mauled by those creatures. You're right. It was a mistake, and a bad one that cost lives. But there wasn't time to think of that, not then. I'd have done the same myself – and maybe, if you were in our place, you'd have done likewise.'

In Galveron's mind's eye he saw Kaita, telling him he was unfit to lead this mission, that his responsibilities lay elsewhere, that Ewald's death had provoked him into making a bad decision. Slowly, he held out his hand to the girl. 'You're right. And whether or not there was any truth in what I said, I shouldn't have said it; not then.

I'm sorry too.' As he held out his hand to her he glanced over her shoulder at her brother, who was still mopping ineffectually at the blood pouring from his nose. The eyes of the sandy-haired young man were flat, hard and unforgiving.

I hope you love your sister enough to keep the peace – at least for now.

'Look, we're all in this mess together,' Galveron said persuasively, 'and we're not out of trouble yet. We can't afford to be fighting amongst ourselves. We must put this unpleasantness behind us, and help each other, if any of us are to survive.'

'You're right.' It was the girl who answered, not her brother. She took Galveron's proffered hand in her small, strong, callused one, and clasped it briefly. 'But you shouldn't have hit my brother.'

He saw it coming, but by Myrial, she was fast. All in a split second her fist came up, she took in the bandages on his face, and brought her knee up into his balls instead. Nausea swamped him. He doubled over, wheezing, blinded for a moment with pain. There was a stunned and frozen silence, and then the Godsword soldiers, enraged by the attack on her leader, moved in to grab the girl. Galveron, still clutching himself, freed one urgent hand to wave them back. If her brother was provoked into pulling out that knife again, there would be no salvaging the situation. Besides, she had pulled the blow. Though it had looked pretty spectacular, and it still hurt like perdition, she could have hit him a damn sight harder, and he knew it.

Straightening cautiously, with an enormous effort, he saw her watching him with wary eyes. Under the circumstances, he couldn't quite manage a smile, but he held out a hand to her again. 'Quits?'

He saw the relief in her face. 'Quits.' This time her handclasp was longer; firmer. Though her green eyes were still swollen with crying, and her mop of tawny curls stuck out in all directions like a scare-crow, she was probably quite pretty, under all the dirt. She was also forthright, brave, and loyal to her brother and her friends. If she came from the Warrens and had not been at the sacrifice, she was almost certainly a thief, but he was ashamed that he had thought of her as scum.

From one side came the acid voice of Areom the miner. 'If you youngsters have all finished playing silly buggers now, do you think we can get on and find the stuff we came for?'

Quaking inwardly, Gilarra stood in the great Basilica, before the screen of silver filigree that concealed the Sanctorium of the eye. She was aware of the weight of history pressing on her; aware that she was doing what every Hierarch before her had done, right back to the founding of the Temple. Had they all been as scared as she was?

The first time you stood here, Zavahl, were you feeling as I'm feeling now? Today I understand you better than I ever did before.

All around, the business of the refugees went on without her: people waiting in lines for food and water; little nests of blankets that denoted territories; homely gossip from one camp to the next; squabbles over living space, and hard-to-come-by goods such as cups and spoons. Children ran about underfoot, playing, or fighting, getting in everyone's way, and on quite a few people's nerves. No-one was taking any notice of the Hierarch. She couldn't remember when she had ever felt so lonely.

Gilarra had left Bevron asleep in the guardroom, exhausted after staying up all night watching Aukil. To her relief the boy was recovering well, apart from a headache that was inclined to make him whiny. Felyss, Agella's niece, was minding him now. She seemed a kind, sensible girl, and was very good with children, making Aukil laugh with the stories she told him. The Smithmaster had taken her aside and told her about the girl's recent ordeal, and Gilarra, touched by her suffering and humbled by her courage, was glad that she had been able to give Felyss some useful occupation to keep her from dwelling on these last few dreadful days.

With her family settled and her people's needs being met for the time being, at least, Gilarra was free to face up to the ordeal she had been putting off since she had first put on the mantle of the Hierarch. Now, she could postpone her fate no longer. Siege or no siege, the other priests were starting to look askance at her, and she knew that they would not fully accept her authority until she had survived her first visit to the Sanctorium of the Eye, that mysterious Holy of Holies that none but the Hierarch was allowed to enter, and heard the voice of Myrial for herself.

Behind the screen, the entrance to the Sanctorium looked like a doorway into pitch black nothingness. The instructions to the Hierarch for this ceremony were recorded clearly in the Temple archives. No lamps, no candles. Frankly, she could have wished they had been a little less specific. That black hole looked more in need of a candle or two than anywhere she'd ever been. Well, it wouldn't do any good to stand here worrying about it. Gilarra slipped her shoes off, according to custom, took a deep breath, and stepped resolutely forward.

Once she was through the doorway there was a loud click, then darkness and thick silence seemed to swallow her, as though the world of light and sound and people had never existed. Looking back, she realised that the portal had closed behind her, despite the fact that when she had entered, she'd seen no sign of an actual door. It was as though she had passed through some kind of barrier that had cut off every vestige of the world outside.

Gilarra stood very still, afraid of confusing her sense of direction, able to see nothing in the profound blackness, and hear nothing but the pulse of blood within her body, and her own thoughts racing in her head. But she couldn't stay there forever. Cautiously she shuffled forward, one step, then two. She could feel nothing in front of her, but there was a wall at the furthest stretch of her fingertips on either side, and she felt a great sense of relief that this void had some limitations. When she took a third step, however, she met with a wall, smooth, cold and solid, right in front of her.

What? But this place can't just be a small black box. There must be something else here!

The ground beneath her dropped away, and she dropped with it. With a terrified squeak, Gilarra went down on her hands and knees to maintain a better contact. Her stomach told her she was plummeting fast, and when she reached out cautiously to the walls, she felt her fingertips burn from the friction of the moving surface.

Suddenly, the floor stopped falling, with much less of a jolt than she had imagined there would be. There was a brief grinding noise, and a hiss of moving air. Her surroundings were still lost in darkness, but when she groped in front of her, she discovered that the wall had gone, and the way ahead was open. With mounting annoyance, she clambered to her feet.

This is ridiculous! Why the bloody blazes couldn't they have put some lamps down here?

Then she realised that if the Hierarch was the only one permitted in this place, there would be no-one to light and maintain them. Besides, there could be thousands of unlit lamps scattered all around the place. How would she ever know?

Very cautiously, Gilarra took another step. Beyond the edges of the box she had come down in, there was nothing: no comforting walls, no structures of any kind. The void around her could have been infinite, or the size of a bedroom. 'Hello?' She called out tentatively. 'I am the new Hierarch.' The words seemed to fall away from her with a hollow reverberation, giving her the impression of a vast space all around her.

Again, she shuffled slowly forward – and her heart nearly stopped. At the side of her right foot, the surface simply ended, leaving her teetering on the brink of nothingness. When she moved over to her left, she found the same. She was standing in pitch darkness, on a bridge about two feet wide, without any handholds or railings. Below her . . . She had no idea what was below her. Water? Rocks? A bottomless pit? A six-inch drop onto a nice soft mattress?

In your dreams.

Very, *very* carefully, she got back down on her hands and knees. Putting her arm over the edge, she felt below her, but without much hope. Sure enough. Nothing.

Better not fall, then. I'd hate to find out just how deep this chasm is.

She didn't know how long the bridge was, either, but there was only one way to find out. Just then, staying on her hands and knees seemed like a very good idea. The bridge was made of what felt like smooth stone, and had a slight upward slope, which suggested that it was some kind of arch, or ramp. Feeling for the edges, she inched her way into the darkness.

Come back, Zavahl. All is forgiven. You can be Hierarch again, any time you like, and I promise I'll never envy you again.

Gilarra could have been crawling for mere minutes or a month: in the silent darkness she had lost all sense of time. At first she had tried counting to herself, but she was too worried about what lay ahead of her to concentrate, and kept losing track. She had reached the apex of the arch some time ago, and started down the other side. Eventually, to her utter relief, she felt the edges broaden out into a level floor. Even so, only pride got her back onto her feet again.

Wherever you are, Great Myrial, I'm not going to meet you on my knees.

The Hierarch groped around her, her hands outstretched, hoping she might encounter something – anything – that would give her a clue how to proceed. Her right hand brushed against some kind of upright shape about waist height. She let her hands trace its outline, and found some kind of plinth, or pedestal. On its slightly sloping top was the sunken imprint of a hand. A shiver of excitement ran through her. Surely this was what she sought!

She spat on her right hand, which surely must be filthy from crawling along the floor, and wiped it down her robes, thinking what Zavahl would say if he could see her dishonouring the Hierarch's sacred vestments thus. For that matter, she'd better hope that Myrial would understand. The ancient texts hadn't been clear about whether or not she should be silent at this point, or should be saying something. No, she decided. If there had been something she ought to say, she surely would have been told what it was. Unless, of course, it was some deadly secret, passed down from one Hierarch to the next by word of mouth . . .

Don't be silly. Surely I can't be the first Hierarch, down all the ages, who has been in this position, or something similar. If there were any words, they would have been lost ages before this.

Trying to keep her hand from trembling, Gilarra placed it on the shallow depression on top of the plinth. She waited. And waited. Absolutely nothing happened, and nothing changed. Gilarra felt cold all over. Had Myrial rejected her? Was she unfit to be Hierarch? Anxiously, her fingers explored the handprint on the plinth. Had she missed something? Oh, if only she could see!

Then she felt it. Beneath the third finger was a small, round aperture. Clearly something was meant to fit there. Something that she lacked. What could it be? It was about the size of . . .

'Oh, dear Myrial, no!' It was exactly the size and shape of the great red stone that glittered on the Hierarch's ring. The too-large ring that had slipped from her finger, and been snatched away into the skies by one of the winged marauders.

Had she not been standing in the most sacred place in Tiarond, Gilarra would have cursed like a fishwife. It wasn't fair! Her mind flashed back to her predecessor. He had been wrong, and so had she. Myrial had not abandoned his people because he was displeased with Zavahl. Clearly it went deeper than that. It seemed as though the God had tired of his worshippers altogether, and had decided to make an end of them for good.

We're finished.

With a heavy heart, Gilarra turned to retrace her steps through that long, dark, difficult route by which she'd come, and all for nothing. She had hardly started her rule as Hierarch, and already she was finished. If she wanted to keep on ruling the Tiarondians, she would have to live a lie. Then when she was about halfway back across the bridge, it came to her like a revelation.

What if it doesn't have to be this way? What if Myrial is testing me? If he really was displeased with Zavahl, maybe he wants to make extra sure that the next Hierarch is worthy?

True or not, at least it was a much-needed ray of hope. But in order to win her place as Hierarch, she would have to recover the ring, though under the circumstances it seemed like an impossible task.

By the time she had made her way back to the noisy, lighted world above, Gilarra's resolve had stiffened. She *would* get the ring back. She *must* get it back. And she would need accomplices to help her, but she would have to choose them very, very carefully. Until the ring was recovered, she must do what Zavahl had done for so long, and pretend to the priests and to her people that everything was all right. Her allies would hold her secret, and if they were not exceptionally trustworthy, they could bring her down at any time.

Nineteen

By the Fireside

Aethon was delighted with Zavahl's progress. Though he could have done without being a helpless passenger at the back of the human's mind while he coupled, there was no doubt that the experience had been fascinating. More importantly, however, he hoped that every step the human took away from his fears and prejudices was one step nearer to communication and cooperation.

The Dragon's opportunity came sooner than he had expected, after the woman had dressed herself and slipped out of the room. Zavahl, left alone, curled up in the disordered bed and fell asleep. This time, Aethon found the inner landscape of the sleeping human's mind to be a very different place. The tarn was still there, ringed with its mountains, but now the sun shone on tranquil, limpid waters. Though the storm clouds still brooded in the distance over the rearing peaks, the immediate surroundings were at peace.

It was easier, too, for Aethon to enter the human's dream. Zavahl was standing on the very peak of Mount Chaikar, looking down on Tiarond, far below. Aethon joined him, once again in his guise of Myrial. 'So,' he said. 'Now you have learned to rise above the past? You are beginning to discover wisdom, Zavahl.'

'I see things more clearly since last we spoke, great Myrial.' His manner was less cringing and more forthright, and Aethon approved of the change.

'So you understand now, that you are being tested?'

'I only wish I had realised sooner. I might have behaved very differently.'

'You have learned, that is the important thing. And you have also been rewarded,' he added slyly. He took a deep breath. 'Are you ready to be tested further?'

Zavahl swallowed hard. 'I will do my best.'

'Then watch and listen.' Without warning, Aethon resumed his true form.

'The Dragon!' gasped Zavahl. 'But it was when I encountered the Dragon that the demon entered my mind . . .' Horror began to dawn on his face. 'A demon,' he said slowly, 'who could come into my dreams pretending to be a Dragon – or Myrial himself.'

He guessed. Well, I might have expected it.

Ever since Elion's conversation with the former Hierarch, Aethon had been lying low in Zavahl's waking mind, taking care not to betray his presence, afraid that he would damage the progress that the human was making. Now the game was up. There had always been that risk, but he could not stay hidden forever.

'Zavahl,' he said quickly, 'trust your instincts. You remember the way you were before: doubtful, afraid, constantly struggling to fight an enemy you couldn't beat. Remember how unhappy you were, and how wretched and bleak your life had become.' Though Zavahl still looked suspicious, at least he was listening. The dragon pressed on. 'Think how much your life is changing since you listened to Elion. Think of that sweet girl who befriended you today. You're not alone in the world any more. Think about that. Does it really feel like such a bad thing?'

Slowly, Zavahl shook his head, though a shadow of doubt remained in his eyes. 'But what of the demon?'

'There *is* no demon.' Aethon told him with infinite patience. 'I am Aethon of the Dragonfolk, no more, no less. Listen. When you encountered the Dragon, he was dying. *I* was dying. But I possess knowledge of the history of this world that may help us in the present crisis. It would have been disastrous if that information had been lost, so when you came so close to me on the mountain, I gambled everything on one last, desperate act. I left my dying body, and lodged my mind, and my memories and spirit, in you. I never meant you any harm, and I'm sorry for frightening you so badly. But I had no choice. It was that or lose everything and, believe me, my life was only the smallest part of what would have been lost. I carry the memories of my people, right back to their beginnings on this world. Had it not been for your assistance, no matter how reluctant, the entire history of my race would have died with me.'

'But that's impossible!'

'You've encountered a lot of things you thought impossible in the last day or two, Zavahl. You were rescued from certain death by a fiery monster. You've passed through the Curtain Walls, to a land beyond.' Aethon's voice took on a tinge of amusement. 'You have also let love into your heart. Now who would ever have imagined that?'

'But how do I know you're telling the truth?' Zavahl was still protesting, but he was beginning to weaken.

Aethon played his trump card. 'You trust Ailie, don't you?'

'Well . . . yes. I do.'

'And she told you that you could trust Elion and Veldan. Why would they risk their lives to rescue you from that pyre, Zavahl? They didn't know you and, with respect, what use could you be to them? It was me they were after, and if they are the good people that Ailie describes, surely they wouldn't be trying to save something evil? Trust me, Zavahl. Trust the people who have befriended you. They have your interests at heart far more than the Callisiorans who sacrificed you on that pyre.'

Aethon paused to let his words sink in. Zavahl said nothing, but he was thinking hard. It was time for a tactical withdrawal.

'Rest now,' the Dragon told his host. 'Dream well, Zavahl. When you awaken, we will talk further, if you wish. I can tell you about my land and my people, or this place to which you have come. I can tell you about Elion and Veldan, and what they represent. More importantly, I can tell you what is going wrong in the world, and what you yourself can do to help your people – without needing to be burned up on a bonfire.' Hoping that he had sufficiently stimulated Zavahl's curiosity, he allowed himself to fade gently from the dream.

Zavahl opened his eyes to find shadows clustering in his chamber, and the fire sunk low and red in the hearth. Stretching, he got out of bed, and poured himself some water from the jug at the bedside. Outside his window it was twilight, the sky a clear and delicate shade of lavender, with one last slumbrous crimson glow, like the dying embers in his fireplace, lingering over the hills at the head of the valley. In the other direction, the first bright stars were appearing here and there. The cool, moist air smelled of evening dewfall, with a rougher trace of smoke from the village fires of peat and wood. Bats, hawking for moths, were banking and looping in exuberant display, and a barn owl flew across the stableyard, pale and silent as a ghost.

Turning from the window, Zavahl lit the candles on the mantelpiece, and the oil lamp on the table. The delicate twilight outside was swallowed up in darkness as the room took on a golden glow. Kneeling on the hearth he made up the fire, blowing the reluctant embers back to life, then he sat down in the fireside chair, and his mind returned to the revelations of his dream.

Not a demon, but a Dragon? Could it be true? Trust your instincts, his visitor had told him. Well, now that familiarity had blunted his fear, he couldn't feel any evil in the other's mind. He knew the intruder must be present in his mind, wanting to speak to him, but prepared to wait until he was ready. It had promised to tell him more, and for the first time since his capture, he was hungry for information about this impossible new world: knowledge whose very existence, only a few days ago, he would have denounced as blasphemy. He knew better now. Or at least, he hoped he did. Zavahl closed his eyes, and sent a thought to the entity that shared his mind. 'Are you there?'

'Always,' the other replied wryly.

'And will you tell me about the history of this world?'

'I will tell you whatever you want – on one condition. That you'll let me take control of your voice for a little while to talk to Veldan.'

For a moment Zavahl wavered.

'Zavahl, this is desperately important.'

'But . . . All right,' he said. 'I'll see if I can get a message to her.'

The door was locked. When had that happened? Zavahl was certain Ailie hadn't done it when she left. He pounded on the wooden panels. 'Is anybody there?' he shouted. 'I need to talk to someone.'

There was the scrape of a key turning in the lock, and the door was opened by a hard-faced man with a sword in his hand. 'What's all the racket about?' he demanded.

Why a guard? Veldan, Elion and Aethon had all told him emphatically that he would come to no harm. Zavahl reminded himself that, up to a couple of days ago, he had been the Hierarch of Callisiora. 'I need to speak to Veldan and Elion,' he said, in tones that were pleasant but authoritative. 'Would you be so kind as to take me to them?'

The guard scowled. 'No, I bloody wouldn't.'

'In that case, will you send someone to bring them here?'

The scowl grew even deeper. 'Listen, matey, I don't know what you was expecting, but Veldan and Elion won't be going anywhere in a hurry. The Archimandrite isn't pleased with them at all, and word is that they've been confined to quarters.'

Plague on it! This was an unexpected setback. His mind raced. 'Well, will you get Ailie for me, please? She told me to give her a shout if I needed anything.'

The guard's face split into a leering grin, and he punched Zavahl jocularly on the shoulder. 'I bet she did, matey. I bet she did.'

Zavahl clenched his fists so hard that his fingernails bruised his palms. In his current situation, hitting the guard (who was much bigger than him) would be a very bad mistake.

Myrial, give me strength.

'Just get her, would you?' he said through gritted teeth. Pulling the door out of the guard's hand, he shut it in the surprised man's face.

'Very wise,' Aethon commented dryly, from the back of his mind.

Veldan pulled back the heavy curtain, and looked out through the narrow gap. 'He's still there – and so was the one at the back door.' She let the curtain drop back into place. 'Has Cergorn gone bloody mad?' she exploded. 'What does he think we're going to do, for goodness' sake? And supposing we did plan to do something, why does he think that putting a guard out there would stop us? Especially when we have Kaz.'

Elion looked up from the depths of a soft chair by the fire. 'Maybe he really wants to impress on us that we're in disgrace. Besides, supposing we did try to go somewhere, and the guards – who are they, by the way? – and the guards say we have to stay put, then we'll be disobeying the Archimandrite, and we'll just be in more trouble than ever.'

Veldan returned to the fireside and sank into her own chair, stretching out with a grateful sigh. She had been on the road long enough to really appreciate life's little luxuries. 'I think Cergorn is trying to keep us away from Toulac and Zavahl,' she said gloomily. 'He seemed so determined not to believe us. What if he decides to remove their memories of this place and send them back?'

'Well, if they try to tinker with Zavahl's memory, at least they'll find Aethon,' Elion pointed out. 'Poor old Toulac won't stand much of a chance, though. Not if Cergorn's dead set against having her.'

'It's so unfair!' She slammed her fist into the arm of the chair, and winced.

'Something hurt you?' Kazairl's head, which had been tucked under his curled tail while he slept, shot up at once.

Veldan rubbed her knuckles ruefully. 'My own fault. I lost my temper.'

'Why?' asked Kaz, with a suspicious glance at Elion.

'Don't blame me.' He held up his hands defensively. 'She's not pleased about Cergorn putting a guard on us, that's all.'

The firedrake's growl rumbled round the room. 'Why, that purulent, maggot-infested lump of offal!'

Veldan chuckled. 'I couldn't have put it better myself. Mind you, you certainly have a way with words. I don't expect it helped our cause any when you called the Archimandrite of the Shadowleague a brain-dead lump of horsemeat to his face.'

'That's not half of what I *could* call that degenerate, disease-ridden offspring of a carthorse and a trollop's bastard,' Kaz grumbled. 'He should think himself lucky that I'm a firedrake of tact and great restraint. What's the matter with him, anyway? Has he gone bloody mad?'

Elion looked from Kazairl to Veldan, the corners of his eyes and mouth crinkling with amusement. 'You two really do think alike, don't you?'

'I don't see what's so funny about that.'

'So what? It's nothing for you to laugh at.'

Woman and firedrake spoke simultaneously, and all three Loremasters burst out laughing. 'Well, that'll give our guards something to wonder about,' said Veldan.

'Who did you say they were?' Elion asked again.

'I didn't. But it looked to me like Trinn at the back and Endos at the front. Why did you want to know?'

'I don't know Trinn very well, but Endos is a decent enough sort, and he won't much care for the idea of guarding us. It'll be a nippy night out there. Why not invite him in by the fire for a drink and a game of cards? He might know more than we do about what's going on, and whatever we eventually decide to do, we can do it more easily with at least one of the guards on our side.'

Veldan rolled her eyes. 'You're being reasonable, Elion. It makes me nervous when you're reasonable.'

'Well, what did *you* have in mind? Hit him over the head with a brick, and vanish into the night?'

She made a rude gesture. 'If I could be bothered to get out of this chair, I'd hit *you* over the head with a brick,' she said lazily. 'No, it just worries me when you start having good ideas. It's so unlike you.'

Elion returned her gesture. 'With knobs on,' he added, for good measure. Then his face grew serious. 'You know, I'd forgotten how much fun you can be, when I give you half a chance. Veldan, I'm sorry I've been such a pain, these last few months.'

'Well, I haven't exactly been all sweetness and light myself.' Unthinkingly, her fingers went to the scar on her face. 'We both had our reasons, Elion, but maybe it's time we put all that behind us, and started pulling together again. We used to be a good team, me and Kaz, and you and Melnyth.'

He nodded, and Veldan realised that he still couldn't really trust himself to talk about Melnyth. 'I suppose I'll have to be thinking about a new partner soon,' he said. 'Up till now, I couldn't even contemplate the idea, but I know I'll have to face it sooner or later. If I stay on my own, I won't be eligible for active service any more, and Cergorn will send me to some duty post at the back end of nowhere.'

'The way old horse-arse feels about us,' Kaz put in, 'I should think we can all look forward to winding up in the back end of nowhere.'

'You know,' Veldan said thoughtfully, 'if only Cergorn would come to his senses, you could do worse than Toulac. She knows everything about fighting and tracking and surviving in the wilds. For the rest of it, you could train her up on the job.'

Elion shuddered. 'Have you lost your mind? She could practically be my granny! How can I possibly train anyone who keeps calling me "sonny" all the time? In the interests of changing the subject, do you want me to go out and rescue Endos from his lonely vigil?'

'Nah.' Veldan grinned maliciously. 'Let's give him a chance to get good and cold first. I don't think there's any desperate hurry. This is such a crazy situation, we don't want to rush into anything without thinking the consequences through. The Archimandrite won't be sending anybody anywhere tonight, and the longer we can give him to cool down, the better. Besides, after the nightmare of the last few days, I'd like to savour the peace and quiet, just for a little while. Cergorn or no Cergorn, it's good to be back home.'

She stretched out her feet, clad in a pair of soft slippers, towards the fire, and looked happily around her. It was an unusual house, constructed as it was to accommodate a human and a firedrake. It was all built on one storey, very long and sprawling, with spacious rooms, wide passages and doorways, and very little in the way of extraneous furniture to get in the way of such a large creature, or be knocked over by a careless tail. The floors were tile or stone – 'we can't have wood,' Veldan had once told Elion, 'not with his claws,' – but were mostly covered with woven rugs of thick wool in vibrant colours, which could be replaced before they wore out. The walls were washed with soft, warm colours, to offset the effect of so much stone.

The main living area, in which the Loremasters were sitting, contained little more than the bookshelves that lined the walls, the two deep chairs, grouped to one side of the fireplace, and a small, low table in front of the fire. On the other side of the hearth was Kaz's place, a haphazard collection of mattresses, quilts, pillows, rugs and sheepskins, which the firedrake had been collecting for years, and had arranged to form a kind of nest, in which he had been curled blissfully all evening.

Earlier in the day, when Veldan had first returned to her home, she had discovered to her delight that it was clean and tidy: certainly a lot tidier than she had left it. Her clothing had been laundered, mended and neatly put away, and there were cheerful fires in every hearth. Appetising smells were coming from the kitchen, and on the table she had found a large basket containing soup in an earthenware jar, a flagon of good ale from the inn, a covered basin of hotpot, a generous wedge of cherry pie, a loaf of bread, a large chunk of cheese and some freshly-picked apples and plums.

On top of this bounty was a note.

Heard you were arriving today, so I came round with a few things. Knew you wouldn't feel like cooking! You'll find a deer out back for Kaz. Dad was twisting his face a bit, but I told him that they can damn well eat pasties in the inn tonight, or starve. Do them good. See you soon, Ailie.

P.S. Glad to have you back.

Veldan smiled. 'Good old Ailie! She's a real friend,' she said to Kaz, who had just poked his head around the kitchen door. He didn't tend to come into that room, which had, perforce, been designed to conform to more human proportions. 'She left me a whole deer?' His eyes sparkled with delight. 'Thank goodness somebody around here knows how to look after a firedrake. There wasn't much meat on that scrawny sheep we had yesterday.'

'Well, you caught it.'

'If I had known you greedy humans were going to eat so much, I would have caught two.' He disappeared out of the back door at speed, just as there was a knock on the other door and Elion appeared, hastily bathed and clad in clean clothes. He was carrying a basket of his own. Veldan grinned. 'Ailie?'

'Ailie. That woman's worth her weight in diamonds.'

Veldan put the food in the oven of her range to warm while she had her own quick bath, promising herself a long soak later, when she was less hungry. They ate in the kitchen, chatting about inconsequential things, enjoying this new tentative accord. By unspoken consent, they avoided the subject of Cergorn. Afterwards, being full of good food had made them drowsy, so Veldan had shown Elion to her guest-room – again, human sized. Though she had a bed of her own in the chamber that she shared with Kaz, she had preferred to curl up with the firedrake in his nest, an even thicker, larger version of the one on the other room. Pulling one of his quilts over herself, she relaxed against the warmth of his hide, and soon fell asleep. All three Loremasters, worn out by their journeying, had slept the afternoon away – and had awakened at dusk to find the guards outside their door.

Damn Cergorn. He should know better than to act like this.

Veldan pulled herself out of her thoughts, and was just about to suggest to Elion that it might be worth trying to invite the guard inside, when Kaz spoke. 'Someone's coming.'

There was a knock on the door. Who could this be? Had Cergorn had a change of heart? Exchanging a glance with Elion, Veldan got up and opened it. There was Endos, chewing happily. 'Gotta visitor for you,' he said, spraying Veldan lightly with crumbs. He stepped aside and there stood Ailie, cloaked against the chill of the evening.

Veldan looked down at what she was carrying. 'Just how many of those baskets do you have?'

Ailie grinned. 'You can never have enough baskets. Well known fact, that. Can I come in? It's freezing out here.'

'Of course you can, and welcome.' Veldan ushered her into the house, and was just about to shut the door, when Endos stopped her. 'I hope the three of you know that this is nothing to do with me,' he said in a low voice. 'I can't think what Cergorn's playing at, but what can I do?'

She patted him on thc arm. 'I understand. These are turning out to be difficult times for all of us, aren't they?' She was about to ask him to come inside, but Ailie caught her eye and gave an infinitesimal shake of her head. Veldan swallowed what she had been about to say. 'I'll let you get on with it, then,' she said instead. 'I'd ask you in out of the cold, Endos, but the mood Cergorn's in, we'd better not risk getting you into trouble. Thanks for letting Ailie visit, though.'

The guard grinned at her. 'Ailie's all right. It wouldn't do to starve you, after all.'

When Veldan had closed the door, the innkeeper went over to the low table by the fire, and began to unpack her basket. 'Pasties tonight,' she said. She winked at the firedrake. 'It was going to be venison, but somebody or other seems to have eaten the deer.'

Kaz cocked his head at Veldan. 'Pass on my compliments and tell her it went to a good home,' he said.

'Got any plates?' Ailie asked. 'Tell you what, let's unpack this in the kitchen. It'll be easier that way.'

As soon as she was in the kitchen, she turned to the others. 'I've got a message for you,' she told them in a low voice. 'I thought it might be safer to talk in here, just in case Endos gets nosey and starts listening at the door.'

'Trinn is stationed out the back, too,' warned Veldan, 'but I shouldn't think he'll hear, as long as we keep fairly quiet. Anyway, what about the message? Is it from Toulac?'

'What is it?' Elion added.

'It's from Zavahl.'

'*Zavahl?*' All three Loremasters, including Kaz, who was listening from the doorway, were utterly dumbfounded.

'Ssssh.' Ailie put a finger to her lips. 'He says that Aethon wants to talk to you, whatever that means. And he says that he's agreed.'

Elion's mouth fell open. Veldan sank slowly down onto a kitchen chair. 'Well, I'll be dipped in dog's dung,' she murmured. 'What can have happened to turn him so co-operative all of a sudden?'

Ailie went rather pink. 'I think it made a big difference to him, finding out that not everyone in this place is his enemy.'

Elion frowned. 'He what . . . ?' Then his eyes widened. 'Oh, well done, Ailie!'

'She didn't *mate* with him?' said the voice of Kaz, in Veldan's mind. 'Humans never cease to amaze me.'

Veldan was stunned. 'You actually . . . I mean, it's not as if . . . Ailie, what in the world possessed you?'

'Mind your own business,' said Ailie promptly. 'What's between me and Zavahl is nothing to do with you lot. I must say, though, I wish you had taken better care of him. He seems to have been through an awful lot, poor thing.'

'*He* went through a lot?' Kaz grumbled. 'I got chased up, down and all over the place, by a bunch of soldiers waving swords and firing arrows. I had to lug not one but *three* passengers right over the mountains to Gendival, with her precious Zavahl kicking me in the ribs for most of the way . . .'

Veldan ignored him. She was too busy being indignant on her own account. 'Why, if you knew half the trouble he'd given us,' she began heatedly.

Elion gave her a dig with his elbow. 'I'm sorry, Ailie, I truly am. The way things worked out, we couldn't help but frighten Zavahl. It's a good thing he had you to help him.'

Ailie narrowed her eyes at him. 'Stop trying to butter me up, Elion. Now, the difficulty is that you're under guard here, and Zavahl and Toulac are also being guarded at the inn. So how do we get you all together?'

Absently, Veldan took a pasty from the basket and nibbled at a corner. 'We might persuade Endos to look the other way, but who's on guard at the inn?'

Ailie pursed her lips. 'Michlin,' she said.

Elion swore. 'That surly bugger. We certainly can't count on him to turn a blind eye.'

Suddenly there was a call from Kaz in the other room. 'Veldan, Elion – get in here quick!'

When the Loremasters came rushing in, a puzzled Ailie at their heels, the firedrake almost had his head in the fireplace. From the chimney came a thumping, scraping noise. Soot pattered down, puffing out onto the hearth, making Kaz jerk his head back quickly in an explosion of sneezes. Something large fell down into the fire, scattering burning embers everywhere, and Elion and Veldan had to rush forward to scoop them up with fire tongs and shovel. Only then did they have a chance to look and see what had caused all the commotion.

Sitting in the midst of the fire was a glorious creature that outshone the flames. In a cloud of sparks it stretched out golden wings, basking in the searing heat.

'Vaure?' gasped Elion.

'Nice of you to drop in,' said Kaz laconically, making everyone groan except Ailie, who was unable to hear mindspeech. She stood with her eyes averted from the fireplace, looking steadfastly into the corner. 'I'm sorry,' she said, when Veldan asked her what was wrong. 'I know that fire is her element and all, but it always gives me the willies to see Vaure doing that.'

The phoenix gave her own equivalent of a shrug, hopped out of the fire and sat cooling on the hearthstone. 'Ah,' she said. 'First time I've been warm in hours.'

'Liar,' said Veldan affectionately. 'You're always sitting in the fire at home.'

'Ah, but I haven't been at home. Bailen, Dessil and I have been talking to Senior Loremaster Maskulu, and you know how cold and damp it is in those Moldan underground dwellings.'

As soon as the phoenix had made her unconventional entrance, Veldan had suspected that some kind of plot was afoot. Now she was certain. She knelt down by the hearth, as close as she could get to the glowing newcomer. 'And what were you doing down there?' she asked softly. 'By and large, Senior Loremaster Maskulu isn't one for entertaining guests.'

Vaure leaned close to Veldan, fanning a hot breeze into her face. They might have been using mindspeech, but somehow the postures of conspirators had survived. 'Maskulu thinks that Cergorn is behaving like an ass, if you'll pardon the expression. And he's not the only one, Veldan. You and Kaz and Elion will find a lot of people on your side, over the way that you've been treated.'

'Ha!' Kaz interrupted with great glee. 'It's about time old Horse-Arse got his come-uppance.'

Elion, who had been in the background translating for their fellow-plotter Ailie, drew close to the phoenix. 'That's all very well,' he said. 'A lot of people in the past have disagreed with Cergorn, but all they've ever done is lurk around in corners, muttering.'

'Not this time.' Vaure's eyes glittered. 'This is the first time a Senior Loremaster has got directly involved. And having talked to him, I'm pretty sure there's more to this business than *we* know. Maskulu wants to get you and those humans you brought away to safety, and—'

'Hold on,' protested Veldan. 'Away to *safety*? That's taking things a bit far, isn't it? I mean, Cergorn might be mad with us right now, and he might be acting like a pain in the backside, but he's hardly going to hurt us.'

Vaure shook her feathers. 'You're probably right, but as I said, there's more going on here than we realise. And whatever it is, I don't think Maskulu wants you caught up in the middle of it. As we speak, your humans are being removed from the inn, and I'm here to see about getting you out. When Cergorn sends for you tomorrow, he'll be in for a little surprise.'

Twenty

The Trap

While the man that Aliana now knew as Commander Galveron went off to the armoury to find what they needed with his troops and the miner, the thief and her friends, much to their disgust, found their field of operations restricted to the kitchens. It was so frustrating. They had found themselves in the very heart of enemy territory, a veritable treasure-trove filled with all sorts of rich pickings, and here they were, assigned to packing up foodstuffs under the keen eye of the archer Corvin.

When they had first been given their orders, Alestan and the others had nominated Aliana to wheedle her way round Commander Galveron. Keeping her expression as innocent as she could manage, she had offered the services of her group to help with the search of the Citadel for useful items, but Galveron had simply given her an old-fashioned look. 'Right now, I don't think there's much point in asking too many questions about the background of you and your friends,' he had told her, 'or whether you were actually at the sacrifice at all . . .'

'Yes we were!' Aliana interrupted fiercely.

Galveron folded his arms and cocked his head to one side. 'If you say so. In that case, what were the former Hierarch's last words before he died?'

'Er . . . We weren't close enough to hear,' she improvised craftily. 'We were right at the back. That was how we managed to get away and hide when those accursed creatures came.'

'I see. It's a good thing the pyre was raised up the way it was. Even if you couldn't hear, at least you would have been able to see Zavahl's death.'

'Oh yes, we saw it all right.'

'Did you really?' said Galveron. 'Well, just for your future reference, in case you ever want to tell this pack of lies to anyone else, the Hierarch wasn't sacrificed at all.'

Aliana's jaw dropped. 'But . . . I saw the smoke myself.'

'Oh, the pyre was lit – when Zavahl was rescued right off the top of it and snatched away by some sort of fire-breathing monster.'

'Get away with you,' Aliana said scornfully. 'Do you think I was born yesterday? There's no such thing as fire-breathing monsters. You're having me on.'

'Am I?' Galveron said. 'Well one of us is playing games with the truth, that's for sure. But it doesn't matter. Aliana, a lot of the men who lived in this Citadel are dead now. They gave their lives trying to protect the people of Tiarond. But there are still a number of survivors, across at the Temple.'

She couldn't see his expression – only his mouth, and his eyes, that showed between the elaborate bandaging on his face. But there was a cold, hard look in those blue eyes that made her gulp and back away a step. He leaned very close to her and spoke quietly. 'And do you know what? I am going to make damn sure that those men have all their possessions to come back to. They don't own much, but by Myrial, they deserve all they've got and more. Now you and your friends will pack food in the kitchen and you'll stay there. If I catch any of you wandering around, brats included, I'm going to throw them out into the courtyard for the fiends to take care of. Is that absolutely clear?'

'All right, keep your shirt on. We'll pack the food, if that's what you want.' Aliana hesitated. 'Look. I'll be straight with you. I know you don't think much of us, but we want to survive this dreadful time just as much as you and your Godswords, and all those other respectable folk in the Temple. We can't do that on our own. No matter how careful we are, those accursed creatures will pick us off one by one. Unless you let us come into the Temple with the others, we're finished.'

She hated herself for begging, but the situation was so desperate that she had no other choice. Too much was at stake. She grasped his arm, her fingers digging into the thick fabric of his sleeve. 'Please, you won't leave us behind, will you? We'll muck in, I promise, and I'll make the others behave if it's the last thing I do.'

Galveron continued to look at her sternly, though she thought she could see a little softening around the corners of his mouth. 'I'm right, aren't I? You lot did come from the Warrens?'

Aliana nodded wretchedly. There was no point in denying it now.

'Then I realise that you don't have anything much in the world, and the only way of life you know is to steal from the people who do. But everyone who survived the attack and took refuge in the Temple is now in the same position as you. We have to share everything, because we have so little. If you and your friends join us, you'll be given a fair allotment of any food, or blankets, or spare clothing that there is, but you can't be permitted to take more than that. That doesn't just apply to you people, it holds true for us all. *Anyone* caught stealing will be cast out to fend for themselves – and remember – if stuff starts to go missing, you will be the first ones I investigate, whether that's unjust or not. Is that clear?'

Aliana bit her lip. 'Yes. I understand.'

'Well, make sure your friends do, too. In the long run, their lives may depend on it.'

So now, for the first time in their lives, the last of the Grey Ghosts were doing honest labour, packing flour and beans, crocks of honey, wheels of cheese and sides of bacon into sacks and backpacks to be transported to the Temple. Though the supplies were not all that plentiful, considering the amount of soldiers in the Godswords, there was considerably more food than Aliana had seen in Tiarond since the endless rains began. She thought of all the people starving in the Warrens and in the poorer parts of the city, and shook her head.

At least Corvin had allowed them to eat while they were working, which was something of a consolation – at least to most of them.

Though Aliana had done her best to soften Galveron's message to the thieves, Alestan had reacted with predictable anger, and it had taken everything in her power to reassure him that the Grey Ghosts would be taken care of, but that patience and co-operation were vital to the safety of them all. She looked across at him now, sighing at his thunderous expression. Everyone had been subdued by Tosel's death, but while Gelina and the youngsters talked to one another in low voices, and exchanged an occasional comment with Corvin, Alestan worked in grim and sullen silence, ignoring the others.

Then Aliana forgot about her brother. Something had been bothering her ever since she rejoined her companions, but she had been preoccupied with Galveron's words, and though something was nagging at the back of her mind, she had paid little attention. Now, as she looked at the others, she realised what it was. Gelina and the youngsters were working hard, but one person was missing from their party. Packrat was nowhere in sight.

Plague on him! I might have guessed he would do this!

Clearly, Corvin had not realised that he was one helper short, so Packrat had probably done his famous fading into the background trick, and had vanished before the work had even started. Which meant, of course, that he could be anywhere in the Citadel by now. Aliana swore under her breath. There could be absolutely no doubt about what the wretch was up to. If Galveron caught him, not only would it mean the end for him, it might also ruin his companions' only chance to be allowed into the Temple.

Aliana's mind was racing. What should she do? Corvin would never give her permission to go wandering off on her own, and even if she could make some kind of an excuse to slip away, where would she start looking? What if she didn't find him, and Galveron came looking for *her*? What if she missed him altogether, and he returned while she was gone? He would have a lot more trouble sneaking back if Corvin was watching the door for her return. There was nothing else for it. Anything she tried to do now stood a good chance of making matters worse. She would just have to wait, and hope, and pray that he would get back undetected.

And when he does – if he does – I'm going to make him sorry he was born.

It didn't take all that long to pack what they wanted. There was only so much that could be carried across in one journey. Just as they were finishing, Galveron and his men returned. Aliana's heart sank like a stone. There, struggling and swearing in the grip of two Godsword soldiers, was Packrat.

Galveron, burdened down by a bulky bundle of what appeared to be clothing, looked grim. 'We caught him snooping round the officers' quarters.' Though he was addressing his remarks to them all, Aliana couldn't help but feel that they were meant for her. 'Didn't you people understand me when I said I wouldn't tolerate thievery under any circumstances? Or didn't you believe I meant it when I told you that anyone caught stealing would be thrown outside for the fiends?'

Beneath the grime on his face, Packrat turned deathly white. 'No,' he gasped. 'Please, I didn't know. I'll do whatever you say, but don't make me go out there.'

Aliana ran across to Galveron. 'I'm sorry,' she cried. 'He didn't know about what you said, honest he didn't! He had disappeared before I had time to warn him. Please give him another chance. If he took anything he'll give it back, and we'll make sure he doesn't do this again.'

The Commander hesitated. Aliana held her breath, watching him, not daring to say any more but trying to put her plea into her eyes.

It was Alestan who broke the tableau. 'Aliana, come away from him. My own sister, grovelling to Godsword offal! Have you no pride?'

Galveron looked at him sharply, his mouth tightening, then turned away as if Alestan was of no moment. 'Search this piece of scum.' He gestured at Packrat with distaste. 'Remove anything he took, and confiscate any weapons, lockpicks, grapnels, or anything else you think he might use to carry out his trade.'

Packrat opened his mouth to protest, but Galveron silenced him with a glance. 'I wouldn't,' he warned. 'Your life is dangling by a very fragile thread, my friend, and it's only thanks to Aliana that I'm not throwing you out of the door right now. I'll be watching you in future, and rest assured, you won't get a second chance.' He raised his voice, including the others. 'That goes for all of you thieves. Any more infringements, and the whole lot of you will be cast out.'

Aliana let out her breath in a sigh of relief. 'Thanks,' she said softly. 'I owe you.'

Alestan spat into a corner. 'Bastard,' he muttered.

Galveron chose not to hear. Glancing down at his armful of clothing as if he had just remembered it was there, he spread it out across the table. 'I don't know if you folk can find anything out of this lot to fit you, but you're very welcome to whatever you want to use. It looks as though you could do with some warmer clothing.' He spoke so pleasantly that the last few moments might never have happened.

'I don't need bloody charity from the likes of you,' snarled Alestan, 'and I wouldn't be seen dead in your filthy Godsword garb.'

'Don't be stupid,' Aliana said sharply, fingering the thick, soft cloth of a tunic. 'This is good stuff. It's clean, it's warm, it's hard-wearing and for a change, it's in one piece. Who gives a damn what colour it is? Still,' she went on, 'if you want everybody in the Temple staring at you because you look like a filthy street-beggar, and saying "There goes that scum from the Warrens," that's your problem.'

'No it isn't.' It had been so long since Gelina had spoken that everyone turned to her in surprise. 'It'll be our problem too, because we're his companions. You know, Alestan, if they think that about you, they're bound to think it about all of us, and despise us. Everyone will suffer for your pride.'

Alestan looked at the anxious faces of his fellow Grey Ghosts. Even Tag and Erla, young as they were, looked grave, as if they understood just what was at stake. 'Oh, all right,' he snapped. '*All right*.'

'But hadn't this better wait until we reach the Temple?' Corvin asked Galveron. 'Surely we don't have time to be thinking about clothes now? It's getting late.'

'I'm afraid that time is no longer an issue,' Galveron said grimly. 'It may not be nightfall, quite, but the sky has clouded right over, and it's snowing hard. It's already dark enough for those winged fiends to be active, and they're swarming all over the place out there. We saw them from the windows on the upper levels.'

'Curse them!' said Corvin. 'How will we ever rid ourselves of such deadly creatures? But thank Myrial, we're safe enough in here for tonight. All the windows in this place are narrow and barred. Not even those stinking freaks could get inside. We'll just have to wait till tomorrow to return to the Temple.'

'If there's any one left there to return to by tomorrow.' Galveron's face was bleak. 'Those creatures will be into the Basilica's upper chambers in a flash, just as they were last night. If our people can't bring the staircase down, because we didn't get back with the blasting powder, then they'll have to defend the stairwell all night long against an enemy that is deadly, swift, and more numerous to count. What chance do you think they'll have of lasting through another night?'

There was a horrified silence.

Aliana's mind began to race. She had been badly unnerved by Galveron's clear and ruthless intent to throw Packrat out to fend for himself. Because he'd seemed a kind and pleasant man, she had made the mistake, as they all had, of thinking he was soft. How wrong she'd been. Courteous he might be, but he was steadfast in his convictions and unswerving when it came to doing what he believed to be right. Now she felt very vulnerable. How long could Packrat last out before his fingers began to itch once more? How long would it take before matters between Galveron and Alestan came to open confrontation? But if Galveron were only in her debt, maybe she could just manage to save her volatile and unpredictable companions.

Could I?

Dare I?

'I can . . .' What had happened to her voice? Aliana cleared her throat, took a deep breath, and tried again. 'I can do it,' she heard herself saying. 'I'll go. If you promise to take care of my friends, *no matter what,* I'll take your blasting powder across to the Temple.'

A laugh came from one of the Godsword troopers, quickly stifled when he found out he laughed alone.

'No!' Alestan shouted. 'Don't be stupid, Aliana. Why risk your life for a bunch of strangers who would spit on you if they knew who you were?'

'Because I want us to have a fresh start in the Temple,' she replied. 'I don't want everyone looking down their noses at us, and picking on us because of who we are.' She turned to Galveron. 'If I go, you've got to promise that you and your men won't tell anyone where we came from. You've got to protect us, or you can forget it.'

The Commander's eyebrows rose. 'You want me to lie to the *Hierarch?*'

Aliana's expression hardened. 'Through your teeth.'

Galveron was looking at her steadily, his shrewd blue eyes never leaving her face. 'What makes you think you can do this?' he said.

'Sneaking is what I'm best at,' Aliana told him without hesitation. 'I make a living out of not being seen. I can find cover, melt into the shadows. And if there's really a blizzard out there, that should help me a lot.'

The Commander shook his head. It was the first time that she had seen him look indecisive. 'Aliana, I don't know. We desperately need to get that powder to the Temple. Hundreds of lives are at stake, and if you're certain you can do it, what right have I to refuse them that chance of survival? But how can I let you go out there and be killed? There are so many of those creatures flying around. One of them must spot you sooner or later, and it would only take one.'

Corvin frowned. 'You're right – and depending on how intelligent they really are, they're probably watching the door. What she needs is some kind of diversion while she's leaving the building. Something to preoccupy those fiends long enough to give her a chance.'

Galveron said nothing, but his eyes went to Tosel's stiffening body. 'There's a trapdoor that leads out onto the roof,' he said, in almost conversational tones.

'Damn you!' roared Alestan. 'That's sick!'

The Commander shrugged. 'Even if it comes down to a choice between him and your sister? And I know it's not pleasant, but what more can they do to him, really? They can't kill him twice, but he could save Aliana's life.'

Alestan said nothing, his face like stone. 'You bastard,' he whispered.

Galveron's eyes were like flint. 'You already called me that once. There is a limit.'

Gelina's voice came softly from the shadows. 'Alestan, the bastard's right. So is Aliana. If she can save all those lives in the Temple, then they've *got* to take us in. And if anybody can do it, she can. You know she's the best of us at moving unseen.'

With difficulty, Aliana's brother nodded. 'I know all that. I know. But . . .' he turned on Galveron. 'If she dies, I'm going to feed *you* to those brutes with my own two hands.'

Galveron nodded gravely. 'If she dies, you'll get your chance to try, I promise, and no-one will interfere.'

By this time, Aliana had had more than enough of them both. 'Shut up, the pair of you!' she snapped. 'I'm *not* going to die, all right?' She hoped she sounded more certain than she felt.

'If I believed you were, I wouldn't let you go,' Galveron said.

Alestan glared at him. 'Well, if she *is* going, she'll need a damn sight better diversion than just sticking poor Tosel out on the roof for those brutes to find. I mean, they've got a courtyard full of corpses outside the Temple. Why would they be bothered about one more?'

'You've got a point,' Corvin said.

'It seems to me,' said Alestan, 'judging by the way those creatures chased us, that they prefer fresh meat to carrion. What we really need is a decoy.'

For a long moment, nobody spoke. Aliana realised that everyone was looking down at their shoes, or up at the ceiling: anywhere save at one another.

He's right, and they all know it. But nobody wants to volunteer.

Then, into the silence, Alestan stepped forward. 'She's my sister,' he said. 'I'll do it.'

Now it was Aliana's turn to protest. 'Alestan, no! I won't let you die for me!'

He grinned, once again looking like the brother she knew and loved. 'Ah,' he taunted. 'You don't like it much when the boot's on the other foot. If you want to take some crazy risk, then I have every right to do it too.' Over her spluttering, he added, 'but I don't intend to get myself killed, not if I can help it. No more than you do. You might be the sneakiest, Aliana, but I'm easily the fastest. And I have an idea.'

He turned to Galveron. 'You said there was a trapdoor on the roof?'

'That's right. It leads onto the stone walkway that goes around the parapets.'

Alestan nodded. 'Good. Right then. This is *my* plan. We take poor Tosel out just like we planned, and lay him down beside the trapdoor. Then I climb out and run around on the parapet until I've got the attention of those damn fiends. When they drop down to attack, I dodge back down through the trapdoor, but they come down to investigate Tosel anyway, because there wasn't a corpse up there earlier, and if one piece of live meat was running around, then this other one might not be dead yet either.'

'Very good,' said Galveron. He broke into a smile, wincing as the movement pulled at the wounds on his face. 'Very good indeed. My compliments to you. It's a great improvement on my first idea.'

Miner Areom, in the meantime, had been staring thoughtfully at Tosel's corpse. Now he looked up. 'I think I can improve it even more,' he said. 'My dear, I can get you the diversion of your life. There's plenty of blasting powder left in the stores, and miles of fuse. Let's take the fight back to those murderous buggers for a change. If they want to prey on our people, I'll give them a meal they'll never forget.'

'Sir?' All the Grey Ghosts gasped to hear Packrat sounding so uncommonly polite. Clearly his narrow escape was having a salutary effect – for the time being, at least.

'Yes, lad?' Areom was clearly trying to hide his distaste.

Packrat gave him an evil, snaggle-toothed grin. 'If you're going to blow Tosel's corpse up anyway, why not include a few surprises? You know, nails, broken glass, that kind of thing?'

Areom burst out laughing. 'Well, well. Whoever would have thought you'd turn out to be a genius?'

Alestan looked on grimly as two of the Godsword soldiers struggled to manoeuvre Tosel's corpse up several flights of stairs. Clearly they were beginning to understand the true meaning of the phrase 'dead weight'. Judging from the looks on their faces, they would have liked to complain about their burden, but with the dead man's friend following close behind, they were forced to restrain themselves. 'Thank Myrial it's only four storeys,' panted one. His companion, lacking enough breath to reply, simply grunted agreement.

'Come on, lads,' Corvin encouraged them. 'Not much further to go.' It was just as well that looks couldn't kill.

The last stretch was the hardest. Even with the assistance of Corvin, Alestan and Areom, it took all their efforts to haul the body up the steep, narrow wooden steps – in truth, not much more than a ladder with wide rungs – that led up to the trapdoor in the roof.

Corvin unbolted the heavy iron panel, pushed it upwards a little, and peered cautiously through the slit. 'Roof seems clear,' he said softly. 'Let's do it. Careful not to lay him too close to the trapdoor. I know it's made of iron, but we don't want to take even the slightest risk of it being damaged in the explosion.'

The trapdoor opened out onto a wide stone walkway beside the parapet. With a struggle, they managed to push the corpse out so that he was lying on his back, partly propped up by the backpack on his shoulders. Tosel had been dressed in dark Godsword clothing, as had Alestan, so that they would show up against the unsullied snow. The backpack, containing a generous amount of blasting powder, carried in addition Packrat's vicious contribution: some nails; a few sharp, splintery chunks of wood; some old arrowheads;

and a generous amount of jagged glass from broken bottles. Tucked securely inside was a length of fuse, which trailed back through the trapdoor to the waiting men. The trap was set.

'Are you ready?' Corvin said softly.

Alestan nodded.

'Good luck.'

The thief eased himself past the Godsword archer, and climbed out onto the roof. He had discarded the ragged bandage around his head, and the icy air made the unprotected cut on his forehead ache. The wind smashed into him like a fist, hurling stinging snow into his eyes, and Alestan rejoiced. Those brutes wouldn't find it so easy to fly in conditions like these. The blizzard would make it more difficult to see Aliana, and harder to catch her.

Get moving! You're supposed to be a decoy, remember?

Drawing the icy air deep into his lungs, Alestan leapt forward. Backwards and forwards he dashed through the blizzard, keeping his footing with difficulty on the slushy ground, and darting glances here, there and everywhere, straining his eyes for a glimpse of the first winged figure to come plummeting down from above.

Nothing. Back and forth, back and forth, nerves stretched to breaking point, careful never to stray too far from the trapdoor, gasping frosty air laden with tiny daggers into his labouring lungs. Running, running . . .

Nothing.

Where in perdition are they? When we were out in the open, the place was swarming with the accursed things. Are they here at all? Has the blizzard driven them away? Dare I gamble Aliana's life on that possibility? What if they aren't stalking me because they're watching the lower door, waiting for someone to come out?

Feeling foolish, he started to wave his arms about as he ran, finding the breath from somewhere to shout at the top of his voice. 'Hey! Hey you! Here I am. Up here. Come and get me, you murderous, stinking, carrion-eating filth!'

They came with blinding speed, just as Alestan had reached the far end of the back-and-forth track he'd trampled in the snow. He caught sight of them first as nothing more than a change in the pattern of the snow-swirl, as the air was buffeted by their great wings. Then he glimpsed a number of dark shadows, swooping down to come in low, and moving fast.

Alestan's shouts became a strangled yelp. He turned too quickly on the slippery ground and felt his legs slide out from underneath him. A black shape went arrowing overhead, just at the height to have broken his neck, had he been standing. It was so close that he could feel the downdraught from its wings, flattening his body against the freezing stone of the walkway. He had no recollection of scrambling to his feet. All of a sudden he was up and running, stooping low, swerving and zigzagging from side to side to avoid the winged shapes that were closing in on every side.

Had it not been for the storm, he wouldn't have stood a chance, but the fiends were finding it difficult to manoeuvre in the gusting, swirling wind, and the snow seemed to confuse their sense of distance and direction. One misjudged a dive and went crashing to the ground behind him. Several of its brethren were on the fallen creature almost instantly, and he heard its dreadful shrieks as they tore out chunks of its living flesh with talons and teeth. Not all of the creatures, however, were distracted by their fallen companion. An instant later, Alestan felt the firebrand lines of claws raking across his back and shoulder, shredding the black Godsword tunic that he had donned so shortly before.

'Come on, come on!'

'Run!'

'You can do it!'

A clamour of encouraging voices could be heard over the whistling of the wind, and Alestan saw the angular shape of the open trapdoor in front of him, even as he felt the talons rake him again. This time, the claws sunk deeper into his flesh, trying to gain a hold. With an agonising wrench he ripped himself free, and with one last, desperate effort, he hurled himself at the trapdoor, diving through headfirst, and hitting the wooden steps a dozen times as he rolled and bounced all the way to the bottom.

With a clang, the trapdoor closed, then he heard a creak as someone opened it a little, to peer through the narrow chink. As his head stopped spinning, he heard voices.

'That's it. They've found the body. They're starting to settle now.'

'Give them a minute,' said another voice. 'Let's get as many as we can.'

There was a pause. Alestan hauled himself to his feet, gingerly flexing his wounded shoulder, and sending a trickle of warm blood down his back. He couldn't move his right arm at all, and when he tried, the pain made him feel faint and sick. Above him, he saw Corvin at the trapdoor. 'All right,' the archer whispered. 'That'll do. Areom, light the fuse.'

There was a flicker of light, a hissing sound, then the trapdoor slammed shut, and Alestan found himself caught up and carried along in a press of bodies, as everyone tried to get as far away from the staircase, as fast as they possibly could. Suddenly, the air was split asunder by the sound of an explosion, and the sturdy stonework of the building trembled all around them. Dust sifted down from the ceiling.

'By Myrial, we did it!' cried Areom.

'Come on,' said Corvin. 'Let's have a look and see how much damage we did to those flying sons of bitches.' But when they returned to the flimsy wooden stairway, they found it had been jolted loose from its underpinnings, and had collapsed into a pile of firewood. To their relief, however, the trapdoor was intact, though somewhat buckled. Two of the Godsword soldiers hoisted Corvin up on their shoulders, and he wrestled with the fastenings of the iron hatch, but there was no budging it. They would simply have to trust and hope that their trap had wrought sufficient damage, and had done its work.

Alestan, who had drawn apart from the others, felt a tremor go through him, like a sliver of ice working its way down his spine. The explosion had been the signal for Aliana to start her run. By now, for better or worse, she was on her way.

Twenty-one

Renegades

Blade awakened after nightfall, just as he had set himself to do. He wanted to approach the Shadowleague headquarters under the cover of darkness, the better to penetrate the heart of Cergorn's realm without being discovered. He poked his nose out of the warm folds of his blanket to feel the fresh, moorland air blow cool against his face, though the small, rock-sheltered hollow in which he lay protected him from the worst of the wind. Nearby, the grey warhorse tugged at its picket rope, as it stretched out its neck to reach a new area of the short upland turf. Apparently, it had been as ready to eat as he had been. Although he was not far from the Gendival wayshelter, and indeed had scavenged it for useful items of equipment, and for food to appease his ravenous hunger, he had not dared to rest there, in case any of the Shadowleague should come along and discover him while he slept.

No matter. It was a long time since he had camped out alone like this, and he had to admit that he was quite enjoying the experience. The journey here had proved to be a much-needed pause for him, a breathing space between the old part of his life and the new, and he had welcomed this time in which to reflect, and clear his mind, and shed the last vestiges of Blade the Godsword Commander like a snake slipping out of its worn old skin. *At long last, I can be Amaurn of the Magefolk once again. Finally I can be revenged on the one who exiled me, and would have had me executed. The one who tore me apart from my beloved Aveole, and indirectly caused her death.*

Watch your back, Cergorn. I'm coming.

He wondered if he dared risk contacting one of his supporters in Gendival. The temptation to find out what was happening in the Shadowleague headquarters at this time was overwhelming, but he restrained himself firmly. Though there was little risk of a clandestine message being intercepted, there was no point in taking any chances. He would be there soon enough now, and then he could find out for himself.

Amaurn would have been very surprised to discover that there were other spies, apart from his own, within the ranks of the Loremasters. Because the Dragonfolk rarely ventured from their own lands, and because the more cloudy, temperate climate of Gendival was unsuitable for their kind, they had taken the precaution of recruiting agents from other species among the Shadowleague to oversee their interests.

No other creature of flesh and blood could have lived in Zaltaigla, the realm of the Dragonfolk. Bordered on one side by the warm southern ocean, and on the others by the impenetrable barriers of the Curtain Walls, it was a landscape harsh, sere and desiccated, composed of arid stretches of black obsidian rock, the air above them rippling and shimmering with reflected heat, and league upon endless league of silvery sand that threw back the ferocious sunlight in a blinding glare. There was no water – it rained only once or twice a year, which suited the Dragonfolk, who drank but rarely, distilling what they needed from the nearby ocean – so there was no plant life to sustain an animal population.

Only Dragons would want such a land, but for them it had always been perfect, with an abundance of sunlight on which they fed by absorbing the energy through the membranes on their outspread wings. The Dragonfolk, because of the racial memory that was passed down through the generations from one Seer to the next, had held a privileged position among the inhabitants of Myrial. Along with the Magefolk, they held knowledge that other races did not, for they were aware that beyond the Curtain Walls were other lands, populated by a host of different creatures.

Beyond their realm to the south lay the Firelands, a range of stark volcanic mountains inhabited by the Phoenix and by the Salamandri, Fire-Elementals who dwelt among the active craters, but apart from this race and those of their own kind, they had no contact with any save the occasional visiting Loremaster of one species or another, usually selected by lot or by misfortune, and only sent in times of direst need, and when there was no alternative available.

Zaltaigla was thinly populated, and though many of the Dragons preferred to dwell in solitary contemplation in the desert, a good number lived in Altheva, their one, great city, created to echo the most stunning achievement of their distant past. Of all the species on Myrial, the Dragonfolk possessed the most information about their origins. Long ago and far away on another world, the cradle of their race had been a desert formed from the dust of myriad shattered gems that blazed so fiercely in the sun that any other eyes save Dragon eyes were instantly struck blind. In the midst of the desert a single peak, a lone, soaring pinnacle of rock like a giant's tower, stretched up into the heavens. On its summit was set a remarkable city, crafted from huge gems with great skill and art. In the racial memories of the Dragonfolk, handed down through the Seers from one generation to the next, it remained a place of magic, awe and legend: the pinnacle of their civilisation. Dhiammara.

How they had come from that world, their own world, to this new place, remained a mystery. Someone, or some *thing*, had tampered with the racial memories of the Dragonfolk, leaving a gap, a void, a puzzle, an aching sense of dislocation and loss. Their magic powers had vanished, and insidious doubt began to creep into their minds. Clearly their recollections had been tampered with, but which part? Were they true, those memories of another world, a greater time? Perhaps the remembered foundations of their race were all illusion. In the atmosphere of uncertainty and confusion, their civilisation faltered, and gradually their great race began to dwindle and fail.

Some of the Dragonfolk, however, refused to doubt. They kept their faith in the other world, the glorious past, the ability of their species to achieve. Led by Kayama, the Seer for her generation, and Phyrdon, Sage and Artisan, they decided to recreate Dhiammara, the wondrous city of their forbears. Then, let the others question their origins!

All manner of difficulties beset Kayama, Phyrdon and those who elected to follow them. The images of Dhiammara were clear in the Seer's mind, but the conditions which had given birth to the city proved impossible to duplicate. The desert in which they now dwelt was mere sand, not drifts of glittering gem-dust. Here there was no great pinnacle, no prodigious work of nature, on which to build their home. On this world the Dragonfolk had no magic to help them in the process of creation, and there were no massive jewels that could be wrought into dwellings, meeting-places, and centres of learning and lore. All they possessed was the skill and ingenuity of their artisans, and countless miles of desert sand. Sand that could be made into glass.

On the western border of Zaltaigla, a long range of stark peaks ran from south to north. On the eastern side the blazing desert ran up into the barren foothills, and on the western side the Curtain Walls delineated the borders of the realm. About midway down the range, a high ridge of obsidian rock, an outthrust arm of the sheltering mountains, jutted far out into the arid sands. Here Kayama, Phyrdon and their followers built their new capital; the echo of an ancient dream, the ghost, wrought in glass, of Dhiammara, city of gems, the original home of their race.

The city of Altheva was a marvel, its streets laid out like a spider web, and lined with the glittering crystalline structures that were residences and meeting-places, wrought in a multitude of colours and shapes. Though the Dragonfolk spent most of the time outside, absorbing the sunshine that meant life to them, there was one place, in the very heart of the city, that was permanently occupied. The Dome of Light had been added to and embellished through countless generations, and had long ago exceeded the original central structure that had provided its name. It was now a vast, sprawling complex of buildings; a maze of chambers, courtyards and wide, dragon-sized corridors whose exuberant design betrayed the fact that they had been constructed for the sheer joy of creation, as much as for any practical purposes.

The Dragons themselves were scattered and independent, and had little need for figures of authority, but their Astaran, their Ruling Council, provided stability and continuity, and an efficient interface for dealing with the outside world. Besides, on the rare occasions when a crisis *did* beset this ancient, stable race, it fell to the Astari, or Wise Ones, to take control. In reality, however, the role of the Ruling council had been mainly ceremonial throughout the ages, and its members had experienced little to challenge or disturb them – until now.

Because the memories of the Seers had been passed down from one generation to the next, the Dragonfolk had a different relation to time than other races. Whereas most species viewed time as a long road reaching from the past to the future, with themselves moving steadily along it, the Dragons saw time as a vast tapestry of repeating patterns whose details altered slightly whenever they recurred. Time, rather than being a straight road, was like a spiral path round a mountain, where the same view had been seen many times on the journey, but the perspective was altered every time the path climbed a little higher.

The roles of the three Council members bore out this slightly different view, representing as they did the past, the present and the future. The Astar for the Past could bring the examples of history and the accumulated experience of the race to throw new light on any situation. The Astar for the future considered how the repercussions of any decision made in the present would affect the Dragonfolk in times to come, and the Astar for the Present dealt with day-to-day details and decisions, always bearing in mind the contributions of the other two. Usually the system worked well, but what would happen now that the Astaran were confronting one of the greatest disasters that had ever happened to their race?

It was a solemn group who convened in the Chamber of Good Counsel, a private meeting room constructed of amber-coloured crystal which changed the cool silver moonlight to a warm, cheerful glow that was completely at odds with the mood of the three Astari. They had just received word from Gendival, concerning the loss of Aethon, their Seer.

Like Amaurn, the Dragons were making sure that no telepathic messages could be intercepted by Cergorn's followers. Instead of mindspeech they were using a rare and precious alseom, one of the artefacts left behind by Myrial's mysterious, powerful creators. It was a sphere of fragile, translucent crystal, slightly larger than a human head, which carried a faint, iridescent bloom on its surface. Each alseom was activated by the utterance of a different password, preserved and handed down through the ages as carefully as the artefact itself. The alseom secreted with the Dragon spy in Gendival transmitted images and words to an identical stone in Altheva, ensuring that the members of the Astaran had a secret and efficient means of finding out what was happening in the private councils of the Shadowleague.

Now, the three Astari were clustered around the alseom in stunned and horrified silence. The news of Aethon's death was a catastrophe beyond words. Xiara, Astar for the past, was the first to rouse herself. Because of Aethon's unique memories, she had always been closely involved with him, and had been very much against sending him away from the safety of Zaltaigla in the first place, though the others had eventually outvoted her. She rustled her great, translucent wings; her jewelled eyes, that could be such lethal weapons, flashed anger and distress. 'There!' she said bitterly. 'Exactly as I predicted. Didn't I warn you again and again that this would happen if you sent poor Aethon off to the accursed Shadowleague?'

Taleng, Astar for the future, growled deep in his throat. 'Yes,' he sneered. 'And I recollect that you were much too busy foretelling doom and disaster to come up with any alternative plan.'

Chandrakanan, Astar for the Present, and therefore the leader of the Council, brought her bickering colleagues to order. 'This won't help,' she said sharply. Turning back to the alseom, she addressed the Dragonfolk spy. 'If this catastrophe happened several days ago, why am I hearing about it from you? Why did the Archimandrite not see fit to inform me immediately?'

The expressionless face of the spy loomed large in the crystal sphere, as it drew closer to the alseom. 'Cergorn feels very threatened at present. As the systems of this world continue to break down, he is coming under increasing pressure from the Shadowleague to use the hidden knowledge of the Creators. His refusal even to consider the possibility is meeting with greater and greater criticism. I believe he knew what your reaction would be to Aethon's death, and was trying to conceal his failure until he could deal with the trouble in his own back yard. Besides, there is more to this business than meets the eye. He sent his own partner, Senior Loremaster Thirishri, to investigate the Seer's death, and she has vanished in mysterious circumstances. It would appear that someone, somewhere, has actually discovered how to kill a Wind-Sprite.'

'*What?*' exploded Chandrakanan. 'Is there no end to your tidings of woe?' The others joined in with her exclamations of sorrow. That there was something in existence which could kill a Wind-Sprite was bad enough, but Shree had been a frequent visitor to the lands of the Dragonfolk, and had been greatly liked and respected.

'In that case,' the Astar continued, 'Cergorn's grief must excuse him much, but if he sent Thirishri to investigate Aethon's death, she herself had not yet perished. So why did he conceal the news of the Seer's loss from us? For surely we must regard his continuing silence as concealment.'

'He claimed that he was waiting for Veldan and Kazairl, the Loremasters who were escorting Aethon, to return and explain exactly what happened.'

'A feeble excuse,' muttered Xiara.

'And?' prompted Taleng.

The eyes of the spy glittered. 'They arrived earlier today, and they came back with the strangest story. They say that in the moment of his death, Aethon managed to transfer his mind and spirit into the body of a nearby human. I have no wish to raise your hopes unduly, but there is a faint possibility that the memories of the Dragonfolk may not be lost after all.'

There was another moment of stunned silence, while the Astari digested this incredible news. This time, they looked at one another with dawning hope. Chandrakanan was the first to speak. 'But if this is true, then what is the reason for Cergorn's continuing silence? We Dragonfolk have been the allies of the Shadowleague for uncounted ages. Why would the Archimandrite put that relationship at risk?'

'Indeed,' Taleng added. 'Surely he must realise the vital importance to our people of this development.'

'He refuses to believe his Loremasters,' the spy replied. 'The human cannot – or will not – permit Aethon to communicate, so the Archimandrite believes that Veldan and Kazairl have concocted the story to lessen their disgrace. Until the human can be persuaded to co-operate, they have no proof.'

'Just who is this human?' Xiara interrupted.

'That's a very good question, but you're not going to like the answer. Apparently the host is Zavahl, the deposed Hierarch of Callisiora. The man is well known to the Shadowleague as a religious bigot of the worst order, so it's not surprising that he won't let our Seer communicate. If Kazairl and Veldan speak the truth, that is.'

Chandrakanan leaned forward. 'And you?' she said softly. 'What do *you* believe?'

'I believe that Cergorn is a fool to discount the possibility. I believe that he is acting irrationally through anger, grief and desperation, but when his wrath has had time to cool, maybe after a night's sleep, I believe that he will investigate more fully.' The spy paused. 'I also believe that if you want your Seer back, or at least his memories, we should act tonight, before the Archimandrite has time to make his move. Aethon's knowledge will be just as useful to the

Shadowleague, even if it *is* couched in a human body, and Cergorn will still want to make use of it. And don't forget that there are others, who no longer support him. They too would find the Seer's memories of great use, and we must act before they do. Also, according to Veldan, the human host is not very stable, and the continuing presence of an intruder in his mind may tip him over the edge into insanity. What if he should escape? What if he seeks to harm himself, or end his life? I would advise that you take steps to get him safely back to you, and as quickly as possible, so that the precious memories can be recovered before they are lost for good.'

Chandrakanan took a deep breath, and looked at the others for confirmation. Taleng nodded briefly. Xiara's hopes and wishes shone out clearly from her jewelled eyes.

'Very well,' the leader of the Council told her spy. 'So be it. Can you accomplish this thing, without betraying your own position?'

'I can. Let me go now, and set events in motion immediately. I'll inform you as soon as the human is safely in our hands. Don't look so worried, Xiara. Within a matter of days, you should have Aethon – or at least his memories – safely back with you.'

With that, the crystal of the alseom grew dark, and the image of Skreeva, Senior Loremaster of the Alvai, faded away.

Skreeva had been right in her guess that other plans were also hatching in Gendival that night. In the home of Veldan and Kazairl, the Loremasters were ready to make their move.

'Are you ready?' Veldan whispered to Ailie.

The innkeeper nodded. 'Be ready to slip out as soon as the coast is clear,' she said softly. Though she was trying her best to look cheerful, her face was very pale, and the Loremaster felt sorry for her. The actions of the next few moments would alter the course of her life irrevocably, and her decision, perforce made in haste, to help the plotters, was not one to be taken lightly. In addition, Veldan knew that she was worrying about Zavahl. Without warning, the man who had lived his entire life around the conviction that there was nothing beyond the Curtain Walls that bounded his land, and no sentient beings in existence other than humans, was about to be thrust into the middle of a major power struggle within the Shadowleague, and there was no way of knowing how he would respond. Nevertheless, Veldan admired the brave front that Ailie was putting on matters. Giving the others a jaunty wave, she hoisted her basket a little higher on her arm, and stepped out into the night.

Ailie was not the only one with a very great deal at stake. Veldan knew that if she and the others left her house against the Archimandrite's orders, they would set their feet on a path from which there was no returning. If the Moldan's plotting failed, if Cergorn was not overthrown, then she and her companions could expect exile or even execution. The centaur had always made it very clear that there was no room in the Shadowleague for rebels. How many times, while she was growing up, had Veldan heard the tale of Amaurn the renegade, held up to her as an example and a warning?

'Cheer up, Boss.' As always, the voice of the firedrake was bracing. 'This contest for leadership is going to happen now, no matter what we do, so there's no point in fretting over it. All we need worry about is choosing the winning side.'

Elion nodded agreement. 'Kaz is right. And it seems to me that there's enough bad feeling against Cergorn in Gendival to make the rebel position very strong.'

The firedrake's head came up sharply in surprise. 'Elion? *You* are saying I'm *right*? Are you sure you're feeling well?'

He grinned. 'Just don't start getting used to the idea.'

'Sssh.' Even though they were all using mindspeech, Veldan held her finger to her lips in the age-old gesture. She was peering out through a narrow chink in the curtains. 'It's started. She's talking to Endos.'

In the light of the glims that were set on poles at either side of Veldan's door, Ailie could clearly be seen, laughing and joking with the guard. She held out her basket. 'Here,' she said, her voice travelling clearly in the evening hush. 'That ungrateful lot in there reckon they've already eaten, and I'm not about to let all my hard work go to waste. There's a whole lot of pasties in the basket. Why don't you give your mate a shout, and the two of you can share them?'

Endos, his mouth already bulging, muttered something barely distinguishable to the effect that his fellow-guard was not supposed to leave his post, and could go to perdition for all *he* cared. Ailie, however, took no notice. 'I'll just go and get him, shall I?' she said brightly, and went tripping away round the corner of the house, being careful to leave her basket behind. After a moment she returned with Trinn, the other guard. He was plainly reluctant to leave his post, but Ailie had hold of his arm and was sweeping him along with her on a flood of cheerful chatter that completely drowned his protests. 'Oh, don't be silly,' she scolded. 'It'll only take a moment. You can pick out what you want, and go right back again.'

Veldan dropped the curtain. 'Let's go.'

Like the rest of the doorways in the house, the back door had been constructed to firedrake proportions. The four Loremasters slipped quietly out and hurried into the concealing shelter of the trees, hastening to get as far away from the house as possible in the shortest time, lest Trinn should return, and glimpse the golden glimmer of Vaure's fiery plumage through the trees. Their need to hurry warred with their need to move quietly, for on such a still evening, any unexpected noises in the forest would arouse the guard's suspicions, and so they must tread carefully, especially the firedrake with his weight and bulk. Kaz, however, had perforce learned stealth in his years as a Loremaster, and in the oak wood there was little undergrowth to impede him. The runaways slipped through the forest, always heading upwards, until they were near the top of the ridge, and could avoid the glim-lit paths that ran between the Shadowleague dwellings. Though they half expected their ruse to be discovered by Endos and Trinn, and to hear, at any moment, the alarm being raised behind them, the night stayed still and silent, and the further they ventured from the main part of the settlement, the better were their chances of reaching the Moldan's house undiscovered.

Swiftly the Loremasters moved up the valley, working their way along the hillside, far above the shores of the tranquil Lower Lake. They didn't want to risk even the light of a glim to show the way: Vaure's plumage was risk enough, though they had agreed that if there was any sign of pursuit, the phoenix would veer off in another direction, to lure any searchers away from them. In the meantime, her glowing feathers gave forth a faint but useful light, and if need be, the other Loremasters could link into Kazairl's night vision.

The entrance to Maskulu's underground home was right on the edge of the Loremaster settlement, high above the reedy neck of land that divided the Upper and Lower Lakes. Here, the topography of the land began to alter, the ridge gradually changing from forested hillside to steeper, harsher crags, with rowan, thorn and stunted, wind-bent evergreens finding a purchase on ledges and in fissures and clefts. The night seemed darker here, for the starry sky was obscured by the veil of cloud that always shrouded the hills around the Upper Lake.

Elion shivered. On the dreadful days following the death of Melnyth, his Shadowleague partner, he had frequently come up to the bleak Upper Lake to brood, and be alone with his grief. Now, this landscape held only tragic associations, and the memory of grim and desperate thoughts which he would rather not be forced to recollect. 'What a barren place to build a home,' he whispered.

'To our eyes, yes,' said Vaure, 'but why should the Moldai care what the landscape is like above the ground? They are only concerned with the rock beneath, with its underlying composition and structure. Underground, their senses find forms of beauty that other races cannot comprehend.'

'Just as we can't understand your habit of sitting in the fireplace,' said Elion.

'Indeed,' said the phoenix. 'And as my people cannot comprehend this urge you humans have to immerse yourselves in water so frequently.'

'This is all very interesting,' said Kaz pointedly, 'but right now it's the centaurs we have to worry about. Let's get safely underground. We can waste time later, comparing notes on our different species.'

Veldan laid a comforting hand on the firedrake's shoulder. No wonder he seemed a little prickly, she thought. He was the only one of his kind that had ever been discovered by the Shadowleague, so he was bound to feel at a loss in a conversation comparing the different races.

The entrance to the Moldan's home was cunningly concealed beneath a slight overhang, where a trick of the light and shadows drew the eye away from the faint outline of a portal. The actual door was a boulder, cleverly shaped and pivoted so that when it was turned on its axis, a space was created on either side to allow ingress. At first it looked as though there wouldn't be room for Kaz, but finally, by dint of much grunting and cursing, he squeezed himself through.

'You know,' said Elion, 'this can't be an entrance that Maskulu himself would use. He simply wouldn't fit.'

'Really,' said the firedrake with heavy sarcasm, licking at the scrapes on his flanks. 'We would never have guessed.'

'Maskulu keeps his own entrances secret,' the phoenix told them. 'He moves them around so much, filling in the old ones and opening new tunnels, that no-one can keep track. Says it keeps him from being spied on.'

I don't think he's in much danger of that,' Veldan snorted. 'Given the aggressive natures of the Moldai, it would take someone very brave or very stupid to even try.'

As Elion swivelled the boulder to block the doorway, the Loremasters were plunged into utter darkness, save for the muted golden glimmer of Vaure's feathers. Veldan pulled an egg-shaped glim out of her pocket, and twisted the two halves against one another, breaking the seal between them. A soft, greenish light sprang out between her fingers, illuminating a beautifully crafted tunnel with smooth walls of polished stone, that wound down and back into the heart of the rocky ridge. The air was cool and dry, without a trace of mustiness, though there were no visible signs of ventilation. The Moldai, masters of stone, were capable of building entire underground cities, with air in abundance for the inhabitants to breathe, so a small tunnel like this must be child's play to them.

The companions followed the tunnel as it wound its way down into the ridge. The floor had a fairly steep gradient, but was smooth and even beneath their feet, and the passage through the rock curved gently, so that it gradually looped round in a spiral, with side tunnels leading off at intervals. They walked in silence for a time, each of them aware of the others' doubts and nervousness, but no-one wanting to be the first to comment. Veldan found herself wondering whether their escape had been discovered yet. She didn't want Ailie to get into trouble for what they had done, and the longer the guards took to find out that their prisoners were missing, the less likely it would be that Cergorn would connect their disappearance with the innkeeper.

After the confines of the tunnel, the Moldan's living area, a great circular chamber some sixty feet across, seemed vast, allowing plenty of space for the lengthy body of the Senior Loremaster. The odd glim glowed here and there at random, scattered around, no doubt, for the benefit of the visitors, for Maskulu had little use for light. The greenish luminescence cast a dim and eldritch light throughout the cavern, making sinister pools of darkness.

There was nothing that a human could identify as furnishing, though various oddly-shaped niches and hollows had been carved into the rock in various places. Some of the stone that comprised the walls and floor was polished smooth and shining as satin, whereas in other places it was undulating, or rough and raised in texture, or incised in alien patterns. Veldan knew that the Moldai had no need for eyesight in the black spaces underground, but their tactile senses, which worked through the many bristles on their legs and at each segment of their carapace, were sufficiently developed so that they could be said to 'see' through every inch of their bodies. This place must appear very different to Maskulu's senses than it did to hers.

As they entered, a figure rose from a dark corner, and came groping its way towards them. For an instant, Veldan thought it must be one of her missing companions, then she heard the voice of Bailen in her mind. 'I'm so glad you're here at last. I was starting to get worried.'

It was only natural, Veldan thought, that the third member of the Listener trio would be here. She wondered where Toulac and Zavahl could be. There was no sign of them in the chamber, but it had taken so long for the Loremasters to slip away from their captives and come to this place that she'd been certain that the others must have got here first. Maybe they were resting elsewhere. No doubt the Moldan would tell her when he came. She was about to ask Vaure who was bringing them, when Maskulu arrived, and put the matter right out of her head.

Set at an angle to the tunnel through which they had entered was another passageway, and with a slithering rush, Maskulu came into the chamber through this alternative entrance. The suddenness of his approach made both Veldan and Elion jump.

'Welcome, welcome,' said the Moldan, communicating in mindspeech though its glittering diamond mandibles clicked open and shut as if in emphasis. 'Though my home is not the most comfortable place for your kind, I hope it will provide you with a refuge in the face of Cergorn's intransigence.'

'Thank you, Senior Loremaster,' said Elion.

'Yes, we're very grateful,' Veldan added. Though she was using mindspeech, she took a deep breath, to buy herself time to think of the right words. 'Would – could you tell us what is happening, please? We've been away so long, Kaz and I, and we feel very out of touch. I know we made an awful mess of our mission, and I'm more sorry than I can say, but somehow I didn't expect so strong a reaction from Cergorn. Surely he, of all people, must know that accidents can happen to any Loremaster. It was a mudslide that killed Aethon, and what could we have done about that?'

'Nothing,' said Maskulu, in surprisingly gentle tones. 'Be easy, Veldan. Of course there was nothing you could have done to prevent the Dragon's death. The Archimandrite would understand that, had he not been concentrating so hard on fighting against the tide of change and the workings of fate. But Cergorn will not accept that his laws of secrecy and isolation are no longer adequate to withstand the current crisis. If the Shadowleague – and indeed, our entire world – is to survive the breakdown of the Curtain Walls, I fear that we must look for a new leader.'

'By which you mean yourself?' Kaz was a great deal less tactful than his partner.

The Moldan made the hissing sound that passed for its laughter. 'Ah, Kazairl. Only you would ever have the nerve to ask me such a question to my face.'

'Somebody had to,' retorted the firedrake, undeterred.

'It is a fair question,' the Moldan agreed. 'If I ask for your support, you have a right to know just who or what it is that you'll be supporting.' He looked down on them with glittering red eyes. 'I have no wish to be the Archimandrite. Of that you may be assured. Later, when the time is right, you will meet the one who has long deserved that name. He will speak to you himself concerning his hopes and plans. In the meantime, you may rest, and await the coming of your human friends.'

'What?' said Veldan. 'You mean that the others haven't come yet? I thought they might be resting somewhere else. They should have been here ages ago.'

'That is strange.' The phoenix sounded worried. 'Dessil was going to release them, and bring them here. If there had been any problem, surely he would . . .' She fell silent, and Veldan knew she must be trying to reach her fellow Listener. Suddenly, Vaure's brilliant plumage dimmed. 'I can't reach him,' she whispered. 'He doesn't answer. Something must have happened to him.'

For a long moment, the Loremasters could only look at one another in horrified silence. Maskulu was rattling his carapace in distress. 'If Cergorn has discovered us,' he hissed, 'then all our plans are in ruins.'

'Well, we can't very well go and investigate,' Elion pointed out.

'We could be walking right into a trap, with Zavahl and Toulac as the bait.'

'Plague on it.' Veldan bit her lip. 'I wonder what has become of them?'

Twenty-two

Cloak and Dagger

Aliana waited with Commander Galveron beside the small postern door of the Godsword Citadel. She was glad that he was keeping silent. Tense and terrified, the last thing she wanted or needed now was useless talk. They had been over the plan. She knew what to do. Galveron had taught her the coded knock which would gain her admittance to the Temple. The heavy backpack on her back was bulged with blasting powder and fuses: a burden that made her very uneasy, though Miner Areom had assured her that as long as she didn't mess about with any fires or candles, she would be all right. Now she only had to wait until the diversion worked – if it worked – and she could get away and get this dreadful business over, one way or the other.

Cutting across her thoughts came the sound of someone clearing his throat. Aliana looked round to see Packrat emerging from the shadows. Giving Galveron a wide berth, the scruffy miscreant sidled up to her. 'I – I got something for you,' he said. In his hands was a tattered looking bundle of cloth. When she made no move to take it, he thrust it at her. 'Here,' he said.

Aliana tried not to shrink away from the disgusting grey object. It looked filthy and verminous and, as it belonged to Packrat, it probably was. So why was he handling it as though it was some precious treasure?

I don't need this. Any minute now I've got to go out and face those nightmare creatures. There's a strong possibility that I won't see tomorrow. Why did he have to choose this particular time to pester me with some disreputable rag that he's scavenged from under a sink somewhere?

There was a slight frown beneath the grime on Packrat's face. 'Go on,' he urged. 'Take it, please. It's a sort of present, for saving my life. It's the most precious thing I own.'

'*That?*' said Aliana, before she could stop herself. 'What is it?' she added hastily, hoping to forestall the injured look that was creeping across his face.

'It's an invisible cloak,' said Packrat proudly.

'But – but Packrat, it doesn't look invisible to me. I can see it perfectly clearly,' Aliana protested.

And I only wish I couldn't.

'No, no. I don't mean that the actual *cloak* is invisible,' he told her impatiently. 'I mean that when I put it on, it makes *me* invisible. It's – what's the word? – it's camouflage, that's what it is. It makes me fade into the background.' He patted the ragged bundle fondly. 'This little beauty has kept me out of the hands of those whoreson Godswords more times than I can tell you.' He flicked a nasty look at Galveron, who stood nearby. 'Honest, Aliana, you've got to wear it if you're going out there. You'll need all the help you can get to hide yourself from those brutes.'

Packrat shook out the cloak and held it up for inspection. Though it seemed to be predominantly grey, it was actually made from hundreds of strips and snippets of cloth in a multitude of hues. Oddly, the overall effect achieved was a blur of no particular colour that confused the eye and seemed to direct it away from the revolting object. In addition, many of the strips of rag had been attached at one end but were left hanging loose at the other, blurring the outline still further. Aliana, looking at it, suddenly understood why her companion was so accomplished at melting into the shadows. But . . .

'But Packrat,' she said gently, 'I'm going out into the snow. Those dusky colours would be perfect in a shadowy room or street, but against a white background, it'll show up almost as much as the Godsword cloak.'

Packrat grinned. 'Ah,' he said, 'but that's where you're wrong. See?' He turned the cloak around, and she saw that the other side was fashioned exactly like the first, but from fragments of cloth in dirty white, the paler blues and greens, and a myriad shades of lighter grey.

Amazed at such ingenuity, Aliana took it from him. 'Thank you, Packrat,' she said. 'This is . . .' she groped for a word. 'It's incredible. So much work has gone into making it.'

'Oh, it wasn't just me,' he said cheerfully. 'It's an heirloom, this is. Handed down from my grandma, and she was the most legendary thief of her day. She left it to my dad, and he gave it to Ma, before they hanged him. She put it by for me, till I was old enough to use it. We've all been adding to it over the years, a bit here and a bit there.'

It's a pity none of you ever washed it.

Aliana told herself not to be so particular. Probably the patina of smoke, grease and dirt added to the camouflaging properties. And if the winged fiends hunted by scent, this should certainly confuse them.

'Better hurry,' said Galveron softly from the doorway. 'They've had long enough now to set the trap.'

'Go on, be quick,' Packrat urged. 'Put it on.'

Aliana gave in. 'But it's only a loan, all right? I'll give it back to you tomorrow.' She handed her precious new Godsword cloak to Galveron, and threw Packrat's disreputable garment around her shoulders, paler side out, over the top of the pack she carried. To her surprise, it was so light that she felt no extra weight at all.

'And the hood,' prompted Packrat.

Aliana's gorge rose at the thought of pulling the filthy cloth, which was infested by fleas, lice and Myrial only knew what else, over her hair. Firmly, she reminded herself that the cloak really *was* good camouflage, and that nits and fleas could be got rid of, but disembowelment was permanent. If putting up with the former was the price of avoiding the latter, who was she to complain?

Myrial help me.

With a shudder, she pulled it over her head, assuring herself that it was her imagination which made her scalp begin to crawl and itch immediately. Seeing Packrat's beaming face, she managed to smile and thank him once again, but inside, she was desperate for her ordeal to be over.

I wish Alestan would get a move on. The sooner I get to the Temple, the sooner I can take this bloody thing off.

It was as though her twin had read her mind. Suddenly, from above, came a booming roar and the stones of the Citadel trembled slightly. Outside, she heard, beneath the shrieks of the winged fiends far above, the faint, wet splats of something raining down on the nearby snow. Galveron unbarred the door. 'Get out of the courtyard as quickly as you can,' he whispered. Rather gingerly, he squeezed her shoulder. 'Good luck.'

Aliana took a deep breath and moved, low and fast, out of the door and to her left, so that she could stay close to the wall, using it as a guide in the darkness, as well as cover. The courtyard, with its high walls, was steeped in darkness, the air thick and icy with a maelstrom of swirling snow. Close to the Citadel, the ground was splattered with dark amorphous lumps which, if she guessed rightly, were proof that Areom's explosive trap had claimed at least one victim.

Obscure dark shadows swept back and forth overhead, making her freeze and cower, but so far, the brutes all seemed intent on the rooftop of the Citadel. Sometimes creeping, sometimes darting swiftly from one sheltered position to the next, the leader of the Grey Ghosts worked her way around the edge of the Godsword courtyard. This would be the easy part, she reminded herself. The vast, open expanse in front of the Temple, choked as it was with the remains of the Tiarondian dead, was still to come.

Oddly, Packrat's 'invisible' cloak gave her extra confidence: not that it made her want to take to take unnecessary risks, but it seemed to help her move even more silently and stealthily than usual. From above, on the roof of the Citadel, the wind brought her the sound of the winged fiends shrieking as they fought for food.

Let it be one of their own they're eating, or even poor Tosel. Please don't let it be my brother.

But she mustn't let herself think of Alestan now. He was a distraction that might easily end her own life. It would be tomorrow before she could find out if he was safe. Somehow, she had to force herself to get through the night and concentrate on taking care of herself, instead of worrying about him.

Aliana reached the arched entrance to the Citadel courtyard without encountering any trouble, and felt her hopes begin to rise. Sheltering in the shadowy archway she peered out into the great open plaza before the Temple – and caught her breath in horror.

The predators that lurked around the Citadel itself had been drawn to the rooftop by the trap, but the rest of their brethren were out here. Wherever she looked, there were winged shapes crouched like sinister gargoyles over the piles of frozen corpses. Bright lanterns burned in the narrow windows of the Temple itself, presumably put there in an attempt to discourage the light-fearing creatures from approaching too close to the building itself. The faint radiance, diffused and reflected by the flying snow, gave her light enough to see that the fiends were engaged in a ghastly orgy of feasting. They were everywhere, hundreds of them. She could see their feral, glittering eyes, reflecting the lamplight with a crimson glow. Every now and again one would raise its head from its grisly banquet, and sweep the plaza with those penetrating eyes which, as the thief knew to her cost, could see so well in the dark.

Panic locked icy fingers around Aliana's heart.

I can't do this! I daren't! I'll have to go back.

But when she looked back again at the Temple, she saw winged figures clustering around the shattered upper windows. If she turned back, then the refugees stood little chance of surviving the night. And if she failed, Galveron might condemn and cast out herself and her friends as thieves, at any time.

He wouldn't!

What's to stop him? He only promised to take care of us if you took the blasting powder to the Temple.

But I tried. Surely that counts for something?

Don't be stupid. He's a bloody Godsword. None of them can be trusted.

In her heart, she knew that the cynical inner voice was right. She had to keep her side of the bargain. That was the only way to ensure that Galveron would keep his word.

Aliana swallowed hard. There was only one way she could think of to get across the plaza undetected – maybe – and the thought of it made her stomach churn. But she had no other option. She removed the dagger from her belt and strapped the sheath around her arm, where she could get at it more easily, without it catching in her cloak. Then, pulling the hood of Packrat's noisome garment well forward around her face, she dropped to her hands and knees, and began to crawl.

She stayed low to the ground, inching along with painstaking caution, worming her way among the mounds of corpses. If she was seen at all, despite the camouflage of Packrat's cloak, she hoped that she would be mistaken for one of the bodies. Hopefully the swirling snow would confuse any signs of her movement, and she prayed that none of the creatures would come near enough to realise that fresh, live prey was lurking amid their store of frozen meat.

It was going to take forever to inch her way across the plaza. It would be necessary to stay close to the wall, with its shadows and its drifts of snow, for it would be suicide to cross the centre of that open space, with the winged fiends all around her. So the journey would take even longer, as she worked her way along the side of the Citadel and then turned to her right to creep along the side of the Basilica. She fretted at the extra time she was forced to take, for the risk to the people in the Temple would increase with every moment's delay, but that was the least of her worries. If she took too long, the cold could prove as lethal an enemy as the winged fiends themselves, for she was forced to move too slowly to generate any warmth, and crawling along the snowy ground, she was losing body heat with frightening speed. Within a moment or two, she had begun to shiver, despite the warm clothing and the cloak she wore. The knees of her trousers were soaked through with freezing slush, and she knew the cloth would wear through in no time, exposing her bare skin to the snowy ground. Soon she was even beginning to feel wetness penetrating the leather Godsword gauntlets that she wore. But she knew she had to keep going, no matter what. Desperately she tried to encourage herself.

This won't last forever. It'll be over before you know it, and you'll be sitting in front of a roaring fire in dry clothes, and they'll give you hot soup, and wrap you in blankets, and you'll be a hero for saving the Temple.

Comforting thoughts – but they were not enough to insulate her from the horrors of that night, as she inched her way among the Tiarondian dead. In order not to be spotted by the fiends, she was forced to stay low on her belly, her face right down amongst the corpses, which lay everywhere; their expressions, where the features still existed, frozen in a rictus of agony and terror. On others, the faces had been eaten away, exposing the delicate white bone of skulls, many of which had been smashed open like eggshells. Aliana was thankful that the snow hid some of the more appalling sights. Bodies had been disembowelled, and the frozen ground was a charnel-house of guts and gore. Limbs were twisted at odd angles. Arms had been ripped right off, and chewed limbs and bones with shreds of bloody flesh still clinging to them littered the snow, where the winged fiends had dined. The crows and rats had also been busy. Holes had been pecked and gnawed in stiffened flesh, and eyes were gone from gaping, bloody sockets. In a way, Aliana was glad of that. She felt that she could not have borne the gelid stare of so many dead eyes. She pictured similar scenes within the Warrens, where so many of her friends had been hunted down and slaughtered, and felt herself beginning to shake.

Don't you dare! Go to pieces later, if you must, but this isn't the time or the place.

Aliana swallowed hard, fighting back nausea. In order to calm herself, she wanted to breathe deeply, but didn't dare. Despite the cold, the air was rank with the rancid, sickly fetor of so many decaying corpses. She was only grateful that the freezing temperatures prevented things from being much worse.

Gratefully, she turned the corner to crawl along the extensive frontage of the Temple. At least she was more than halfway to her goal. Now it would be as easy to go on as it would to retreat.

I'm going to have nightmares about this for the rest of my life.

I'll just be grateful if I have the rest of my life.

Doggedly, Aliana crawled on. She knew she must have scraped the skin from both her knees, but her flesh was too numbed with cold to feel any pain. Now, so close to her goal, she was running out of patience. Why was it taking so long to reach the doors of this accursed building? Why did they have to make the wretched thing so big?

Cautiously raising her head a little, she risked a quick look round, and found, to her relief, that the doors were only a few yards away. But looking up like that had been a mistake. She had assumed that the fiends would want to avoid feeding in the vicinity of the Temple, because of the lights, but she had been wrong. Not far away, certainly closer than she would have guessed, one of the predators was squatting over a dismembered corpse, tearing out great mouthfuls of flesh.

Damn!

Aliana ducked down quickly, but it was too late. The creature, glimpsing the movement out of the corner of its eye, turned its head towards her. She froze, not even daring to breathe, pretending with all her might to be just another corpse among the many.

Go away. Please, go away! There's nothing here.

But she could hear it creeping towards her: the hissing sound of its breathing and the rustle of its leathery wings as it moved. It didn't bother to take off, and Aliana suspected that it didn't want to warn its fellows that there might be something interesting here.

That's right. Let's keep this between ourselves.

Lying still as a corpse, Aliana worked her dagger loose from its sheath, and eased the hilt into her hand. Suddenly the fiend exploded into movement, darting towards her in a kind of crouching scuttle. She waited until it was right on top of her, and struck. As the creature stooped down to tear at her flesh with its talons, she rolled over and went straight for its throat with her knife. She felt the jar as her blade bit into flesh, and the next moment she was covered in a gush of warm and stinking blood. The creature rolled aside, thrashing in its death throes, and Aliana scrambled to her feet. There was no point in hiding now. Already she could hear the drumming of wings as a host of the creatures took to the air to investigate the disturbance. Moving as fast as her cramped and frozen body would let her, she made a desperate dash for the Temple doors.

Impelled by fear, Aliana moved faster than she had ever done before, slipping and sliding, her sheer momentum keeping her upright as she scrambled over the bodies of the frozen dead. She would never have made it, had the Temple doorway not been so close, and had there not been the storm to hamper the predators in flight. To one side of her and behind her, winged forms hurtled into the ground as two of the creatures misjudged the strength of the wind as they struck. Another was caught in a freak updraught, and was tumbled over and smashed into the wall of the Temple. Some of their companions immediately attacked the fallen, choosing this easier prey over the small, moving target, clad in the colours of the wintry ground, which was so difficult to see against the background of flying snow.

Aliana scrambled up the last few steps, and fell against the Temple doors. For a panic-stricken instant she thought she had forgotten the coded knock, but found that her knuckles were hammering it out almost of their own volition, thundering out the rhythm against the icy bronze of the doors, which rang like a gong beneath her hand. 'Let me in,' she shrieked. 'For Myrial's sake, let me in!'

The skin between her shoulderblades was crawling. The fiends would be on her any moment now. Aliana turned at bay to face her attackers, pressing her back against the Temple doors. Seemingly, the predators had learned from the fate of her companions, and had given up trying to swoop down on her from the air. Instead, she found herself faced by a cluster of menacing, cadaverous figures, who ringed the bottom of the steps, their rustling, leathery wings folded close against their backs, their foetid breath hissing out from between bared and jagged fangs, their mad eyes ablaze with a glittering red light. Slowly, they edged closer to her, wary of the dagger in her hand, knowing that the first one to reach her would very likely die. She wondered how intelligent they were. They seemed to have no concept of working together. How long would it take for them to work out that they only needed to rush her all at once?

With her free hand behind her back, Aliana beat a frantic tattoo on the Temple doors. As if enraged by the noise, the fiends came rushing forwards, snarling and hissing horribly, their clawed hands reaching out for her; reaching to pull her down. She made a wild swipe with her dagger and the foremost creature fell back, clutching at a bleeding arm – and at her back, the doors came open, and unseen hands dragged her through the narrow gap.

She'd been yanked in with such force that she overbalanced. Sprawling on the floor, she was almost trampled as people rushed forward to force the doors shut against the mass of attacking predators. After a moment, much to her relief, she heard the slam, and the scrape and click of bars and bolts shooting into place. Then the crowd seemed to melt away, leaving a clear space all around her. In the ensuing silence Aliana struggled to her knees – and found herself facing a little woman who looked swamped by the rich robes of the Hierarch. She stood, hands on hips, tapping her foot impatiently. There was a scowl on her face that looked like the dark front of an approaching thunderstorm. 'Who in perdition are *you?*' she demanded.

Aliana's visions of hot soup, glowing fires and warm blankets suddenly vanished like a dream, but she was too angry at this unjust reception to be cowed. Scrambling to her feet, she shrugged out of Packrat's disreputable cloak – which had not been improved by having the winged fiend's blood splattered all over it – and tore off her backpack, dropping it at the woman's feet. Only the fact that she was a little nervous of the blasting powder kept her from hurling it. 'There,' she said. 'I've brought your bloody blasting powder. And if I'd known that this was all the thanks I'd get, I wouldn't have bothered to risk my life for you miserable bastards.' Then her knees gave way beneath her, totally ruining the whole dramatic effect. 'Damn,' she said, and crumpled to the ground.

Gentle hands were supporting her shoulders, and she opened her eyes to see a thin, pale face with a firm, wry mouth, and sparkling, shrewd green eyes, all framed in springy dark curls which had escaped in tendrils from the ragged strip of fabric that tied them back.

'I didn't faint,' Aliana said muzzily. Suddenly, she felt incredibly tired.

The woman smiled. 'Of course you didn't,' she replied briskly. 'You don't look like the fainting sort to me. But my dear girl, you're frozen to the bone!' Her voice grew sharp. 'I'm Healer Kaita. Is any of that blood yours, do you know?'

'Don't think so.' Despite her best efforts, her eyelids began to droop again.

Kaita turned to the Hierarch. 'With all due respect, my lady, this isn't the time for questions. What does it matter who she is? The girl is a hero, and that's what counts.'

Gilarra's face coloured, and her mouth went tight. 'Very well. But I'll want some answers later. And there's one thing we must know at once.' She looked down at Aliana. 'What happened to Commander Galveron? Why couldn't he come himself?'

'He's all right. They're trapped in the Citadel.' She saw both women's faces brighten with relief, and smiled to herself. What was it about that man? He seemed able to charm anything in a skirt!

'I'll speak to you later,' said the Hierarch. 'I need to get this to the Godswords at once.' She gestured for someone to pick up the backpack, and bustled off without a backward look, confident that she would be followed.

'Not very big on thanks, is she?' Aliana muttered.

'She's got a lot on her mind,' said the healer. 'But no, you're right. She isn't.' She gave the thief a conspiratorial smile. 'What's your name?'

'Aliana.'

'Come on then, Aliana. There's a nice big fire in the guardroom. Let's get you warm, then we'll clean you up a bit and let you rest. I'll get someone to carry you.'

'I can manage,' Aliana insisted stubbornly. Carried indeed! She was made of sterner stuff than that. A Grey Ghost would never be so feeble. With Kaita's help, she struggled up onto legs that felt curiously shaky, and she had to lean heavily on the healer's shoulder as she was led away. Never mind. She was getting along on her own two feet, and that was the main thing. Despite the severity of the Hierarch, it looked as though she'd get her fire, her hot soup and her blankets after all.

Twenty-three

The Dierkan

Something had gone badly wrong. Toulac was certain of it. There was a feeling of trouble in the air, as distinct as the uneasy, oppressive atmosphere of an approaching storm.

At first, trusting that Veldan would be back in no time, the veteran had been quite happy simply to rest herself and conserve her energy. After working her way through Ailie's generous midday meal – she still had the soldier's habit of making the most of any food that was around, because you never knew where the next meal was coming from – she had abandoned herself to the luxury of the feather-soft bed, and had fallen into a deep and dreamless sleep. She slept as she had always done, with a knife under her pillow and her sword to hand, but nothing happened to disturb her, and she had finally awakened just as it was getting dark.

After she had lit the lamps, had a quick wash in her basin of cold water and built up the fire, Toulac began to feel that it was time for something else to happen. Whatever had become of Veldan? She had expected her younger friend to come back for her ages ago. By the thunderous expression on that horse-man's face, the veteran had known that her new companions were in all sorts of trouble, but Veldan had seemed confident that any difficulties would be sorted out in no time. It looked, however, as though she'd been mistaken.

Toulac decided to nip downstairs and find Ailie. Inns were always first with all the local gossip. Surely *she* would have some notion of what was going on. It was only then that the warrior discovered the guard outside her door.

Luckily, the habit of a lifetime had prompted her to open the door cautiously and quietly, and peep out through the narrow gap before going out onto the landing. Even more luckily, the burly man with the sword had his back to her at the time. Toulac closed the door with the same careful stealth she had used to open it, muttered a lurid curse under her breath, and sat down on the edge of her bed to think.

Plainly Veldan, Kazairl and Elion were in a lot of trouble. Obviously, any unpleasantness was going to extend to the two outsiders they had brought with them. So what should she do? It wasn't clear, as yet, whether Toulac and Zavahl should stay put, or escape – but one thing was for sure. If it turned out that escape *was* the best option, they had better be ready. Then something else occurred to her.

Hold on! Do I really want to saddle myself with Zavahl at this point? He doesn't like me, and he trusts me even less. If we stay put, he'll be a pain in the backside, and if we escape together, he'll be nothing but a liability.

Toulac sighed. Unfortunately she had a conscience, and it was reminding her that she and Veldan had been the ones who'd got Zavahl into this mess in the first place: notwithstanding the fact that, in doing so, they had extricated him from an even worse one. He had found it far more difficult than she had, to adjust to the idea strange of lands and alien races outside the Curtain Walls. The beliefs in which he'd been steeped had directly contradicted such things, and no-one could really expect him to throw away the central tenets of his life in a couple of days without there being some sort of denial. In a way, she felt responsible for him. She and the others had brought him here against his will, and if Veldan, Elion and Kaz were out of the picture now, that only left her.

All right, Zavahl. But you'd better not mess me around.

Toulac made her preparations swiftly. Thankfully, Ailie had found her some sensible clothes: trousers, slightly big and baggy, but all right when held up by a belt, in the sturdy weave favoured by the working folk; a thick cotton shirt and a woollen jerkin. Now . . . If the guard found her wandering round with a sword, he would certainly try to take it off her, and she was hoping to avoid any bloodshed if possible. She dipped into the capacious pockets of her old sheepskin coat and rummaged through a miscellaneous collection of useful little items, until she found a couple of lengths of thick twine. With these, she strapped her sword in its scabbard firmly to her back, so that it lay, most uncomfortably, down the length of her spine, with the hilt nestling between her shoulderblades. When she put the long, thick, fleece-lined coat over the top, there was no sign that the weapon was there, apart from a certain awkwardness and stiffness in her movements that she could probably blame on old age.

There was a crust of bread and a chunk of cheese left over from Ailie's generous meal: Toulac wrapped them in a linen napkin and thrust them into one of her pockets, adding, as an afterthought, a couple of spare candles from the box on the mantelpiece. *Right. Here we go.*

This time there was no attempt at subterfuge. Toulac strolled out of the door as if she hadn't a care in the world. Instead of turning in the direction of Zavahl's room, however, she headed the opposite way, towards the stairs.

'Here, Granny! Where do you think you're going?'

Toulac arranged her features into what she hoped was an expression of doddering vacuity, and turned to face the guard before he had a chance to put a hand on her shoulder and feel the hidden sword.

'Evenin' sonny,' she said brightly. 'And a lovely night it is to be taking a walk. I'm just off for a little stroll.' Again, she gave him that vacant smile, adopting the frank and guileless stare that had made her the most feared card player from one end of Callisiora to the other. 'That's all right, isn't it?' she added.

For a moment, she thought she was going to get away with it. The guard actually seemed to be wavering.

Myrial in a handcart! He's never going to let me, is he?

That would be a better outcome than she had dared to imagine.

If she could only get out of here, she could go and find Veldan. That would be the best plan, even if it did mean leaving Zavahl here for the time being.

But no, the guard was shaking his head. 'Sorry, Granny. I've orders from the Archimandrite himself, to make sure that you and your friend stay put.'

Toulac's eyes widened. 'Is that right? Fancy your Archa, Archi . . . whatever you said . . . being interested in a little old woman like me. Still, I expect it's Zavahl he really wants you to guard.' Taking hold of the guard's arm, she drew him close and spoke in low, confiding tones. 'He's the Hierarch of Callisiora, you know.'

'Is he?' Obviously, this was news to the guard. From the way his eyes lit up, Toulac suspected that he enjoyed a good gossip. 'Oh, yes,' she said. 'Very important man, the Hierarch. It'll be him you're guarding, depend on it.'

'I'm sorry, but I still can't let you go wandering off,' said the guard. 'I have my orders.'

'That's all right, sonny. I was getting a bit bored, that's all. You don't mind if I just slip in and have a little talk with young Zavahl, do you? After all, if we're both in the same room, we should be just as easy to guard, if not easier. And some company would be very welcome for a while. Unless *you* might like to spend some time chatting with me? I could tell you all about the old days, when I was a girl.'

'No, I'm sure that will be fine,' the guard said hastily. 'You go right on in, Granny. No problem at all. You stay as long as you like.'

Toulac had her back to him as she went to the Hierarch's door, so he did not see her vacant smile turn into an evil grin.

Granny, indeed!

Aethon was deep in conversation with Zavahl. The Dragon knew that he was still finding it difficult to believe that his own view of the world could have been so wrong, but the longer they conversed, the more the former Hierarch was persuaded that he had been living blind for so many years. 'So let me get this straight,' he said. 'You're telling me that when Myrial wanted a home for his children, he created a race of beings in whom he invested his power and his knowledge. Is that right?'

Aethon considered for a moment. If Zavahl wanted to see the facts in the context of his beliefs, he supposed he could live with that. 'It's just as reasonable an interpretation as some others I've heard,' he conceded. 'Now, we don't know what this race of Creators looked like, or the extent of their powers, but it was they who fashioned this world.'

'According to Myrial's instructions, no doubt,' Zavahl put in.

'I dare say,' Aethon agreed. Well, so what if his host needed to hold on to the idea of this deity? When it came to explanations, it might even might make matters a little easier. 'Though the world was to be a home for many races,' he went on, warming to his story, 'Myrial wished to keep them apart from one another, and so he divided the lands between them according to his wisdom, and created the Curtain Walls to keep them apart. His children were brought here, each to their rightful place, and left to thrive and prosper.

'But Myrial did not leave his people entirely. Into the very stone that makes up the heart of the world, he infused part of his mind and spirit. And he left a portal, hidden underground, through which he could be reached. Now listen well, Zavahl. That portal, I believe, was located beneath the Temple in Callisiora. To one special person, out of all the beings in the world, Myrial gave a gift, so that his children could come to him in times of need, and receive his wisdom. He took a stone, a red gem that was part of the stone at the heart's core of the world. Whoever holds that stone possesses part of Myrial's spirit, and that is the key to saving this world. I believe that stone is the very same one that's in the Hierarch's ring.'

'*What?*' gasped Zavahl. 'You mean I had the answer all the time, and I didn't know?'

'How could you have known? You only knew it made the Eye come to life, but you never knew why. I believe that the stone is part of whatever system keeps this world in balance and, most importantly, keeps the Curtain Walls in place. If we can only find out how to use it, I think we may be able to fix whatever has gone awry in the heart of our world. The question is, how are we going to get the ring back from Gilarra? She has no idea of what she's holding, no more than any Hierarch has ever done.'

Zavahl hesitated. 'You think I should go back?' Clear in his mind was the memory of the sacrificial pyre.

Aethon understood his fear. 'Not yet,' he said, 'and not alone. It'll take more than just you to sort out this problem, Zavahl. Whether it tallies with Cergorn's ideas of secrecy or not, we'll have to put a team together from the best minds in the Shadowleague . . .'

He was brought up short by the sound of the door opening. Immediately, the Dragon withdrew into the back of Zavahl's mind. It was up to the human to deal with any unexpected visitors.

Toulac barely recognised Zavahl. Gone was the ornate mantle of the all-powerful Hierarch; gone was the sacrificial victim's robe of white. He looked like a different person entirely, clad in the practical, everyday clothing of an ordinary man. Ailie had found him similar garments to those that Toulac wore: dark, sturdy pants, a thick cotton shirt and a heavy woollen overtunic. She had even managed to produce a belt for him, and boots. Looking at him, the veteran suspected that the transformation went far deeper than a simple change of clothing. Gone was the bitter, closed expression, and the indefinable air of loneliness which had always surrounded the former Hierarch. He seemed more relaxed now; more confident and certain. Gone was the bitter, fearful, driven man that she remembered.

Myrial in a wash-tub! What happened to him? And whatever it was, can I have some?

Then she thought about Ailie's obvious interest in the man, and her jaw dropped.

Well, may I be dipped in dog's dung! Don't tell me she actually succeeded? Whoever would have thought it?

When he heard the door, Zavahl started as though she had awakened him, and leapt up from his chair by the fireside. 'What are you doing here? Is there any news?'

Toulac shrugged. 'News from where? Apart from that guard out there, I haven't seen a living soul since Ailie brought my midday meal.'

He sighed. 'I wish she would hurry up and come back.'

'Who?'

'Ailie.' Suddenly, Zavahl was finding it hard to meet Toulac's eyes. 'She went off to look for Veldan.'

A weight lifted from Toulac's shoulders. 'Thank goodness for that. It's comfortable here, but I'd feel a damn sight safer if we could be with the others.'

'You're not the only one. Come and sit by the fire,' Zavahl ushered her further into the room.

'Thanks.' She shrugged out of the sheepskin coat, and his eyes widened at the sight of the sword tied to her back. 'Make yourself useful, will you?' she asked him in a low voice. 'I had to smuggle it past ape-face out there, but I don't like having my weapons where I can't get at them. We'll need it if we want to escape, and that's what I came to talk to you about. Of course,' she continued, as she buckled on the sword in its proper position, 'I didn't know about Ailie then. If she has gone to find Veldan, we're probably better off waiting here for her to come back.'

Zavahl nodded. 'You're right. But I'm glad you came, anyway. In our current position, two are definitely better than one, and at least we don't have to sit around and wait alone.'

Toulac stared at him. If he had sprouted wings and flown away out of the window, she couldn't have been more surprised. 'Who are you, and what have you done with the real Zavahl?'

He glowered at her. 'If it comes to that, *you're* a damn sight more friendly than I remember.'

'I suppose I am, at that,' the veteran conceded. 'It just goes to show you how greatly our circumstances have altered.'

'Mine certainly have,' Zavahl agreed wryly. 'Your friend told you about the Dragon, didn't she? Well, he and I have been having a long conversation. It seems that just about nothing in the world is as I believed it to be.'

They were interrupted by a heavy thud from outside the room. 'What in perdition . . . ?' Toulac muttered, her hand going instantly to the hilt of her sword. She was halfway to the door when it opened. In came one of the large, otter-like creatures she had seen that morning.

A strangled exclamation came from Zavahl. 'What in Myrial's name is *that?*'

Toulac remembered some of the bizarre-looking denizens of Gendival that she had seen on her arrival. She thanked providence that their strange visitor was one of the cute ones, and not a centaur, or the hideous centipede monster that she was sure would haunt her nightmares. 'There are all sorts of weird and wonderful-looking folk living around here,' she explained to Zavahl. 'Elion warned you, remember? That was why you were wearing the blindfold when you came. At that point, you didn't seem to be ready for too many shocks all at once.' She grinned at him. 'I reckon you are now, though. At least, I certainly hope so.'

The visitor sat up on its hind legs, reaching to about Toulac's waist, and gazed at the two humans with an uncannily intelligent expression. 'We must hurry.' She heard the voice quite clearly in her mind. 'I've come to get you out of here, and there's no time to lose.'

Silently Toulac cursed the fact that she was unable to broadcast in mindspeech. 'Who sent you?' she asked it aloud, hoping it would understand.

'My name is Dessil. I've been sent to take you to Veldan and the others. You'll be much safer with them than you are here.'

'It'll be a relief to get back to our companions, that's for sure,' the veteran said. 'But why hasn't Veldan spoken to me directly? You know that I can understand mindspeech. I just can't send it. I've been waiting all afternoon for some kind of word from her. Is she all right?'

'She is. But she dared not contact you herself. Already, Cergorn is very unhappy about you being here. If he had intercepted any messages between you, it could only lead to more trouble. That's why I came. To guide you and to bring you word.'

Turning to Zavahl, she translated Dessil's message.

'You can understand that creature?' His voice rose on a note of incredulity. 'How?'

'I hear it in my mind,' she told him. 'I can hear the firedrake just the same.'

Zavahl was frowning. Toulac thought he didn't believe her, so his next words took her by surprise. 'But I can hear the Dragon. So why can't I hear this otter-thing?'

Of course. He had mentioned the Dragon earlier, just before they had been interrupted by Dessil's arrival. Toulac shrugged. 'I think we'd better sort that one out later. He says there's no time to waste.'

She turned back to Dessil. 'What happened to the guard?'

'He met with an accident.' He made a whistling sound through his teeth, and there was a bright edge of humour in his mental voice. 'I reached up through the bannisters and rolled a handful of pearls towards him. They mean nothing to my people – we find them by the hundreds – but you humans seem to value them. When he bent down to gather them up, I sneaked up from behind, and hit him over the head.'

Toulac chuckled. 'Then let's get going,' she said, 'While we have the chance.'

'Wait a minute.' Zavahl was frowning. 'How do we know that we can trust our friend here? What if he's lying?'

He never got an answer. Without warning, the window shattered in an eruption of flying glass. A creature beyond the lurid imaginings of Toulac's worst nightmares burst into the room. It looked like a gigantic insect, so large that it just fitted into the window frame; its shining body as long as a man is tall. In that first, frozen instant of horror, Toulac's mind flashed back in memory to when she had been a little girl. She had been throwing stones for her dog, and had hit a hornet's nest . . .

Though the invader was iridescent, glistening black instead of striped, it had the same predatory outline, from its wicked, triangular head with the waving antennae, to the bulbous, teardrop-shaped abdomen ending in a cruel sting. Its legs were barbed to grasp and hold, its huge, compound eyes glittered evilly, and the great, curved mandibles with their sharp, serrated edges twitched and clicked, as if in anticipation of feasting on vulnerable human flesh. And over everything was its snarling, high-pitched buzz: a menacing sound that turned the blood to ice.

Even as Toulac took in these details, she was starting to move. But before her sword could clear her scabbard, the door behind her exploded inward, and three more of the creatures poured into the room, moving with deadly speed and trampling Dessil as they came. Even as she whirled to face the new threat, barbed forelegs closed around her, pinning her arms to her sides. Zavahl, his face grey with shock, was writhing in the grasp of another gigantic insect, while a third was standing over the prostrate form of Dessil. The bulbous abdomen curled down. The sting lanced out and penetrated his prostrate body once. Toulac cursed helplessly as Dessil's lithe, furry body convulsed, then went limp.

The last of the creatures was enlarging the window, knocking a way out through the wall beneath. Toulac was appalled at such strength. Her own captor's forelegs enclosed her like iron bands, so tightly that she was struggling to breathe. The buzzing rose to a crescendo as the attackers unfurled their translucent wings. One by one they took to the air, and flew out of the enlarged window opening. Toulac made one last, despairing effort to struggle free, but to no avail. She felt herself being lifted from the ground, then there was cool air against her face, and she was swallowed by the night.

There was a growing air of uneasiness among the conspirators in the Moldan's cavern. Everyone was worried, and the waiting was made all the more difficult by the discomfort of their surroundings. They had no light but the cold and eerie radiance of the glims. The

Moldan wouldn't let his visitors light a fire. He had no need for heat or light himself, and he didn't want his tunnels filling up with smoke. Veldan huddled close to the firedrake's warm flank and shivered in the chill, damp atmosphere. What could have become of Dessil and the humans he had gone to fetch? How much longer could she and her companions stay in this miserable place and do nothing?

Vaure's mind had obviously been working along similar lines. After a time she rustled her wings impatiently. 'I've had enough of this. I'll be careful, Maskulu, and I'll do my best to stay out of sight, but I'm going to find out what has happened. We've wasted enough time already.'

The Moldan raised its formidable head. 'There is no need.'

'I say there is, and—'

'There is no need,' Maskulu repeated. 'Someone has entered my dwelling, and I can feel footfalls heading this way.'

A moment later, Ailie stumbled into the chamber. She looked like a wild woman, with her blonde hair tangled like a nest of snakes, and her tearstained cheeks flushed from running. There was mud on her shoes and a jagged tear in the front of her skirt, and she had fallen over more than once, judging from her abraded palms and the dirt smeared on her clothing.

'What's wrong?'

'What happened?'

The Loremasters clustered round her, the Moldan, with his massive body, almost knocking her over in his anxiety for news. Veldan and Elion half-dragged, half-supported her into a corner, and made her sit down and catch her breath. After a few moments she had regained sufficient breath to speak. 'They're gone,' she gasped. 'Zavahl and Toulac. Dierkan took them.'

Pandemonium broke out, with everyone talking at once, using their normal voices – most alarming when it came to the hisses and clicks of the Moldan, the shrieks of the phoenix and the bellows of the firedrake – and mindspeech, which was no good to Ailie whatsoever.

'QUIET!' Elion shouted, both aloud and in his mind. 'Give the poor woman a chance.'

When the uproar had subsided, Veldan sat down beside Ailie and put an arm around her shoulders. 'Now,' she said. 'Tell me what happened. You said it was Dierkan?'

Ailie nodded. 'You know how they're bred to be specialised to the needs of their Alvai masters? Well these were warriors, the winged sort. You know, those evil-looking bastards with the stings. I had just got back – I hadn't even had time to take my cloak off. I heard a horrible buzzing noise, and five of them came swarming in. It's an inn after all, so the door was open. There was nothing to stop them. I was in the passage and they knocked me over . . .' A shudder ran through her. 'Oh, Veldan, I was sure I was going to be stung. But they just ignored me. One scuttled right over the top of me.'

She took deep breaths, struggling to pull herself together. 'Two of them went and guarded the doors to the taproom and the common room, so that no-one could get out. The other three went straight upstairs. There was a lot of buzzing and banging, then an awful yell. Then it all went quiet again. The two Dierkan that were downstairs went out the way they had come, and flew away. Dad came running out, and the customers. When we all got upstairs, there was no sign that Toulac's room had been disturbed, but I'm sure she must have been with Zavahl, because we found her coat in his chamber. Not to mention a great hole where the window had been. Dessil was unconscious on the floor, and Zavahl and Toulac were gone.'

'Dessil!' Vaure exclaimed. 'Where is he? Is he all right?'

Bailen passed on her mindspeech to Ailie in spoken words, and the innkeeper shook her head. 'I'm sorry, but I don't know. The Healers are with him now. He was still alive when I left, but he wasn't looking too good.'

'The Dierkan venom is designed to paralyse, not kill,' Elion said, 'but that's if they only sting once. Dessil is quite small, and that won't help.'

'I'll go to him at once.' Without waiting for a reply, Vaure went streaking out of the cavern.

The Moldan reared up in agitation, lifting half its elongated body off the ground. 'Dierkan!' he hissed. 'So the Alvai are responsible for this. What is Skreeva up to?'

'You mean you don't know?' Kaz asked in surprise. 'She isn't one of your lot?'

'She most certainly is not. The Alvai have always kept their own counsel.'

'Never mind whether she is or she isn't,' said Veldan. 'Somebody will have to tackle her. We've got to get Toulac and Zavahl back, and right now, we don't even know which way they've gone.'

'Do not worry,' the Moldan told her grimly. 'I will have an explanation from Skreeva, or I will crush her head like an egg between my jaws.'

'That'll really help,' snorted Kaz. 'Just how will she be able to tell us anything with her head crushed? And how do you plan to do it without coming to Cergorn's attention? Right now, because she used Dierkan, Skreeva will be under suspicion, but you won't. If you really want to pull this rebellion off, you need to be free to act, for the time being at least.'

'Which is exactly what we won't be,' said Veldan bitterly. 'Since Toulac and Zavahl have been taken, the first thing they'll do is check on us. Once Cergorn discovers we're missing, he'll either think we've been abducted too, or suspect us of being in league with Skreeva. They've probably started searching for us already. If we weren't fugitives before, we certainly are now.' She rubbed a weary hand across her face. 'Why in the name of providence didn't we just stay put? Now our movements will be more limited than ever. And how are we going to find Toulac and Zavahl? What are we going to do?'

'We're going to get them back,' said a calm decisive voice. 'That's what we're going to do.'

From the shadows of the cavern entrance, a lone figure walked forward. All the breath went out of Veldan in a gasp as she recognised Lord Blade.

Twenty-four

Promises

Oh, for a hot bath, an enormous breakfast, and a long, long sleep.

Since Gilarra knew that her chances of getting any of those things were nonexistent, she told herself firmly to stop thinking about them.

Just be grateful that you've got your people safely through another night.

A shudder ran through the Hierarch. How close they had come to disaster! Had it not been for Galveron's blasting powder, they might all be dead now, and those winged abominations rampaging unchecked through Myrial's Temple.

Not that Myrial's sacred Temple would ever be the same again. Sadly, Gilarra looked at the pile of rubble and shattered stonework that choked the staircase, cutting off the upper storeys. The ornate, luxurious chambers belonging to the Hierarch were gone, before she'd even had a chance to move into them.

Try telling that to the families of the dead and wounded, and see how much sympathy you get.

In order for the Miners to place the powder and fuses in the right position, the Godswords had been forced to mount an all-out attack, to drive the winged invaders back from the stairwell for a few vital moments. Three men were dead, and five more seriously injured. Kaita and her helpers were stretched to the limit.

But at least it's over now, and for the time being, we're safe. Myrial be thanked for getting the blasting powder to us in time.

But Myrial had needed some help. Gilarra's brows knotted together in a frown as she remembered the strange waif of a girl, with her verminous, disgusting cloak. Who was she? Where had she come from? Why had Galveron relied on her, instead of sending one of his men, or coming himself? Though she was desperate for sleep, and longing for her family, the Hierarch resolved to have some answers.

Grey daylight had begun to glimmer through the high, narrow windows of the Basilica, and throughout the building, people were relaxing after the dangers of the dark hours. Most of them had been wakeful and scared all night, guarding their pathetic, makeshift little territories – marked out with odds and ends, blankets and bits of clothing – with whatever crude weapons came to hand. Now, the exhausted refugees of Tiarond were settling down to sleep, relieved that they had lived to see another day.

Gilarra picked her way between the crowded little camps, and headed for the guardroom, where Healer Kaita had her domain. As she reached the door she saw, to her dismay, that a new makeshift territory had been set up just outside. Her surprise turned to anger when she recognised her own family, with a tired-looking Bevron sitting with his back against the wall, watching over little Aukil, who was curled up asleep in a nest of blankets. 'What happened here?' she demanded. 'Why isn't my son in his bed?'

Bevron, who had clearly been in a dream, started and jumped to his feet at the sound of her voice. 'There was no more room in there. Aukil will be all right, love. I've made him as cosy as I could . . .' He was talking to empty air.

Gilarra went storming into the guardroom, where Kaita and her helpers were hard pressed to tend to those Godswords who had been injured in the defence of the stairwell. 'Where is the Healer?' she demanded.

Kaita, who had been stooping over the bed in the far corner, straightened up and came out of the shadows. She had the guarded look of one expecting trouble, but her voice was low and pleasant as she spoke. 'Lady Hierarch. What can I do for you?'

'You know perfectly well,' Gilarra stormed. 'Will you explain to me why you saw fit to turn an injured child out of his bed?'

Kaita's chin came up. There was a dangerous glint in her eye. 'There are plenty of injured children out there, Lady Hierarch, who've been forced to sleep on the floor since we came here.'

'That's no concern of mine!'

'Really?' said the Healer softly. 'Strange, I could have sworn it was.'

'Damn you, Kaita, don't twist my words,' Gilarra snapped. 'You know perfectly well what I mean. If there were beds for those children, I would move mountains to see that they got them.'

'And if I had a bed for your son, the same thing would apply,' Kaita told her. 'But you can see for yourself, there's just no more room. We need all the beds we have for the Godswords wounded from last night. Aukil is recovering now, Lady Hierarch. He doesn't need a bed as much as these poor men who, I might remind you, were injured because they were protecting us.'

For a moment, Gilarra was nonplussed. There was no answer to that, and she knew it. Then her eye lit on the quiet corner bed, and the sleeping form of the strange girl who had come the previous night. 'What about her?' she demanded. 'As far as I know, she wasn't wounded at all. Why should *she* have a bed?'

'She was deeply and dangerously chilled, she had a touch of frostbite and was utterly exhausted,' Kaita said stiffly. 'And considering what we owe her, I certainly wouldn't begrudge the poor thing a bed for the night.'

Gilarra was so angry that she didn't notice the warning edge in Kaita's voice. Again, she rallied. 'I disagree. A ragamuffin like that has probably slept on the floor her entire life. A few blankets near the fire would have served her. My son was badly hurt the other night, and he still hasn't recovered. He needs a bed. And why did you send him outside into the cold? If you were determined upon this insanity, at least you could have let him stay in here, in the warmth.'

Kaita's eyes flashed. 'First of all, it doesn't matter a damn to me whether that girl has had a bed before. She's getting one now, because in my opinion, she needs one and she deserves one. Secondly, we're just too busy in here to have people camping out all over the floor. Frankly, your family would be in our way. Thirdly, there were things taking place in here last night, with those wounded men, that no child should ever be allowed to see. I got Aukil out for his own good, and his father agreed with that.' She took a deep breath, and moved a step closer. 'And there's one thing more, Lady Hierarch. Out there, you rule. In here, *my* word is law. And the sooner you accept that, the better it will be for everyone concerned.'

Galveron walked in on the tableau. Hierarch and Healer were squared off against each other like a pair of duellists, and glaring so savagely that he could almost feel the air scorching between them. He sighed. Now what? As soon as daylight had cleared the last of the fiends from the courtyard, he had brought his ill-assorted group of thieves and Godswords across as fast as he could. The Smithmaster, delighted to see him in one piece, had opened the door to him, and he had very gladly received the news that Aliana had arrived safely the previous night. Having asked Agella to take care of Alestan and his people, he'd set off to find Gilarra.

But I certainly didn't anticipate a scene like this!

At any moment, one or both of the women would let their anger get the better of them, and things would be said which could never be forgotten or forgiven. Close confinement, the constant threat of danger, and the crowded conditions within the Basilica, were winding up the tensions like a crossbow string. While simply crossing from the main door of the Temple to this rear guardroom, he had witnessed two fist-fights and a handful of vicious quarrels, mostly over living space. The tedium of incarceration, coupled with the lack of privacy, was taking its toll on everyone. Nevertheless, there could be no excuse for the leaders to be fighting among themselves. It was their duty to set an example to the other refugees.

Absent-mindedly, he rubbed at the healing wounds on his face, which were itching beneath their grimy bandages. It was up to him to put a stop to this nonsense, before it got out of hand.

'Lady Hierarch,' he said loudly. 'Healer Kaita. You can't imagine how good it is to see you again.'

'Galveron!' Both women spoke together. Both turned towards him, their faces transfigured with relief, their quarrel forgotten.

No, not forgotten. Just shelved for now. But it's better than them having a stand-up fight where everyone can hear them.

Remembering the dignity of their rank, neither woman ran to him. Kaita, he noticed, was the first to get her detached, professional mask back into place, with Gilarra following an instant later. Judging from the dark hollows under their eyes, the lines of strain around their mouths, and the weary droop to their shoulders, both women had put in a tough night.

'Come over to the fire and get warm,' Kaita said. 'We've been using some of our precious tea ration to keep ourselves going all night.' She grinned. 'It should be like boiling pitch by now.'

'Just the way soldiers like it. Thank you, Kaita, you've saved my life.' Galveron accepted the cup from her with gratitude, using it as a hand-warmer while the contents cooled enough to drink. 'You got the blasting powder all right, I see,' he said to Gilarra. 'How well did it work?'

'It did what we wanted,' the Hierarch said. 'We lost three of your men though, Galveron. I'm so sorry. They were assaulting the staircase, forcing the fiends back far enough for the miners to get up there and position the powder and the fuses.'

'Five more were seriously injured,' Kaita put in. 'We should pull four of them through all right. As for the other . . .' She shook her head. 'But we'll do our best.'

Galveron sighed. 'I lost one too. Poor lads. May Myrial keep them. Do you know who was hurt?'

Kaita nodded, rummaged in her pocket, and brought out a list of names.

'I got the names of the dead men, too, from Quartermaster Flint,'

Gilarra added. 'He's finding out if any of them have surviving families.'

'If there are, maybe the two of us can have a talk with them later, and see if there's anything they need,' Galveron said. 'In the meantime, I'll go and have a word with the wounded.' He paused, and looked at Kaita. 'If I may?'

'It's fine by me,' the Healer said. 'You've got more sense than to disturb them if they're sleeping.'

'Of course not. And what about Aliana? Where is she? Will she be all right?'

Kaita smiled. 'She's a tough little thing, that one. Do you know, she found the plaza full of those abominations, and so she actually *crawled* here on her belly, in the snow, through all those corpses. And she killed one of the fiends with just a little knife. She was badly chilled and exhausted, with a touch of mild frostbite, but nothing to worry about. She'll soon bounce back.' Her expression grew pensive. 'Though I get the feeling that she's going to have some bad nightmares for quite some time to come.'

Unwisely, Galveron grimaced, and felt the stitches on his face pulling tight once more. 'She doesn't lack for courage, that's for sure, but I wish it hadn't been necessary for me to send her. Poor little thing! What an ordeal to put her through.' He turned to Gilarra. 'Oh, by the way, I have some of her friends with me. Her twin brother, two children, a woman, and a – well, you'll see. We came across them at the Citadel.'

The Hierarch frowned. 'Did you indeed? Galveron, I would like a word with you concerning this girl and her friends. In private. But first, let me meet these strays.'

As she turned away to lead him out of the room, Galveron grimaced in dismay. Kaita caught his eye, and grinned.

The Smithmaster had found a place for the newcomers, near her own unpopular corner that was, as far as most folk were concerned, just too close to the great doors. Though Agella was trying to put them at their ease, they were huddled together, plainly nervous of their new surroundings and the situation in which they found themselves. Gilarra got the strong impression that they were unsure of their welcome.

And they may be right, at that. There's something about this lot, and the circumstances in which Galveron found them, that makes me very suspicious.

What made her more suspicious was that the whole lot of them were wearing cast-off Godsword uniforms, to comical effect in certain cases. So what had happened to their own clothes? As Galveron had said, there were two gap-toothed urchins who could badly use a wash, a wild haired woman with bold eyes and an exotic beauty to her face, and a young man who was clearly Aliana's twin. Though his hair was blond instead of tawny, their elfin features and compact bodies were unmistakable. He had his arm in a rough sling.

'As you see,' Galveron said, 'Alestan needs the attentions of Healer Kaita. He dived head first through a trapdoor and fell down some steps last night, while he was being chased by one of the abominations. He was acting as decoy, attracting their attention while his sister got away. When all the excitement died down, he found that his arm hurt like perdition, and he could barely move it. I think it must be broken.'

'I'm sure the Healer will help.' Kaita was the last person the Hierarch wanted to talk about just then. As a distraction, she looked at the last member of the odd little group – and froze in horror. Gilarra shuddered at the filthy, unkempt – and if he wasn't infested, she would boil up her Hierarch's robes and eat the lot – specimen that met her eyes. His hair was lank and greasy, and flopped across his eyes, he was sporting several days' worth of stubble, and though he wore the same dark tunic and pants as the others, he somehow managed to make his clothes look ragged and scruffy. Her words of welcome died on her lips.

Galveron stepped into the breach. 'Let me make some proper introductions. Of course you folk already know that this is Lady Gilarra, the Hierarch of Callisiora. My Lady, the two young scamps—' – the two young scamps exchanged a look of pure disgust at this, and raised their eyes to the heavens – 'are Tag and Erla. This is Gelina, and this is Alestan, Aliana's twin brother. And this is Packrat.' He looked pleadingly at Gilarra. 'His cleverness saved all our lives yesterday.'

'Really,' said Gilarra coldly. Again, she gazed in disbelief at the disreputable figure, who gave her a nervous grin with a mouth full of black and rotting teeth. 'You must tell me all about it some time.'

In the background, she saw the Smithmaster put a hand up to her mouth to hide a smile, which didn't improve her mood at all.

Though the young man Alestan was grey-faced with pain, he stepped forward, and gave her a decent approximation of a bow. 'My Lady, I can't tell you how grateful we are to have finally found sanctuary here with our fellow townsfolk.' Somehow, Gilarra just couldn't seem to tear her horrified gaze away from Packrat. With an effort, she pulled herself together.

'I hope you'll be comfortable here – at least, as comfortable as any of us are in these conditions.'

Alestan hesitated. 'Lady? Is my sister all right? Where is she?'

Galveron cut in swiftly. 'Don't worry. The Healer says she'll be fine. She's just very chilled and exhausted, and she's sleeping it off.' He gave the thieves a reassuring smile. 'According to Healer Kaita, Aliana is a bit of a hero. Not only did she get the powder here safely, but apparently she killed one of those winged fiends with just her knife. You'd better not all go trooping in to see her, or Kaita will have my hide, but if you want to go, Alestan, I'm sure that would be all right. You can have your arm tended at the same time. In the meantime, the others can be settling in, then you can come back and tell them how she's doing.'

'Indeed.' Gilarra seized the chance to escape. 'We will show you they way. Then, Galveron, you and I will have that little talk.'

There was nothing to be done but comply with her, but Galveron wasn't looking forward to this conversation one little bit. He was torn between his loyalty to Gilarra and his promise to Aliana. He knew that the Hierarch should be told about the dubious background of the thieves, but how could he betray them now, after giving his word that he would protect them? Especially after Aliana had shown such courage in keeping her side of the bargain. As they walked back to the guardroom, he found it impossible to look Alestan in the eye.

Kaita welcomed Aliana's brother, pronounced his arm broken and, giving in to his pleas to let him see his sister before she set it, led him off to the bed in the corner. Unhooking a lamp from its bracket on the wall, Gilarra ushered Galveron through the back door of the guardroom, following the escape route of the creature who had snatched Zavahl away. When they reached the deserted tunnel leading to the upper caves where the food was stored, the Hierarch halted him with a hand on his arm, and balanced her lamp on a rough ledge about three feet from the ground, where the wall of the cave shelved down.

'Now,' she said. 'I want to know what's going on. Just who are these strays you've picked up? Why are they wearing Godsword uniforms? Where were they when the abominations interrupted the Sacrifice? Not with everybody else, it seems. And why did you send that girl here last night, in preference to one of your own men?'

Galveron racked his brains for an answer that would satisfy, marginally, at least, his obligation to both women. 'Aliana had experience of dodging the fiends,' he said at last. 'She had been surviving out on the streets since we were first attacked. She's small, fast and agile, and she convinced me that she would have a better prospect of sneaking past them unseen than one of my men.'

'What? A slip of a girl like that?'

Galveron kept his face impassive. 'It was vital that I get the blasting powder to you, so I chose the one with the greatest chance of getting through. Besides, she volunteered.'

Gilarra's eyebrows went up. 'So in other words, she convinced you that she'd be good at sneaking around in the dark. And have you any idea how she acquired that particular skill?'

Damn.

Galveron shrugged. 'Not everyone has led your privileged life, Lady Hierarch. Impoverished folk are at the whim of those more powerful than they are – and when you come right down to it, that's practically everybody. It often pays the poor people of this city to be inconspicuous.'

Gilarra looked at him through narrowed eyes. 'It certainly does when they are thieves. You said that the girl and her companions survived the abominations *out on the streets*. That's enough to tell me that they did not attend the sacrifice. Why not? Could it be that they planned to make the most of everyone's absence, so that they could break into houses undisturbed? Why were they so ill-clad that you had to clothe them in the uniforms of our soldiers? None of our refugees were in quite such desperate straits. Even the poor folk had put on what few good things they had, to attend the ceremony. Why is your little friend so good at creeping around at night without being seen? It's a necessary skill in her trade, I expect.'

Gilarra's eyes were blazing, and her face was hard with anger. 'Galveron, you are a hopeless liar. You're too fundamentally honest to succeed at this duplicity. Now, I will have the truth from you. Are those new people genuine refugees? Or have you brought me thieving scum from the Warrens?'

Now it was Galveron's turn to be angry. 'It doesn't matter where they came from, they are still genuine refugees, sharing the same risks as we do, and needing the same shelter and sustenance. And no matter how they have been forced to make a living in the past, my Lady Hierarch, *they are your subjects*. Or has Myrial started to discriminate between the rich and the poor?'

'Myrial discriminates between the honest and the dishonest,' she flung back at him.

'And since when has petty thievery carried a sentence of death?' snapped Galveron. 'Because if you deny them shelter now, you are killing them just as effectively as if you had me carry out their executions here and now.'

Gilarra stepped back, breathing heavily, her rage so great that Galveron steeled himself for a blow. Somehow, she managed to regain control of herself. 'Of all the people here, I never thought I would have cause to doubt your loyalty.'

That hurt. He wished that she had hit him instead. 'Because I tried to defend the weak and helpless, does that make me a traitor?' he demanded.

'Don't twist my words, Galveron. You know it does not. Though I would dispute the weak and helpless part. But if you didn't exactly lie to me, you deliberately concealed the truth. What does that make you?'

She had him there. Galveron sighed. 'Lady, I'm truly sorry. But Aliana and her friends are desperate to make a fresh start. They know how perilous their position is. They can no longer afford to live outside the rules. She begged me to let them start here with a clean slate, and volunteered to deliver the blasting powder if I would agree. I felt bad about concealing the truth from you, but it seemed a small thing to ask of me, in comparison to the tremendous risk she was taking. They all promised that there would be no more stealing, and I trust them all – except maybe Packrat – to stick to their word. I told them that if there was any trouble whatsoever, they would all be cast out immediately, with no appeal.'

Seeing a slight softening in Gilarra's expression, he reached out and took her hand. 'My Lady Hierarch, let them stay, I beg you. Don't make me break my word. I'll keep a very close eye on them, and I'll stand surety for their behaviour myself.'

For what seemed an age, Gilarra stood, lost in thought, then she nodded. 'Very well, Galveron. I will let them stay, and I will even keep their identity to myself, and give them their fresh start. But remember that I hold you responsible for their behaviour. If they are found guilty of any misconduct, I will expect you to carry out your threat, and eject them from the Temple at once.' She took a deep breath. 'As for you, Commander, I am very disappointed with the way you've handled this. You should never have given your word to anything that meant concealing the truth from me. Did you really trust me so little, that you thought I would refuse to honour an undertaking you'd given in good faith? I can understand why these folk should want to keep their background secret. Now that they have come here, they have to live with the rest of us, and be accepted. But I am Hierarch here, and as such I am responsible for the welfare of everyone in the Temple, not just a bunch of itinerant thieves. I should have been informed at once. By choosing to conceal matters of such importance, you may prevent me from discharging my responsibilities to the community as a whole. Do you understand?'

Galveron bowed his head. 'Yes, Lady Hierarch.' In his heart, he knew she was right, but the reprimand had stung his pride. 'May I be excused now?' he added coldly.

As he looked up, he was astonished to see the glimmer of tears in her eyes. 'Not you too,' she whispered, and started to sob.

This was the last thing Galveron had expected. For a moment he forgot that she was the Hierarch, and reacted just as he would with any other women in distress. Putting an arm around her shoulders, he led her to the protruding ledge of rock where she had left the lamp, and sat her down. 'You've been having a bad day, I see,' he said calmly.

As he had expected, that was enough to loosen her tongue. It all came flooding out: her worry over her son's injury, and her subsequent fight with Kaita over the business of the bed. 'To be honest,' she said, 'telling it to you now, I can see that I was thinking like a mother, not a Hierarch. But it's so hard to balance everything, Galveron! I used to think it would be much easier than this. I would see Zavahl making so many mistakes, and I would think *why can't he see?* I was always firmly convinced that I could do a much better job – but now that I'm wearing the Hierarch's robes myself, I've found out that it's not so easy after all.'

She shook her head. 'You know, I used to get so angry with poor Zavahl when he told me I had no business having a family; that my duty was to my role as Suffragan. Maybe he was right after all.'

'Maybe he was,' Galveron said, 'but if you could go back and live your life over again, would you change things? Would you really want a life without Bevron and Aukil?'

'Never!'

He smiled. 'Well then. There's no sense in fretting about whether or not you made the right decision years ago. Things are as they are, and you'll learn to cope, and we'll all help as much as we can . . .' He hesitated. 'At least, we will after you and Kaita have apologised to one another. You know very well that the leaders in this place can't afford that kind of squabble. It lowers morale and sets a bad example.'

'But she—' Catching the stern look on his face, Gilarra subsided. 'Oh, all right. But she's got to apologise to me, too. I might have been in the wrong, but Hierarch or no Hierarch, she had no right to talk to me like that.'

'I'll talk to her,' Galveron promised. 'And after you've both apologised, you can go and have something to eat, and march straight off to bed. And stay there for the next few hours. You've been acting as if you could go on forever – no wonder the two of you are so short-tempered. I'll arrange a couple of bunks for you up here in the far guardroom, at the end of this tunnel that comes out on the mountain. That should keep you out of mischief until you've had a chance to rest. And don't worry, Gilarra,' he added, concerned that he had failed to lift the frown from her face. 'Things will look better after a good sleep. As you just said, being Hierarch isn't as easy as it looks. You're doing as good a job as any of us could, given these difficult circumstances, and you'll do it better and better as time goes on.' He patted her hand. 'Once we've got ourselves out of this mess, you'll have plenty of time to practice.'

'Oh, Galveron, I don't think I will.' He was startled by the anguish on her face. 'There's something you don't know,' she whispered. 'I shouldn't really be telling you. It's a closely-guarded secret passed down from one Hierarch to the next. But there's no-one else I can trust to help me . . .'

Galveron's eyes grew wider and wider as she told him, in a low voice, of her lone pilgrimage beneath the Temple, and her failure to make the eye of Myrial function. 'And so you see,' she said at last, 'nothing will work without the ring. Without it I can't really be

Hierarch. No-one can. And it's not just myself I'm worried about. You talked before of loss of morale. Just think how it would affect the refugees if they knew that Myrial had truly abandoned them. We must get it back! We've just got to!'

'But Gilarra, how can we?' Galveron frowned. 'It was snatched up by one of the winged fiends when you dropped it in the attack. Why, it could be anywhere by now. Even if we didn't have the abominations to contend with, where would we start to look?'

Gilarra dropped her face into her hands. 'I don't know,' she whispered. 'But without it, everything I do is a lie.'

Kaita adjusted the bandages on the arm of a wounded Godsword and straightened up, rubbing her aching back. With a twinge of guilt, she remembered Alestan, Aliana's brother. He'd had long enough for his reunion with his sister. It was high time she saw to his arm. But when she looked into the quiet corner where Aliana lay, she discovered that the girl was still asleep, and Alestan was nowhere to be seen. 'Oh, for goodness' sake,' she muttered in exasperation. 'I could do without this.' He must have gone back to his friends, in the main part of the Temple. She was just turning away, when a movement in the shadows caught the corner of her eye. There was that wretch, sneaking – and even the most charitable of observers could have described it in no other way – *sneaking* out of the back tunnel where Galveron and Gilarra had gone to have what looked like being a very private conversation.

'And just where have *you* been?' she thundered, and had the satisfaction of seeing him jump like a startled deer.

He covered it up well, though. 'I was just looking for somewhere to relieve myself,' he explained with wide-eyed innocence.

'Oh, were you indeed? And why didn't you ask me where you had to go?'

He looked down at his feet. 'Didn't like to,' he mumbled. 'And you were so busy, I didn't want to bother you.'

'Look here,' said Kaita severely. 'That won't wash. It's perfectly obvious where you've been, and why. For Aliana's sake, I'll give you one chance, and turn a blind eye this time, but if I ever catch you creeping around again, trying to eavesdrop on people's private conversations, I'll go straight to Commander Galveron. Do you understand?'

He nodded – and disarmed her completely by giving her a guileless and delightful grin. 'I won't. I promise.'

Beware of this little charmer. He's more dangerous than a rattlesnake – and a damn sight more cunning.

'Make sure you don't,' she told him severely, annoyed by the near success of his attempt to manipulate her. As she turned away to get the splints and dressings for his arm, she heard him mutter something that sounded suspiciously like, 'I won't need to.'

Twenty-five

Amaurn

The girl with the face from the past. Now that he was finally confronting her, Amaurn had no idea what to say. Nor did her situation seem to be any easier. She was staring at him as if he were a ghost. Her companion, however, had no such difficulty. It was fortunate for Amaurn that firedrakes came from his own homeland, and he was familiar with their habits. He heard the deep intake of breath, and flung himself flat to the floor.

A long jet of flame, hot enough to sear the flesh from his bones, roared overhead to blast against the opposite wall. In the same instant the Moldan, in defence of his leader, hurtled towards the firedrake, diamond jaws agape. Time slowed to a crawl for Amaurn. The firedrake was gathering himself to leap, but he had no hope of getting out of the way in time. He might be quick on his feet, but the Moldan was bigger and faster. Its momentum alone was probably enough to kill. Veldan shouted, and started to run forward. Despite a lifetime that included betrayal, bereavement, exile and murder, the expression on the woman's face was the most agonising thing that Amaurn had ever seen.

'STOP!' He shouted, throwing every scrap of his will at the charging Moldan. Then time flicked back to its normal course, and somehow, he was on his feet again, and he found himself diving forward into Maskulu's path – only to collide with the woman. They went down hard, all in a tangle, just as the Moldan dug in his feet, ploughing great furrows in the stone of the cavern floor. Losing control of his rear end, he skidded sideways, and was almost slowing to a halt as he reached Amaurn and the woman, knocking them back to the floor just as they were beginning to rise. Shakily, they helped each other up. 'Are you all right?' he asked her. She must have been bruised and shaken, but she nodded anyway.

'Thank you,' she said softly, with a little nod of acknowledgement. 'You didn't have to jump in front of Kaz like that. I appreciate it.'

Before he could think of an answer, she ran to the trembling firedrake, who crouched beside the wall, still clearly shocked by its narrow escape. She hugged the great head to her, and Amaurn could sense that they were communing silently with one another. Then to his dismay, she scrambled up onto Kaz's back, and turned to Maskulu with a look of contempt. '*This* is your mysterious leader? Well, I suppose it serves me right for consorting with Cergorn's enemies. I don't believe I could have made such a mistake, and I don't want any further part in it. Especially not if *he* is involved.' She gestured at Amaurn. 'I'm sorry I came here now. Don't worry. I'm not going back to Cergorn. I'm finished with the lot of you. Kaz and I will find somewhere of our own.'

Just like your mother. And she never came back.

He reached out involuntarily, but let his arms drop as she vanished into the tunnel.

Don't think you can run away from me. I won't let you get far.

'You can't mean to let her go!' the Moldan protested. 'What if she betrays us?'

'If she did, it would be your fault,' Amaurn snarled. 'But she won't betray us. She told us that. Anyway, I'm going after her. She's upset and angry, but when the shock wears off, she'll soon calm down. Hey, you! Where do you think you're going?'

The other Loremaster, the dark, bearded man, was sidling towards the tunnel. 'I'm going with Veldan,' he declared. 'I was with her in Callisiora. I know who you are, and what you did to Zavahl, and poor Tormon's wife. I don't know what you're doing here, but I'm not about to get involved with murdering scum.'

Amaurn signalled to the Moldan to move across the doorway. 'You don't need to go with her. She's not going anywhere yet,' he said. 'It'll take her forever to find her way out of here, and before she does, I'm afraid I owe her some explanations.' Turning away from Elion's puzzled stare, he addressed the Moldan. 'If you want to apply your aggression to something useful, it's time we had a little talk with that Alva. I also want to keep Cergorn from knowing what we're up to for as long as possible. Do you think you could tunnel underground and come up right in Skreeva's quarters?'

Though there could be no expression on the chitinous mask of the Moldan's face, his mental tones were positively ringing with delight. 'It's as good as done. It will take me about an hour, I should think, to get right through.'

'Excellent. That gives me time to win Veldan over.' Amaurn indicated Elion and Bailen. 'In the meantime, can you make sure our friends here don't go anywhere?'

'Easily.' The Moldan snapped his diamond jaws.

Amaurn raised his eyes to the heavens. He wanted to go after Veldan, and he was finding all this delay intolerable. 'No, no, Maskulu. I know you come from an aggressive species, and normally you have to spend the whole time suppressing your natural instincts, but you're getting too carried away with all this. It's about time you remembered that first and foremost, you are a Senior Loremaster. I meant, pull down the exit tunnels to keep them here for a little while.'

The Moldan sighed in a surprisingly human fashion. 'I suppose you are right. At least with regard to these humans. But what of Skreeva? What if we cannot persuade her to bring her captives back?'

Amaurn felt his face settling back into the old, bleak expression of Lord Blade. 'Then we kill her.'

When Blade had left, it took no time for the Moldan to pull down the ceilings of the two exit tunnels, destroying the second one behind him as he left. Only Bailen, Elion and Ailie were left alone in the dim light of a single glim, waiting for the dust to settle. Elion shook his head. 'I can't believe Blade did that,' he said. 'Where's the sense? He might have kept us from escaping, but he can't prevent our thoughts from getting out. I thought he was supposed to be so clever, but surely he must have known that the first thing we'd do if he left us in this fix was contact Cergorn.'

Bailen turned his sightless eyes in the direction of Elion's voice. 'Is that right? Well, maybe Amaurn understands more about us than you think.' He took a deep breath. 'I'm sorry, Elion, but Vaure and poor Dessil are too deeply involved in this. Right or wrong, I can't betray my partners, and I can't let you do it, either.'

As a Listener, and one, furthermore, who had been deprived of sight and needed to compensate in other ways, Bailen had spent most of his life developing the power of his mind. His thoughts and will were stronger, even, than Elion had realised. Suddenly the Loremaster found his own mind clamped tightly in the grip of Bailen's far more powerful thoughts, kept immobile and inactive beneath the force of the blind Listener's will. Without his volition, his body folded beneath him and he sank down until he was lying, limp and helpless, on the cavern floor.

Bailen sat down a little distance away. 'Forgive me, Elion, but things have gone too far for us to start interfering. We must leave this business to Amaurn and Cergorn to settle.'

Ailie, at his side, was nodding. 'I agree,' she said. 'The Moldan's friend is the only person who can get Toulac and Zavahl back for us. Cergorn won't trouble himself about them.'

'And what about poor Veldan?' Sweat sprang out on Elion's forehead with the effort of projecting the thought to the mind that grasped his own. 'What does that bastard want with her? If he harms her, I'll kill him with my own bare hands.'

Bailen's surprise was clear. 'You've changed your tune, haven't you? The last time I spoke to you, you were wanting to kill her yourself.'

'I know.' Elion's thoughts were bitter. 'It was mutual. And

through my stupidity and hers, we both denied ourselves a friend when we needed one most. Why didn't any of you think to tell us that it was really ourselves we hated, and ourselves we blamed?'

'We're lost, aren't we?' Kaz's question lacked a lot of his normal ebullience. 'All these cursed tunnels look alike.'

Veldan peered around her in the faint glim-light, and sighed. 'So much for a dramatic exit,' she said in disgust. As the firedrake stopped she slid down to the ground and came round to his head. 'Are you feeling all right now?'

'Me?' said the firedrake, his mental tones tremendously hearty and cheerful. 'Nothing wrong with me. I'm fine, I am.'

'Right. Of course you are.' Veldan came around to face him. 'Oh, Kaz, you idiot. You stupid, stupid fool. Will you never learn to think before you act? If the Moldan is backing Blade to become Archimandrite, you might have guessed he would defend him. And you know how aggressive they are. Even a young one would be too much for you to fight, let alone a full-grown, fully-armoured adult.'

'I was only defending you,' Kaz said softly.

Veldan realised that he was still very shaken. She also knew that she was only feeling angry because he had given her such a fright. 'I know,' she said, 'and I'm grateful. But maybe next time you should save it until I'm actually under attack.'

'The last time we saw that festering sack of offal, the bastard *was* trying to kill us,' the firedrake pointed out with a flash of his old spirit. 'What did you want me to do? Wait until he'd stuck a knife in you? It would have been too late to protect you then.'

Just like last time.

Veldan caught the thought he was trying to hide from her. He had never truly recovered from the guilt of not being there when she was attacked in the caves of the Ak'Zahar. Gently, she took his head in her hands and looked into his opalescent eyes. 'Now look, Kaz. You didn't want me to go where you couldn't follow. I ignored you and went anyway. It's not your fault, or Elion's, or even poor Melnyth's that I was wounded. It was mine. If you remember, you were the one who ripped your claws to ribbons digging through a solid stone wall to get to me. You saved my life, Kaz, and Elion's too. You have nothing more to prove . . .'

She was interrupted by another voice. 'Veldan, I need to speak to you.' Blade stepped out of the shadows.

Kaz, more wary this time after Veldan's remonstrances, let out a soft, drawn-out hiss, and curved his long neck protectively across the body of his partner. Veldan strove to keep her voice calm, and matter-of-fact. 'You know these tunnels very well, for someone who makes their home in Callisiora.'

He shook his head. 'I'm afraid not. I'm just picking up a plan and instructions from the mind of the Moldan as I go along.'

Only then did Veldan realise that he had not spoken aloud. She replied in the same way. 'Of course. You would have to understand mindspeech if you wanted to be Archimandrite. But who are you? Lord Blade of Callisiora can't also be a Loremaster, and I've never seen you in Gendival.'

'Ah,' he said softly. 'I used to live here once. But I haven't been back for a long, long time. I disagreed with Cergorn over the way the Shadowleague was keeping secret so much of the knowledge that could really help this world, and after that, I wasn't welcome here anymore.' He paused. 'You may have heard of me. Amaurn the renegade. Amaurn the traitor. But remember, you've only heard Cergorn's side of the story. I could tell you a very different tale. And so could your mother.'

Veldan's jaw dropped. 'You're Amaurn? And you knew my *mother*?'

He nodded. 'She helped me. No-one ever knew how I escaped, but it was Aveole who arranged it all. If it hadn't been for her, I would have been executed that sunrise as Cergorn planned,' he said softly. 'You have her face, did you know that? When I first saw you up on the mountain, I could hardly believe my eyes. I thought I was seeing a ghost.'

'Beware.' Veldan heard the firedrake's warning voice in her mind. 'Remember who he is, Boss.'

Kaz was right. There were a thousand questions she wanted to ask him, but firmly, she pushed them aside, and glared at Blade – or was it Amaurn? 'I don't care who you claim to be, or who you knew, or didn't know, and I couldn't care less about your past,' she said. 'I know what a cold-blooded, ruthless killer you are now. Zavahl told me what you did to him. Toulac has mentioned a few of your more notable activities through the years. Elion says you had a trader woman murdered in cold blood, and would have done the same to her lifemate, had he not escaped. And it's not so very long since you were shooting at me and Kaz with crossbows, and trying to hunt us down like prey.'

For an instant, his eyes flashed cold as steel. 'I was hunting Zavahl, not you. It was nothing personal. I was shooting at you because you had ruined all my plans, and because you got between me and my quarry.'

'Oh, that's all right then. That makes me feel a *whole* lot better.'

Blade ignored her sarcasm. 'I don't suppose Zavahl also told you *he* was the one who ordered the traders silenced in the first place? They had discovered the dragon, and he wanted to pretend he had found it himself, so the people would believe that he still had the favour of Myrial.'

Veldan frowned. 'He certainly didn't. But even if that is true, what about the rest?'

'I expect that Toulac was telling you the truth.' There was a wry twist to Blade's mouth. 'After what Cergorn did to me, I needed to build a power base so that one day I could return and be revenged. In order to gain that power, I had to learn ruthlessness.' His eyes grew distant. 'Unfortunately, I learned it all too well. Ruthlessness is like an insidious drug. Once you find out how simply and quickly it can gratify your needs, it becomes more and more necessary, and it becomes increasingly easy to appease your conscience as time goes on.'

'I bet that's a real comfort to the people who got in your way over the years,' Veldan snapped. 'Just as Kaz and I are doing now. When you let me walk out of the Moldan's cavern, I didn't think you'd let us out of here without some sort of trouble.'

'When you left the cavern, you weren't thinking at all. You were simply reacting,' Blade told her. 'But you're wrong if you think I followed you to harm you in any way.' He stretched his arms out to his sides. 'Do you see any weapons?'

'What about hidden knives?'

He roared with laughter. 'What – with poison on them? Veldan, you've been reading too many romances. Think about it. Your friend Kaz would incinerate me long before I could draw a knife. In fact, he could kill me at any time.'

Kaz rumbled deep in his throat. 'That's the best idea you've had so far.'

Blade shook his head. 'No. The best idea I've had so far is getting your friend Toulac back for you. Because I'm the only one who can.'

Suspicious as she was, Veldan couldn't quell the hope that leapt up at his words. But how could she trust this man? Wasn't it Toulac herself who had warned her he was tricky? 'What do you mean, the only one?' she said quickly.

He shrugged. 'Do you think for one minute that Cergorn will act? Why should he? His policy in general is inaction, and the worse this crisis becomes, the less he seems prepared to intervene. Besides, you didn't manage to convince him that Toulac should join the Shadowleague or, more to the point, that Zavahl carries the spirit of the Dragon Seer. If he thinks the ones who've been taken are so insignificant, why should he lift a finger?'

'How did you know about all that?' Veldan demanded.

He waved her question away impatiently. 'Maskulu told me, of course. The point is, am I right? And think carefully before you answer. Toulac's life might depend on it.'

'He certainly has a point,' Kaz said to his partner in their private mode. 'If we want Toulac and Zavahl back, old horse-arse will be more of a hindrance than a help.'

'I know.' Veldan frowned. 'But he's not doing this out of the goodness of his heart.' She turned back to Blade. 'So why are you doing this? What's the bigger picture?'

'I told you already. I've been waiting all these years to get my revenge on Cergorn, and to take the Shadowleague in a new direction. This is the time.'

Veldan shook her head. 'But if you're suggesting what I think you are, the implications are colossal. We have information here with the potential to do great harm, as well as good. I know that's what Cergorn was afraid of.'

He waved his hand impatiently. 'I'm not saying that we should release information at random.' He made a wry face. 'The twenty years or so have taught me *that* much wisdom, at any rate. We'll have some kind of council of our most experienced Loremasters, who'll discuss the implications, and decide each case on its merits. But that's for later. The real crisis at this moment is the destruction of the Curtain Walls. The Shadowleague need a leader who's not afraid to use whatever knowledge is at his disposal, and to take swift action. Only when our world is safe again, can we afford to debate the other matters.'

'And you really think that *you* can do this?' Veldan asked incredulously.

'I'm sure I can. The key lies in the Dragon's knowledge, if we can only unearth it from all that mountain of information he carries. That's why we *must* get Zavahl back. We can't afford not to. I'll be completely honest with you, it's really him I'm after, but we'll get your friend Toulac back for you at the same time, I promise.' He leaned towards her. 'It's time to make a decision, Veldan. Are you with me?'

Veldan looked at Kaz. 'I already know what you're going to say,' he told her. 'I agree. I can't say I trust him, but he's a better option right now than old horse-arse.'

She nodded curtly to Amaurn. 'All right. We're in.'

He let out his breath in a sigh of relief, and briefly, she wondered why it mattered so much to him. 'Good,' he said. 'Then let's get going. Maskulu is already tunnelling so that we can come up under the Alva's quarters undetected. She controls the Dierkan slaves who have Zavahl and Toulac. Either she'll return them to us . . . Or we'll take them back ourselves.'

Twenty-six

Grim Warning

It didn't look like a triumphant entry to the lands of the Reivers. Tormon and the others were soaked, chilled, and spattered with mud from the trail. All through the night, he had driven them hard with scarcely a respite, and now they were wilting and short-tempered from a lack of sleep, aching in every limb, famished as winter wolves, and footsore because he had made them get down and walk for half the night, to spare the exhausted horses.

By the time they reached the valley that was home to Arcan's clan, the trader's companions, with the exception of the loyal Scall, were almost in a state of mutiny. Tormon had finally stopped driving them and let them stop briefly so that they could make themselves slightly more presentable before they met the chieftain. He realised too late that he had made a mistake. It would have been wiser to have kept them going.

Scall was nodding as he checked the feet of the little chestnut mare for stones. Seriema was swaying on her feet like a drunkard, clinging to the drooping neck of the great black gelding to keep herself upright. 'Don't sit down, don't sit down,' she was muttering over and over.

Presvel and Rochalla had no such compunctions. Letting their knees fold beneath them, they sank down into the wet bracken, where they would stiffen up in no time, and have considerable difficulty in rising again. Tormon raised his eyes to the heavens. City folk! Hadn't the sense of a fieldmouse. (Except for Lady Seriema, of course, he amended hastily, who seemed to have a pretty level head on her.) Presvel had actually dropped the reins of his horse on the ground, and it was only sheer good luck that the animal was too exhausted to stray.

Annas, more fortunate than the rest, had spent most of the night asleep in her father's arms. She was wide awake now, and had been complaining about hunger for the last hour or so. Tormon handed her to Seriema. 'Look after her for a minute will you, while I sort out those damned idiots.' He noted with approval that she put her arm through the loop of the reins before taking the child, and thanked Providence that someone in the party had some common sense. Relieved of his precious burden, he stretched his aching arms, and rubbed them hard to restore the circulation. They felt like limp string – if string could be this painful.

Dear Myrial, I'm getting as bad as the rest of them. My mind is starting to wander.

The trader took several deep breaths to clear his head, and strode over to Presvel and Rochalla. He snatched up the trailing reins of the horse from the ground. 'Hey! You two!' he barked. 'Get on your feet right now!'

Presvel simply ignored him, but Rochalla burst into tears. 'I can't,' she sobbed. 'Please don't make me get back on that horse again. Let me rest. Just let me sleep for a little while. I'll be all right then.'

In the short time he had known her, Tormon had been impressed by the courage and common sense of this slight young girl. She was proud, too, and he knew that she would never have broken down like this except in the deepest extremity. But he couldn't let her collapse here, in the middle of a wet and windswept moor. 'Come on, lass,' he said gently, holding out a hand to help her to her feet. 'Just make one last effort. We're nearly there now, I promise. Within the hour you'll be full of hot food and tucked up in a nice warm bed.'

Rochalla sniffed, and wiped her face on her sleeve. 'All right.' She let him pull her up, but her knees were so shaky, he doubted that she could stand unaided. He was about to help her back onto the horse that she shared with Presvel, but was stopped by pity. The poor beast had struggled valiantly through the night beneath the weight of two riders, and it too was on the verge of complete collapse. The trader made a quick decision. Scooping up the weary girl into his arms, he carried her across to his own sturdy Sefrian, and boosted her up onto the broad, black back. Rutska turned his regal head to give his master a long-suffering look, and let himself sag a little. Tormon stroked his neck and nose. 'You old fraud,' he said affectionately. 'Why, she's no weight at all for the likes of you.'

Putting the girl up on his own horse had also had the effect of getting Presvel to his feet. He advanced on Tormon, fists clenched and eyes ablaze with anger. 'What the bloody blazes do you think you're doing?' he yelled. 'She rides with *me*!'

'That poor horse of yours can't carry the two of you any further,' the trader told him calmly. 'I'll take the little lass up to Arcan's stronghold.'

'Liar!' Presvel shouted. 'You want her for yourself! It's just an excuse for you to put your hands on her, you foul, filthy—'

'Presvel!' Seriema thundered, cutting across his tirade.

Tormon looked at him through narrowed eyes, and fought against the anger that swept over him. 'I don't want anybody for myself except my soulmate Kanella, and she lies dead in your accursed city,' he said in a cold, quiet voice. 'Now let me put you straight on a thing or two. I have safe conduct among the Reivers because I'm a trader, and you'll only have it as long as you're with me. One more word from you, just one, you jumped-up little clerk, and I'll leave you out here on the moor to fend for yourself. The Reivers don't tolerate trespassers on their territory, and they can't afford to feed prisoners. So if you want to come with us, you'll shut your mouth and get on your horse right now. And remember, you've been warned. One more outburst like that, and Lady Seriema or no Lady Seriema, you're on your own.'

Turning his back on Presvel, he went to Seriema, who had been standing quietly beside her horse with Annas in her arms, watching events unfold. The expression on her face warned him against making any comment. She was furious with one of them, that much was clear, and he hoped it wasn't him. 'Will you take Annas, please?' he asked her. 'Just until we get there.'

She nodded. 'Of course. Let me get mounted, and you can pass her up to me.' She handed the child back to him. Annas opened her mouth, about to say that she didn't *want* to go with Lady Seriema, but caught the look in his eye and shut it hastily, allowing herself to be lifted up onto Avrio's back without a murmur.

'You ready?' the trader asked Scall, but the lad was already mounted, and tugging on Esmeralda's lead rope to get the tired donkey to move.

He's a good lad. I wonder if Kanella and I would ever have had a son like that?

Tormon thrust the painful thought away from him and swung up into the saddle beside Rochalla. 'Let's go,' he said.

Seriema glanced across at the wilting Rochalla with scorn. Despite her weariness, despite all her losses and the terrible scenes she'd left behind in Tiarond, she found herself enjoying the ride beside Tormon on the glorious black horse he had loaned her. Though she too was bone-tired from the long night of walking and riding, she could never bring herself to blubber and whine about it the way that ridiculous girl was doing. She had too much pride for that. If Avrio had not been so tired, if she had not been carrying the trader's little daughter before her, she would have loved to gallop for miles on these wild moors, with the wind like cold water sluicing over her face, and her tangled hair flying out behind her.

It all came down to freedom. For so many years, Seriema had believed that power and wealth had given her the freedom to do whatever she wished. Now, stripped of all she had accomplished and everything she'd owned, she finally recognised them for the shackles that they were. For years, ever since her father's death, in fact, she had been a slave to her responsibilities: the business, the mines, the property and the Mercantile Assembly. She had worked morning and night to amass more power, gold and prestige, and in doing so had simply created more drudgery for herself.

And when all's said and done, Myrial only knows what I was trying to prove. I didn't give a fig what the Consortium of Miners and the Mercantile Assembly thought, so long as they lacked the power to interfere with my plans, and as for my father: well, if I couldn't gain his respect when he was alive, I'm damned if I can impress him now he's dead. I've wasted some of my best years on all that idiocy. Maybe it's time I came to my senses and enjoyed the rest of my life.

For as long as those winged abominations let me.

Annas squirmed in her arms. 'Are you all right?' Seriema asked her. 'I'm not squeezing you too tightly, am I?' She wasn't very good with children – to be honest, she didn't like them – and she and Tormon's daughter had got off to a disastrous start, but she was determined to reach some kind of accord with the little girl. She was sick of having Rochalla's easy friendship with the child paraded in front of her, while Annas looked on *her* as some kind of gorgon.

At some time during the night she had reached the conclusion that she was absolutely sick of the way all the men, even young Scall, seemed to run around after bloody Rochalla. Even Tormon, today, was carting her around on his horse and was neglecting his own daughter to do so.

Just because the little dimwit's pretty, and I'm not, and never have been. Well, I can do nothing about that, but I'm damn well going to be better than her at everything else – well, except maybe mending, and cooking and stuff. She can have those, and welcome.

Seriema was honest enough to admit that, with her life becoming so chaotic, she was desperately searching for something that *could* be under her control, even if it was such a small thing as winning the trust of a child. So she had set herself to make friends with Annas, and make friends she would. Just as soon as she found out how to start.

She had been so deep in thought that she hadn't realised that

Annas was trying to talk to her, until the child started to tug at her sleeve.

Well, that's a good start, you idiot!

'Sorry, Annas.' She dredged up a nervous smile. 'I was miles away. What were you saying?'

'It's all right. I just said you weren't squeezing me, thank you.'

'Good. I don't think it will be much further now.'

'It isn't,' said Annas, with great authority. 'We just came from here, in the wagon, before . . . When my mama . . .' Suddenly her fists clenched tightly on Seriema's arm.

'You must miss her,' Seriema said softly. Somehow, she couldn't seem to get the hang of talking down to the child, but it had struck her that Tormon didn't, either. Annas was used to having fairly adult conversations, and it was a relief to be able to approach her on those terms. It made life much easier. She was still very young, though. Now, she simply nodded, and her eyes filled with tears.

Blast!

Seriema thought quickly. 'I missed my mama a lot when she died,' she said. 'I was a bit older than you – seventeen – but I can remember how lost I felt without her.'

Annas considered this. 'Oh. Is that why you're so grumpy sometimes?'

Well, of all the—

She opened her mouth, and closed it again. How the bloody blazes could she respond to something like that? With honesty, she supposed. 'No. I get grumpy sometimes when I'm worried, or I'm tired. I wish I didn't, but sometimes I can't help it.'

The little girl nodded. 'I get grumpy when I'm tired, too. Or hungry, or bored. I'm hungry now. Are we there yet?'

'I don't know. You're the expert. I thought you said we were.'

Annas made a face. 'I think I might have been wrong about that.'

'Well, let's hope you weren't.'

Luckily, she wasn't. Soon Seriema, following Tormon, found herself looking ahead into the mouth of a broad valley, hemmed in on either side by slopes covered in bracken and heather, with patches of turf between grazed by shaggy, black-faced sheep. In the distance, she could see a cluster of low, turf huts. Suddenly, without warning, a knot of riders came galloping towards them on sturdy, stocky little horses who were clearly bred for the rough terrain. She saw the dull gleam of unsheathed steel, and firmly told herself that there was nothing to be scared of. But as a merchant, she had suffered just as much as her fellows from the depredations of these Reivers, and the high cost of caravan guards proved that they were dangerous indeed.

Tormon knows these people. We'll be all right.

Sure enough, the trader rode forward, calling out to the wild-looking warriors in greeting. She heard a murmur of surprise as the Reivers recognised him, then he went into a huddle with the men, and there was a spate of urgent talk. Several of the riders set off at a gallop, heading back up the valley, and one stayed behind with Tormon, who beckoned the rest of his little group to follow.

When Seriema drew level, she saw a pleasant-faced man with piercing green eyes and a square, determined chin. His long hair, tied back in a tail, was the colour of dark copper. Tormon performed the introductions. 'This is Cetain, son of Arcan, the clan chieftain.' He grinned. 'At least one of the sons. There are so many of them, it's hard to keep track.'

When he discovered her identity, the warrior's eyes widened. 'By my blood! So it's your carts that things are always falling off. Have you come seeking your missing merchandise, my Lady?'

Seriema laughed. 'I would have once, maybe, had I thought it would be any use. But now I'm just content that my merchandise went to a good home.'

His eyes twinkled. 'You may be sure of that.'

He fell into place beside her, and his eye fell on Rochalla who slumped against Tormon's chest, apparently asleep. 'What ails the lassie?' he asked. 'Is she hurt?'

Not again! *I don't believe this!*

Seriema forced a smile. 'No,' she answered, trying not to clench her teeth. 'We rode and walked all through the night, scarcely stopping at all. She isn't used to it.'

'What? Is that all? Well, it doesn't seem to have done *you* much harm, my Lady.' He waved a dismissive hand at Rochalla. 'There's no place for all that nonsense among the Reivers. We require our women to be strong. They must be able to ride with the men and fight with the men if need be.' He frowned at Rochalla. 'A woman who can't ride all night is of no use to anyone out here, least of all to herself.'

Yes!

Seriema felt a broad grin spreading across her face. She had a feeling she was going to like it here.

Arcan, clan chieftain, was not a big man, but he had an air of strength and power that gave the impression of greater stature. When he was displeased, a fire would come into his eye that was enough to quell the fiercest Reiver warrior. Right now, however, Grim was refusing to be quelled, which was not improving the chieftain's temper.

At least young Dark has the sense to keep quiet.

Grim's assistant, glad, no doubt, that his master was the one who had to face up to Arcan's ire, had edged his chair back out of the circle of firelight, and was trying his best to fade into the background. Grim felt sorry for him. Poor Dark had been dragged along here without a word of explanation and had no idea what was going on. Grim had simply put on his skull mask and all his Summoner regalia that morning, marched up to the stronghold, and demanded to see the chieftain in private.

No-one would refuse a Summoner, though Arcan did not seem too happy about being disturbed at breakfast. In no time the three of them had been settled in the comfortable chambers of the chieftain, a very different place from the rough turf hut in which the dying child had dwelt. The furniture was crafted from priceless carved wood, plundered, no doubt, as were many of the chamber's luxuries, from sundry luckless merchant caravans, though some of

Arcan's possessions had been purchased from trader Tormon, or bartered for fleeces and hides. Thick bear skins covered the cold stone floor, and the wall hangings were rich with fine embroidery which was clearly not the local patterned weave. Despite the early hour, wine was served, and it came in precious glass goblets, instead of the usual vessels of pewter or horn.

Arcan, who even looked short-tempered, with his short-cropped silvering red hair, his bushy eyebrows and his bristling beard, leaned back in his chair and glared at the Summoners. 'Well?' he barked. 'You've dragged me up here, Grim. Now what is this grave news that I had to hear in private?'

'I've had word that disaster has befallen Tiarond, my Chief,' said Grim, in a tone of voice that matched his name. 'The city has been invaded by hordes of winged predators. They are large, fast and lethal, their prey is human beings, and I firmly believe that once they have exhausted their current food supply, they will start to spread out into the surrounding regions.'

He took a deep breath. 'My Chief, this valley is in easy reach of a creature with wings. You must take precautions now. You must prepare for a siege. The livestock must be brought in from outlying areas, so that they can be sheltered here in the stronghold if we come under attack. Your folk must be prepared to flee their homes at a moment's notice, and come here for shelter. You must stock-pile food and weapons, and—'

As the Summoner spoke, Arcan's face had been growing more and more thunderous. 'I *must?*' he growled.

Thank Providence Amaurn is letting me join him soon. Arcan isn't such a bad fellow, but after years of pandering to his ego, I've had enough.

With that thought in his mind, Grim shrugged. 'You must please yourself, my Chief. But if you choose to ignore my advice, you will soon find yourself chieftain over a valley full of rotting, half-eaten corpses.'

Behind him, the Summoner heard Dark gasp in horror. The look on Arcan's face reminded him of a dog he had once owned, who was in the habit of snapping at flies, and had one day caught a wasp instead. The chieftain's eyes glinted coldly. 'You have a privileged position in this clan, Master Summoner,' he said. 'You should consider your words very carefully.'

'And *you* should consider your actions very carefully,' Grim retorted. 'You are facing the most serious threat that has ever been known in these lands. Make no mistake about that. If you wish your clan to survive, you must take action immediately, while there is still time. Once the skies have been darkened by the wings of the abominations, it will be too late.'

Arcan had grown very still. Beneath the bluster and bravado which was so necessary for a chieftain in these rough lands, he was not a stupid man. 'You mean,' he said at last, 'that there is no way in which these creatures can be fought?'

'No, I did *not* say that,' Grim replied. 'But you can only fight them from a fortified position. If they catch your people out on the open moor, they will hunt them as the eagle hunts the hare.' He leaned forward. 'I know that bows and crossbows are weapons not generally favoured by your people.'

Arcan nodded. 'We call them the coward's choice. We teach our warriors to use them for hunting, though, as you know.'

'Well, my Chief, I suggest your warriors start practising. They will soon hunt a quarry such as no man has ever seen before.' Grim took a deep breath. Now for the last, and most difficult part. 'There is one thing more, my Chief. In this crisis, it is time to set clan rivalries aside. The other chieftains must be warned.'

'WHAT?' Arcan leapt from his seat. 'Do you take me for a fool, to be helping my enemies? The more they are weakened, the stronger I become.'

Grim sighed. This was exactly what he had been expecting. 'My Chief,' he said patiently, 'though the Reivers raid and fight among themselves, there is a tradition that they would always band together to repel any invaders from the outside. The hilltop beacons are the ancient signal that called the clans to arms. They have not been used for many a long year, but they are still in place. I urge you to use them now. Light the beacons. Spread the word. Send two swift riders under a flag of truce to neighbouring clans, and let them in turn send messengers to others, until everyone has been warned. My Chief, these are desperate times, and this is like no emergency you have ever known. This has nothing to do with man contending against man. It is humanity itself against something alien, something other than ourselves. And believe me, if we are to survive, there is no time to lose.'

Arcan's eyes narrowed. 'You say these creatures are alien,' he said softly. 'So where do they come from? The priests from Tiarond say that nothing exists outside the Curtain Walls. Have they been killed by their own mistake?'

Damn. He's too shrewd by half. But if Amaurn becomes leader of the Shadowleague, surely it's all right to tell Arcan the truth?

But what if he fails?

To Grim's relief, he was saved from having to answer, as the door flew open and Lewic, Arcan's oldest son, burst in. 'Trader Tormon is back from Tiarond,' he cried. 'His soulmate, Kanella, has been killed, he lost his wagon, and he says the city has fallen to winged creatures terrible to behold. He says that nearly everyone is dead. He only brought a handful of survivors with him. Only half a dozen, from the entire city.'

Arcan looked at Grim. His face was bleak. 'I only half-believed you,' he whispered. 'I'm sorry I doubted, Master Summoner.'

Grim nodded his acceptance of the apology. 'I only wish I had been wrong.'

The stricken man took a deep breath, straightened his shoulders, and as he got to his feet, he became the clan chieftain once more. 'Come with me, Lewic. Master Summoner, will you come too, and your assistant? We have much to do. But first, let us go and greet our friend trader Tormon, and his companions. They will have a welcome here for as long as we hold out.'

The beast quarters were on the ground floor of the stronghold, in dark, cavernous spaces supported here and there by walls and square, sturdy pillars. Following Tormon's news about the fall of Tiarond, the Reivers were already starting to bring in the beasts from the settlement and the moors around. There were cattle, sheep and pigs coming in, with additional animals in covered yards outside. All were individually marked with the sign of the owner. Some of them, Tormon pointed out, had more than one brand or dye mark, with a line through one of them to cancel it. These had been animals taken in raids from other clans. Arcan had explained to them that no torches or candles were allowed down there because of the risk of fire, and lamps were used only in an emergency, such as if someone arrived after nightfall, or a beast was sick or giving birth in the night. As a rule, all tasks were done in the daylight, which filtered through a series of narrow slit windows set high in the walls, which ventilated the place as well as providing dim illumination.

Scall was glad to be down here with Tormon, just the two of them. Though the chieftain had made them all very welcome, the lad had been overawed by the many tall, fierce-looking warriors that had filled the great, torchlit hall of the stronghold – and the women, most of them regally beautiful, were just as overwhelming. Damaeva, Arcan's small but stately soulmate, had found rooms for everyone, and the others had immediately gone to bed, but Tormon had refused the chieftain's offer to have his men see to their animals, and had insisted on taking care of them himself. 'They brought us so far, and worked so hard,' he'd said. 'It's the least I can do.' Immediately, Scall had offered to help.

The horses were kept separate, with their own roomy area. Some were kept in boxes, but most were simply tethered, well apart, to iron rings bolted into the rough walls. An area had been given over to Tormon, and he and Scall led their tired beasts into position, and tethered them securely. For Rutska, Tormon used a length of lightweight chain that he had brought with him. 'If he smells a mare in heat, or he takes against a strange stallion, he'll bite straight through a rope to get to them,' he explained.

'I know,' Scall said ruefully. 'You should have seen the wreck he made of the Godsword stables.' He forbore to mention that the stallion had killed a man. There was no point in upsetting the trader for something that was done and in the past. Besides, as far as he was concerned, Rutska had been provoked, and had every reason to act as he did. When he had recovered his horses, Tormon had narrowed his eyes at the lash marks on the stallion's withers, but at the time he had been too distressed by the death of his wife to think of asking where they had come from. And as long as he didn't bring up the subject, Scall certainly wasn't going to.

They settled the horses in deep beds of bracken, fed them from Arcan's precious stores of hay and grain, and started to brush off the worst of the mud. 'We'll just make them dry and comfortable for now,' Tormon said. 'We can come down and groom them thoroughly later, when we've had a sleep ourselves.'

Scall was glad to hear it. But the trader's words about mares in heat had started him thinking. 'Tormon?'

'Yes?'

'You know Firefly?'

'Is that your little mare? It's a good name.'

'Elion told me that was her name. He had some other names for her too, that I would be embarrassed to repeat. They weren't very nice.'

Tormon went on brushing Avrio. 'Elion was no horseman,' he said. 'You are. You might be only learning, but it's in your blood, none the less. Anyway, what did you want to ask me about your mare?'

Scall hesitated. He had wanted to ask the next question for some time, but had been afraid to. 'Is – is she really mine? I mean *mine*, mine? Or is she yours, and you're letting me borrow her? Or will Elion want her back one day?'

'Why, bless you, boy, Elion gave her to you, didn't he? Of course she's yours. All yours, every bit of her. The first of many, I hope, if we get through these bad times.'

For a moment, Scall couldn't speak. He hugged the mare's neck to hide the tears of joy in his eyes, and she turned her head and gave him an affectionate nip on the arm – at least, he interpreted it that way. 'Tormon?'

'Yes, Scall?'

'Er . . .' He felt himself going red. 'You know when Firefly comes into season?'

Tormon looked up in surprise at that. 'Yes,' he said cautiously.

'Well, what I mean is – well, Rutska is a truly magnificent stallion, and all that, but don't you think he might be a bit big for Firefly? The foal, I mean. They had a mare up at the Godsword stables whose foal was too big. She couldn't give birth to it, and it killed her. What if that happened to Firefly?' He couldn't keep the tremor out of his voice.

Tormon smiled across at him. 'You did well to be thinking of that before the crisis hits us, as you might say. Yes, I would say that Rutska's too big for her. I wouldn't like to take the risk.'

'But won't we have an awful job to keep them apart? Especially if we're out on the road. I wouldn't like to get between Rutska and anything he really wanted.'

'We'll manage, son. We might find somewhere safe for you and the mare, and leave you there until she's all right again. Or we may still be here. Arcan has stacked up a lot of favours that he owes me, over the years. Or,' he smiled, 'we might even find another stallion for her, one of a more suitable size. What would you reckon to that?'

Scall looked in horror at the shaggy Reiver ponies that surrounded them. 'Not one of *these*,' he said in dismay. 'Sawn-off little runts.'

Tormon laughed. 'Well, we'll wait, then, until we find her a mate magnificent enough to suit her picky owner.'

'I am *not* picky,' Scall protested. 'It's just that she's a very special mare, and she's going to have a special foal.'

Tormon chuckled. 'If you say so.'

They worked in silence for a while, and by the time Scall had finished with his mare and started on the donkey, his mind was straying to other subjects. 'Tormon?'

'What?'

'You know that weird thing I found when I was trapped by the floods? The one that looks like a little silver nut and it shows you maps, like tiny pictures of places?'

'You did mention it, yes. I'm not sure it's wise to play around with stuff like that, Scall. Goodness only knows what it is, but it might be dangerous.'

'I suppose. I was just wondering if I could get it to show me pictures of the city, and if it would be the city as it is now.' He bit his lip. 'It's awful not knowing whether my family are alive or dead.'

The trader shook his head. 'Myrial only knows, son. I couldn't begin to guess. Why don't you take it to Grim, or his young assistant? That sort of thing would be right up their street. And if it is dangerous, they can warn you before you carry it around any longer.'

A chill went through Scall. 'The Summoner?' he squeaked. 'I wouldn't *dare*!'

Tormon shook his head. 'It's a mistake to judge things by their outsides, Scall. Thosc skull masks are only there to impress the ignorant. The rest of us know better. Don't we?' He shot a piercing look towards the youth.

'But . . .'

'I've known Grim for years. He's a good man and a good friend, and he could certainly tell you a lot more about your find than I could. I think you and his assistant would get along too, though he's a bit older than you are. Why don't you talk to them when you've rested?'

'Maybe.' Scall cast around for a change of subject. 'Tormon?'

'That's my name.'

'You know Rochalla?'

'Yes.'

'She's really pretty, isn't she?'

The trader's eyebrows went up, and he stopped working. 'Yes, she is. She seems a nice, kind, level-headed girl, too, and that's a lot more important than you probably realise at this point.'

'Do you think she likes me?'

'Well, it's early days yet, but I think she's getting to like you. She gave you a kiss, didn't she, when you came back from being trapped all night in the floods.' With a sudden frown, he looked across at Scall. 'There's just one thing, lad. If your thoughts are tending in that direction, be very wary of Presvel. I think the last few days have unhinged him, and if you've noticed, he's very possessive of the little lass. Seriously, Scall, beware of him. He's a dangerous man, and becoming more unstable as time goes on.'

'*Presvel?*' Like most people of his age, Scall had never considered anyone over the age of thirty as being prey to jealousy and lust. 'But he's too old for her.'

'Well, that's not what *he* thinks, lad, so watch your step. Or better yet, ask one of Arcan's warriors to teach you how to fight.'

'But . . .'

'Scall?'

'Yes?'

'Shut up.'

'All right, but . . . Tormon? You know when we first met, up in the Snaketail Pass?'

'Yes, I remember.'

'Well . . . If I had to run into anyone that day on the mountain, I'm really glad it was you.'

Tormon smiled. 'So am I, son. So am I.'

Twenty-seven

The Hoard

Surely I'm dreaming. That sounds like Alestan's voice.

Aliana opened her eyes – not such an easy task as it sounded, because while she slept, someone had weighed her eyelids down with several pounds of lead. They must have had a lot of lead, she thought drowsily, because apparently they had done the same thing to her arms and legs. She was just about to give it up and go back to sleep when she heard her brother's voice again.

'It was very hard. To be honest, when we parted, I thought that was the last I'd ever see of her.'

'She was very brave, and so were you, to act as decoy like that.' The other voice sounded vaguely familiar. Aliana groped through the fuzzy mists of recent memory, and came up with a name. Healer Kaita. Of course. She'd been very kind. With that memory, a whole host of others came flooding back, of a less welcome sort. Contorted bodies, gnawed limbs, the blank, hollow stare of gouged-out eyes. The stench, which still clung faintly to her hair and body, even now. The endless, bone-deep cold. The mad, red eyes of the winged fiend, as it loomed up before her, and the spray of hot, stinking blood as her knife bit into its throat . . .

Without quite knowing how it had happened, Aliana found herself out of bed, blinking in the welcome lamplight. The dark, snowy plaza and its grisly inhabitants had been replaced with the subdued, reassuring bustle of Kaita's sickroom. She was wearing nothing but her Godsword shirt, big enough on her to hang down to mid-thigh, and spare her modesty. Its sleeves had come unrolled while she slept, and flapped down over her hands.

The sudden movement must have alerted the Healer and Alestan, who were sitting nearby. They both turned in the same instant.

'Aliana! You're awake,' her brother cried, but subsided as Kaita shushed him. He came rushing over to enfold her in a lopsided hug, and Aliana saw that his right arm was splinted and bound tightly to his body in a sling.

'Alestan,' she cried softly, 'what in the world have you done?'

He shrugged, and winced at the injudicious movement. 'I jumped headfirst through the trapdoor on the Citadel roof, while I was dodging your winged pals. I wish I could have taken a leaf out of your book, and cut the bastard's throat.' Then he brightened. 'But it did get blown to smithereens shortly afterwards, which made me feel a whole lot better. I didn't even realise I'd injured myself at first. We were all too busy running away from the explosion. It was only afterwards that I realised how much my arm was hurting. But what about you? How are you feeling now? Healer Kaita said that what you did last night was one of the bravest things she'd ever heard of.'

Aliana felt herself blushing. 'It didn't seem like that at the time,' she confessed. 'But I was so scared that the only thing I could do was keep going. If I had stopped to think, I would have panicked, and made a run for it, and the fiends would have caught me for sure.' She shuddered. 'I would have been one more corpse out there, among hundreds.'

'But you aren't,' a voice said briskly. 'You're here in my sickroom, safe and warm. Your brother is with you, your friends are close by, and you're just about to have some breakfast.' They both looked around to see Healer Kaita, carrying a tray. 'Try not to dwell on what might have been, Aliana,' she said. 'Probably you won't ever forget what happened, and maybe it's not right that you should. But don't go complicating matters with what *didn't* happen. That way lies insanity. What you did was a triumph. You got the better of those abominations, and showed the rest of us it could be done.

Look at events in that light, and you'll come to terms more easily with all the horror.'

Aliana didn't want to talk about it any more. There must be some way to get Kaita off the subject. 'What's in the soup?' she asked.

Kaita put the tray, with its two bowls, down on the bed. 'As you can see, it looks like dishwater with bits in it – and as to the nature of the bits, I prefer not to speculate. If I had some of my own spices, I could have improved it for you, but you'll just have to be brave, I'm afraid.'

'And the rocks?' Alestan pointed to the two small, greyish lumps on the tray.

'Ah, well. Our cooks haven't yet got the hang of making bread for so many people in a place with no real facilities. Still, you're young. You've got good teeth. You'll manage.'

'Well, *I* certainly will,' Aliana said. 'And if Alestan doesn't want his, I'll have that too.'

'No you bloody won't!'

Kaita laughed. 'I must go. Commander Galveron is wanting a word with me. He'll be glad to know that you're awake, Aliana.' She hurried off.

They sat for a while, eating their soup, gnawing on the rock-hard bread and drinking hot, black tea with honey in it. Gradually, they filled in the details of what had happened while they had been apart. Then Kaita's assistant, a tall, serious-looking young man, came and chased them out. 'I'm sorry,' he said, 'but we need the bed. 'One of the women in the Temple has gone into labour, and it looks like there are complications. Anyway, I'm sure you'll be glad to see your friends again.'

When he had gone, Alestan looked gravely at Aliana. 'It's about time we got everyone together. I found something out before that concerns us all. Commander Galveron has betrayed us.'

It had seemed to Packrat that the bundles and sacks that he and his friends had carried across from the Godsword Citadel were far more welcome than themselves. In a whirl of activity the goods had been pounced upon by various people: the food and blankets were commandeered by a big bald man with one arm; the blasting powder and fuses were taken off by a group of folk that the thief recognised as miners, from the black dust in the pores of their faces; the weapons were gathered up by Corvin and his men, and taken away. That only left the thieves, in a defensive huddle near the Temple door.

Smithmaster Agella had done her best to help them settle in. She had taken them through a door at the back of the Temple, past the rubble of the staircase which, she said, had been blown up last night with the blasting powder Aliana had brought. There was another staircase, still in one piece, leading downwards, and they followed her obediently down the worn, steep stairs, then along a passage leading to the vast cavern which held the underground lake that was the reservoir for the city's water supply. From here, the highest point, the water was diverted down through the city via a complex system of valves and pipes, actually into the houses of the rich, and to a pump on each street corner for the poorer folk. Chains of hard-working people were carrying the water away in buckets. 'Some goes along that tunnel to one of the Temple vaults, where the cooks are working,' Agella explained. 'I'll show you in a minute where to go for your rations. Some of the water goes upstairs, where it's put into casks, so that people can dip out water as they need it for drinking.'

'Where did you get the casks from?' asked Packrat curiously.

The Smithmaster shrugged. 'There are plenty in the food storage caverns, holding apples and stuff. We just emptied a few out.'

After all the months of rain, there was certainly enough water coming down off the mountain. Some of it overflowed the lake, forming a stream that went through another cavern, which had been curtained off, with some of the Temple hangings, into private areas for washing.

'This is amazing,' Gelina said. 'I had no idea that all this was underneath the Temple.'

'The story goes that in the dim and distant past, before there even was a Temple, these caves were here,' Agella told her. 'They actually go down into the mountain for such a long way that no-one has ever explored them all. Some say they were made by our ancestors, mining the mountain for precious stones. Others say that they were created by Myrial himself and they were used as a place of worship before the Basilica was built. Anyway, they're proving useful now. We'll run out of food sooner than we'd like, but at least we'll never die of thirst. Oh, and if you need to relieve yourself, by the way, there's a place just along here, with a crevice in the floor that goes way down. For now at least, we're using that.'

'It's a long way to come,' Packrat grumbled.

'Think of the alternative,' Agella said grimly. 'If everyone started doing it in the Temple itself, we wouldn't be able to stay there for long.'

After the Smithmaster had shown them everything, and found them something to eat and a blanket each (just one – and after Packrat had lugged a great sack of the bloody things all the way from the Citadel!), she took them back upstairs to the area that was to be their very own. Then she left them alone, and feeling very much out of place among the crowded refugees.

It seemed to Packrat that the numbers of the Grey Ghosts were diminishing all the time. Now that Alestan had been led away to see his sister, only Erla, Tag, Gelina and himself remained.

The other two will be coming back soon. Not that I care.

He added the last part hastily, wondering what had come over him lately. Packrat liked to see himself as a lone wolf, living always on the edge, beholden to no-one, relying on his wits to survive. He had grown up among the rag-pickers, the community of pathetic human scavengers who were despised even by the folk of the Warrens. They dwelt outside the city on the west side of Tiarond, where the high walls were built out from the end of the great ridge that cradled it on that side. There was an open space between the walls and the river; a strip of gravel and mud about fifty yards wide which vanished under water every spring, when the river was swollen with snow-melt from the mountain's higher slopes. Over the centuries, this area had become the city's midden, where rubbish, household waste and broken or worn out items were dumped. Every year, the spring floods swept the waste ground clean, and the process began again.

This was where the rag-pickers lived, in rough hovels constructed from cast-off bits and pieces. Each day they combed the midden for any useful items, competing with the birds and rats for anything edible and trapping and eating the rats and crows themselves. Each spring, when the floods came, they scrambled to the higher ground of the promontory itself, perching precariously on cold, damp, narrow ledges for days at a time while the waters raged below. When the floods had subsided, no trace remained of their miserable homes, or the discards upon which they lived. Spring was always a bad time, until the refuse had time to build up again. Each year, many died, but somehow, there always seemed to be replacements. A succession of Hierarchs had tolerated this state of affairs because the rag-pickers performed a useful function as scavengers, and were scarcely viewed as human at all.

Packrat had not started his life in this appalling place, but when he was six years old, his father had accidentally killed a merchant in a struggle for a purse, and had been hanged. Not long afterwards, his mother had been cast out of the Warrens for the ultimate crime of stealing from another member of the little community. Protesting her innocence in vain, she was exiled to live among the human scavengers of the midden, and her little son with her. Only Packrat knew the truth – that her chief accuser had stolen the items himself – and who listened to the word of a little child?

Packrat's mother did not survive long in the midden, and after that, he was left to his own devices, owning nothing in the world save his father's ragged cloak. Somehow he survived, spurred on by the need to avenge his mother's death. He became so good at scavenging that in the course of time his original name was forgotten, and he became known among the rag-pickers as Packrat. When he was ten years old, he smuggled himself back into the city, hidden in a trader's cart. He tracked down the man who had been responsible for his mother's exile, and stabbed him in the back one night as he relieved himself in a dark alley. As the wounded man crumpled to the ground, Packrat darted in and cut his throat.

His revenge accomplished, he stole a change of clothing and wormed his way back into the Warrens by claiming to be an orphaned miners' child, down from the mountains to seek a new life in Tiarond. No-one remembered the little boy who'd been cast out so long ago, and he was given a guarded welcome. Though they accepted him, he always remained something of an outcast. Nobody wanted him, and he belonged to no-one. Somehow, the taint of the midden always seemed to be upon him, and because no-one cared what he looked like, he didn't care himself. To ease his loneliness, he had set out to become the very best thief he could, and the years turned him as wary and mistrustful as a wild animal – until Alestan and Aliana had come along and formed the Grey Ghosts, the elite among the city's thieves.

Packrat knew he was as good as any of them, and burned to join their number, but he knew that they would not have him. Why should they? He had never been accepted anywhere else. So he pretended to despise the Ghosts, to show them that he didn't care. But he had reckoned without Aliana. When the skill of the scruffy outcast came to her attention, she worked tirelessly to persuade her brother and the others to welcome him, until they finally gave in to her wishes.

Though he remained distrustful and suspicious, Packrat never forgot what she had done for him. Even after he became a Ghost, he had kept up his tough, uncaring act, with Aliana as much as the others, but she was, in truth, the only person he had cared about since his mother's death, so long ago. And now he owed her again. Yesterday she had saved his life, even putting her own at risk to stop that bastard Godsword Commander from throwing him to the mercy of the winged fiends. He owed her, and he was determined to find a way to pay her back. Not that it would be easy, under the current circumstances. Normally he would just have stolen her something nice, but right now, it seemed wiser to keep his head down and his nimble fingers to himself for a while.

Should I give her what I found yesterday?

Packrat smiled to himself. He had put one over on the Godswords then, all right. When they had searched him on his return from his unauthorised explorations of the officers' quarters in the Citadel, there was one item they had missed. He had hidden it in his trousers, and search or no search, no soldier had been about to go *there*. The item was still there now, nestled safely against his skin: a large sack, it looked like, of some kind of silky, silvery material that weighed absolutely nothing, and folded up smaller than the palm of his hand. And though it had seemed impossible that there *could* be anything inside it, all his instincts, developed over a lifetime of pilferage, were telling him that there *was*. When he looked at it, it made his fingers itch to get inside. He hadn't worked out how to get it open, but there hadn't really been much time to try.

So should he give it to Aliana instead? Nah, Packrat decided. For a start, he wasn't going to give it to anyone until he'd found out what it contained. That would be stupid. Besides, since his wanderings in the Citadel had been the cause of the dreadful ordeal she'd been forced to undergo last night, it might be more tactful (and wise) not to remind Aliana of what he'd been doing. She had promised Galveron that there would be no stealing, and if she knew he'd actually taken something and kept it, she would probably be furious with him. Women could be funny like that.

Nah, I'll find something else to give her. I'll keep it for myself, and make sure nobody finds out I have it. When I get the chance, I'll work on opening it.

Though there seemed no obvious way to get inside it, he had no doubt that he would succeed in the end. Nothing had ever beaten him yet. It was only a matter of time.

When Alestan and Aliana returned to the others, they found them huddled together near the Temple doors, in the middle of the open floor: the worst possible place for a thief who was used to lurking all the time under whatever cover was available. Packrat was sitting with his blanket wrapped around him like a cloak and hood, plainly trying to hide beneath it. He was ignoring the others, and looking across the little campsite in the niche opposite, where a tall, red-haired girl was telling a story to a cluster of small children. Aliana's brother poked her with his elbow. 'Oh no,' he whispered. 'Look at that. Don't tell me he's started fancying Smithmaster Agella's niece. I can't see that going down very well.'

It didn't look to Aliana as though *anything* was going down very well. Tag and Erla seemed to be taking it in turns to keep up a constant barrage of whining, and Gelina, her lovely face haggard with fatigue, looked as though she was within a hair's breadth of thumping them both.

This is what I risked my life for?

Aliana was filled with dismay. Firmly, she reminded herself that things could be a damn sight worse. A fleeting memory of the corpses in the plaza made her shiver. At least she and her companions were still alive, and safe, and fed after a fashion.

When she and Alestan joined the others, they received a delighted welcome from everyone, but soon the weary and dejected Ghosts were back at their former occupations. It appeared to be Tag's turn to whine. 'I don't like being here. Why can't *we* be closer to the wall, instead of those stupid people over there? It's horrible here. It would feel a lot safer *there*.'

'Maybe when we see the Commander again, he'll find a better place for us.' Aliana suggested.

'Him!' Alestan spat on the floor, drawing disapproving looks from some of the people in camps nearby.

'What's wrong with him? Why shouldn't we ask him? When I volunteered to bring the blasting powder back last night, he gave his word that he would keep our identity a secret, and help us.'

Alestan scowled. 'Yes – and the bastard broke his word the first chance he got. Before you woke up, I overheard him telling the Hierarch who we were.'

'*What?* But he promised he wouldn't!'

'Well, he did. I heard him, I tell you. He probably doesn't think that promises made to the likes of us are worth honouring.'

Aliana felt as though someone had kicked her in the stomach. 'I can't believe it. After everything I went through last night! How could he do this?' She seized her brother's arm. 'Alestan, tell us everything they said to one another. We've got to know what we're up against here.'

Somehow, in the face of this crisis, all the ghosts were united once more. Packrat had dragged his attention away from Agella's niece. Gelina was sitting up straighter, and some animation had come back into her face. Tag and Erla, blessedly, had stopped whining. The Grey Ghosts listened with growing dismay as Alestan repeated the conversation he had heard. 'And then she burst into tears,' he finished, 'and she started talking about some ring or other that was lost. It was stolen by the abominations when they attacked during the sacrifice, and apparently she can't be Hierarch without it.'

'What?' Packrat said sharply. 'She lost a ring?' His eyes gleamed. 'Just think. If we could get our hands on that ring, we could make her do anything we wanted.'

'That's all very well,' Aliana argued, 'but we don't even know what it looks like. And even if we did, I'm not about to go and fight the fiends for it.' Memory cast a fleeting shadow across her face. 'Last night was enough for me.'

Packrat shrugged. 'It was just a thought. It would be useful, though, if we could find out what it looked like, on the quiet.'

Alestan gave him a hard look. 'Packrat, do you know something that we don't? Remember what Galveron said about stealing.' He rubbed his broken arm, bound tightly in its sling. 'It cost us more than enough to get in here, and I don't intend to be thrown out again, just because you're playing silly buggers. If I find you've been hiding things and putting the rest of us at risk, I'll throw you out myself.'

Aliana gave her brother a quelling look. He should know by now that threats had never been the way to get Packrat to co-operate.

'Please, Packrat,' she coaxed. 'I did as much as I could last night, and so did Alestan, but though we managed to get into the Temple, we're still in a fix if the Hierarch doesn't want us. If you know something that might give us the advantage, then you're the only one who can help us now. We're all depending on you.'

Packrat made a great show of thinking it over, and Aliana smiled to herself. When he did that, it meant that he was going to let himself be persuaded. He looked around furtively, as if someone might be listening. 'Gather round close,' he whispered. 'Make a kind of shield for me, so that nobody else can see what I'm doing.' Obediently, the other thieves closed round, with Packrat somewhere in the centre of the huddle. He rummaged around, and all at once, Aliana noticed that he was wearing the new Godsword outfit on top of his normal clothing, which consisted of layer upon layer of ragged shirts and tunics, which not only kept him warm, but created a positive labyrinth of pouches, pockets, hidden caches and secret hiding places.

'Just a minute . . . I know they're in here somewhere.' After a little more rummaging, he pulled out his closed fist in triumph. 'Now before you say anything, I didn't take these from the Citadel *or* the Temple. I found them on top of the wall when we climbed down into the Precincts.' Slowly, he opened his fist. 'What do you make of that little lot?'

There was a collective gasp from the assembled Ghosts. There, glistening in a colourful heap on Packrat's palm, were an assortment of jewels set in gold: rings, brooches, earrings, necklaces and bracelets. Some still had bits of skin and hair caught in them, others were encrusted with what looked suspiciously like dried blood, but still their glowing beauty shone through. Rubies like the first glimmer of sunrise, garnets the darker red of glowing embers, the dark mystery of sapphires and the bright star-twinkle of diamonds. Emeralds the colour of spring leaves, ice-blue topaz, the royal purple of amethyst; it looked as though Packrat held a handful of rainbows.

Aliana gasped. 'Myrial's teeth and toenails! Put them away, Packrat. Quick, before anyone sees them.' Yet when they vanished back into the mysterious recesses of his clothing, she felt an odd pang of loss. 'I *knew* you were up to something, when we were on that wall,' she said. 'Did you find them in that oddly-shaped rock with all the holes in it?'

Packrat looked chagrined. 'Bollocks. I thought no-one had noticed. But I could feel a whole lot more stuff in there. I only had time to grab that one handful. It seems as though the fiends like to pick up shiny things, like the magpies used to do on the midden.' Aliana gave him a sharp glance. He never talked about the midden. But he was too excited to notice. 'That must be their hoard, right up there on top. What if the Hierarch's ring is there?' His eyes gleamed. 'What if it's right *here*, in the handful I managed to take?'

He was right. Suddenly, Aliana knew what she must do. 'I'm going to have it out with Galveron,' she said, 'and find out why he betrayed us.'

'But you can't,' Alestan protested. 'He'll find out that I was spying on him.'

'So what if he does?' she shrugged. 'Under the circumstances, he's hardly in a position to protest about *us* being untrustworthy. While I'm there, I'll get a description of the ring from him. Then we'll see where we go from there. If we can produce it, we'll have that bloody Hierarch eating out of our hand.'

Twenty-eight

The heights of ambition

Aliana found Galveron sitting on a stool in Kaita's sickroom, having his wounded face tended. It was the first time she had seen him without the masking bandages, and she was surprised at how good looking he was, despite the livid scars on his forehead and right cheekbone where Kaita had done her best to stitch the torn flesh back together.

As she approached, the Commander half-turned his head to see her better, and earned a sharp reprimand from the Healer. 'Keep *still*, will you? You're worse than little Aukil for your fidgets. It'll only take a moment more.'

It did. Kaita bandaged his forehead again, where the skin had been so badly torn, but she left the wound on his cheekbone as it was. 'There are no signs of infection there, and it'll heal quicker if you let the air get at it,' she told him. 'Just try to keep it clean, will you? And don't go picking at those stitches.'

He opened his mouth to protest, but she cut him short. 'Yes, I know they itch, but you're just going to have to be brave and put up with it.'

'Yes, Healer Kaita,' he said meekly.

Galveron greeted Aliana with pleasure, though he looked puzzled when she asked if she could have a private word. He led her off up the passageway behind the guardroom, and she smiled grimly to herself at the irony. According to Alestan, this was the place he'd chosen to betray them to the Hierarch. A lamp had been left burning on a low stone shelf that looked somewhat like a bench sticking out of the wall. Galveron sat down, and patted the stony surface beside him. 'Well?' he asked, with a smile that was even more charming now that Aliana could see the rest of his face. 'What can I do for you?'

The thief took a deep breath. She had thought of several ways, some more tactful than others, in which she could broach her subject, but in the end she had decided it would save time, (though possibly not trouble), if she came right out with what she wanted to say. 'Alestan was eavesdropping when you were here talking to the Hierarch,' she told him flatly. 'He heard you betray us, after you had given me your word that you wouldn't.'

Galveron had turned very pale. 'Plague on him!' he snarled. 'How much did he hear? Was the little weasel listening the whole time?'

Aliana leapt to her feet. 'You've got a nerve, calling my brother names! I can think of a few for you, too. How could you do it? After everything I went through, how *could* you betray us? Do you think that just because we come from the Warrens, a promise doesn't count?'

His mouth tightened. 'Maybe it shouldn't, if you can't be trusted to behave in a civilised fashion.'

Aliana was so angry that she could barely speak. 'Alestan only followed you because he's responsible for the others, and he was trying to make sure that they'd be treated well. He doesn't make a habit of spying on people. He wasn't sure *you* could be trusted – and all you did was prove him right.'

'Don't you think she has a point, Galveron?' a voice said softly. Aliana looked round to see the Healer, who had approached unheard while they were arguing. 'By the way,' she added wryly, 'if you choose this place for any more private talks, you might want to keep the noise down a bit.'

Galveron glared at her. 'You didn't *have* to listen.'

'I could scarcely help it,' Kaita retorted. 'It's a damn good thing I sent my helpers out to take a break, or your private business would be on its way around the Temple by now.' She held up her hand to forestall before he could speak again. 'Considering the subject of your discussion, I thought I had better confess to something at this point. Aliana has very kindly been shielding me, but I expect she's aware that I knew what her brother had done. In fact, I gave him the fright of his life when I caught him.'

Galveron looked stunned. 'You *knew*? Then why the bloody blazes didn't you tell me, Kaita?'

'I had to use my judgement. I knew he wouldn't repeat what he had heard to anyone but his friends. He neither knows nor trusts anyone else in the Temple. And he gave me his word he wouldn't do it again.' She shrugged. 'I happen to believe that Alestan is a young man who'll keep *his* promises.'

Galveron groaned. 'I suppose I deserved that,' he admitted. 'You're right, Aliana. Whether your brother is at fault or not, I owe you and your friends an apology.' He spread his hands. 'But if Alestan heard the whole conversation, he must have known I couldn't help it. Really, it was your fault.'

'*Mine?*' Aliana bristled.

'I'm afraid so. It was just one of those things that couldn't be helped. If I had just brought you all in together the following day, we might have got away with it, but when you were so clever at creeping and dodging through the darkness, it made Gilarra suspicious. She wanted to know why I'd sent you, and not one of my men. She wanted to know why you were all wearing Godsword uniforms, and where your own clothes were. Because I very stupidly let something slip about you surviving the abominations out on the streets, she decided that you couldn't have been at the Sacrifice.' He sighed. 'She was just too astute, I'm afraid. She worked out for herself that you must have come from the Warrens, and when she asked me outright, what could I say? I have sworn an oath of loyalty to her, you know. Sooner or later she'd have been bound to find out I had lied to her, and then she wouldn't keep me as Commander. How could she? And it's only as Commander that I have any power to help you and your friends if things become difficult.' He held out his hands to her. 'Forgive me, please? At least I got her to let you stay, and I persuaded her to keep your identity secret from everyone else in the Temple.'

Aliana blinked. 'You *did?*'

'Didn't Alestan tell you that part?'

Now, her anger was directed at her brother. 'No, he bloody well didn't,' she growled. 'I'm sorry, Galveron. I didn't know that part.'

'Well, I'm glad that's settled,' Kaita said briskly. 'Now you can forgive each other, and start again with a clean slate.' She treated the two of them to her most flinty look. 'Can't you?'

'Yes.'

'Yes, we can.'

They looked at each other, and both smiled. Aliana, knowing that she would never find a better moment, took a deep breath. 'Galveron, there's something else you've got to know.'

'Don't mind me.' Kaita turned to go. 'I've done enough sticking my nose in where it doesn't belong for one day.'

Aliana waited until they were alone once more before she spoke. 'It's about the Hierarch's lost ring, Galveron. I think we can help her. She'll have to leave us alone then, won't she?'

The Commander's jaw had dropped. '*You* know where the ring is? But how can you possibly? The fiends took it.'

'I know where it might be,' Aliana said cautiously, and began to tell him about the climb into the Sacred Precincts, and how Packrat had discovered the predators' hoard. 'He only got a chance to grab a handful out of the hole,' she finished, 'but he says there was a whole lot more. So we wondered, would *you* recognise the Hierarch's ring if you saw it?'

Galveron's dumbfounded expression had changed to one of keen concentration. 'I would. As Lord Blade's second-in-command, I came into contact with the Hierarch – Zavahl, that is – pretty often. That ring is unmistakable.'

'Was it one of these?' Aliana rummaged in her pockets for Packrat's little hoard, which he had entrusted to her with the greatest reluctance. Galveron gasped as she spilled the jewels onto the stone bench, where they lay glistening in the lamplight. 'Holy Myrial!'

Feverishly, he rummaged through the glittering pile, disentangling the pieces one by one. Then with a sigh, he shook his head.

'It's not here, I'm afraid. I didn't think so, but it was worth a try. The stone is huge. We would have seen it right away.' He reached for the pile of gems. 'I'll just put these somewhere safe . . .'

'No you bloody won't!' Aliana knocked his hand away. 'These are going back to Packrat.'

'What? Now hold on, Aliana. They don't belong to Packrat.'

'Then who *do* they belong to?' she demanded. 'If they're from the fiends' hoard, then their previous owners are all dead. Packrat found these. He risked his life to get them. If it wasn't for him, you and the Hierarch could have been searching for that wretched ring for the rest of your lives, and you still wouldn't have come close. He didn't have to tell you, you know. Now at least you have a chance.' Her hand closed over the bright tangle of gold and jewels. 'These belong to Packrat now. You owe him that much.'

Galveron nodded reluctantly. 'All right.' He sat there quietly for a moment, deep in thought. 'Aliana,' he said at last. 'Do you think Packrat could show me where he found that stuff?'

She shook her head. 'I don't think wild horses with wings of fire could drag him up that cliff a second time. He's had enough, Galveron. We all have. We aren't like the folk who've been sheltering in here. We've been running, hiding, and fighting for our lives ever since those creatures first attacked. Packrat is a superb thief, but physically he's not in very good shape. You don't ever recover from a childhood as hard as his. I doubt that he could manage that cliff again even if he wanted to. Not so soon after the last time.'

'But this is so desperately important. You have no idea . . .' Galveron grasped her hands so hard that she grimaced with pain.

Aliana sighed. 'I could show you.'

'Aliana, no! Not after what you did last night. It wouldn't be fair. You haven't had time to recover.'

She shrugged. 'I'll be all right. Besides, there's no-one else. Alestan has a broken arm, Gelina can't climb to save her life, and you can't send the children. Tosel was your man – he was the best climber I've ever seen – but he's dead now. I'm your only option, take it or leave it.' She rounded on him fiercely. 'But I'll tell you something. If I do this thing, you and that wretched Hierarch will be in my debt for the rest of your lives. I want the *best* place in the Temple for my friends, and the *best* clothes, and the *best* food and blankets. And no-one had better ever look down on us again as Warrens scum!'

Galveron squeezed her hands. 'If they do,' he said, 'they'll answer to me.'

The Hierarch stared at the heap of jewels. Could it really be true? She hardly dared to hope. She turned back to Aliana. 'And your friend said there were lots more up there? He's really sure?'

The girl grinned pertly. 'If he says so, my Lady, then I believe him. When it comes to loot, Packrat doesn't make mistakes.'

Packrat! Gilarra felt a curl of distaste in her stomach when she thought of the filthy, unkempt wretch with the sly eyes. She didn't relish being in his debt. But the hope held out to her was so shining, so marvellous, that it tempered her repugnance. Why, she could even put up with this bold-faced girl. Once she had her ring back, and was Hierarch in truth, she need no longer be dependent on such creatures.

By the time Gilarra had pulled her thoughts back to the here-and-now, Galveron was speaking again. 'I told her we ought to put it off until tomorrow, when she's had more time to get over last night's little adventure, but she won't listen.'

'Well, you've seen the sky for yourself,' Aliana said. 'The clouds are quite high today, and there's even reflected light from the snow on the ground. This may well be the brightest day we'll get for a long time. And I don't want to wait, Galveron. I don't want this hanging over me – apart from the fact that once Alestan hears about it, I'm going to get my ears chewed off. Being cooped up in here day after day being nagged at by a worried brother is *not* my idea of a good time.'

Gilarra's heart leapt. 'If you feel that way about it, then I think you should go as soon as you can,' she said, 'and your point about the sky is well taken. Does Kaita say you're fit now?'

Aliana nodded. 'She says I'm very resilient.'

'But she didn't know why you were asking her,' objected Galveron.

'Surely, Galveron, Aliana is the best judge of whether she's fit or not,' Gilarra said firmly. She knew that her judgement was being affected by the fact that she was desperate to find out whether the ring was really there, but she couldn't help it. Besides, the girl would take no harm. These street-urchins were tough little creatures.

Galveron shrugged. 'Very well. If I'm to be outvoted by the pair of you, we'd better break the happy news to your brother and get ready no leave. It's getting close to noon already, and I don't want—'

'Just a minute!' the Hierarch interrupted. 'What do you mean, *we*? You certainly won't be going, Galveron. I have no intention of risking you again.'

The Commander's eyes hardened. 'I certainly am going. If Aliana wants to put herself under such a strain so soon after yesterday, someone will be needed to keep an eye on her.'

'Then someone else can,' said Gilarra dismissively. 'It's not so long since you were wounded too, or had you forgotten? Besides, you are the Godsword Commander. You can not be spared. Yesterday's escapade was bad enough, but I won't have you making a habit of such jaunts. It's not your place to put yourself at risk. That's what your men are for.'

'That may be true, my Lady: nevertheless, I'm going this time,' Galveron said firmly. 'Have you forgotten the secret nature of this mission? How can you possibly send anyone else? No-one can know that the ring is missing.'

Damn him! He's right.

Gilarra sighed. 'Very well,' she said. 'It seems that I have no choice. All that remains is for me to wish you good luck.'

When Galveron and the thief had left her, Gilarra let her anger show in a scowl.

Dear Myrial, what am I going to do? I can't keep letting him undermine my authority like this. Yet how would we manage without him as Commander? His men worship him, and the people have such respect for him.

She realised, with dismay, that if it ever came to a real conflict between them, she wouldn't stand a chance.

Maybe I should let him take as many of these stupid risks as he likes. Somehow we would learn to manage without him. He's a fine man and I would hate to lose him, but it would certainly solve a lot of problems for me.

Godsword Commander and thief threaded their way through the Sacred Precincts and emerged from between the artisans' houses, close to the black maw of the tunnel entrance. The hairs on the back of Galveron's neck prickled. Surely they were being watched. Anxiously he scanned the towering walls of the canyon, though he knew the exercise was futile. There must be hundreds, maybe thousands of ledges and niches weathered into the soft, golden stone. The winged abominations could be hiding anywhere.

A sharp elbow poked him in the ribs. Aliana had been edgy ever since the unpleasant confrontation with her brother, before she left. Galveron could have strangled the man, for upsetting her at such a critical time, even though he knew it was love that had made Alestan so determined not to let her go.

The elbow poked him again. 'Come on, stupid,' she hissed. 'I told you they would be dormant now, but we'd better make the most of it. We don't have forever.'

They chose the western side of the tunnel mouth, where Aliana and her companions had climbed down before, and ducked into the shadow beneath the cliff. Galveron swallowed hard and glanced at the sky. They had picked the best possible day to make this attempt. As usual there were clouds, but they were high and racing in the strong wind; hurtling across the sky in ever-changing patterns. It was one of the brightest days that the Godsword had seen for a long time, and the snow was melting on the ground.

'Sssst!' hissed an impatient voice from somewhere above him. The nimble-footed thief was already scaling the cliff, going up the rough surface like spider up a wall: a quick upward scramble for a few yards, then freeze and vanish among the shadows until it was time to move again. Galveron watched, marvelling at her skill. After a time she found a deep ledge and disappeared from sight. A rope came slithering down, uncoiling as it fell. He jumped back as the last few feet unravelled, beautifully judged to reach the ground. Up above, Aliana's white face, framed in its short, tawny curls, appeared like a star in the gloom. A slender arm beckoned. Galveron, his pride and the reputation of the Godswords at stake, spat on his hands and began to climb.

It seemed to take an eternity before he finally hauled himself level with Aliana's ledge. Panting, he swung himself up onto the wet surface and sat down gratefully, rubbing with burning hands at arms that felt as if they had been pulled from their sockets. Aliana watched him, grinning, her eyes sparkling with mirth. Galveron, short of breath with which to comment, contented himself with an obscene gesture.

'And the same to you with bells on.' The girl hauled up the rope, unfastened it, and slung it over her shoulder. 'You don't climb badly, for a flatfooted Godsword,' she told him condescendingly, 'but you want to use your legs more. There's plenty of little ledges and cracks'll take your weight. Have a rest now, while I do the next bit.'

Before Galveron could answer she was gone again on her upward scramble, one foot swinging perilously close to his ear as she searched for a hold. After a quick scan of the skies, the Godsword settled back, determined to make the most of his respite. He refused to complete the next section puffing and blowing like a broken-down carthorse. He was damned if he'd give that brat of a thief the satisfaction!

It turned out that he needed all of his resolve. Four times they repeated the climb, with Aliana skimming ahead to secure the rope, and the Godsword Commander hauling himself up behind her.

There were times when pride was all that kept him going, and when he finally reached the top of the cliff, it was the most welcome sight he had ever seen in his life.

When Galveron pulled himself over the edge, all he could do was collapse for a moment, until his breath came back and strength and feeling returned to his stiff arms. Though he had rolled over on his back to see the sky, it was doubtful whether he could have dealt with an approaching threat just then. At any moment he was expecting some mocking gibe from Aliana, and it was only when it did not come that he realised she was not in sight. Forgetting his fatigue, the Godsword sprang to his feet. After a moment, Aliana emerged from behind an eminence, picking her way carefully over the uneven ground. She dropped out of sight again, then materialised right at his feet, popping up out of nowhere like a rabbit from a hole.

'Why didn't you wait for me?' Galveron demanded.

'What for? We don't have all bloody day, you know.' She planted her hands on her hips. 'Now listen here. Thieving's my territory, we agreed that. Up here I outrank you, so shut up and listen.'

Galveron was too good a soldier not to see the sense in this. Reluctantly he nodded, and was rewarded by a flash of brilliant smile. She leaned close so that he could hear her over the shrill whine of the wind. 'Right, then. We should leave the rope tied here in case we need a quick escape, so you'd better stay and guard it. It's only sensible,' she added quickly, interrupting the protest that sprang to his lips. 'There's no sign of those cursed abominations now, but you know how fast they can appear. If they take the rope we're buggered. It's an awful long way to jump.'

The Godsword sighed. 'All right. But be careful. And don't stray out of bowshot.'

Aliana shrugged. 'How far is that? But don't worry. Their hiding-place isn't far away. I'll be back before you know it.' Without waiting for an answer she ducked away again, vanishing without a trace among the labyrinthine dips and ridges.

Galveron unstrapped his crossbow from his back and, turning where he stood, surveyed the skies. He could see no trace of the enemy, but he worried none the less. Though it appeared to be true that the winged horrors were sleeping and dormant during the brightest part of the day, that still seemed a slender thread to hang their lives upon in the clouded gloom of Myrial's perpetual rain. He looked out across the Sacred Precincts, remembering the great square before the Temple packed with the entire population of Tiarond as they attended the Hierarch's sacrifice. In his nightmares, he still saw the blood and heard the screaming as the demons fell upon the defenceless townsfolk.

Don't look down there. Don't think about it.

Scanning the skies instead, he settled down to wait for Aliana's return. Where the blazes had she gone? Could he trust her? Would she be all right on her own? He hoped that he had not made a mistake in letting her leave him.

Aliana, in the meantime, had found what she was looking for. There was Packrat's odd-shaped rock, looking like a cloaked and kneeling figure. She soon found the deep hole that Packrat had described. Her quick glance swept the surrounding skies and the mountain peak above her for any signs of movement. The air was cooling as the day grew older, and she noticed that the dark clouds were beginning to mass again, just as they had done the last time she was here. She cursed under her breath. Why hadn't she realised that the weather might have a fairly regular pattern over the mountain and the canyon below?

Never mind that. Just hurry.

Having assured herself that all was quiet, she turned back to the rock, took a deep breath, and plunged her hand inside.

Her arm went in up to the elbow. At the bottom, her groping fingers found the hard, cold shapes she sought. Working quickly, emptying the first aperture then moving on to the surrounding holes, Aliana pulled out fistful after glittering fistful and stuffed them into the bag tied round her waist. There was no time now to pick through the hoard in search of the Hierarch's ring. She would have to take all she could find, and hope for the best – and just as well, too. Until it had been cleaned, her find would not bear much close examination. Many pieces, taken from corpses, were still encrusted with the blood of their previous owners. Others came with hanks of hair and bits of stinking carrion flesh wedged between the dull, stained gems. More than once, she recoiled to find a ring with a decaying finger, still clasped within its loop of gold.

At last there were no holes left to clear. 'Well, if it's not here, I'm damned if I know where it is,' Aliana muttered. Balancing the weight of the heavy bag that swung from her waist, she hurried back to the edge of the cliff, where Galveron stood on guard.

The Godsword looked pleased to see her. 'About time you—*DOWN!*'

Aliana flung herself to the ground. She heard the whine of the crossbow bolt as it passed over her head, almost parting her hair. Behind her she heard the wet crunch of a body impacting with the ground. A glance over her shoulder showed her two more swooping winged shapes, coming in low and fast.

'Go!' Galveron shouted, rewinding the crossbow with feverish haste. This was no time to argue. She made a dive for the rope and began to scramble down, hand over hand, as quickly as she dared. Above her the bowstring twanged as the Godsword fired again. She heard a shrill scream. He'd wounded one, at least, then. An instant later the rope was almost jerked from her hands as Galveron followed her, sliding down insanely fast. Aliana winced. He would take the skin right off his hands! Clearly, the danger wasn't over. The other fiend must have gone to alert the rest.

With Galveron catching her up too quickly, Aliana let go of the rope and dropped the last dozen feet, sliding down the sloping stable roof and feeling the impact jar through her knees and spine as she landed. Within seconds Galveron was also down. 'Run. We don't have much time.'

Together they fled into the maze of narrow laneways between the artisans' homes, even as the skies above them began to darken with winged shapes. There was no chance whatsoever of them reaching the Basilica, or even the Citadel. Aliana scanned the area frantically for somewhere they could take shelter. 'Not there,' she yelled at Galveron, as he headed for the nearest of the little houses. 'We need somewhere without windows.'

For a moment he hesitated, looking about him, then he took a sharp turn to the right, and headed straight across the open green. Aliana glanced back over her shoulder, and from somewhere, found an extra spurt of speed.

Oh, Galveron. I hope you know what you're doing.

'Through here!' He yanked her into a long, low building before she had the chance to protest about its windows. Then she saw the door at the far end, and followed him down. The daylight was blocked out behind her as the first winged demon entered. Windows shattered as more of them took their own route in. Galveron shoved her in front of him, straight through the further door, and she went headfirst down a shallow flight of steps. All in a split-second, an image of Alestan's bound and splinted arm flashed into her head, and she tucked in her limbs and head as best she could and let herself roll down to the bottom. Above her, she heard a slam as the door closed, and the grating sound of iron bolts sliding into place.

She sat up, her head spinning. After a moment she heard the scrape of flint on metal, and a light blossomed around her as a small lamp was lit. Galveron came down the steps towards her. 'Are you all right?' he said softly.

Aliana nodded. 'Apart from a new lot of bruises to add to my collection. I'm just grateful to be alive.' For the first time she looked around her, and to her surprise, saw a complex tangle of piping, shining metal vats, the dark arches of fireplaces, and a series of wooden tubs and casks against the further wall. Close by, near the foot of the steps, the lamplight slid over the curves of bottles, all stacked neatly in racks. 'Where in Myrial's name are we, anyway?'

'The Precincts' brewhouse.' Galveron grinned. 'We may not be able to get back to the Basilica until it's light tomorrow, but we can light the fires in here, and if we want to drown our sorrows, we've come to the right place.'

Aliana listened to the pounding and scratching on the door above, and shuddered. 'Not with those fiends so near. I wouldn't dare.'

'Don't worry.' He grinned at her. 'Brewmaster Jivarn is – was – very jealous of his secrets. If any place is intruder-proof, this is it. And I don't suppose there's any food down here, but there'll be plenty of water to get us through the night.'

In a short time they had fires lit in one of the three great fireplaces that ran down the length of the building. Though the temptation had been to light all three and really warm the place up, they had decided to conserve the coal supply to last them all through the night. The warmth was welcome, and Aliana huddled as close to the fire as she could get, actually sitting on the edge of the high hearthstone. Galveron sat down beside her, and blew out the lamp now that the flames were providing enough light. 'That's better.' With a sigh of relief, he stretched out his legs. 'Dear Myrial, but I ache! Another climb like that would finish me off.'

'Try doing it twice in two days, *then* come back and tell me you ache.'

By now, the pounding and scratching on the cellar door had ceased, and they had both begun to hope that the creatures had given up, though Aliana couldn't shake off the uneasy feeling that they must be looking for another way in. She hoped that Galveron was right about this place being so safe. She decided that she needed something to take her mind off the predators. 'Why don't we take a look at our ill-gotten gains?' she suggested.

They spilled out the glittering contents of the bag into the little pool of firelight on the hearthstone, and began to sort through the gruesome contents, washing the blood off in a basin of warm water as they went. Aliana kept getting distracted. She had never seen so many beautiful things in all her life. Galveron, however, was sifting through the pile with care and concentration, his mind fixed on the single item that he sought. Suddenly, he gave a cry of triumph. There, in the palm of his hand, lay a ring with an enormous red stone which glowed as though he had picked up an ember from the fire.

Aliana looked at the ring, and to her surprise, felt nothing but disgust. So this was what they had risked their lives for. This lovely bauble was what made a Hierarch. Not ability, or intelligence, or strength, or leadership, or skill at arms. Just this, and endless tradition. She looked up from the stone to Galveron's face, and the scars he had earned fighting against the enemy.

You'd make a better leader than that Gilarra will ever be.

She couldn't leave the idea alone. 'Galveron,' she said softly. 'I know this goes against tradition, but many traditions change with time and need . . .'

He looked at her sharply. 'What goes against tradition?'

She hesitated, then plunged on. 'Both Alestan and Kaita said that Gilarra is having difficulty coping with all the responsibility, and everybody in the Temple seems to look to you. You have the stone now. You hold the power. If you kept it, couldn't *you* be Hierarch?'

His eyes widened, and his fist closed tightly over the glowing stone. 'Don't be ridiculous! I'm the Godsword Commander. My loyalty is to Gilarra.' But to Aliana's mind, he spoke a little too loudly and too fast, and she noticed that his eyes remained thoughtful long after he had put the ring away. She knew better than to mention it again. After all, he had all night before him to think about what she had said.

And who knows? Maybe tomorrow, Gilarra will be in for a surprise.

Twenty-Nine

One Chance for Redemption

It was a nervous group who waited in the cold darkness of the Maskulu's newly excavated tunnel. Ahead and above, they could hear the grinding of his diamond jaws as he pulverised his way through the last few yards of rock beneath Skreeva's dwelling. The sound was setting Elion's teeth on edge, and he could well have done without it. He was already tense and apprehensive enough. So, apparently, were his companions. Kaz crouched in the tunnel, flicking his tail from side to side like an uneasy cat. Bailen, perched on the firedrake's back, was frowning as he listened with his mind, as well as with his ears. He was awaiting word from Vaure, in the lakeside settlement, who probably had the least enviable task of all of them at present. She was with the healers, watching over the unconscious Dessil, while at the same time fielding a whole spate of awkward questions from the Archimandrite.

Ailie stood beside the firedrake. Her face, with its worried frown, was pale and haggard in the eldritch light of the glim. It was unheard of for a villager to interfere in the affairs of the Loremasters. If this plan failed, she stood to lose everything. And she wasn't the only one, Elion thought grimly. This business with the Alva would force an immediate confrontation between Cergorn and the renegades. Within the next hour, not only would the fates of Zavahl and Toulac be decided, but the immediate future of the Shadowleague hung in the balance.

And what am I doing here? I never meant to get caught up in this!

Yet there was no running away from the events that were now

unfolding. Amaurn or Cergorn? Every Loremaster would have to make that decision before the day was out. He was only being forced to make it sooner than most. When Bailen had disabled him, he had been astonished to find that Blade, of all people, had such loyal and wholehearted support among the Shadowleague. But more surprises were to follow. When the confrontation took place between Veldan and the former Godsword Commander, Kaz, unknown to the two protagonists, had been relaying their conversation back to Elion as it happened. He had been as shocked as Veldan to discover that Blade was none other than Amaurn the renegade, but as time went on he had found himself being swayed, just as she had, by the force of his arguments. By the time the Moldan had reopened the tunnel into the cavern at the insistence of Veldan, who had been emphatic about coming back for him, Elion had already made his own decision.

And the irony is that Cergorn, by the way he acted towards us on our return, has made us into renegades himself. He proved his own undoing, as far as I'm concerned. Whether he had agreed with us or not in the end, if he had only been willing to listen to what we had to say, I would have been much more likely to have supported him now.

Elion knew that he was still smarting from the monstrous unfairness of being blamed for Thirishri's loss. Though the Archimandrite's very obvious worry and distress were mitigating factors, a leader could not be permitted to let such personal considerations cloud his judgement. It might not be fair, but it was the dark side of the power and prestige: the price that had to be paid.

And will this new incarnation of Blade be any better?

It was an uneasy thought. Only time would tell.

Elion glanced across at Amaurn, and found him looking, not up ahead to where the Moldan worked, but at Veldan, who stood nearby. She must be talking privately to Kaz, for her eyes were far away, and she was completely oblivious of the scrutiny. There was an odd, speculative look in those cold, grey eyes, and a shiver of alarm went though the Loremaster. What was the purpose of such intense scrutiny by a man who was known as a cold-blooded killer?

Plague, pox and pestilence! He can't possibly fancy Veldan, can he? When they were talking he said she looked exactly like her mother.

Then Elion gasped as a new thought struck him.

No! Don't be ridiculous. He couldn't be! After all, it's her mother she resembles, not him. But no-one knows who Veldan's father is . . .

Firmly, he put the whole idea out of his head. It obviously hadn't occurred to Veldan, and there was no way *he* was going down that road. Why, the whole notion was ludicrous. He was letting his imagination run away with him, and besides, it was none of his business. Nevertheless, in that moment, he would have given a fortune just to know what the would-be leader of the Shadowleague was thinking.

After all that, I can't believe I didn't tell her.

Amaurn wondered what had become of his courage. When he had set out to talk to Veldan, he had meant to let her know what had happened between himself and Aveole. He had thought to tell her about his Magefolk origins, and where Kaz had come from. And hadn't he also meant to tell her that she surely must be his daughter, conceived on the night of their final parting, when he and Aveole had known that they would never see each other again?

It wasn't time to do that. I don't have her trust yet. Why should she believe me?

Or was I just afraid? What if I'm wrong? What if there was someone else, someone to whom Aveole turned for consolation after I was gone?

To survive the long, hard years of his exile, he had been forced to put Aveole out of his mind, partly because he had missed her so desperately, and he couldn't afford to have that weaken him, and partly because he knew that she would hate and despise what he had become. Only the sight of Veldan's face had brought her back to him, and with her memory came the recollection of the innocent idealist he once had been.

Well, this was not the time to be thinking about such things. Amaurn pulled his attention firmly back to his current situation.

The business with Veldan would keep until he had the leisure for private affairs – though the fates only knew when that might be. Right now he needed to concentrate on gaining control of the Shadowleague. Wasn't that what he had been working towards all these years?

'I'm almost through.' The tidings, spoken in the Moldan's mental voice that sounded like gravel and broken glass, came as a huge relief.

Amaurn took a deep, shuddering breath. 'Then let's do it.'

A spear of light pierced the darkness of the tunnel, as the final barrier crumbled away. Instantly, Maskulu's clustered eyes responded, overriding the spatial information received from the vibrissae that protruded from each section of his body. Without warning he exploded into motion, propelling himself up and out through the floor of the Alva's dwelling, the others at his heels. Amaurn followed him quickly, scrambling over the sloping ramp of rubble that the Moldan had created to reach the chamber above.

The house was situated on the wooded hillside, not far from Veldan's home. From the outside, the hemispherical dwelling looked like part of a wasp's nest; from the inside, the papery walls of the single chamber looked delicate and translucent. But Skreeva's home was constructed of chewed pulp and the Alva's saliva, which dried the resulting material to a hard, tough surface, and the edifice was much more robust than it seemed.

Skreeva was in the corner, in a tangle of leafy vegetation which had been planted directly into the ground. Silken threads formed a nest among the branches, and there she sat, seemingly at rest. She barely turned to look at the intruders who were erupting into her home from underground, and her chitinous face and bulbous, compound eyes conveyed no expression.

Amaurn emerged behind the Moldan, who moved aside to let him pass. The Alva's body glistened emerald green. She fastened those glittering cold eyes on him, and moved her head slightly, so that light flashed along the edge of her gleaming mandibles. Though she scarcely moved, the air between herself and those who confronted her was charged with menace. 'Amaurn. After all this time, you have the temerity to return. Cergorn will be very pleased to see you. He has never forgotten your unfinished business.'

'He might also be interested to learn that *your* loyalties lie elsewhere, Alva,' Amaurn replied levelly. 'For whom did you kidnap Zavahl? Was it the Dragonfolk, perchance? They would be the obvious choice.'

'What difference can it make to tell you now?' Skreeva replied carelessly. 'Their Seer is vital to their race. They wanted him back, where he would be safe, and it is only right that they should have him.'

'The Shadowleague needs him here,' Amaurn said flatly, in a tone that brooked no argument. 'He has knowledge vital to the restoration of the Curtain Walls. You must bring him back, Skreeva. The entire future is at stake; not only for the Dragonfolk, but for all of us.'

'I cannot. I gave the Dragonfolk my word.' Though tension was mounting among the watchers, Skreeva's voice and the gleaming, triangular mask of her inhuman face remained devoid of all emotion. She had remained utterly still during their conversation, like a statue carved in jade. 'The Seer will be returned to the Dragons. If you want him, you must negotiate with them.'

Amaurn pinned the Alva with his compelling grey gaze. 'Recall your Dierkan servants now. I will not ask again.'

'Or what?' This time, there was a touch of mockery in the Alva's voice.

'OR THIS!' The impatient Maskulu was done with debate. Without warning, he launched himself forward, and suddenly the Alva was transformed. She sprang from her corner, her glistening wings extended like a rustling cloak, her formidable forelegs, with their saw-toothed edges sharp as daggers, extended to grasp and kill. As the Moldan charged forward she leapt to one side, one foreleg shearing down to slice through a section of his rippling fringe of legs, while the other darted at his face, extinguishing a cluster of his eyes.

Maskulu barely faltered, though his gait had developed a perceptible lurch to one side. Inexorable as an avalanche, he charged through the deadly barrier of the weaving forefeet to close with his adversary, and with an earthshaking crash, the titanic protagonists met in the centre of the chamber. Skreeva staggered from the impact, her elaborate jaws thrust out to snap at his face, her razored forelegs scraping and screeching on the Moldan's scaly carapace as she attempted to gain a hold. Occasionally, luck would favour her, and she would slice through another section of legs, interfering with her enemy's grip on the ground, and the force of his attack.

Maskulu was trying to lunge forward, his terrifying mandibles extended to tear and crush, but the Alva's forelegs held him back, pushing him away from her softer body. Her massive, muscled hind legs were planted firmly into the ground, giving her leverage against even his tremendous strength.

For what seemed an eternity, they grappled back and forth in a deadly dance, each looking for an opening, each seeking to be the first to gain even a small advantage. As they reeled and twisted, they blundered into the side of the chamber, which was not designed for such abuse. Moldan and Alva went crashing through the wall and burst into the hillside clearing beyond, as the house collapsed around the others in a blizzard of papery fragments.

As if nothing had happened, the fight went on among the trees, but clearly, Skreeva was tiring now, and as she weakened, her peril increased. She could only survive as long as she could hold the Moldan at bay. The lesser fear of Cergorn discovering that she was a Dragonfolk agent was lost in larger concerns. In fear for her very life, she took a desperate gamble, and called for help.

Damn!

Amaurn ground his teeth in frustration. The last thing he needed now was the Archimandrite's interference. Veldan exchanged a glance with him and scrambled up onto the firedrake's back, in front of Bailen, and they moved forward to shield Ailie, while Elion closed the distance between them. In the meantime, the Moldan and the Alva continued their deadly struggle, neither one of them daring to break the deadlock, in case they gave the other the advantage.

'Cergorn comes!' Each one of them heard Vaure's warning. At full gallop, it would take the centaur only moments to reach them. Soon afterwards, the sound of rapid hoofbeats could be heard approaching through the woods, and the Archimandrite hurtled into the clearing. The phoenix was in hot pursuit, streaking like a comet between the ranks of trees. 'Quick!' she shouted. 'He has outstripped his guards. This is your chance!'

Across the clearing, there was the sound of splintering wood, as Moldan and Alva, still locked in combat, crashed into a tree, but their struggle was ignored now. All eyes were on the meeting taking place between Cergorn and Amaurn.

'*You!*' Leaves and clots of earth flew up as the centaur came ploughing to a halt in front of Amaurn. 'So, traitor, you have returned at last to face your punishment.' His eyes slid past the renegade to his other Loremasters: Veldan, Elion, Bailen and Kazairl. His eyes lingered on Veldan, and he spat upon the ground. 'Like mother like daughter,' he snarled. 'You corrupt everything you touch, Amaurn.' Reaching behind his shoulder, he drew an enormous broadsword from its sheath.

Good. He's so much against using the knowledge we guard, that he didn't have the sense to fetch one of the advanced projectile weapons from the forbidden armoury. Fool.

Amaurn called out quickly in mindspeech, addressing his companions behind him. 'Don't interfere unless the guards come. This is between him and me. Don't soil your hands and consciences with the blood of an Archimandrite.' They would obey, he knew. He had convinced them to follow him, but he was yet to win their loyalty.

Without warning, the centaur was moving, and there was no more time for speech.

Cergorn was fast. Amaurn barely had time to unsheath his own weapon and get it raised to block the first stroke. He caught the broadsword on his blade, deflecting the blow, though the power of it drove him to his knees. For an instant he feared that his sword would be broken by the heavier weapon, but it was of Smithmaster Agella's forging: sharp and strong, and capable of withstanding more abuse than most. Before the centaur could strike again, Amaurn jabbed at his underside, forcing him to leap away. Despite his cumbersome appearance, he moved so quickly that the sword tip only made a shallow cut across his ribs and belly, instead of a disembowelling slash. Nevertheless, first blood had gone to Amaurn. He could waste no time in following up his advantage. The guards and other Loremasters would be here at any moment, and then it would be too late.

Cergorn wheeled and came charging back towards him, the massive broadsword cleaving down through the air. Amaurn hurled himself aside, and the great blade went whistling past his shoulder to embed itself deep in the forest floor. He rolled, almost cutting off his leg with his own sword, and scrambled to his feet while his opponent was wrenching the broadsword loose from the ground. He moved in fast and low behind the centaur, aiming for the hind legs in an attempt to cripple, but Cergorn was ready. One hind hoof lashed out, with deadly accuracy and force. Pain exploded up Amaurn's arm, and his sword went flying right across the clearing as the blow struck it neatly from his hand.

One mistake. And one is all it takes.

He had only fought humans for the last twenty years. He had forgotten that the power of a horse, coupled with the intelligence of a man, were such a lethal combination.

But there was still a chance. The other battle, the one between the Alva and the Moldan, passed close to Cergorn, making the centaur turn his head for a moment. Gathering himself, Amaurn made a desperate leap, and gained Cergorn's back, in a move that sent agony shooting through his injured hand. The centaur bellowed a curse and reared, but Amaurn managed to get one arm across his throat, and clung on desperately while his free hand groped for his knife.

With a roar of rage, the centaur dropped to his knees and rolled, intending to crush and maim. Amaurn barely flung himself off in time, though a flailing hoof caught him a glancing blow beneath the ribs and winded him so that he could barely stagger upright.

In a shower of fallen leaves, Cergorn scrambled to his feet. With a laugh, he pointed his weapon at his disarmed and fallen foe. 'I won't kill you now,' he said with quiet menace. 'Not unless you try something really stupid. It will be done in front of the assembled Shadowleague, as it should have been before. You deferred your execution for twenty years, traitor, but the time has come at last.'

Breathless with pain, Amaurn backed away. There was no sign of his sword. It was lost in the deep leaf litter. Beyond him, he heard Veldan's sharp intake of breath, and from the other side the sound of voices and running feet. That must be the guards, and other Loremasters, on their way at last.

Suddenly there was a fiery blur, and Vaure swooped down, making the centaur jump back in startlement as he caught the motion from the corner of his eye. She burrowed down into the leaves and tried to snatch Amaurn's fallen sword up in her talons, to give it back to him, but it was far too heavy, and dragged her to the ground.

'I'll remember that—' Cergorn's voice was cut off in mid-sentence. Amaurn had gauged the position of the sword and leapt that way. Lifting his blade, the centaur thundered after him – just as the Moldan, sensing that Skreeva was growing weaker, managed to push himself beneath her and lever her off her feet. She went crashing over, her great wings unfurling like fans, with the Moldan's weight on top. Green lifeblood spurted as the diamond mandibles closed around the Alva's head. There was a horrible crunch as her exoskeleton gave way, and the great toothed forelegs thrashed wildly in her death throes. One of them caught the charging centaur right across the midriff, where his human torso joined the body of the horse. With a howl he dropped his sword and crumpled, blood spurting from the dreadful injuries, his limbs folding under him at awkward angles. As he toppled, there came the dry crack of a foreleg snapping.

The other Loremasters, a group of assorted beings, human and otherwise, came running up from the settlement, but faltered at the sight of such carnage: the mangled body of the gigantic Alva, and their leader lying in a pool of his own blood. There was a stunned silence as they looked in horror at the bodies. Veldan was the first to come to life. She slid down from the firedrake's back and ran across to Cergorn, feeling the side of his throat for a pulse. 'Fetch a healer, quick,' she shouted. 'He's still alive!'

There was a sudden stir among the crowd as mental messages flashed forth, summoning not only a healer, but Syvilda too. At the same time, the guards made a doubtful move towards Amaurn, who by this time had joined Veldan beside Cergorn's inert form – and stopped when they found themselves face to face with the titanic, nightmare form of the Moldan.

'Listen to me, all you Loremasters!' he cried in mindspeech. 'Cergorn is hurt, and cannot lead. But there is one here who would have become Archimandrite many years ago, had Cergorn not defeated him. Perhaps now, his time has finally come. For the present at least, consider Amaurn for the leadership of the Shadowleague. When first he made his challenge, so long ago, we were not ready to embrace his plans, and he was condemned by Cergorn to a traitor's death. Now, in these chaotic times, I say to you that his revolutionary ideas may be all that will save us, and the world we are pledged to protect, from utter disaster.'

The Moldan's move was bold indeed, to be suggesting such things at this moment. Due to the current crisis, the resident population of Gendival was very much depleted, with most of its Loremasters scattered far and wide around the troubled lands. A goodly proportion of those who remained were old enough to remember Amaurn, and many of them had sympathised with him at the time, or supported him outright. There might never be a better opportunity to win them over – but how would they react to all the violence that had taken place?

At that moment the healers arrived, and with them Syvilda. Tears were streaming down her lovely face, and she looked on Amaurn with repugnance and contempt. 'Scum!' she spat. 'If anything happens to him, I'll kill you myself.'

Amaurn shrugged. 'He was the one who sought my death, not the other way around.'

She turned her back on him and knelt by the inert form of Cergorn, but as the healers and their helpers prepared to carry him away, she faced the assembled Loremasters once more. 'Don't be fooled by him. He's nothing but a heartless, murdering bastard, who twists everything he touches. We should have killed him long ago, when we had the chance. If you let him, he'll bring down the Shadowleague in ruin.' She turned her cold gaze on Veldan. 'After all we've done for you and Kazairl over the years, I might have expected more loyalty from you. But blood will out, they say.'

After Syvilda had left with the healers and their frail burden, there was a long silence. The thoughts of the Loremasters, unshielded, came clearly to Amaurn. Most of his covert supporters, who remembered him from the past, were joyous at his return despite Syvilda's words. Many of the others had been concerned about Cergorn's policy of inaction, but they hadn't counted on replacing their Archimandrite with a merciless killer.

While a frantic spate of thoughts sped back and forth between them, Amaurn looked down the hillside to the peaceful settlement at the lake's edge, the place he had dreamed of for so many years, then back at the clearing, with its gore, its gouged and trampled ground; its broken trees and the mutilated body of the Alva. Uncertainty assailed him, and for the first time, his brutal and merciless acts of the last two decades appeared in a new, and different light. What if the doubters were right?

'You don't have to do it that way in the future.' The voice had come from Veldan. 'There's no undoing those dreadful deeds, and you'll pay for them all eventually, in one way or another. So you should. But if you really seek redemption, saving a world isn't such a bad way to start. Besides, the Shadowleague won't let you go around acting like Lord Blade, and there are plenty of us with the power to deal with you if you try. But maybe we've had it soft for too long, hiding here in Gendival and hugging our secrets to ourselves. You may ruffle a few feathers, but a certain amount of ruthlessness is what we need right now – in moderation, of course.'

Amaurn gave her a wry smile. 'Ruthlessness in moderation? Now there's a rallying cry.' He paused. 'And you? Could you forgive a cold-blooded killer so easily?'

Gravely, she shook her head. 'No. But I'll work on it. That's probably as much as you can ask of any of us right now. But everyone should have at least one chance to atone for their past.'

'I'll do my best – if they give me the chance.' Amaurn got to his feet, and faced the accusing eyes of the Shadowleague. 'I regret the death of Skreeva,' he said, 'but it had to happen. She was an agent of the Dragonfolk, and though Cergorn was not convinced that the human brought in by Loremaster Veldan bore the spirit of the Seer Aethon, the Dragons had no doubts, and nor have I. In Aethon's ancient knowledge lies the only slender hope we have of unlocking the secrets of the Curtain Walls. If we had allowed him to go south to Zaltaigla, we would have lost that chance for good.'

'But . . .' Vaure spoke hesitantly, from the crowd. 'I thought you didn't *want* to restore the Curtain walls. Surely you always used to say that it was wrong to pen up the inhabitants of this world like cattle.'

Amaurn nodded. 'Maybe it is. And maybe later we can arrange for some kind of information flow, or even the passage of occasional people, between the lands. But we've seen what is happening now that the Curtain Walls are failing. Whether or not we approve of them in political or moral terms, we've found out the hard way that they are an integral and essential part of our world, and we need them to keep our environment in balance.'

'So Cergorn was right?' someone asked.

Amaurn felt, in that instant, the future hanging in the balance. 'He was right about maintaining the Curtain Walls, but I firmly believe that he was wrong to withhold so much information from the people of this world. With greater understanding, they might have been better equipped to deal with the various calamities they're facing now. But this is neither the time nor the place to debate such grave matters. Our first task must be to ensure that we *have* a future. Only then can we discuss what form it will take.' He took a deep breath. 'For the duration of this crisis the Shadowleague must have a leader who is prepared to get things done, and make some very hard decisions. Back me now, until we've set our world to rights. Then, if Cergorn survives, and if he or anyone else wants to become Archimandrite, we can take another vote.'

He was surprised to find that he meant it. As Lord Blade, he had taken what he wanted by force, and achieved his aims by any means he could. As Archimandrite of the Shadowleague, he wanted the respect and support of his Loremasters, or his victory was hollow.

Sensing the waiting silence around him, Amaurn tore himself away from his thoughts. 'Well?' he challenged. 'Are you with me?'

In mindspeech and aloud, the Loremasters voiced their hesitant acceptance. Though the response was not as wholehearted as he might have wished, he knew it was as much as he could rightfully expect, and more than he deserved. There was no undoing what he had done during his exile, and when word of his deeds seeped out among the Shadowleague, as these things always did, he knew he could expect more trouble.

And I'd better pray that they never discover who was responsible for the Curtain Walls becoming unbalanced in the first place. They'll tear me to pieces.

He looked across at Veldan. There might be no way of altering his past, but he could certainly change the future. What was it that she'd said? Everyone should get one chance to atone.

Amaurn turned back to the waiting Loremasters. 'Let's not waste any more time,' he said. 'We've got a lot of work to do.'

Thirty

The Voice of the Future

Though Toulac's plight didn't look any better in daylight, it was good to see the sun, none the less. If she could have seen it from the ground, however, instead of from midair, she would have felt a whole lot happier.

Myrial in a midden! Don't these bloody creatures ever get tired?

Held tightly in the Dierkan's barbed grasp, she couldn't move, let alone fight. And even if she could have wriggled loose, it would have been suicide to try it this far above the ground.

But just you wait, you bastard. You've got to land sometime, and when you do, I'll be ready.

The creatures might seem formidable, but apparently they were pretty stupid, otherwise they would have noticed that she still had her sword. Surely it must only be a matter of time before they would have to land. She wished they would hurry. Neither she nor Zavahl were wearing coats or cloaks, and the air was incredibly cold at this height. She could only keep going for so long before she became so enervated that she would be unable to function even if they did land.

Toulac wondered if Zavahl was all right. She had not seen him move, or heard him make a sound since the gigantic insect had snatched him up, but he might have been following her own example. She had elected to play dead, and was letting herself dangle limply in the creature's grasp. The less mobile she seemed to be at this point, the greater her chances of taking it by surprise when the opportunity finally arose. There was only one drawback to her plan.

After all this time in the air, the truth had caught up with her dissembling, and despite her best efforts, she found herself falling asleep.

It was the sudden change in movement that aroused her. Toulac jerked awake as her head was jolted on her shoulders, and opened her eyes to see the ground coming up at her, fast. To her horror, she saw that they were flying along the edge of a shallow cliff, and on her left there was nothing but open ocean. Dear Myrial, if there was something wrong with this creature, and it fell into sea . . .

Before she had time to draw breath, the gigantic insect went zooming upwards once more, taking an irregular, zigzag path that sent the landscape tilting and swinging below, now land, now ocean. Instead of the usual, purposeful drone, its buzzing had changed to a rough, uneven rattle. Toulac felt the icy touch of fear. What ailed the thing? It was almost as though it had been drinking! Was it sick, or had it been wounded somehow? But though she scanned the skies as far as she was able, she could see nothing that might have harmed the creature.

Not far away, Zavahl's captor was behaving in a similar erratic manner, its flight as blind and blundering as that of an autumn bluebottle. He was certainly awake now. She caught a glimpse of his eyes opened as wide as they would go, as he stared at the revolving ground and water in stark terror. Poor man, she thought, with an unexpected stab of pity. These last few days had simply gone from bad to worse for him.

Then suddenly, Toulac was getting a better view of Zavahl than she needed, as her captor veered blindly towards its companion. Forgetting all about playing dead, she jabbed frantically at the underside of the creature with her elbow.

Move, you stupid creature! We're going to crash! We're going to—

The buzzing stopped abruptly as the two great insects collided in midair. Toulac felt a wrenching jolt run through her body, then her stomach was up in her throat as she went spiralling down. How near the ground were they? The rushing wind was making her eyes water, and she couldn't see . . . Without warning, she felt the clutch of the barbed legs loosen, as the creature dropped her.

A gigantic fist slammed into her, hard. For an instant she lay there, stunned and gasping, then relief surged through her as she realised that she must have been very near the ground when she fell. The luck which had preserved her life through forty years of campaigning must still be holding out.

Not so fast, old girl. Better see if anything's broken, first.

She sat up cautiously, but everything seemed to be more or less in one piece, though several bits of it hurt like perdition. She was going to have some very interesting bruises in a while, but she could live with that. Then, as her head began to clear, she saw how close to the cliff edge she had fallen, and suddenly felt sick.

All at once, she heard a drunken buzzing from somewhere to her right. Looking around, she saw her captor crawling lopsidedly towards her, its antennae askew and one iridescent wing bent at an awkward angle. It had seen her, it was making for her, and it wasn't happy. The jagged mandibles twitched and clicked as though they could hardly wait to sink into her flesh, and on the end of its abdomen the great sting, like a sinister, gigantic thorn, was pumping in and out.

Toulac's pain and stiffness vanished as a jolt of pure terror shot through her, ready to help her flee – or fight. Already her sword was in her hand, without her knowing how it had got there. There was no point in caution. At this point, her opponent was weakened and disorientated. She would never have a better chance. With a wild war cry, the warrior darted in. Before the creature could react, the wicked, triangular black head was bouncing away, to spin over the edge of the cliff.

But even as she yelled in triumph, her true danger become apparent, as the body of the insect went into violent spasm. Its momentum carried it to her, and before she could get out of the way, it knocked her off her feet. Toulac rolled, but the body was moving in such a haphazard way that she didn't know if she was moving in the right direction. She felt something catch in the cuff of her pants, and saw the vile black sting, pinning a fold of the loose material to the ground. Quicker than blinking, it withdrew, then stabbed down again . . .

Toulac wrenched her leg to the side and rolled away – and found that she was right on the edge of the cliff. Digging her fingers into the tangled growth of the plants along the edge, she slowed herself, scant inches from disaster. Her feet swung round, went over the edge, and kicked wildly in midair – but her body had stopped moving, and there was enough of her on the brink of the precipice to prevent her balance from tilting over. Below her, she could hear the clatter of stones and gravel, as the edge began to crumble . . .

'Quick! Take my hand!' The hand, coated with black mud and greenish slime, appeared in front of her, and seized her wrist. She felt a similar grip around the other arm, and she was jerked forward, almost wrenching her arms out of their sockets, as the cliff edge crumbled away behind her, and a large piece detached itself and slid down into the sea.

Her rescuer had pulled so hard that he overbalanced backward, and the two of them ended up sprawling in a heap on the ground. It had to be Zavahl – who else could it be? – but he was unrecognisable, his hair plastered to his head by stinking muck, and his face and body glistening black, with livid green streaks of weed and slime. Behind them, another bit of the cliff edge had begun to crumble and, helping one another, the two of them staggered to their feet and reeled away from the danger until they were sufficiently far away from the edge. Then both of them folded to the ground again, breathing hard.

Toulac shook the former Hierarch's hand. 'Thanks,' she said. 'You saved my life. I'm in your debt.'

He smiled one of his rare smiles, his teeth gleaming white in his black face. 'No. You saved me from the pyre in Callisiora. That makes us quits.'

Toulac stared at him in amazement, then gave him back a grin to match his own. 'Well, may I be dipped in dog's dung! You've finally decided that life is sweet after all.'

He shrugged, and looked away, embarrassed. 'It took a long time to sink in, but when I was hurtling to the ground with that ghastly creature, I thought I was a dead man for sure. And I suddenly knew I didn't want to die.'

'So what happened?'

He smiled again. 'You'll never guess. It appears that after all this time, Myrial has answered one of my prayers after all.'

Toulac couldn't believe her ears. Had Zavahl just made a joke about *Myrial*?

'Well, it's a damn good thing he chose to answer that one,' she said solemnly.

'Yes, but did he have to answer it by dropping me into a *bog*?' Zavahl said plaintively. 'Granted, it was nice and soft, and granted, it drowned that creature, but . . .'

'It did the trick, then,' Toulac told him briskly, 'and that's the main thing. We're both extremely lucky to be alive. Come on, let's find a way down this cliff. We can get you cleaned up a little in the sea, though there's nothing much we can do about your clothes. It's too cold for you to do without them while we wash them. I suppose you'll just have to wait until the stuff dries, and then we'll brush it off as best we can.'

They had reached the water's edge, and Zavahl was cleaning his hands and face in a rock pool near the edge of the ocean, when Toulac first heard Veldan's voice.

'Toulac? Toulac, can you hear me? Don't worry, we're coming to get you.'

The veteran's heart soared.

I might have known that girl wouldn't let me down. If only I could tell her where we are.

And suddenly, she was sure she could. Afterwards, she joked that it was being dropped from a height that had done the trick. In reality, she was never sure whether her great need or her intense relief and joy had provided the key she needed to unlock her mental voice, but it seemed to her that her need released the ability to send her thoughts forth, and her joy had given her voice wings to take it to her friend.

'Veldan?' she cried – and felt the young woman's start of shock. Delight poured like sunlight into her mind.

'Toulac? I can hear you. Well done, well done indeed. Are you all right?'

'We're fine so far. We're on a sea coast somewhere, with cliffs, and a rocky beach. As far as I could tell from the stars last night, we seemed to be heading roughly south-east, from the Gendival valley, and we certainly didn't pass through a Curtain Wall.'

'Wonderful. That gives us some idea, at any rate. I suspect that the stupid Dierkan were simply following the line of the Evalnor River until they reached the coast, then if necessary they could work their way all around the coast to Zaltaigla, the realm of the Dragonfolk.'

'Myrial up a pole!' gasped Toulac. 'How far is *that*?'

'Too bloody far. But apparently the Dragons have agents all over the place. I suspect they might have arranged for a boat to pick you up and take you across.'

Toulac shuddered at the narrowness of her escape. 'But why did they take me, as well as Zavahl?' she asked. 'Surely, it was only him they wanted?'

'I suspect that the Dierkan were confused by your presence in Zavahl's room,' Veldan replied. 'They aren't very intelligent. They were told to take the human from that room, and when they found not one but two humans, they didn't know which one they wanted.'

'So they took us both.' Toulac shook her head. 'That'll teach me to mind my own business in the future, and stay where I'm put.'

Even in mindspeech, Veldan's chuckle came through. 'That'll be the day. But it's just as well for Zavahl that you're there. You can take care of him for us until we find you.'

The veteran cast her eyes to the heavens. 'My oh my. Lucky me. Still, he's not so bad now. Ailie has been training him a bit. You'll be astonished at the change in him.'

'Funny, that's exactly what *she* said. Thank Providence I can tell her he's in one piece, and that we'll have him back to her soon.'

'If you're coming to get us, I don't want to delay you,' Toulac said, 'but there's one thing that puzzles me about those damn great insects. They were flying along quite purposefully, then suddenly they were buzzing aimlessly around in circles. They seemed completely confused, and I had very little trouble killing one of them. The other one dropped Zavahl into a bog, then proceeded to drown itself. What did you do to them?'

'They were merely slaves, controlled by Skreeva of the Alvai. You may have seen her when we arrived: the one like an enormous green insect. We had to kill her, because her mind controls all of her Dierkan slaves. Once she was dead, they no longer had any sense of purpose.'

Toulac whistled. 'From what I remember of the jaws on that Skreeva thing, it must have been quite some fight.'

'It certainly was.' Veldan sounded almost hesitant, as though she'd been about to say something, but had changed her mind. 'Anyway, I'll tell you the details later. All sorts of things have happened, but there's no time for all that now. We ought to be moving. We'll find you soon, I promise. Will you be all right until then?'

'We'll be fine,' the veteran told her firmly. 'When it comes to surviving in the wilderness, I know a trick or two, and there's always plenty of food to be had around a beach. Don't you worry, girlie. Everything we need is here. Tell Ailie I'll take good care of Zavahl.'

'I'll be sure to let you know, from time to time, how we're getting along. You take care of yourself, do you hear?'

'Veldan, this is me you're talking to. I'm too mean and tough to be finished off by a couple of days camping out. After all the running around I've been doing since I met you and Kaz, it'll seem like a holiday.'

The Loremaster laughed. 'Well, don't get too used to a life of leisure, because we're on our way.' With that she was gone, and Toulac found herself released from the thrall of mindspeech. It had required all her concentration, and had left her with a slight headache, but she hoped it would get easier with practice. She came back to her surroundings, to see Zavahl sitting on a nearby rock, apparently brushing flakes of drying mud from himself, but also eyeing her surreptitiously, with some concern. 'Are you all right?' he asked her.

'Of course I am. Why shouldn't I be?'

'The way you were screwing up your face, I thought you were in some kind of pain.'

She glared. 'I was talking to Veldan, if you must know.'

'Thank Myrial for that. You looked as though you were going to lay an egg.'

Toulac made a rude gesture at him, but in reality she was impressed by Zavahl's calm acceptance of her words. He certainly *had* changed. Finally he was adjusting to the wider horizons, physical, emotional and mental, of his new world.

'So what did the other Formidable Female have to say?' he prompted.

'I managed to give her a rough idea of where we are, and they're setting out to look for us right now. So we should have you back with your girlfriend in no time,' she added with an evil leer.

She was impressed anew when Zavahl didn't rise to the bait. 'Good,' he said cheerfully. 'I'm missing her already – she's a lot less cantankerous than you.'

'And a damn sight prettier,' Toulac said. 'Though I thank you for being too much of a gentleman to point that out. I'll tell you something, though. Ailie wouldn't be able to keep you fed through the next few days, but I can.' Suddenly, she was all business. 'Come on, let's get moving. It takes a lot of work to survive in a god-forsaken place like this. As well as food, we'll need a huge stock of firewood and some kind of shelter before nightfall. There's no time to waste.'

Just as they were scrambling to their feet, Zavahl froze, his eyes on the sea. 'Look! We've got company.'

Toulac followed his pointing finger with her eyes. In the green ocean, just beyond the surf line, a cluster of neat, compact, round heads were bobbing on the swell, while large dark eyes watched them curiously.

'Do you think they're friendly?' whispered Zavahl. He looked very white, and his pointing finger trembled a little. In that moment, Toulac realised that though he was putting a commendably brave face on things, his abduction by the Dierkan had left its mark.

'They look just like Dessil, or very similar, at any rate. *He* was friendly enough.' She did her best to sound reassuring. 'After those damned insects, they look positively cute. Anyway, we'll soon find out.'

Concentrating hard, she switched to mindspeech. 'Ho there!' she called. 'I'm Toulac. Can you understand me?'

The wave of curiosity and amazement that followed almost knocked her off her feet. 'A Loremaster?' said a voice in her mind. 'Then we have come to Gendival at last?'

'More or less,' Toulac answered cautiously.

There came a confusion of mental voices, all exclaiming in relief and delight. 'Please wait,' the creature said. 'Though we Dobarchu very seldom come ashore, we will join you for a time. We are the last refugees to escape from the Archipelago of Nemeris, and maybe the last survivors of our race.'

'I'm truly sorry to hear that,' said Toulac. 'We're sort of refugees ourselves, but some people are coming from the Shadowleague headquarters in a couple of days, to take us home. I'm sure they'll do whatever they can to help you, too.'

A dig from Zavahl's elbow interrupted her concentration. 'Who are they?' he hissed. 'Can you understand them? Are they friendly?'

'They certainly are.' Toulac clapped him on the shoulder and grinned. 'Isn't it wonderful, the way our lives are getting more interesting every minute?' She looked at the sleek, brown-furred figures scrambling clumsily ashore, and was aware of a great feeling of contentment. The despairing Toulac of a few days ago, who felt old, and useless, and spent, was gone for good.

Thank you, Veldan, for showing me this magical new world. I was born for this. After a lifetime of wandering, I've found where I belong.